skinny legs
and all

Books by Tom Robbins

Another Roadside Attraction
Even Cowgirls Get the Blues
Still Life with Woodpecker
Jitterbug Perfume
Skinny Legs and All

Tom Robbins

skinny legs and all

BANTAM BOOKS
NEW YORK · TORONTO · LONDON · SYDNEY · AUCKLAND

Some of the works of art described in these pages are fictionalized exaggerations of pieces originally created by Patti Warashina, Fred Bauer, and Norma Rosen. The author salutes them.

SKINNY LEGS AND ALL
A Bantam Book / May 1990

Copyright © 1990 by Tibetan Peach Pie, Inc.

Book design by Richard Oriolo.

Library of Congress Cataloging-in-Publication Data
Robbins, Tom.
 Skinny legs and all / Tom Robbins.
  p.   cm.
 ISBN 0-553-05775-8
 I. Title.
PS3568.O233S55   1990
813'.54—dc20   89-18309
                                      CIP

Published simultaneously in the United States and Canada

Bantam Books are published by Bantam Books, a division of Bantam Doubleday Dell Publishing Group, Inc. Its trademark, consisting of the words "Bantam Books" and the portrayal of a rooster, is Registered in U.S. Patent and Trademark Office and in other countries. Marca Registrada. Bantam Books, 666 Fifth Avenue, New York, New York 10103.

**For Alexa d'Avalon and Ginny Ruffner
and their pink shoes.**

*The Messiah will only come
when he is no longer needed.*

—Franz Kafka

It's the end of the world as we know it
(And I feel fine.)

—R.E.M.

prelude

This is the room of the wolfmother wallpaper. The toadstool motel you once thought a mere folk tale, a corny, obsolete, rural invention.

This is the room where your wisest ancestor was born, be you Christian, Arab, or Jew. The linoleum underfoot is sacred linoleum. Please remove your shoes. Quite recently, the linoleum here was restored to its original luster with the aid of a wax made from hornet fat. It scuffs easily. So never mind if there are holes in your socks.

This is the room where your music was invented. Notice the cracked drumhead spiked to the wall, spiked to the wolfmother wallpaper above the corner sink where the wayward wife washed out her silk underpants, inspecting them in the blue seepage from the No Vacancy neon that flickered suspiciously out in the thin lizard dawn.

What room is this? This is the room where the antler carved the pumpkin. This is the room where the gutter pipes drank the moonlight. This is the room where moss gradually silenced the treasure, rubies being the last to go. Transmissions from insect antennae were monitored in this room. It's amazing how often their broadcasts referred to the stars.

A clue: this is the room where the Painted Stick was buried, where the Conch Shell lay wrapped in its adoring papyrus. Lovers, like serpents, shed their old skin in this clay room. *Now* do you remember the wallpaper? The language of the wallpaper? The wolfmother's blood roses that vibrated there?

Enough of this wild fox barking. You pulled up in the forest Cadillac, the vehicle you claimed you'd forgotten how to drive. You

1

parked between the swimming pool and the row of blackened skulls. *Of course*, you know what room this is.

This is the room where Jezebel frescoed her eyelids with history's tragic glitter, where Delilah practiced for her beautician's license, the room in which Salome dropped the seventh veil while dancing the dance of ultimate cognition, skinny legs and all.

the first veil

It was a bright, defrosted, pussy-willow day at the onset of spring, and the newlyweds were driving cross-country in a large roast turkey.

The turkey lay upon its back, as roast turkeys will; submissive, agreeable, volunteering its breast to the carving blade, its roly-poly legs cocked in a stiff but jaunty position, as if it might summon the gumption to spring forward onto its feet, but, of course, it had no feet, which made the suggestion seem both empty and ridiculous, and only added to the turkey's aura of goofy vulnerability.

Despite its feetlessness, however, its pathetic podalic privation, this roast turkey—or jumbo facsimile thereof—was moving down the highway at sixty-five miles an hour, traveling faster, farther on its back than many aspiring actresses.

The turkey, gleaming in the callow March sunlight, had been a wedding present from the groom to the bride, although the title remained in the groom's name and he was never, in fact, to relinquish ownership. Actually, it was the fashioning of the turkey, the phenomenon of its existence, that was his gift to the bride. More important, it was the manifestation of the turkey, the squealy, swoony surprise of the creation of the turkey, that had precipitated the marriage: the groom, Boomer Petway, had used the turkey to trick the bride, Ellen Cherry Charles, into marrying him. At least, that was what Ellen Cherry was thinking at that moment, less than a week after the wedding, thinking, as she watched the turkey suck the thawing countryside into its windshield and blow it out its rearview mirror, that she'd been tricked. Less than a week after the wedding, that probably was not an excellent indicator of impending decades of marital bliss.

Some marriages are made in heaven, Ellen Cherry thought. *Mine was made in Hong Kong. By the same people who make those little rubber pork chops they sell in the pet department at K mart.*

Mockingbirds are the true artists of the bird kingdom. Which is to say, although they're born with a song of their own, an innate riff that happens to be one of the most versatile of all ornithological expressions, mockingbirds aren't content to merely play the hand that is dealt them. Like all artists, they are out to *rearrange* reality. Innovative, willful, daring, not bound by the rules to which others may blindly adhere, the mockingbird collects snatches of birdsong from this tree and that field, appropriates them, places them in new and unexpected contexts, recreates the world from the world. For example, a mockingbird in South Carolina was heard to blend the songs of thirty-two different kinds of birds into a ten-minute performance, a virtuoso display that served no practical purpose, falling, therefore, into the realm of pure art.

And so it was that in the dogwood branches and lilac bushes on the grounds of the Third Baptist Church of Colonial Pines, mockingbirds were producing art, were "making a joyful noise unto the Lord," while inside the building, a Georgian rectangle of powdery brick and prissy white trim, several hundred freshly scrubbed, well-fed human beings concerned themselves not with creation but destruction. Ultimate destruction.

In east-central Virginia, where Colonial Pines was located, spring was quicker on its feet than it was out in the Far West, through which Boomer and Ellen Cherry's roast turkey was transporting them ever eastward. Pussy willows had already come and gone in Virginia, and sickly faced dogwood blossoms, like constipated elves, strained to take their places. From underground silos, jonquil bulbs fired round after round of butter-tipped stalks, all sorts of buds were swelling and popping, birds (not just mockingbirds) strung ropes of birdsong from treetop to fence post, bees and other insects were waking to the unfamiliar alarm of their own faint buzz; all around, the warming natural world was in the process of rebirth and renewal, almost as if to deliberately cast some doubt upon the accuracy of the sermon being concluded at that moment in the church.

"God gave us this sign," said the preacher from his oak veneer podium. "The Lord gave us a *sign*! A *sign*! It was a warning, if you will. A word to the wise. He gave his children a big easy-to-read sign, words in tall black letters, maybe golden letters—maybe it was a *neon* sign. In any case, there's no mistakin' its message. The Lord shoved this sign before the countenance of his beloved disciple, John, and John, being a righteous man, John bein' a *wise* man, John didn't blink or scratch his head or ask for details, Saint John didn't call up a lawyer on the phone and ask for a legal interpretation, no, John read this sign and copied it down and passed it on to mankind. To you and I."

The preacher's voice was reminiscent of a saxophone. Not the cool, laconic sax of Lester Young, but the full, lush, volatile sound of, say, Charlie Barnet. There was a marvelous, dark lyricism in his voice, the kind of defiance that is rooted in deep loneliness. His pockmarked face was lean and hungry looking, a beat face poisoned by boils and the runoff from rotting teeth. Yet the voice that rolled out from that face, from underneath the boyish shock of damp, black hair, the voice was fecund and round and gloomily romantic. Females in the congregation, especially, were touched by the preacher's voice, never stopping to consider that it might have been hot pus that fueled its grand combustion.

"What the Almighty Father told John was this: that when the Jews return to their homeland—yea! when the Jew is once again at home in the land of Is-ra-el—the end of the world is at hand!"

The preacher paused. He gazed at the congregation with his starving eyes. Verlin Charles was later to say, "Sometimes when he looks down at us like that, I feel like he wants to eat the flower right outen my buttonhole." "Uh-huh," his wife, Patsy, replied. "Makes me feel like he wants to chew the elastic outta my underpants." Verlin Charles did not appreciate Patsy Charles's interpretation of the preacher's voracious stare, and he told her so.

Off to the left of the altar, a radio engineer raised three fingers. The Reverend Buddy Winkler caught the gesture out of the corner of his eye, immediately thereupon aborting the penetrating scrutiny of his flock and returning to the microphone.

"When the Jew has returned to his homeland, the *end of the world* is at hand! That is the sign God gave unto us. Why? I want to ask you somethin'. Do you think God just threw out that crumb of information offhand like it was gossip, like it was an interestin' item outen the *Reader's Digest*? Or did God have a *purpose* in the showing of this sign to John? Did God have a *reason* in ordering John to write down this prophecy in his Book of Revelation? Are we intended to act somehow upon this message?"

The engineer raised two fingers. Buddy Winkler nodded and quickened the tempo. Blowing Charlie Parker style, blowing a swift freight of harmonic rhetoric, blowing his sax-voice at about fifty-eight bars per minute, blowing alto now—his usual tenor abandoned at the gates of syncopation—the preacher swung into a dazzling diatribe against Semite and anti-Semite alike: instructed his brethren (with a sputter of grace notes) to turn their attention to Jerusalem, the city of their eternal fate; bade them prepare themselves for physical entry into Jerusalem, where they that were righteous among them were to accept their promised rewards; reminded them that on the following Sunday he would describe to them what conditions they might expect to encounter in the New Jerusalem; and further reminded them that next week's sermon, as each of the sermons in this series concerning the Rapidly Approaching End, would be broadcast over the Southern Baptist Voice of the Sparrow Network, of which WCPV was the local affiliate. He then stitched on a reedy coda of prayer, timing an "amen" to perfectly coincide with the wag of the engineer's single digit.

Sequins of spittle were scattered along his smile as he accepted compliments at the door.

"Powerful sermon, Reverend Winkler."

"God bless you, Roy."

"Reverend Winkler, you are just eloquence itself. You move me, you stir me up inside, you—"

"It's the Lord that speaks through me, Miz Packett." He squeezed her hand. "The Lord does the movin'."

"Right nice, Bud. Frogs are out."

"Don't know if I'll have time for any jiggin' this spring, Verlin."

"You got other frogs to jig, right, Bud?"

His boils waxed a deeper red. "Patsy now."

"As in 'other fish to fry.'"

"Patsy." He said her name laboriously, as if he were coaxing a lone low note from his saxophone bell. It was both censure and plea. Patsy grinned and left him to his flock.

Verlin and Patsy Charles walked to their Buick Regal in the parking lot.

"You hadn't ought to mess with him here, Patsy. In God's house . . ."

"He was out on the steps."

". . . on the Sabbath."

"Bud's Bud, on Sunday or the Fourth of July."

"How about on Judgment Day?"

"We'll see soon enough, I reckon," said Patsy, and Verlin, safely behind the lilac hedge, smiled.

"You know," Verlin said, as he stopped to admire a new Ford pickup that he knew to belong to an acquaintance, "the end of the world is not gonna be coming right away. You know why? Because the fact is, there're more Jews in New York City than in the entire country of Is-ra-el." He tried to pronounce it the way his cousin Buddy did, but Verlin's voice was more kazoo than saxophone.

"So, you wanna deport 'em?"

"No skin off my pecker if New York's more Jewish than Jerusalem. I'm not ready for Armageddon. I got bills to pay."

"You got a daughter fixin' to live in New York City."

A tremendous frown wadded up Verlin's face. It was a pink face, occupied neither on its west bank nor its east by a single whisker. Verlin was one of those men who seemed to shave internally. His build was rangy, as was his kin's, the preacher's, but his face was round, smooth, satiated (which is not quite the same as "content"), and it smelled perpetually of mildewed washrag, no matter what quantities of Old Spice aftershave were tossed at it. "You would have to remind me," he said.

"Millions of people live in New York. It must not be that bad."

"Perverts. Puerto Ricans. Muggers. Terrorists. Whatta ya call 'em: bag ladies."

"Terrorists in New York? Honey, New York is located in the U.S.A., for your information."

"They will have 'em if they don't already. Jews attract terrorism like shit attracts flies. Always have."

"I swear, you sound like Bud. The Jews didn't walk off some boat last Tuesday. New York's been full of Jews since I don't know how

9

long. And they've been returned to Israel since back in the nineteen-forties sometime. I don't know why you two are all of a sudden so worked up about Jews."

"Oh, must be the Middle East on the news." He sighed. "Seems like any more that's all there is."

"Besides, Boomer'll take care of Ellen Cherry. You said so yourself."

"Once upon a time I said it. Not anymore. That damn contraption he drove out to pick her up in! I think she's finally made him as kooky as she is." Verlin spat. *"Artists!"*

As the couple walked up to their Buick, two mockingbirds flew away from its grill, one of them tweeting in a little-known dialect of the goldfinch, the other mixing a catbird cry with a raspy chord borrowed from a woodpecker. For centuries, mockingbirds had hunted live insects and foraged for seeds, but when motorcars began to appear in numbers on southern roads, they learned that they could dine more easily by simply picking dead bugs off the radiators of parked autos. Mockingbirds. Turning modern technology to their idiosyncratic advantage. Inventing new tricks to subsidize their expression. *Artists!*

Before static finally fried it to a crisp, a portion of the Reverend Buddy Winkler's Sunday sermon had crackled out of the roast turkey's radio. "Uncle Buddy," sneered Ellen Cherry. Although he was, in fact, what is called by southerners a mere "shirttail relation," she had called him "uncle" since she was a tot. "Ol' Uncle Buddy's gone nationwide."

Boomer was perfectly aware of that. In recent years he had been closer to her father's family than she. Boomer didn't appear to notice when she switched the Motorola to a news broadcast. ("In the Arab quarter of Jerusalem today, Israeli soldiers fired into a group of . . .") Boomer appeared to be counting cows. The cows that were stuck like gnats to the fly strip of the horizon. When he counted up to a certain number, he smiled. Thought Ellen Cherry, *I will probably never really know how many little faraway cows it takes to make my husband smile.*

Strange, but in country such as this—dry, bare, and wide; country given to forage crops, flat rocks, and sidewinders—Buddy Winkler's apocalyptic rant acquired a certain credibility. West of the Cascade Range, back around Seattle, where they had begun their journey, trees were so thick, so robust and tall, that they oozed green gas, sported mossy mustaches, and yelled "Timber, yourself!" at lumberjacks. Those chill forests, quietly throbbing with ancient vitality, seemed to refute the firmest eschatological convictions. Here, however, trees were wizened, drab, and thinly distributed. The road, clear and straight, uncoiled ahead of the turkey, recoiled behind, locking its passengers in a drowsy, lifeless rhythm from which the granulated yellow-brown layer cake to either side afforded scant relief. Distant cow-specks, raisins in the receding frosting, outnumbered pussy willows; and, indeed, the imprint of the hoof was on everything.

In country such as this, Ellen Cherry always rather expected the golden clock to go off. The clock with the alarm that sounded like firestorms and flügelhorns. Followed by the voice of Orson Welles reading from *The Book of the Dead.* "It'd be just like the world to end," she said, "when we're out here in the boondocks miles from a telephone."

Boomer didn't respond. His attention was fixed on an approaching cattle truck. As it drew nearer, the truck slowed and began to weave. It nearly sideswiped them in passing. The driver was hanging his head out the window in disbelief. Boomer swerved and honked the horn.

"Ignorant cowboy," muttered Boomer. "Nearly took a drumstick off."

Colonial Pines was a suburb without an urb. At a distance of twenty-two miles, it was too far from Richmond to truly function as an appendage thereof, yet it lacked the autonomy of a separate city. It boasted no industry to speak of, and while excellent tomatoes were grown in abundance in its immediate vicinity, it certainly couldn't be characterized as a farming community. Oddly enough, it had no downtown. What passed for a business district in Colonial Pines was a four-lane highway that, despite the turnpike that nowadays allowed traffic to skirt the place, still carried thousands of Yankee tourists to Florida and back. As it passed through Colonial Pines, that highway, three miles of it, was lined cheek to jowl with motels, service stations, and restaurants—although *restaurant* might be too dignified a word for the barbecue pits, ice cream stands, truck stops, and so-called "family" inns (whose blank, almost totalitarian cuisine could be trusted never to excite or confuse a repressed taste bud with flavors novel or bold). Presumably, inhabitants of this quasi-town earned their income from the Strip, as it was known (comparing it to the Las Vegas Strip would be akin to comparing Marie Osmond to Mae West), though we may also presume that they benefited from the proceeds of their traffic court: the reputation of the Colonial Pines speed trap stretched from Boston to Miami.

Exactly how an almost exclusively Caucasian lower-middle-class residential community of nineteen thousand supported itself, how it paid for its green shutters, power mowers, and ubiquitous American flags, is a question fit to occupy a demographer for a useless month or so, but it is not, thankfully, a concern of ours. Suffice for us to establish that Ellen Cherry Charles was born and reared in Colonial Pines, Virginia, that she loathed it from the cradle on, plotting even as a little girl to flee the vapors of unrelieved boredom that she believed were stifling her there. Eventually, and with some difficulty, she did escape. The tentacles of home place are as tenacious as they are stealthy, however, and the fact that she had yet to cut completely free of their coils was attested to by the weekly telephone calls she aimed at the Charles household. She made one on that March day.

"Hi."

"Honey!" exclaimed Patsy. "Good to hear your voice! Listen, I oughtta go pull my robe on 'fore we commence. You caught me nekkid as a jaybird."

" 'Nekkid' or 'naked,' mama?"

"What's the blessed difference? Are you making Yankee fun of the way I talk? The way you *used* to talk?"

"No, no, mama, let me tell you. *Naked* means you just don't have any clothes on. *Nekkid* means you don't have any clothes on and you're fixing to get into trouble."

Patsy giggled. "Lord, chile, I've already done that." She lowered her voice to a notch above a whisper. "The fact is, your daddy just had his way with me, as is his custom on a Sunday afternoon. I understand that most of these once-a-weekers do it on Saturday night, but your daddy's gotta be different in *some* category, I reckon. I swear, I think it's Buddy's sermons get him heated up, just like they do half the good Baptist ladies in this town. Or maybe it's the football, I don't know. He does watch the football first." Patsy stopped and cleared the giggle out of her voice. "Anyways, I shouldn't be gabbing to *you* about it. Except you *are* an ol' married woman now."

"Boomer's fine, mama."

"Good. Where y'all callin' from?"

"Some rodeo town. Close to Idaho, I think. A person would believe they'd have nice hamburgers in towns like this, cows practically grazing on Main Street, but I swear the patties have more sawdust in them than they do in Colonial Pines. Boomer's had two, though, and working on a third."

"You watch that boy. Don't let them pretty muscles go to fat."

At that, Ellen Cherry glanced over her shoulder toward the snack-bar blacktop where she had last seen her muscular groom. A half-dozen or more men had gathered to gawk at the great turkey, and Boomer was standing in their midst.

"They still refer to you gentlemen as cowboys?" Boomer asked. He gnawed at a ragged rind of burger bun the way a howling wolf sometimes seems to gnaw at a gibbous moon.

Apparently, the teenager at whom he'd directed his inquiry was too shy to respond. The young fellow seized the opportunity to examine his boots. Likely need new soles by summer.

One of the older men, raising his neck, gooselike, up out of his denim, took it upon himself to extend the courtesy of a reply. "How might you think they'd be referring to us?" His voice was slow and deliberate, like a mouse-fattened adder crawling over a rock pile.

"Oh, I thought that this day and age you maybe would be known as bovine custodial officers." Boomer chuckled. He snapped at the last of the mustard-lit crust. "I did read somewheres," he said through a mouthful, "that the most accurate job description of your ol' wild west cowboy would be 'boorish Victorian agricultural worker.' Don't reckon *that's* a handle that'd stick."

There was a general shuffling of boots.

"Uh-oh," said Ellen Cherry.

"Honey, let me slip a robe on," said Patsy.

"Mama, I think we have to go. Right now. Love you. Bye."

Perhaps admiration of the cowboy as the quintessential American hero is, indeed, not as universal as it was once. Traveling among the "bovine custodial officers" of Wyoming, Can o' Beans was to remark that a comparison between the American cowpoke and, say, the Japanese samurai, left the cowboy looking rather shoddy. "Before a samurai went into battle," Can o' Beans was to say, "he would burn incense in his helmet so that if his enemy took his head, he would find it pleasant to the nose. Cowboys, on the other hand, hardly ever bathed or changed their crusty clothing. If a samurai's enemy lost his sword, the samurai gave him his extra one so that the fight might continue in a manner honorable and fair. The cowboy's specialty was to shoot enemies in the back from behind a bush. Do you begin to see the difference?" Spoon and Dirty Sock would wonder how Can o' Beans knew so much about samurai. "Oh, I sat on the shelf next to a box of imported rice crackers for over a month," Can o' Beans would explain. "One can learn a lot conversing with foreigners."

Ah, but we are getting ahead of our story. The immediate news is that Boomer and Ellen Cherry were obliged to depart the rodeo town in a bit of a rush. As a matter of fact, a mob, made mobile by a fleet of Japanese pickup trucks, chased the turkey across the state line and some twenty miles deep into Idaho.

After the phone went dead in her hand, Ellen Cherry's mother, moderately puzzled and freshly laid, wriggled into a robe, poured a cup of coffee, and went out on the sunporch to have a good think. She wished to consider, once again, the possibility that her daughter might have erred in marrying Boomer Petway and that Verlin and his cousin, Buddy Winkler, might have meddled insidiously in Ellen Cherry's life, not just where Boomer was concerned but generally.

She had had her own secret plans for Ellen Cherry, and it vexed her that Verlin might yet succeed in thwarting them.

If she makes it in New York as an artist, it's due to me, Patsy thought. She parted her robe slightly so that the late afternoon sunlight might warm her between her legs, where she was leaking a rivulet of the manly fluid in which she sometimes suspected her own artistic life had drowned.

As a young woman, Patsy had been a cheerleader who yearned to become a dancer. Why, at fifteen she was Grapefruit Princess of Okaloosa County! At seventeen, she met and married Verlin Charles, a navy pilot flying out of Pensacola. Discharged, Verlin moved her to Virginia, where he had resumed his career as a civil engineer. For the rest of her life, when Verlin was at work, Patsy would dance at home alone in cute white boots.

Ellen Cherry liked to watch her dance, but, to be honest, it wasn't Patsy's fancy-stepping that had channeled Ellen Cherry toward art. Rather, it was vertigo. And Colonial Pines.

Twice each year, the family would drive down to Florida to visit Patsy's folks. Inevitably, Ellen Cherry got carsick. To keep from vomiting, she had to lie on her back in the rear of the station wagon and look up. As a result, she began to see the world from a different perspective.

Telephone poles went by like loops. She would register the light from signboards first, then the tops of the signs, then their blurry message: the melting Marlboro man, the expanding slice of pie. Gradually, she experimented. Played what she called her "eye game." By squinting, and controlling the squint, she could achieve a figure-ground reversal. Figure-ground, ground-figure, back and forth. She could make herself color-blind. For miles, if she wished, the landscape would be nothing but red.

"How's Daddy's girl?" Verlin would ask from the driver's seat. "Need to pee-pee?" Often, Daddy's girl failed to reply. Daddy's girl was busy, sliding her focus to muffle or distort the normal associative effects of object and space, stripping them of common meaning or symbolic function, forcing them to settle in the highly mysterious region that lies between the cornea and the brain—and fooling with them there. The parallel lines of electrical wires, under her dynamic gaze, would tend to overlap, so that they would break their continuity and magnify the open areas between them. This was especially interesting when a flock of blackbirds could be stirred into the optic mixture. Or, she would be looking at the field of vision itself, refusing to favor a central form, such as a water tower, but concentrating instead on the zone surrounding the tower, finding pattern and substance in areas our eyes tend to regard as secondary, vacant, vague. And all the while viewing everything upside down, sideways, and nauseated. Is it surprising, then, that she would be a trifle contemptuous of Boomer Petway's practice of tallying cows?

From kindergarten through high school, Ellen Cherry could draw better than anyone in her class. With all respect to Patsy's boasts, it was a talent inherited from her father, the engineer being a whiz at site sketches and schematic renderings. (What she inherited from her mom, aside from a certain feisty dreaminess, was an animated rump, perfectly round breasts that, Grapefruit Princess or no Grapefruit Princess, were closer to the tangerine end of the citrus scale; a pert nose, a pouty mouth, wide blue eyes, and a tangle of caramel-colored curls that no matter how it was styled, always looked as if it had starred in the first reel of *The Wizard of Oz*. It was hair that did its own stunts.) Every school has its unofficial "school artist," does it not, and, there, Ellen Cherry was it. Over the years, as the optic ore she mined on her trips to Florida was refined, her art projects became increasingly adventurous and complex. She started to lose her local following. Kids made cruel comments. She didn't care. She had decided to be a painter.

There was less art in Colonial Pines than there was porn in a Quaker's parlor. As is sometimes the case, the very absence of cultural stimulation was culturally stimulating. For Ellen Cherry, art was a signpost pointing away from Colonial Pines. It would magic-carpet her out of that community where the single movie theater was a ratty drive-in whose existence was perpetuated solely because of its convenience as a surrogate lovers' lane.

During her senior year, suffering from a chronic case of what Patsy, as a result of prolonged personal experience, termed "mosquito britches," Ellen Cherry attended that drive-in's cinematic exhibitions Friday night after Friday night in the company of Boomer Petway. When she went off to art college the following autumn, she would never see ol' Boomer again, she was convinced, and that was fine with her. Alas, on her very first night in the freshmen girls' dorm, there was a commotion at her window toward two in the morning—and in climbed Boomer, a can of Pabst in his fist and a rose in his teeth, having sped to Richmond aboard his brother's

Harley motorcycle and climbed three stories up a treacherous ivy-covered wall. Boomer, you see, was thunderously, dizzily, and—this should be said in his favor—sincerely in love.

"You can't do this," blubbered Boomer, as Ellen Cherry attempted to push him back through the window. "You gotta come home. Be with me. After what we been through! We—we signed into that motel as man and wife! You put—you put your *mouth* on me."

"Shoulda checked the fine print, hon," whispered Ellen Cherry, trying to assist him back onto the ivy vines as quietly as possible. "That blow job did not come with a lifetime warranty."

Ultimately, the roast turkey must be regarded as a monument to Boomer's love.

Look at it now, plump and glossy, floating across Idaho as if it were a mammoth, mutated seed pod. Hear how it backfires as it passes the silver mines, perhaps in tribute to the origin of the knives and forks of splendid sterling that a roast turkey and a roast turkey alone possesses the charisma to draw forth into festivity from dark cupboards.

See how it glides through the potato fields, familiarly at home among potatoes but with an air of expectation, as if waiting for the flood of gravy.

The roast turkey carries with it, in its chubby hold, a sizable portion of our primitive and pagan luggage.

Primitive and pagan? Us? We of the laser, we of the microchip, we of Union Theological Seminary and *Time* magazine? Of course. At least twice a year, do not millions upon millions of us cybernetic Christians and fax machine Jews participate in a ritual, a highly stylized ceremony that takes place around a large dead bird?

And is not this animal sacrificed, as in days of yore, to catch the attention of a divine spirit, to show gratitude for blessings bestowed, and to petition for blessings coveted?

The turkey, slain, slowly cooked over our gas or electric fires, is the central figure at our holy feast. It is the totem animal that brings our tribe together.

And because it is an awkward, intractable creature, the serving of it establishes and reinforces the tribal hierarchy. There are but two legs, two wings, a certain amount of white meat, a given quantity of dark. Who gets which piece; who, in fact, slices the bird and distributes its limbs and organs, underscores quite emphatically the rank of each member in the gathering.

Consider that the legs of this bird are called "drumsticks," after the ritual objects employed to extract the music from the most aboriginal and sacred of instruments. Our ancestors kept their drums in public, but the sticks, being more actively magical, usually were stored in places known only to the shaman, the medicine man, the high priest, or the Wise Old Woman. The wing of the fowl gives symbolic flight to the soul, but with the drumstick is evoked the beat of the pulse of the heart of the universe.

Few of us nowadays participate in the actual hunting and killing of the turkey, but almost all of us watch, frequently with deep emotion, the reenactment of those events. We watch it on TV sets immediately before the communal meal. For what are footballs if not metaphorical turkeys, flying up and down a meadow? And what is a touchdown if not a kill, achieved by one or the other of two opposing tribes? To our applause, great young hunters from Alabama or Notre Dame slay the bird. Then, the Wise Old Woman, in the guise of Grandma, calls us to table, where we, pretending to be no longer primitive, systematically rip the bird asunder.

Was Boomer Petway aware of totemic implications when, to impress his beloved, he fabricated an outsize Thanksgiving centerpiece? No, not consciously. If and when the last veil dropped, he might comprehend what he had wrought. For the present, however, he was as ignorant as Can o' Beans, Spoon, and Dirty Sock were, before Painted Stick and Conch Shell drew their attention to similar affairs.

Nevertheless, it was Boomer who piloted the gobble-stilled butterball across Idaho, who negotiated it through the natural carving knives of the Sawtooth Mountains, who once or twice parked it in wilderness rest stops, causing adjacent flora to assume the appearance of parsley.

Randolph "Boomer" Petway was a welder by trade. He was seven years older than Ellen Cherry Charles. He was husky, dark, and, in a broad-faced, silly-grinned, thuggish sort of way, handsome. He drank a lot, guffawed a lot, and walked with a moderate limp, a piece of equipment having crushed his anklebone in the welding shop. In spite of the lameness, he boogied to country-rock more flamboyantly than any man in east-central Virginia. Some dance critic, who worked behind the bar in a honky-tonk, said that when Boomer danced he looked like a monkey on roller skates juggling razor blades in a hurricane.

"He's a complete idiot," reported Ellen Cherry to Patsy, "but I have to admit he's a hill of fun."

In addition to what she considered an unseemly excess of body hair, what displeased Ellen Cherry about Boomer was that he knew zip about art, cared zip about art, and, moreover, discouraged her from pursuing *her* interest in it. (Nevertheless, whenever the young philistines of Colonial Pines fired sarcastic barbs about her "weird" paintings, Boomer threatened to remove the plaque from their gums with his steel-toed workshoes, a promise they were sure he would keep.) He was a high-school dropout.

Suspended for a week for drinking beer in biology lab—and for various instances of insubordination—he went home from school, never to return. The track coach almost wept, almost bribed him to come back. Because by that time Boomer had already broken state records in both the shot put and the discus. Half of the universities on the Atlantic Seaboard had offered him scholarships. He was deemed to be Olympic material.

"Supposin' I'd devoted the best years of my life to field events," he said to Ellen Cherry. "After all that trainin' and sweat and pain and never thinkin' or dreamin' 'bout anything else but shot puts, which at the world-class level is the way it's done, what'd I been fit for in the end but the front of a Wheaties box?"

"So what are you fit for now, darlin'? The side of a Pabst Blue Ribbon can?"

Indeed, Boomer was world-class at pumping aluminum. He guzzled beer—and an almost equally large volume of RC Cola. He gobbled pizza, watermelon, and chocolate doughnuts. With rough delicacy, he guided his torch, pouring its earnings into a hot-rod Camaro that never seemed to run right. He danced and brawled and read espionage novels. Once he bragged that he had read every international thriller ever written, many of them twice. He smoked cheap cigars. He worried his thinning hair. He took secret tango lessons. He courted Ellen Cherry Charles.

That the courtship was encouraged, even aided and abetted, by Verlin and Buddy appeared contradictory on the surface of it, considering Boomer's rowdy reputation, considering that the older Verlin's daughter grew, the more strict Verlin became with her. Advised by Buddy, Verlin enforced a conservative dress code for Ellen Cherry. He censored her reading, monitored the television she watched, imposed a curfew, and forbade her to dab herself with the faintest trace of makeup or perfume. Surely, Verlin and Buddy could not have pictured her every Friday night at the Robert E. Lee Drive-in, her panties down around her shins, squirming on one of Boomer's big shot-putter's fingers. Or could they?

The Petways were a fine old Virginia family. There were judges and legislators in the clan. Verlin and Buddy had jigged many a bullfrog with Boomer's daddy. They understood a boy like Boomer. They did not understand Picasso.

"Art school is nothin' but a waste of your time and my money," Verlin protested. "It's flat-out silly. Bud claims art's Satan's way of belittlin' God's handiwork, and Bud may be on target. I do know it's silly. Why don't you go to a decent Christian women's college and study to be a teacher? Or develop some secretarial skills? Somethin' to fall back on. Some security. Marry yourself a good provider—"

"Like ol' Boomer?"

"A woman needs a strong, hard-workin' man. You wanna end up with some sissy makin' mudpies in a attic fulla rats?"

Ellen Cherry smiled. She was remembering the rodents that fought over spilled popcorn alongside the steamed-up cars at the Robert E. Lee.

It was only because of Patsy's militant support that Ellen Cherry was permitted to enroll at Virginia Commonwealth University in

Richmond, which had one of the top fine-arts departments in the nation. She was happy and successful at VCU. She was excited there. She learned to properly stretch and prime a canvas, to ink a lithography stone. She discovered post-painterly expressionism and Georgia O'Keeffe. O'Keeffe became at once her ideal, her heroine, the subject of a paper for which Ellen Cherry earned her first collegiate A. The eye game of her childhood she played with fresh zeal, finding it increasingly a pitchfork with which to puncture what Melville labeled the "pasteboard mask" of visible reality. She was beginning to comprehend what de Kooning meant when he said, "Whatever I see becomes my shapes and my condition."

On weekends, she Greyhounded to Colonial Pines—Daddy's orders—where she continued to date Boomer Petway. Drinking beer and motel-hopping with Boomer provided a relaxing contrast to the intensity of classroom and studio. She had herself a fairly sweet little setup. Until something happened that busted her deal, leaving her with an emotional limp more pronounced than Boomer's jerky gait.

Among the congregation of Colonial Pines Third Baptist Church, a rumor had been circulating that art students at VCU were forced to draw naked bodies. It was said that men as well as women paraded around totally nude in front of mixed classes of boys and girls. Essentially, the report was correct, except that nobody was "forced" to enroll in life classes and that the male models always posed in jockstraps. At any rate, dissatisfied with the school's response to their letter of inquiry (Ellen Cherry, in self-defense, had denied the existence of the life classes), the Reverend Buddy Winkler and Verlin Charles decided to find out for themselves.

So dramatically did Bud and Verlin burst into the classroom that many of the students laughed and shouted, "Rambo! Rambo!" But Ellen Cherry wasn't laughing. Her protests took on a hysterical edge as Verlin pulled her from the room (Buddy Winkler remained to lambast the professor and preach to the thoroughly embarrassed model). Wails, as piercing as meat hooks, as black as swamp water, spiraled from her breast when Verlin commenced to pack her belongings.

Buddy soon joined them in the dormitory. In a frenzy, the two men seized dry washcloths and scrubbed the lipstick, rouge, and eye shadow from her face. So harsh was the scrubbing that it peeled the skin from her cheeks. Like a boiled tomato, her lips split. Her eyelids swelled until it was as though she looked at her room through a blizzard of cinders. She felt as if she were caught in a firestorm and that the purest, smoothest part of her was being pitted.

All the while, as the men scrubbed at her, they uttered one word, over and over.

"Jezebel," they chanted.

"Jezebel!"

Jezebel rode with Ellen Cherry and Boomer in the big roast turkey. Wherever Ellen Cherry went, Jezebel went, too. If Georgia O'Keeffe had been her temporary heroine, Jezebel was her eternal double, her familiar, the bright wound she swung in like a hammock, the ceramic skeleton that clacked inside her flesh. From the day of her humiliation at VCU until the present, a tambourine rang in her blood, and while it just as easily could have been Salome's tambourine, Ellen Cherry identified it as Jezebel's. As a rule, its ringing was soft, its beat distant: months would pass during which she and her invisible twin did not so much as brush past each other in the hall. No sooner had the turkey entered a colored canyon in southeastern Idaho, however, a place where the sandstone appeared to be painted with lavender eye shadow and pomegranate lip balms, than the latent frankincense of Jezebel filled the turkey like an effluvial stuffing and . . .

But hold on. Jezebel has waited this long, she can wait a little longer. First, we should deal with the turkey itself; its origins, its destination, its raison d'être.

For days following her forced withdrawal from college, Ellen Cherry stayed in her room and cried. Downstairs, Patsy and Verlin quarreled viciously. Verlin called Patsy a strumpet, a mother who influenced her daughter to behave lasciviously. Patsy called Verlin a hypocrite who enjoyed lasciviousness but lacked the backbone to admit it.

"God created my body," said Patsy. "I'm not ashamed of its nekkidness."

"Fine," Verlin said. "Why don't you get undressed, and I'll call up all my friends to come paint pictures of you."

"Your friends couldn't paint a shithouse wall."

Patsy charged that she might have become a dancer if it hadn't been for Verlin. Verlin countered that she ought to fall on her knees and thank him for saving her from disgrace.

At one point Ellen Cherry overheard Verlin say, "She's been shut up in her room for damn near a week. When's she gonna come downstairs?"

"Oh, probably when her face heals," answered Patsy.

"Her face is not that bad. We cleaned it, for God's sake! It's not like we flayed her."

"In any case," Patsy said, "she can come down whenever she's good and ready to. She's free, white, and eighteen."

So I am, thought Ellen Cherry. She bolted upright in the tear-smeared bedclothes, propelled by the surprise of the obvious. "So I am!"

When she was certain that Johnny Carson had signed off for the night, she slipped downstairs—Verlin imitated alligators in the bedroom, Patsy tossed and turned on the sofa—and cooked a four-egg omelet, washing it down with the brandy Patsy used to flavor fruitcakes, the only alcohol allowed in the house.

Morning found her in the welding shop, where she somehow persuaded Boomer to loan her five hundred dollars. Maybe she threatened to tell his drinking buddies that he took tango lessons on the sly. Maybe she twisted her tongue in his ear.

That midnight she once again crept downstairs. Patsy had moved to the bedroom, Verlin snored on the sofa. For a while, she stood over her father. Floating upon a pond of sleep, his pink face reminded her of a Monet water lily. She thought him an honorable man damaged by dogma. Patsy and Uncle Buddy were vying for his uncertain soul. Buddy had the lead, but Ellen Cherry would bet Boomer's five hundred on Patsy. Bending to kiss his cheek, she smelled the mildew and changed her mind.

Ellen Cherry boarded the next Greyhound to pass through Colonial Pines. That was at four in the morning. It carried her to Cincinnati. From there, she set out hitchhiking, heading for New Mexico to do something girlish and romantic, such as setting up her easel beside Georgia O'Keeffe's grave. She hadn't counted on the vagrancies of the road, however, and she landed in Seattle, where she was forced to modify her eye game to accommodate hissing curtains of rain.

Working nights as a waitress, Ellen Cherry earned a degree in three years from the Cornish College of the Arts. In only one way did graduation alter her fortunes: she was now eligible for membership in the Daughters of the Daily Special, a local organization of waitresses with college degrees. Paying relatively stiff weekly dues and raising additional funds with bikini car washes and bake sales (most of the bakery goods were pilfered from restaurants in which the women worked), the Daughters established a fund that awarded grants to deserving members so that they might lay down their trays and devote some time to their true calling. When Ellen Cherry won hers, she painted for six months without interruption. The work she completed was hung in a restaurant. "I escaped, my paintings didn't," she told the girls. It may have been the happiest period in her life.

For several years, Seattle's art scene, like New York's, had been dominated by the Big Dumb Ugly Head School of painting. Dealers and collectors too insecure to buck fashion were obliged to cover their walls with clumsy portraits of the aggressive victims of urban angst: those angry, tormented sourpusses for whom the next pluto-nium enema apparently was right around the corner. In the back-ground was the compulsory burning building, skull-and-crossbones, or rabid dog with a hard-on. The world of art is seldom slow to rotate on its gelt-greased axis, however, and—wham!—overnight, connoisseurs were interested in integrity, vision, and technique again. Because of nostalgia, perhaps, an unconscious yearning for a country-side not damned by pollution and development, landscape painting began to be taken seriously for the first time since the Great Depres-sion. And a path began to be beaten to the door of Ellen Cherry Charles.

Sure, she depicted cattails growing out of the side of ferry boats; sure, her trees were loops in space, her mountains sky-blue and her skies as tan as stone: they were recognizably landscapes, nonetheless, and they acquired an audience. She hadn't the trendiest gallery, the most chic patrons, but she was launched, as they say, and down to two shifts a week at the War on Tuna Café.

Generally speaking, that was her situation when Boomer drove into Seattle in the turkey.

Approaching retirement, Boomer's father had purchased an Airstream motor home with the notion that he and his wife might spend their golden years touring the United States. "We'll drive this sucker from sea to shining sea," he said. "And not miss a one of our favorite TV shows," added Mrs. Petway.

Alas, midway through his retirement party, at the apex of merriment, Mr. Petway collapsed and died. His widow sold their house and moved in with a sister, but not before signing over the Airstream to Boomer.

"What the hell am I gonna do with an eight-ton silver egg?" Boomer wondered.

His metaphor was apt. Except that it had a cockpit with steering wheel, Airstream's motor home looked almost exactly like its famous trailer. Which is to say, it looked like the ovoid deposit of a metallic dragon-bird, the hard-boiled cackleberry the Statue of Liberty was about to peel for her breakfast. Silvery as starlight, bulbous as a porpoise nose, the Airstream was an elongated pea, a bean, a sausage skin inflated with mercury, a land blimp, a lemon (in shape, not performance), the football of the titans.

Each morning before he went to work, Boomer would stand in his driveway, hands on his hips, scrutinize the Airstream, and shake his head. Some days, if he wasn't late, hungover, or both, he would circle it, tracing its curves in the dust with his lame foot. One morning, a funny picture popped into his mind. From then on, every time he saw the motor home, he thought of that image.

This continued for approximately a year, until one Friday he awoke in a mood that could best be described as operatic. Overwrought, melodramatic, exploding with energy, his head swimming in a kind of ornate, fatalistic overture, he frightened away the soprano with whom he'd spent the night, fetched a six-pack, and drove the Airstream to the welding shop. There, ignoring work orders and the hoots of his assistants, he spent a month fabricating a pair of giant metal drumsticks and two stumpy metal wings, then welding them to the motor-home body in appropriate positions.

"There," Boomer said. "If that ain't the spittin' image of a roast turkey, what is?"

"It's cute," the girls all said. "How'd you ever think of that?" They giggled nervously.

"You've goddamned ruined a highly expensive piece of equipment," his buddies accused. They were embarrassed for him.

Calmly now, he packed every thread of his wardrobe (six pairs of jeans, five Hawaiian shirts), his welding paraphernalia, and collection of spy novels into the forward storage bin. He loaded on a cargo of Pabst. And then he aimed the glimmering breast of the thing northwestward.

"If Ellen Cherry's not with me on this," he said, "I'll just motor on down to Mexico and tequila myself into a stand-up fossil."

Women were more interested in sex than men were, Ellen Cherry was convinced of that. True, men talked about sex more. Men were forever making a big deal about it with jokes, *Hustler* magazines, aggressive advances, and transparent braggadocio—but in her opinion that was largely for the benefit of other males. They thought that to be masculine, they had to be copulative dynamos, and it was largely to prop up their insecure masculinity that they resorted to sexual display, whereas, in fact, it was their relatively mild interest in actual physical contact that was largely the *source* of that insecurity. Why am I not more horny? Why isn't my pecker bigger? Why am I washed up after one orgasm when *she* can have a dozen and still be ready to go (to go with some fresh man)? How do I know that kid's really mine? It's got red hair! Ellen Cherry had to laugh.

Typically, her own interest in sex was abiding and deep. And incognito. In a patriarchal society, the abiding sexuality of the healthy female was obliged to wear a prim disguise. Unaware of the irony, men flaunted their pale desires, while the stronger passions of the woman were usually concealed. Nobody could tell Ellen Cherry otherwise.

The only thing that interested Ellen Cherry more than sex—in her five years in Seattle, she had drained the night drops from at least eight swains, none, she discovered to her dismay, half as satisfying as Boomer—was love. And art. Well, sex, love, and art intermingled when Boomer eased the remodeled Airstream into her apartment house parking lot.

Its honking drew her to the kitchenette window. The notorious raindrops of Seattle blistered the fire escape, and the sky looked like bad banana baby food. But there it was! Shining in the gray. Thirty-two feet long, sixteen thousand, five hundred pounds. Emergency lights blinking, windshield wipers chasing themselves. And beside it, Boomer Petway doing his wild and gimpy dance, splashing puddle water almost as high as its appendages.

"I made it for you!" Boomer yelled. "Made it for you, little sugar britches!

"Wahoo!"

After combing her curls with the most convenient implement, which happened to be a tofu-encrusted chopstick, she raced downstairs. Oblivious to the shotgun drizzle, incandescent with surprise and wonder, she circumambulated the outlandish turkeymobile, hand in hand with its creator. Around and around they went, in a glow of amused admiration, until they had practically worn a path in the wet asphalt. Eventually, he swept her up in his arms and carried her into the belly of the beast. Her panties were off before she hit the bed.

He tricked me, Ellen Cherry was thinking now. *With art and sex, he tricked me into love.*

Trouble was, she had scant faith in her love for Boomer. Married less than a week and already it was slipping like a frayed fan belt. Lust she feared would also leave in time. Just fly out the transom one morning on its salty red wings. Whatever happened, though, her art would see her through. She was confident enough in it to take it to New York. Give her the big time. Give her a big break. Give her Manhattan. The Bronx and Staten Island, too. Give her this day her daily bread. Boomer's welding, for the time being, would bring home the bacon and the turpentine.

Boomer had asked her once, in a telephone call from Virginia, "Why does this stuff, these hand-painted hallucinations that don't do nothin' but confuse the puddin' out of a perfectly reasonable wall, why does it mean so much to you?"

It was a poor connection, but he could have sworn he heard her say, "In the haunted house of life, art is the only stair that doesn't creak."

Mr. and Mrs. Petway, tricked and trickster, were turkey-trotting through a loop of the Bible Belt. Slogans of the death cult were everywhere. "Jesus Is Coming," the billboards announced. "Prepare to Meet Thy Maker." "Repent for the End Is Near." Can o' Beans had the feeling that if doomsday didn't arrive quite soon, those people were going to take up a collection and send for it.

"Time Is Running Out." "Have You Reserved Your Place in New Jerusalem?" Echoes of Uncle Buddy and his ilk. It gave Ellen Cherry the Hebrew-jeebies. Especially since the brightly hued cliffs and craters that surrounded the billboards had succeeded in releasing her doppelgänger, old Jezebel, from her rouge jar.

"Bring Him the Bleeding Head of the Whore," read one sign, and that one really escalated the willies, because Ellen Cherry was positive that the "Whore" to whom the sign referred was Jezebel.

She had outgrown her susceptibility to car sickness, but she squinted anyway, intending to employ the eye game as a distraction. Instantly, the rough, irregular contours of the sandstone landscape, the interlocking configurations of mesa, gully, and natural chimney, began to soften, to sift, to close off the background space so that the countryside was projected forward, millimeters in front of Ellen Cherry's nose, where it presented itself as laced webs of scrambled color. Alas, since the jumbled color was both powdery and decorative—it tended toward salmon, grape, and ivory—it was even more evocative of cosmetics than when it was in hard-edged perspective, and Jezebel's presence was reinforced rather than denied. The artist called off the game.

Soon after arriving in Seattle, the incident at VCU still painfully alive in her mind, she had procured a bible and gone searching for the lurid details of Jezebel's debauchery. From Sunday school, she had a hazy picture of a thoroughly immoral harlot who costumed herself like a rock 'n' roll vamp, but she couldn't recall a single biographical fact. Imagine her surprise when the Old Testament Book of Kings informed her that Jezebel was a royal—and faithful—wife.

Actually, the biblical story of Jezebel is only a few sentences long. It seems that she and her husband, King Ahab, were accused of practicing idolatry by a young right-winger named Jehu, who had designs on the throne. Earlier, Ahab had acquired by devious means some real estate belonging to a neighbor, and Jezebel was said to have sparked a rumor that led to the neighbor's death. Ahab, a Hebrew, was king of northern Israel; Jezebel was the daughter of a king and queen of Phoenicia. Being a foreigner, she didn't wholeheartedly worship the god of the Jews, which may have led to the "idolatry" charges, but aside from loyally supporting her husband in his suspect land deal, she apparently had been as properly behaved as, say, Queen Elizabeth.

Then, there was a curious and fatal episode. The ambitious Jehu, having secretly murdered Jezebel's son (Ahab, in the meantime, had died in battle), came riding up to the palace. When Jezebel heard of his unscheduled visit, she, according to Scripture, "painted her face and tired her head and looked out a window." Another translation had her painting her "eyes" and "arranging her hair." In any case, there she was, freshly groomed, looking out at the Hebrew rebel, when he incited "two or three eunuchs" to "throw her down." "Her blood splattered the wall," according to the gory old Bible, and Jehu left her in the courtyard for the dogs to eat while he went inside and helped himself to the wine. After a few flagons, he must have felt a prick of guilt because he ordered his flunkies to go bury her, but by that time the mutts had left nothing but "her skull, her feet, and the palms of her hands."

Ellen Cherry was as mystified as the fly that wasted a day following a plastic horse. What had Queen Jezebel done to earn the distinction as our all-time treacherous slut? In the Bitch Hall of Fame, Jezebel had a room of her own; nay, an entire wing. For fixing her hair and applying makeup? Was it implied that she went to the window to *flirt* with the rebel warrior? And if so, was that so wicked that it should wreck her reputation for three thousand years? The trimillennial lash-bat?

As Ellen Cherry walked the rain-rippled pavement of Seattle, bumbershooting from restaurant to restaurant in search of a job, she bore upon her back the weight of a skull, a pair of feet, and the palms of two hands. The nails of the feet were lacquered vermilion, a pretty ribbon fluttered from a lacuna in the skull. And she would wonder as she walked, "What is the Bible trying to tell us?"

That Satan is a hairdresser?

That Elizabeth Arden ought to be fed to the poodles?

"Spooky around here, don't you think, Boomer?"

"Well, it's kinda like the moon."

"We should have taken the direct route."

"What's the hurry? This is our honeymoon. Honeymoon on the moon."

"Are you nervous about New York?"

"Why, hell no. No reason for *me* to be nervous. New York's just a big pile of iron and steel. Perfect for a welder." He focused on the countryside. They were either in Wyoming or Utah now, he wasn't sure which, and the rock formations looked like furniture in the lobby of the Eternity Hotel. "Out here," he said, "a welding torch could atrophy. Just wither away and die from lack of use." He stared at his bride. There was no danger in staring. The road was as straight as a shot of grain alcohol, and the jackrabbits, well, each individual rabbit had the right to make his or her own choice when it came to crossing the path of an onrushing Airstream turkey. "There's a part of me gonna atrophy and drop off, too, if you and me don't make a rest stop pretty soon."

"Oh, Boomer! You just had some this morning."

"That was this morning." He squeezed her thigh.

"Oh, Boomer!"

He turned back to the highway but continued to grip her leg as though it were a misshapen shot put that he might at any second hurl into the record books of western Wyoming. Or was it Utah? "Maybe New York is making *you* a little nervous, huh, babe?"

She shook her tumbleweed, her butterscotch maelstrom, but she answered, "Yeah, I guess. Famous artists, dealers, collectors, curators, critics. I'll be involved with some high-powered people, rich, sophisticated hard-ball players; me, Ellen Cherry Charles, the painting waitress, the little Jezebel of Colonial Pines."

Boomer snatched his eyes off the road again, allowing a jackrabbit to fulfill its pact with destiny. "Mrs. Randolph Petway the Third—of the Virginia Petways—and don't ever let 'em forget it."

He wished that she wouldn't link herself to Jezebel like that. No matter how lightly she phrased it, it struck him as self-deprecating. A person can't make a career out of somebody else's invective. Only recently, an observer had called him a hydrocephalic lummox, and he hadn't even bothered to look it up. Was Ellen Cherry just picking scabs or what?

Confused by the Bible's portrayal of Jezebel—it appeared to contend that cosmetics were witchcraft, and coquetry a capital offense— Ellen Cherry had asked Patsy (lines of communication with her parents had been reopened approximately six months after she settled in Seattle) what she knew about the queen's sordid reputation.

"Just a real tacky woman, I reckon."

"Mama! Is it possible you could be more specific?"

"Your daddy didn't mean it, honey. Calling you ugly names. Bud just had him all festered up. Bud makes him feel guilty about stuff they did when they were boys, mischief they got into, and then he manipulates him. But—"

"Mama, please, do me a favor and just ask Uncle Buddy what Jezebel did that was so bad. I'd like particulars."

The next time the Reverend Buddy Winkler stopped by for dinner, Patsy had, indeed, raised the subject. There was silence, except for the musical sizzle of pork chops in the skillet. Slowly, the preacher got up from the kitchen chair, a chair whose green enamel contrasted vividly with his berry-domed boils, and he laid his hungry expression upon Patsy like the tongue of a steer. She could almost feel strings of cold saliva dripping to make paste of the flour on her apron.

"You tryin' to spoil my appetite, Patsy? Ain't there enough pork chops to go 'round? Utterin' the name of that shameless fornicator, that painted hussy before we've sat down to our supper. I want you to lead our grace tonight, so's to scour the scum the name of Jezebel may have left in your mouth."

"My mouth's spic and span, thank you, Bud." She opened it wide and held it open for a while, close to his face, to see if looking into her pink yawn would set off his tic. It did. "Jest tell me, who all did this ol' hussy fornicate with?"

Buddy stepped back. Something about the way she said "fornicate" unnerved him. "Patsy now."

"Well, *who*, Bud?"

When he spoke again it was in his pulpit voice, his saxophone voice, his blue flame voice, although the jaw tic that Patsy had inspired caused him to miss occasional stops and to blur the higher registers. "It is written in the Book of Revelation, chapter two, verse eighteen, that God Almighty sent a message to the church in Thyatira—"

"Where?"

"Thyatira."

"Where's that?"

"It don't matter! It don't exist anymore. God said unto them, 'I have a few things against thee, because thou sufferest a woman named Jezebel, which calleth herself a prophetess, to teach and to seduce my servants to commit fornication.'"

"So, she didn't do the fornicating herself. She tried to get other folks to do it."

"Patsy, you're missin' the point. Jezebel was a prophetess of Baal. She was a pagan fanatic, she was a filthy idolator who led the Is-raelites away from Jehovah. For twenty-seven years, that woman used her power as queen to try and overthrow Jehovah and replace him with the idols of her native country."

"What was the king doing all this time?"

"Ahab was under her thumb. It's the same ol' story. A connivin' woman influencin' a weak man to commit crimes he never woulda had the gumption to commit by hisself."

"Uh-huh."

"She wanted to convert Is-ra-el to Baal worship. I'm talkin' the golden calf, Patsy. You know what I'm talkin'? I'm talkin' strange shrines in the woods. I'm talkin' nekkidness and orgy and human sacrifice. Little children by the hundreds sacrificed to some stupid, smelly dairy animal. Babies hacked to pieces on a greasy altar in the moonlight—"

"Gross!" Patsy suddenly held the plumping pork chops in vomitus regard. "I don't wanna hear about dead babies."

"Oh, we hear a heap of ugly things when we speak of Jezebel. Her lies sent an innocent neighbor to a horrible end so that Ahab could annex his vineyards."

"Hubby's little helper went too far, you say? But tell me now, Bud, where does the makeup figger in?"

"The makeup?"

"You know, the painted woman thing. Isn't that what she's remembered for?"

"Patsy, have you never seen a baboon's bottom?"

"I thought we agreed not to spoil our supper."

"A baboon's rump is redder than your apron. Sometimes there's yellow and blue thrown in. Why does your baboon have a colored rump? To attract other baboons to mate with it. Why did Jezebel color her face? I'll wager you can make the obvious connection." He paused. He returned the saxophone to its case.

"Taters are done, I see. Maybe I should call Verlin in. Monday night football, he'll be wanting to eat and scat."

Later in the week, Patsy had telephoned Ellen Cherry in Seattle and catalogued, as faithfully as she dared, Jezebel's vices.

"Neat," Ellen Cherry had said. "I'm delighted to learn that I've been compared to a heathen fornication instructor, a husband corrupter, and a baboon's ass, all in one lump."

Patsy, who had purposely omitted the part about diced babies, cautioned her, "You've got to accept some of Buddy's preaching with a grain of salt. Granted, he's a man of God, but ol' Bud has got . . . *ambition.*"

"Mama, you say it like he's got a disease."

"Well, ambition's not as bad as AIDS, I reckon. But it can be a whole lot worse than the measles."

 ⌣

They were making good time. Saying adios to the rock stacks. Boomer hated to leave them behind. He admired the way the paladins of pumice seemed intent to stand on their own wide feet, to stand tall, face their gods, and one day ascend from this chatty planet to a world more worthy of their silence. Look at 'em back there, rugged and unwavering, not a *Pouilly-fumé* sipper in the lot. No, those rocks were not artists but working stiffs, heroic welders who could mend the hinges of hell, yet if need be, if their loved ones required it, could transform a motor home into a traveling juggernaut entrée basted by the butters of the sun.

The rock formations were thinning out, however. The land was starting to jut less and roll more. Rolling toward the Rockies. It was less arid here. In fact, the road was running parallel with a stream, a tributary of the Green River, perhaps. Juniper sprouted from the hillocks, and barely budding aspen huddled along the creek like ghost squaws come to launder their sheets.

There weren't any settlements, not even on the map, but sure enough, around the next bend a billboard stood, quoting, in archaic English, the apocalyptic rantings of a long-dead Middle Eastern prophet. It made Ellen Cherry shudder, and then it made her mad. "Anybody," she said to herself, "who would erect a garish billboard in a beautiful setting like this would fart in a phone booth, dynamite a hummingbird feeder, use the Mona Lisa for a dartboard, consult a Japanese light meter at the burning of the Hindenburg, or name their firstborn after Richard Milhous Nixon."

On they rolled, turkey and hills. The dire prophesy did not slow them down, nor did it relieve the driver's grip on the passenger's thigh. Suddenly, Ellen Cherry brightened.

"Boomer, you realize you and I can't fornicate anymore?"

He looked astonished. "We can't?"

"Why, no. We're married now. Dictionary says fornication is between unmarried persons. From now on, we've got to call it something else."

"When did we ever call it fornication in the first place? That's a dumb word: fornicate. Sounds like something lawyers do. Government lawyers."

"Well, we've fornicated for the last time, darlin'." She placed her small hand atop his huge one. "So what're we going to do from now on?"

"Same thing but call it something friendly." He was trying to remember if anyone in a spy novel ever spoke of "fornication." Certainly not Bond.

"What would you call it, then? What friendly thing are we going to do from now on?"

"I hadn't thought about it."

"Well, think about it." With her nails, she raked the hair on the back of his hands. "What would you *like* to call it?"

"I don't wanna call it anything. I just wanna do it."

"Then let's do it."

In teasing him, she had gotten herself aroused. While she kissed the right corner of his mouth, he pulled the vehicle off the road, concealing it behind the last mesa in the wilderness.

• • •

"**W**ill the New Jerusalem look like Richmond, the lovely capital of our most lovely state? Nay. Will it look like Washington, D.C., the great capital of this great nation? Nay. Will it look like London or Paris or even—even, what? What's another city that everybody thinks is hot stuff in the beauty department? Uh . . . Venice. Will it look like Venice? Nay. Am I using too many 'nays' here? Oh, no! All these grand cities will shrink beside the New Jerusalem; Rome at the height of its glory will, no, *would,* be but a slum in comparison to . . . Tallahassee. Tallahassee, you moron!"

Despite the prodding of the Reverend Buddy Winkler, the contestant identified the capital of Florida as Miami Beach—"Miami *Beach*? The moron must be a Jewish moron."—thereby losing out on a set of fine Wedgwood china and a year's supply of margarine.

"Now, let's see. Where was I? Ever' last city that man has built in this world, including the fabulous showplaces of the Oriental potentates, that's good, 'fabulous showplaces of Oriental potentates,' will pale into ghettos. . . . Hmmm, I guess your ghetto is not exactly, *pale,* is it? Heh. Will pale beside the transformed Jerusalem that God Almighty will bring down from heaven to serve as the capital of his kingdom on earth, the city where, in which, you and me—you and I—will for all eternity . . . rumba. Come on, stupid. Rumba! Oh? Okay, samba. What's the blessed difference? Nobody dances like that anymore. Let's see. For all eternity dwell. Dwell or live? Ummm . . ."

3 5

The Reverend Buddy Winkler was experiencing some difficulty with his powers of concentration. The game show was not to blame. He always watched television game shows while working on a sermon. As a rule, they proved more inspirational than distracting. All that energetic yearning. Each contestant standing at the gate of wealth, hoping to be judged worthy of admission. No, it wasn't "Wheel of Fortune" that was slowing his pen, it was the good news from the Baptist network. Only that morning, he had learned that two stations in California and one in Oregon had agreed to air his weekly broadcasts. California, yet! Talk about your going forth among your whores, publicans, and sinners. At the rate that his radio exposure was expanding, could a TV contract be long in coming? He couldn't afford to keep postponing a dental overhaul. On the tube, your smile was your mustard-cutter and not a penny less. "Right, Bob?" He grinned at the game show host. And then, the merry saliva turning to roach powder in his cheeks, he drew a despairing hand over his candy jar of boils. "Heal!" he almost shouted, but he was not that kind of preacher.

Buddy's mind wandered to the house call he must make the following day. A member of his local congregation had recently, at the age of eighty-two, undergone surgery to restore her sight. She had been blind since four. The operation was an unqualified success, yet when she looked in a mirror for the first time and observed her corduroy complexion, observed the fissures and puckers that caused her countenance to resemble a close-up photograph of a Laplander's scrotum, she ignored the miracle of vision and flew into a fury. Having never seen an old person's face, she thought the doctors had done it to her, that the epidermal wasteland was an unnatural consequence of the surgery, and she was intent upon filing a malpractice suit. Neither her family nor her attorney could dissuade her, so it fell to Buddy, as her minister, to explain how and why God routinely made prunes out of his little sugarplums.

"For seventy-eight years, that woman sat in the dark, unaware that the cream was curdling. At least I wasn't ambushed." He let his fingers glide over the pustules again, then it was back to the sermon.

Of the New Jerusalem, the Lord revealed to John that its gates were pearls; its foundations garnished with precious stones. Buddy underlined the Bible verse: "The city was pure gold, like unto clear glass."

He supposed that he was obliged to defend that description. There would be debunkers out in California who would object that pure gold wouldn't stand up as construction material. Even in Colonial Pines, the unrighteous, the troublemakers might raise issues of practicality. Patsy might, for example.

Well, he'd be ready, he'd head them off at the pass. "If I was one of these so-called modern preachers, I might say to you, don't get literal on me. John's vision of the New Jerusalem is not meant to be taken at face value. We're dealin' with your symbolism here. John was shown a city that was so beautiful, so glorious, so overwhelmin' to his senses that he compared it to jewels and gold because he lacked the language to describe its reality. John just helped hisself to the most high-sounding metaphors he could come up with. Well, if you wanna believe that the saints and prophets of biblical times went around talkin' like English professors, you're welcome to it. I believe the Holy Bible means exactly what it says. True, you or me couldn't build a house outta pure gold and have it hold up. Donald Trump couldn't build a skyscraper outta gold and have it last. But, brothers and sisters, *God* can do anything he wants! It was God that made gold in the first place. God could build a city outta . . ." Buddy was about to say "grits" until it occurred to him that there were folks listening nowadays who probably were unfamiliar with grits. He surely wasn't going to substitute tofu, California or no California. The idea of a tofu city was both sacrilegious and repulsive. "God could build a city outta . . . *cobwebs* if he took a notion to, and it would outlast Pittsburgh." Yes, indeed, the Reverend Buddy Winkler would stand tall and say to the doubters and modernizers, "Pancreas! Sweetbreads are your gourmet term for your cow pancreas. Come on, Bob, out with it. That sturdy plastic lawn furniture by Bessie of Beverly Hills is *mine!*"

Alas, Buddy Winkler never learned for certain if "pancreas" was the correct answer, for at that instant the game show was interrupted by a news bulletin. Another bomb had exploded on a crowded bus in Jerusalem, killing nineteen and wounding fifty-four.

Boomer thought that they would simply make love in the turkey, back in the rear of the bird on the corner double bed in "blush" color scheme with deep innerspring mattress and color-coordinated quilted bedspread (ample storage tucked away beneath the bed with "pack-at-home" removable trays). Ellen Cherry had other ideas. The sun was shining, it was the first week of spring, there was little traffic and no inhabitants—she wanted to do their friendly thing outdoors in the open air, in the zone of vegetation beneath a gulping sky.

"We'll have a picnic, too," she announced, and she swept into a paper bag a box of crackers, a tin of sardines, a can of pork and beans, a jar of dill pickles, cheeses of both the cheddar and jack varieties, a can opener, a knife, and a spoon. Boomer added four frosted beers.

Hand in hand, she short, he tall, she bouncy, he lame, they walked along the stream. The bank was shaded and many degrees cooler than it had appeared from inside the motor home, so they left the creek and set out across a sun-sprayed hill. Releasing her hand, Boomer walked a few paces ahead of her, meaning that Ellen Cherry, the brisker walker, was forced to throttle her gait. He meant to protect her from any venomous reptile awakened from hibernation by the bells of spring. To that end, he brandished a hefty stick, with which he swatted the bushes and clumps of grass that they passed. From time to time, as they searched for an ideal spot to spread their blanket, he glanced over his shoulder at her, regarding her, as he often did before they made love, as if she were a lost continent about to be rediscovered.

It was sweet of him, she thought, to be protective; sweet and typically southern. In her experience, southern men tended to be charming that way. Protective as Brink's, polite as tea, respectful as a job applicant during a recession. Yet, just beneath the surface of that inviting lagoon, fierce green lobsters clanged brutal claws. Possessive and pugilistic, even the most educated and aristocratic of them—lawyers, psychologists, investment bankers—engaged in fisticuffs with some regularity, usually at swell parties where ponds of bourbon were drained, and frequently over a harmless flirtation. Southern men were trapped in a backwater of masculine ethics, a classical male image that the rest of the population had largely outgrown. To be sure, their code of honor precipitated their chivalrous charm, but it also fostered the primate-band competitiveness that prevented them from relaxing unless dead drunk. Their strength was a facade, for it emanated from rules and protocol rather than from self-knowledge or inner resources. They were paper tigers, these Dixie white boys, though Ellen Cherry would ever prefer them to Latino males: *those* guys—Mexicans, Puerto Ricans, some Italians, even—had absolutely no sense of humor about themselves and got angry over offenses so small a woman required a microscope to identify them.

As for Greek men, she was on the verge of tarring them with the Latino brush when her southern Anglo-Saxon groom, who, she was concluding, was preferable to many Mediterraneans, most South Americans, and all art critics, interrupted with a wave of his club. "Look there," he called, pointing toward a cavity in the hillside just below a rocky overhang. "A cave."

Indeed, it was. Due to the manner in which Ellen Cherry automatically looked at landscapes, squinting and widening, focusing and fuzzing, employing her eye game to drag God's patio furniture from one retinal lanai to another, she probably would have missed it. For that matter, a conventional hiker might have passed it by, as well, since the cave was small and its opening partially obscured by juniper bushes and fallen shale.

As they climbed the slope to its entrance, they entertained similar ideas. The afternoon breeze had stiffened, and spring or no spring, it was chilly enough to pave their backsides with goose bumps at the very thought of undressing. Perhaps the cave would shelter them, provide a warm, cozy haven where they might launch their carnal canoe. They would still be out in nature, but as snug as if swallowed up by the turkey.

Naturally, Boomer insisted on scouting it first. Because the hillside was steep, a fair amount of light angled into the cave's opening. "It's shallow and right dusty, but it looks okay," he reported when he was positive there were no rattlesnakes or bears lying in wait for his tasty bride. She dropped to her hands and knees and followed him inside.

Once in the chamber, they could have stood upright, but standing upright was not what they were there for.

"Have you ever done any spelunking?" Ellen Cherry inquired as she arranged the picnic.

Boomer knew perfectly well what speleology was, since Trevanian's *Shibumi*, with its cave-exploring protagonist, was his favorite spy novel, but he replied, "Is that a fancy form of fornicatin'—or is it something married people can do?"

Ellen Cherry set down the pickles and regarded him drolly. For all of his rowdy bluster, she knew him to be actually rather shy in the trenches. "Oh," she said finally, "*some* married men are expert spelunkers." She took his left hand and, lubricating his ring finger by licking it, removed his wedding band. His protests dwindled into grunts when she gave the finger a bonus suck.

Hiking her skirt up to her waist and pulling her panties down a few tantalizing inches, she slipped the wedding ring into her vagina. She gave it a poke to, well, ascertain that it was securely hidden; then, with a kind of reverse flourish, like a magician who has pulled a rabbit *into* a hat, she snapped her elastic and announced that he could try his luck at spelunking whenever he felt fit.

The um, the oh, the ah; the rubbery slap slap of bare bellies, damp as cavern walls; the clink of gold against tooth enamel as they passed the salty wedding ring from mouth to mouth; the almost audible vibration of her tiny stalactite.

He was lost among glowworms, among silky sprays of bats. Down the shaft of his explorer, he sensed a trickle, like mineral solutions slowly dripping into the eternity of a subterranean lake. There had been other spelunkers in these hollows, that she had confessed, but he took solace in the knowledge that he'd been first, that his was the brush that had left the hunting scenes upon her labial Lascaux.

Um oh ah, this troglodyte love was for him, he reckoned; this cave within a cave, this paleolithic pussy, this descent into the deepest dark of fuck. With what intensity they stared into each other's eyes, their gazes roped together like the discoverers of Carlsbad! Boomer felt that they were squeezed into a narrow crevasse that any moment now would expel them with a rush into a fabulous undiscovered chamber, resplendent with polychrome columns and calcite organ pipes—but, alack, Ellen Cherry chose at that instant to utter a word that jarred him as rudely as a collision with a dripstone.

"Jezebel," she whispered.

"Uh?"

"Please, darlin', call me Jezebel."

Oh, no, he thought. *Not this. She's turning kinky on me.* He said nothing, but increased the power of his thrust.

"Come on, honey."

"Huh-uh." He wished she'd be quiet. That wedding ring trick was cute, but this . . .

"Come on, now. Call me your Jezebel."

"Aw, gee, Ellen Cherry." He pumped with even greater velocity, but she persisted in her demand, and he could tell that if they continued to argue he would lose his erection. Already, it was bowing in the middle like a maître d's tie. "Jezebel," he grunted.

"I can't hear you."

"Jezebel." There was a detectable shortage of enthusiasm.

She sunk her fingernails into his buttocks, her teeth into his shoulder. "Say it, Boomer."

Against his better judgment—was this the way women behaved once they married?—he called it out, loud and clear. "Jezebel!" It echoed: "Jezebel! Jezebel!" The name rattled in the little cave like a die in a cup.

Digging her nails in deeper, Ellen Cherry bucked against him. A moan wobbled out of her throat like an overweight dove.

"Jezebel!" he yelled. "You cheap slutting cunt-whoring Jez-a-fucking-bel!"

With that, he lost consciousness. As for her, her orgasm had been lent the necessary dynamic gradient that in classical theater promises its audience catastrophe, immortality, or both.

Of course, there was no audience there in that funky, obscure little burrow in the disappearing American wilderness.

Or was there?

They lay in silence, barely touching, their postcoital reverie edged with mild embarrassment. Each was waiting for the other to speak, each secretly hoping that when the other did speak, his or her remarks would be cheerful and loving, with no trace of the shame that muzzled the other—and with absolutely no reference to a certain maligned queen from the ninth century B.C. They might have lain like that until the sun went down but for the fact that three or four minutes after their sex cries subsided—it seemed considerably longer—there was a stirring at the rear of the cave.

Ellen Cherry froze. Boomer bolted to a sitting position and made a frantic search for his club.

There it was again, a dry rustle followed by the sort of noise Boomer's work shoe made when he was tired and given to dragging his bad foot. Ellen Cherry's eyes widened, and not in the service of some arty game. Her protective southern husband turned in the direction of the sounds.

At most, the cave was twenty feet deep. To be sure, the light was dim, but they could see easily to the back wall. There was no place for anything, man or beast, to hide. Unless. . . . For the first time, Boomer noticed a small niche, a vaginal slit in the left corner. It was about eight feet from the floor, up near the ceiling, too high to peer into. It hardly seemed adequate to conceal an animal, although he supposed one or more snakes might have called it home.

The noises weren't quite right for snakes, however, nor for the ghost of Injun Joe. Imagine, if you will, that a naive girl has accepted the invitation of an older gentleman to peruse his etchings. Imagine the leather-bound book being dragged from a shelf, the turning of its heavy, expensive pages. Then, imagine the young girl, in her nervousness, knocking over the quart of mescal with which the gentleman would ply her, freeing the mescal worm, which comes to life and tries to organize a revolution in a basket of nacho-flavored corn chips. Those were the kind of noises they were.

Comes to life. . . . There was an accompanying sensation, a feeling that overtook our couple the instant they heard the noises, and that they were later to agree was a sensation of something *coming to life,* although what they couldn't guess. It was spooky, more spooky even than the prospect of some fat fang-snapping reptile sliding down from the niche on its squamous stomach. They pulled on their clothes, snatched up their picnic things, and vacated that den in a flash.

All the way back to the highway, they kept checking to determine that they weren't being pursued, and it wasn't until they were safely inside the turkey that they could laugh.

"You're only wearing one sock," Ellen Cherry pointed out.

"Lucky to get *one* on," Boomer said. "You manage to put on your underpants?"

"Of course. What do you think I am, some Jezebel?"

They stared at each other for one tense moment, then, giggling, fell into a long and tight embrace.

"Must've left that sock behind as an offering to the cave monster," said Boomer.

"As I recall, honey, you'd been wearing that sock for three days."

"Jesus. You're right. How offensive! We better haul on outta here."

Joking aside, they drove quite a distance before they felt comfortable. Even then, they were too flustered to realize that in addition to Boomer's sweat-caked sock, they had left behind in the cave a fine silver spoon and a can of beans.

For approximately a quarter hour after the couple fled the cave, the stirring continued in its niche. None but Dirty Sock, Spoon, and Can o' Beans was privy to it now.

"I'm frightened," said Spoon.

"Nothin' in there can hurt us," said Dirty Sock. The idea of a viper biting an old purple sock struck him as funny. Were there a possibility of a puppy in the niche, he would have been less amused.

"Shhh," shushed Can o' Beans. "Hear those sighs. Whatever is waking up in there is waking up slowly because they've been asleep a long, long time."

Can o' Beans was correct. In fact, nearly two thousand springs had come and gone since that which was awakening was last awake. Obviously, more than a simple vernal equinox was required to interrupt such slumber. What had awakened that which was awakening was the sexual intercourse of Mr. and Mrs. Boomer Petway, combined with the echoing shouts of a familiar and treasured name.

Oh, yes, Jezebel was well known to those that hibernated in the nook. Any questions that Ellen Cherry had concerning the "painted hussy" could have been answered by them in accurate detail.

They could, for example, have supplied the following information:

Except in an entirely secondary manner, Queen Jezebel never worshipped Baal. *Baal* was the ancient Semite word for "lord" or "husband." The god referred to by the Bible as Baal had divine status primarily because he was husband to Astarte. It was Astarte whom Jezebel worshipped.

Who was Astarte? She was a goddess; rather, she was *the* Goddess, the Great Mother, the Light of the World, the most ancient and widely revered divinity in human history. Shrines to her date back to the Neolithic Period, and there was not one Indo-European culture that failed to remove with its kiss the mud from her sidereal slippers. In comparison, "God," as we moderns call Yahweh (often misspelled "Jehovah") was a Yahny-come-lately who would never approach her enormous popularity. She was the mother of God, as indeed, she was mother of all. As beloved as she was for her life-giving and nurturing qualities, the only activities of hers acceptable to the patriarchs, she was mistress over destruction as well as creation, representing, according to one scholar, "the abyss that is the source and the end, the ground of all being."

In Jezebel's native Phoenicia, the Goddess's name was Astarte. In Babylon, she was Ishtar; in India, Kali; in Greece, Demeter (immature aspect: Aphrodite). If Saxon was your indigenous tongue, you would address her as Ostara; if Nordic, you'd say Freya; if Egyptian, Isis—or Nut or Hathor or Neith. Oh, the Goddess had many names, and many roles. She was virgin, bride, mother, prostitute, witch, and hanging judge, all swirled into one. She had more phases than the moon. She knew the dark side of the moon like the palm of her hand. She shopped there.

Because the Goddess was changeable and playful, because she looked upon natural chaos as lovingly as she did natural order, because her warm feminine intuition was often at odds with cool masculine reason, because the uterine magic of her daughters had since the dawn of consciousness overshadowed the penis power of her sons, resentful priests of a tribe of nomadic Hebrews led a coup against her some four thousand years ago—and most of what we know as Western civilization is the result. Life still begins in the womb, cocky erections still collapse and lie useless when woman's superior sexuality is finished with them, but men control the divine channels now, and while that control may be largely an illusion, their laws, institutions, and elaborate weaponry exist primarily to maintain it.

In Jezebel's time, a full millennium after the patriarchal revolt, Yahweh had managed to establish no more than a precarious foothold. Today, each and every ejaculation, each and every earthquake or harvest moon may remind the deep male unconscious of the Goddess's continued presence, but in the ninth century B.C., she was openly worshipped in the lands surrounding Israel, and covertly in Israel itself. Small wonder, then, that when King Ahab's Phoenician bride started building shrines to Astarte, and when the Israelites started flocking to those shrines—the populace apparently favored Astarte's voluptuous indulgence over Yahweh's rigid asceticism—the patriarchs reacted violently against her. Interestingly enough, one of the crimes charged to Jezebel, according to the historian Josephus, was the planting of trees. Since the Goddess always has been honored in sacred groves, it is understandable that patriarchs, then as now, leaned toward deforestation.

Incidentally, Astarte's Hebrew appellation—Ashtoreth—is mentioned in the Bible only thrice. In carefully patriarchalized incarnations, the Goddess does appear in Scripture as Eve and the Virgin Mary (the one a wily temptress, the other an asensual, passive vehicle); John refers to her as the whore of Babylon, identified with the fornicating "Beast" whom the innocent, nonorgasmic "Lamb" will defeat in the battle that climaxes history. But the mouthpieces of patriarchy were far too freaked out by her, by her openness, her variability, her magic and carnality, to so much as write down her name. Thus, they substituted her husband, her *baal*, realizing, too, that only to a male divinity could the alleged sacrifice of babies be convincingly attributed.

Lest it be misconstrued here that those that stretched and yawned in the underground niche had some historic ax to grind, it should be established that they were . . . well, agents of reality, not scholars or proselytizers, and hardly would have bothered, even were they able, to reel off names of goddesses as if announcing the lineup of a soccer team. Yet, while they undoubtedly would have been less loquacious about it, they would willingly have revealed to Ellen Cherry the true character of Jezebel's transgressions. To wit: her misdeed was her devotion to Astarte. Because that devotion was contagious (being an instinctive human reflex), because it weakened the grip of the Yahweh cult, she was slandered, framed, and finally murdered.

When the moment arrived, Jezebel was thoroughly aware that she was to be assassinated. She put up her ergot-black hair, donned her tiara, rouged her cheeks and lips, applied kohl to the lids of her huge Phoenician eyes, and went to face her killer with the style, dignity, and grace befitting a reigning queen. So much for painted hussies.

The dog-sucked bones of Jezebel may be the skeleton that bangs its knobs in the closet of our race.

Why wasn't Ellen Cherry aware of all this? Why wasn't the mass of humankind aware of it? Because veils of ignorance, disinformation, and illusion separate us from that which is imperative to our understanding of our evolutionary journey, shield us from the Mystery that is central to being.

The first of those veils conceals the repression of the Goddess, masks the sexual face of the planet, drapes the ancient foundation stone of erotic terror that props up modern man's religion.

But, listen now. If Painted Stick and Conch Shell are permitted to leave the cave where they've been sleeping—and what stands in their path but a spoon, a smelly old sock, and a can of beans?—Salome might dance in the Temple again. And if nobody stops Salome from dancing, that first veil may one day soon be dropping.

the second veil

"**W**hy is it," Boomer asked, "that beer goes to your head faster in the daytime than it does after dark?"

The man to whom he had addressed the question tugged at his scraggly beard, nodded, said nothing.

"It's a fact," Boomer went on. "I can drink triple after sundown what I can hold in the afternoon. You notice that, too?"

Ellen Cherry was in a Speedy Wash doing their laundry. From now on, she insisted, Boomer would go forth into the world attired in the freshest, most sanitary footwear that detergent and hot water could provide. Should ever she break that vow, he would have only to remind her of the sock he'd left in the cave the previous day, the one whose foulness was offending, they half-kiddingly suspected, some chthonian spirit creature whose hospitality they had violated after it stood guard over their marvelous fuck. While she watched the stockings and underwear flap and churn, dive and surface in the suds, directing her eye game through the porthole in the washer door, Boomer had repaired to a tavern across the street.

"It's a common phenomenon," Boomer said, "but I've never heard it explained on the education channel or anywheres. How 'bout you?"

There were only three people at the bar: Boomer, the man to his left, and the man to *his* left. Boomer's neighbor was large and seedy looking, shirted in wrinkled plaid flannel that gave the impression it had been repeatedly run over by farm machinery. His beard might have endured an identical ordeal. He nodded at Boomer but did not speak. His pal, obscured from Boomer's view by the first man's bulk, stared straight ahead. The bartender, an elderly woman, was at the far end, assiduously polishing, inspecting, and repolishing cheap glassware, as if the Queen of England and her entourage were due by any moment for a round of brews. From its lonesome perch, an unwatched TV set flicked frizzy pictures of a soap-opera character weeping for her boyfriend who had been dispatched to help keep peace in the Middle East. The girl on the show was wondering why the Arabs and the Jews couldn't learn to live in harmony.

Boomer, like most Americans, had wondered about that himself once or twice. Today he was wondering about something else. "Must have something to do with light. The alcohol refracts the sunlight somehow, causing a reaction in the brain. Bang! Right behind the eyes."

Still the big man was reticent. Boomer leaned toward him.

"Of course, the effect might be different up here in the Rockies for all I know. Altitude. I understand that peacocks can't squawk above five thousand feet. Altitude makes 'em mute as doorknobs. I'm assuming that doorknobs are mute. They're widely acknowledged to be deaf. Regular little Helen Kellers." Boomer flashed an understanding grin. "Say, maybe that's *your* problem." Placing his mouth close to the fellow's ear, he screamed, "Annie Sullivan calling!", confident that the man would recognize the name of the therapist who taught Ms. Keller to speak.

With one slow but unavoidable paw, the man flung Boomer from the bar stool. As he struggled to right himself, brushing spilled beer from the palm fronds on his aloha shirt, Boomer exclaimed, "If God didn't prefer for us to drink at night, he wouldn't have made neon! Am I right or wrong? And that is *not* a rhetorical question."

They exchanged grazing blows, grappled, clinched, and fell to the floor, Boomer on the bottom. Boomer had just linked his fingers around the man's arboreal throat—which had yet to produce a peep—and was commencing to squeeze when Ellen Cherry marched in, swatted them both with her loaded laundry bag, and pulled them apart. The third man slipped off his stool as if inclined to interfere, but a newly washed pink lace brassiere tumbled, A cup over A cup, from the laundry bag and landed at his shoes. He backed away from it like a vampire from a garlic bulb.

Ellen Cherry retrieved her undergarment, assisted the combatants to their feet, and pushed Boomer toward the exit. "Gentlemen, I

apologize," she said. "My husband is a complete idiot." They nodded.
"But you've got to admit, he's a hill of fun."

As the couple was backing out the door, the big man at last broke
his silence. In a hoarse whisper, he croaked, "I kicked your ass."

Boomer whirled, shaking an angry fist at his opponent. "You never
kicked nothin', Dumbo! You use steroids! You've been disqualified!"

With a yank that could have ripped the beak off a toucan, Ellen
Cherry snatched him into the street. A full foot of snow remained in
the village gutters. When they saw the blaze in Ellen Cherry's face,
each little compressed crystal in the drift whimpered with anxiety.
"Where, oh where, will we be come August?" they cried in unison.

Ellen Cherry had a question of her own. "Goddamn it, Boomer!" she
swore. "Are you going to be pulling these stunts in New York City?"

Inside the tavern, normalcy returned. On television, a jilted lover was
sobbing; on the jukebox, a jilted lover was crooning; on a beer glass,
a flyspeck was disintegrating; on the ceiling, a Marlboro cumulus was
gathering; on wire racks, beef jerky was moldering, and on bar
stools, the two patrons were frescoing their tonsils with the Bavarian
brush. They drank as one.

"You know," said the smaller man, rimming his Coors can with an
index finger, "that asshole was right."

"Whaddya mean?"

"Brew treats you different in the day than it does at night."

"Maybe some people."

"Makes you sleepy. Makes you see stuff."

Habitually, the big man's laugh so resembled choking that he
couldn't watch "Hee Haw" in public without some stranger trying the
Heimlich maneuver on him. When his derisive chortle had finally
humped its way through the mucilaginous layers that webbed his
throat, he added, "See stuff," as if repeating his friend's remark was
enough to refute it.

"My sister called me this morning. Now, I've knowed her to put
down near as many brewskies as me and you. And you'd need a
damn Breathalyzer machine to know she hadn't been sipping Bosco.
I'm talking night drinking. Well, this morning, about noon, she
called from way over near Pocatello, where they been living. She'd
had a couple already. And she seen stuff."

"Stuff?"

"You know. Things."

"There's things all around us, Mike. Every damn place you look, there's things. Things on that fool's shirt whose ass I kicked. Whud your sis see—things from outer space?"

"They was regular things, ordinary little usual things. You're missing the damn point. It was morning, and she'd had, the most, four beers, and she was driving along and thought she saw this stuff walking the side of the road. That's all."

The big man shook his big head slowly from side to side. He was quiet for so long one might have imagined that Anne Sullivan, indeed, would have been required to restore his powers of speech. Eventually, he gave his whiskers a sort of snappy tug and asked, "What kind of stuff walking the side of the road?"

"Let's jest forget it." Mike summoned the bartender from her jihad on flyspecks, ordered another round of Coors, and offered the opinion that Uncle Sam ought to just wade in and take the oil fields away from the Arabs and be done with it. "Not that I favor the Jews over the Arabs, they're both lower than the tits on a sow, far as I'm concerned. But we ought to stop the terrorism and take the damn oil."

Mike really didn't want to discuss foreign policy, but how could he sit there and tell anybody that his sister had seen a seashell that morning walking alongside a country road? And a fork or a spoon. And a red stick and a sock. A sock, for Christ's sake! And what looked like a can of beans.

There are landscapes in which we feel above us not sky but space. Something larger, deeper than sky is sensed, is seen, although in such settings the sky itself is invariably immense. There is a place between the cerebrum and the stars where sky stops and space commences, and should we find ourselves on a particular prairie or mountaintop at a particular hour (the wispiest little pasta of cloud can spoil the effect), our relationship with sky thins and loosens while our connection to space becomes as solid as bone.

Near that raised stitchery on the map where the quilt scraps of Idaho, Utah, and Wyoming are sewn together, Can o' Beans rested in the twilight, taking in, and being taken in by, an overflowing vault that was not so much sky as space.

It was the end of their first day's journey but also the beginning of their first night's journey. Following the events of the morning—the tipsy woman who almost wrecked her pickup truck when she spotted them along the highway, the hunters who fired at them (thinking them rabbits or what?) not long after they moved away from the road and into the countryside—Painted Stick and Conch Shell had decided to take Can o' Beans's original advice, which had been to travel by night. Painted Stick was naive even to consider that their band of objects might, with impunity, move across America in broad daylight. Welcome to the modern world, Painted Stick.

Having spent the afternoon hiding in a tiny arroyo, they would soon be under way again, and now Can o' Beans stood on the gully's lip, looking past a darkening sky into the dominions of stillness and grace. With a serene, if tinny, shiver, he/she centered him/herself at that spatial crossroads where Intimacy and Elsewhere intersect, and reviewed from a philosophical vantage, the strange situation in which he/she found him/herself.

Conch Shell had been first out of the niche. She had dropped in such a manner that she landed on the hard tip of her spire, thereby avoiding any cracking or chipping of her body or lips. For a second, she had stuck there in the cave floor's soil, balanced upright on her spire. Then, slowly, she had fallen over to rest on the low ridges of her body whorls. She had lain like an odalisque, lounging upon her whorled side, affording an unobstructed and, perhaps, immodest view of her tannish outer lip, her creamy inner lip, and the heavenly pinks of her opening, her aperture.

To Can o' Beans and Dirty Sock, who had been expecting something scaly and wired, the pink glow of Conch Shell was heavenly indeed. Can o' Beans thought she might have been the most lovely thing he/she had ever seen. He/she issued a sigh that spun every single bean in his/her sauce. Dirty Sock whistled in the style of a construction worker and called, "Hey now, hey now, foxy lady!" or something like that.

As for Spoon, she registered such a pang of jealousy that it very nearly turned her as green as if she had spent a night in mayonnaise.

The conch shell is the voice of Buddha, the birth-bed of Aphrodite, the horn that drives away all demons and draws lost mariners home from the sea. Colored by the moon, shaped by the primal geometry, it is the original dreamboat, the sacred submarine that carries fertility to its rendezvous with poetry.

Shaped by the primal geometry? No, the conch shell *is* primal geometry. Its perfect logarithmic spiral coils from left to right around an axis of fundamental truth. A house exuded by the dreams of its inhabitant, it is the finest example of the architecture of imagination, the logic of desire.

A calcified womb, a self-propelled nest, the conch shell outlasts its tenant, its builder, to go on alone, reminding the world's forgetful of their watery sexuality.

Mermaid's tongue. Milkmaid's ulcer. Courtesan's powder box. Ballerina's musk. With its marvelous pinkness, the glow from Conch Shell's long, smooth, folded aperture saturated the cave. It was a bonbon pink, a tropical pink; above all, a feminine pink. The tint it cast was that of a vagina blowing bubble gum.

As the three forgotten articles were admiring Conch Shell, and puzzling how she came to be in that dry place, Painted Stick flew out of the nook and gave them each a fright. Conch Shell had dropped as elegantly as a parachutist. Painted Stick, on the other hand, leapt with reckless abandon—so reckless, in fact, that he landed on top of her.

No harm was done her, for he hit her backside, which was as rough as her front was slick. Hardly a puny periwinkle, Conch Shell weighed a full five pounds and measured eleven and a half inches from apex to lip curl. Her spire was spiked in the manner of a mace, and the whorls that ribbed her bulk were thick and tough. It was almost as if she were naked in front, around the pinks and creams of her aperture, yet protected elsewhere by a tan suit of armor that would have made a knight rattle with envy.

Speaking of iron tuxedos, one of the religious billboards passed by the giant turkey had commanded its readers to "Put On the Whole Armor of God." Boomer and Ellen Cherry failed to guess that it was a motto borrowed from the Crusaders, although Ellen Cherry eventually was to learn that it was the Crusaders, those barbarous European knights, who, in the sweet name of Jesus, had done as much as anyone or anything to lock the Middle East in the lapidary machine of hellfire in which for all these centuries it has been painfully tumbling.

Painted Stick bounced off Conch Shell's armor plate, then rolled to within several feet of our abandoned trio. "Greetings," he said, at no loss for breath or words (although, obviously, objects do not, in the animate sense, breathe or speak). "Greetings. I assume from the likes of you that you were not responsible for the great fucking that summoned us from our rest."

Spoon blushed and Dirty Sock chuckled. "There were humans here," said Can o' Beans. "They've run away."

"How unfortunate," said Painted Stick.

"Why's that?" asked Dirty Sock, who was rather pleased to be free of Boomer's twisted foot.

"They would have taken us to where we must be going," Painted Stick replied.

"Don't bet on it," said Dirty Sock.

It turned out that Painted Stick had assumed that Boomer and Ellen Cherry were a priest and priestess of Astarte, from the way they had addressed Jezebel while making love. Painted Stick had had no intentions of walking across America. He thought that he and Conch Shell would be carried to their destination in the arms of the Goddess's adorers, as had been their experience in former times.

When, on the following morning, against Can o' Beans's warnings,

Painted Stick had led the group toward the roadway, the can had confided to the seashell, "I'm afraid Mr. Stick is naive."

"Not naive," Conch Shell had corrected him. "He simply has not been taught to fear the things you fear."

In her hysteria, Mike's beery sister had described the stick as "red." Actually, its original coating was a strong, rusty umber, but the passing centuries had sapped the mineral pigment of its oxidic potency, leaving it a flat, dull rose, like a dance hall memory, and so thin that the original wood showed through it like the night sky through a canopy of fishnet. In addition, there were five blue bands— four narrow, one broad—around the stick's middle, although these, too, were badly faded. Painted Stick's top end was notched, as if someone had tried to carve little horns there, little bull's horns. These crescent-shaped nubs once had been gilded, and flecks of gold leaf still clung to them, like spinach to teeth. His length was under a yard, but he was long enough to have been a cane for a blind jockey or a baton for a conductor with an overbearing personality. In circumference, he equaled a mature carrot, although he was not tapered in any direction.

As the World Tree stands, so stands its child, the sanctified stick. Shamans climb it. Maidens dance around it. Men use it for pointing. It points to thunder, to comets, to the migrating herds. Sometimes it points to you.

Once there was a man who carried a stick that he swirled in a stream until a hair clung to it. The direction in which the hair pointed led to satisfaction. But who deserved credit, the hair or the stick?

Stick is the magic penis. When waved, it sows sons and daughters. Stick is also lethal. It cracks a skull nicely.

Guns have been called "magic sticks," but guns are only half magical: they take life but can't create it.

If a stick is twirled under proper conditions, it makes fire. If rubbed against another stick, it makes fire. Once a stick is painted, however, it is assigned to other duties.

Sigmund Freud observed children rolling hoops with sticks. Freud made notes in his journal.

T.S. Eliot wrote:

> Crossed staves in a field
> Behaving as the wind behaves.

In a deck of cards, there are four suits: diamonds, spades, hearts, and sticks. The card stick was both the rod of the peasant and the wand of the magi. Whip the donkey. Stir the moon.

Like a sword, or a phallus, it feels quite good to hold a stick in your hands. If held correctly, with maximum consciousness (and that is difficult to do), the stick may suddenly flower.

There is a sense in which a painted stick is a stick in bloom. This stick points to the hidden face of God. Sometimes it points to you.

Later, when Dirty Sock asked Painted Stick what he did, meaning exactly what people mean when they ask at a cocktail party, "What do you do?", Painted Stick answered that he was a navigational instrument.

Although his description of his function was an understatement, a simplification, it wasn't precisely a lie. Dirty Sock accepted it at face value, and, up to a point, Can o' Beans did, too. After all, despite his errors of judgment in some areas, it couldn't be denied that Painted Stick marched them unwaveringly eastward.

Almost as abruptly as they had presented themselves, Conch Shell and Painted Stick had asked to be excused.

"Forgive us if we are rude," said Conch Shell, "but we have lain in this foreign place for a very long time."

"And unless the globe has shrunk while we lay in our trance," added Painted Stick, "we have a very long journey ahead of us."

"Where is it that you're headin'?" asked Dirty Sock.

"Why, to the Holy City," said the stick, as if it had been a silly question.

"That would be the Vatican," whispered Spoon, who had spent most of her life in the jelly bowl of a strict Catholic household. Ellen Cherry had acquired her at a diocesan rummage sale.

Dirty Sock nodded in agreement, but the can shook its contents, *slosh gurgle*, as if it weren't so sure.

"Without human assistance," Painted Stick complained, "we probably shall arrive too late."

"Oh, you must not worry so," said the seashell. "I feel in my whorls that we've time to spare." Then, before Can o' Beans could spit out any of the many questions burning his/her sauce, Conch Shell inquired, in her compassionate manner, about the others' circumstances and how they happened to be in that desolate den. After they had given their account of the aborted picnic, she asked, "What will happen to you now?"

Spoon and Dirty Sock looked blank, but Can o' Beans, who had obviously thought about it, replied, "Well, it's fairly dry in here. That's to our advantage. But, unless some human stumbles upon us and takes us away . . ."

"Who'd want just one solitary ol' sock?" asked the soiled one, suddenly morose.

"Unless a peg-legged human stumbles upon us and takes us away, we'll gradually pay our dues to the elements. Miss Spoon should fare okay. She'll tarnish, of course, she'll turn as black as Aretha Franklin, but otherwise, she'll be healthy and whole."

"No, I won't," said Spoon, with a sob in her voice. "What good is a spoon that nobody eats with? To be eaten with is—is all that I exist for." Through her tears, her private longings had unintentionally surfaced. The others could sense the extreme sensual pleasure this dainty utensil had enjoyed in the jelly, in the ice cream—and in the mouth; forever being slipped into soft, sweet substances, then licked and sucked affectionately and repeatedly, followed by a bath in warm, bubbly dishwater.

"As for me," Can o' Beans went on, "I suppose that as the years go by, my label will peel off, and slowly I'll rust. Or, my contents could ferment and cause me to burst. But I'm optimistic. Some adventurous lad will find me and carry me off to his hungry scoutmaster." He/she paused. "Poor Mr. Sock, though. He can only look forward to dry rot and disintegration."

Conch Shell made as if to comfort the distressed stocking, but Painted Stick stopped her. "We wish you the fortune that we wish for ourselves," he said, "but we really must depart now. Matters of mighty importance are about to transpire, and our presence is required."

"At least, we would like to think so," said Conch Shell. Reluctantly, she followed the wooden relic out of the cave. "Have faith," she had called back. "We shall petition the elements in your behalf."

They were alone then, the three of them, really alone. And as silent and useless as Mozart's inkblots.

Within an hour, the exotic objects had returned.

"Greetings again," said Conch Shell. "We have come to beseech you . . ."

"We have come to *invite* you," Painted Stick corrected her.

". . . to accompany us."

"How far?" asked Can o' Beans.

"As far as we are going," replied Conch Shell.

"Except into the Holy of Holies," said the stick. "You cannot follow us in there."

"There is no guarantee that *we* shall be going into the inner sanctum, either," said Conch Shell.

"What has happened twice will happen three times," argued Painted Stick, quoting an ancient law.

The bean tin was obviously a bit bewildered; its companions even more so.

"You are natives here," said Painted Stick. "Without priestesses to transport us, and so far I have seen none, you can provide valuable assistance in the crossing of this broad land."

"Besides," said the pretty univalve, "having frightened away the lovers, it is our fault that you are stranded here. We cannot in good conscience desert you. I am positive that you shall be good company."

"Hey, that's a swell deal!" exclaimed Dirty Sock.

Spoon glanced hopefully at Can o' Beans.

"Miss Spoon here thinks that you are off to visit Vatican City," said Can o' Beans. "I have a feeling that it's not that simple. You just don't strike me as papist types."

In human terms, it would be said that the foreigners smiled. And it occurred to Spoon that Can o' Beans was quite right.

"So," continued the bean tin, "two questions. Where, precisely, are you going? And how do you propose that we accompany you? You know that we lack the power of locomotion."

"Our destination is Jerusalem," said Painted Stick. "I thought we made that clear."

"As for your locomotion," Conch Shell put in, "we believe that we can boost your vibrations."

Like all inanimate objects everywhere, the three displaced articles from the Airstream turkey knew instinctively what the seashell was talking about.

"We need a little while to mull this over," Can o' Beans had said.

"What the hell for?" objected Dirty Sock.

"*Please*, Mr. Sock," said Can o' Beans, somewhat exasperated.

"Very well," Conch Shell said. "We shall leave you to discuss the matter in private."

"But do be quick about it," snapped Painted Stick.

Can o' Beans had stopped the pair as they were leaving the cave. "About this place, Jerusalem," he said. "You might be interested in knowing that there's a lot of strife and unrest there nowadays. In fact, I get the idea that it's a dangerous place to be."

"Oh, dear," said Spoon.

"Yeah. How 'bout that?" asked Dirty Sock.

Painted Stick barely paused in his exit. "Jerusalem has *always* been torn by strife. If the blood in the streets does not reach to my first blue band, then it could not be as dangerous now as it used to be."

To Painted Stick's liking, the election had been fast and favorable: two votes to join in the journey, one abstention. Can o' Beans was far too curious to turn down an opportunity to see more of the world, perilous or not, while the sock couldn't see where he had much to lose: anything was preferable to dry rot. Numb with apprehension, Spoon was incapable of decision. While her companions briefly argued the pros and cons, she daydreamed about chocolate pudding soaking up cream, about the spray from the young Jesuit's trigger-tight mouth, whitecapped inside with eager saliva.

Once informed of the trio's compliance, Painted Stick and Conch Shell immediately began preparations for the frequency-raising ritual. It would require intense effort and concentration on the part of everyone involved.

The inertia of objects is deceptive. The inanimate world appears static, "dead," to humans only because of our neuromuscular chauvinism. We are so enamored of our own activity range that we blind ourselves to the fact that most of the action in the universe is unfolding outside our range, occurring at speeds so much slower or faster than our own that it is hidden from us as if by a . . . a veil.

We regard the objects that polka-dot our daily lives as if they were rigid, totally predictable solids, frozen inferiorly in time and space. Yet, how can we be so sure that we know what things are doing when we aren't looking at them? When our eyesight is inadequate to truly look at them?

For example, here is a can of Van Camp's pork and beans. Familiar? Take a closer look at the label. Forget the ingredients list (including the sugar and corn syrup you may not have guessed this product contains); forget the heating instructions, the declaration of weight (twenty-one ounces or 595 grams, a little heavier than the brain of a horse); forget the modified Old West typeface in which this information is printed, cow-face white and rodeo yellow against a background of bandanna red. Look deeper.

You'll require a magnifying glass, which, incidentally, glass being essentially a liquid, is hardly the passive, inactive object we regard it, either: it just drips and flows at rates we normally fail to register. In any case, the label is paper. When seen close up, it is a rough, tangled bog of wood chips, fragments of hemp, linen fibers, asbestos fibers, wool fibers, and clots of ink, oil, and glue. Each of these substances has its own formal characteristics, and if you look more closely (you must switch to an electronic microscope), if you examine the molecular structure of each, the variety in form—pyramids and rings, spirals and stacks and zigzag chains—is dazzling. And that's the opening act. For the main show, you must look deeper still.

On the atomic and subatomic levels, weird electrical forces are crackling and flaring, and amorphous particles (directly related, remember, to the composition of the bean-can label) are spinning simultaneously forward, backward, sideways, and forever at speeds so uncalculable that expressions such as "arrival," "departure," "duration," and "have a nice day" become meaningless. It is on those levels that "magic" occurs.

The magic performed by Conch Shell and Painted Stick consisted of focusing their own force fields to raise ever so slightly the velocity of the others' electron recoil, to widen by a fraction of a degree the scattering angles of their photons. A quantum jump start, if you will. They had always been capable of movement. Now, after hours of energy exchange, controlled power surges, and meticulous synchronizations, they were able to move at rates detectible to human measure, at rates that allowed them to depart the cave as absolutely, if (from an anthropomorphic perspective) not quite as efficiently, as Boomer Petway and Ellen Cherry Charles.

So, Can o' Beans stood then on the rim of the little arroyo, watching the stars drop, one by one, into view, like baked beans spilling over the side of a camp plate, and reflecting upon the day's adventures and upon the relative freedom that the relative increase in relative locomotion had granted.

The bean can was exhilarated, to be sure, yet its initial experience with the animate brand of mobility succeeded in enlarging its appreciation of its former condition of arrest. There was a lot to be said for stillness (relative stillness), Can o' Beans conceded, a statics characterized not so much by an absence of ability to move as by a serene balance of forces. It is because inanimate objects, in their stillness, turn back upon themselves that they are exactly identical with themselves. The frantic confusions of the organic realm wash over them. The universe moves around them. The Divine lines up with them. Their solidity may be spiritual as well as physical. In the immobile whirls the infinite.

A gentle nudge from Conch Shell's spire punctured the bean can's musings. "We must depart now," Conch Shell said. "Painted Stick has taken his fix on the guide star."

"Hey!" yelled Dirty Sock. "Round 'em up and head 'em out!" He was certainly enjoying himself.

Spoon popped up tentatively over the gully edge. She was nervous but under control.

Very well, thought Can o' Beans. *On to Jerusalem.* The Holy City might sizzle with contention, quaver with explosions, and buzz with bullets, but at least the chances of his/her being opened and consumed were appreciably less than in Ellen Cherry's cupboard. Jerusalem, for the moment, was the capital of a Jewish state, and while the actual amount of pork in a bean can's contents was minimal, as everyone knows, it was sufficient to hold the most ravenous rabbi at bay.

Thus, it was with general good humor and optimism that the band of objects set off into the American night. Before the sun would next strike their various surfaces, however, they would face a terrible ordeal.

Under cover of darkness, they scooted, toddled, and bounced along, slowly but steadily gaining altitude as they followed the creek into the foothills. Although unaccustomed to the rigors of locomotion, Spoon, Dirty Sock, and Can o' Beans held up reasonably well. Nevertheless, when the group paused for a rest about midnight, the three were more than thankful to set themselves down.

"Damn, good buddies!" said Dirty Sock. "This locomotin' is neat. But I tell ya, I'm feeling pretty spaced out."

"Pardon me for saying so, Mr. Sock," Can o' Beans counseled, "but you really ought not to use that slang."

The stocking was stung. "What's the damn matter with it?" he asked.

"Well," said Can o' Beans, a bit hesitantly, "imprecise speech is one of the major causes of mental illness in human beings."

"Huh?"

"Quite so. The inability to correctly perceive reality is often responsible for humans' insane behavior. And every time they substitute an all-purpose, sloppy slang word for the words that would *accurately* describe an emotion or a situation, it lowers their reality orientations, pushes them farther from shore, out onto the foggy waters of alienation and confusion."

The manner in which the others were regarding him/her made Can o' Beans feel compelled to continue. "The word *neat,* for example, has precise connotations. *Neat* means tidy, orderly, well-groomed. It's a valuable tool for describing the appearance of a room, a hairdo, or a manuscript. When it's generically and inappropriately applied, though, as it is in its slang aspect, it only obscures the true nature of the thing or feeling that it's supposed to be representing. It's turned into a sponge word. You can wring meanings out of it by the bucketful—and never know which one is right. When a person says a movie is 'neat,' does he mean that it's funny or tragic or thrilling or romantic, does he mean that the cinematography is beautiful, the acting heartfelt, the script intelligent, the direction deft, or the leading lady has cleavage to die for? Slang possesses an economy, an immediacy that's attractive, all right, but it devalues experience by standardizing and fuzzing it. It hangs between humanity and the real world like a . . . a veil. Slang just makes people more stupid, that's all, and stupidity eventually makes them crazy. I'd hate to ever see that kind of craziness rub off onto objects."

Spoon, who, like the bean can, had caught a few movies on television, appreciated the analogy. Painted Stick and Conch Shell didn't even know what a movie was. Among them, only Dirty Sock had ever been inside a movie theater, and his view had been limited to the gum on the bottoms of the seats. Dirty Sock was quiet for a while. One might even say that he was pensive. Then he grumbled something about every damn one of them knowing exactly what he meant when he said locomoting was "neat" and that he didn't see any need to go into a lot of boring detail about it. Folding his saggy elastic over his crusty heel, he curled up to rest.

Unable to contain herself, Spoon turned to the stick and the shell and gushed, "Wasn't that wonderful?! Can o' Beans is as wise as Solomon."

The foreigners looked at each other. "Did you hear that?" asked Conch Shell. "King Solomon still has a reputation for wisdom."

"Why, yes," said Spoon, her frail voice propped up by sincerity. "Solomon was the wisest man who ever lived."

Conch Shell turned politely away, but Painted Stick laughed right in Spoon's ladle.

Believing that she had made some kind of faux pas, Spoon blushed and withdrew. Can o' Beans, on the other hand, moved closer to the foreigners. "Excuse me, please," he/she said, "but you seem to suggest that Solomon was less wise than his considerable fame maintains."

"In truth, we do," said Painted Stick. "Solomon. Ha-ha."

Conch Shell was more specific. "King Solomon was as vain and prideful a man as ever lived. His sole purpose in life was the elevation of his own name, the perpetuation of his own esteem. He enslaved his subjects and exploited all around him so as to erect monuments to his personal glory. Surely you cannot consider this to be wisdom."

"But he *did* have plenty of glory, didn't he?" asked Can o' Beans, remembering tales of fabulous grandeur.

"Israel, under Solomon, was impoverished and backward. Its 'cities' were mud villages. Even Jerusalem failed to impress Europeans and Arabians who visited there."

"But the Temple," protested Can o' Beans. "What about Solomon's Temple?"

"*Solomon's* Temple," repeated Painted Stick. "Ha-ha."

"First, it was not *Solomon's* Temple," Conch Shell explained. "It was Hiram's Temple, Hiram of Tyre; Tyre being a great city of Phoenicia. The Temple bore Solomon's name, 'tis true, but Hiram erected it, furnished it, decorated it, influenced the activities therein. Although the Temple sat in Jerusalem, it was actually Phoenician."

"As are we," Painted Stick chimed in.

"Yes," admitted Conch Shell. "Many from Phoenicia served Israel: Hiram, Jezebel, countless priests and priestesses of our Goddess, and, in a minimal way, we, your humble guests."

Up to that point, the exotic pair had been quite vague about its reasons for traveling to Jerusalem, and the beans in the can were practically farting with curiosity. Seizing the opportunity, Can o' Beans moved even closer. "Wait a second," he/she said. "Do you mean to tell me . . ."

But they meant to tell nothing, at least not at the moment. A cloud bank pulled away from the moon, like a . . . a veil from a face, and in the sudden rush of pale, almost tinkly, spring moonlight, Painted

Stick spun on his end, sending up a shower of pine needles, like splinters of blue glass. His little horns turned and twitched, as if he were a tuning fork varying the pitch of the stars. Like the heart of a great animal bursting open, Conch Shell released a vapor of pinkness that, as it evaporated in the moonlight, smelled both of honey and the sea.

"We must continue now," the shell said tenderly.

Can o' Beans roused his/her friends, and soon they were off again, scooting, toddling, and bouncing along through the soul-testing, teeth-chattering forests of the night.

For another three hours, they climbed rocks, scaled logs, challenged shadows, and waded through owl-hoots so raw with enigma they would have sent half of urban America grabbing for the Valium bottle. Then, they paused again. It was obvious that Spoon, Dirty Sock, and Can o' Beans were exhausted. Painted Stick announced that under the circumstances they would retire early, a good three hours before dawn, and hope to make up for lost time on the following night.

They had stopped in a flat place, upholstered with moss. It was secluded there, in the blackest part of the forest, although moon rays were strewn through the pine boughs like rolls of toilet paper hurled from the upstairs windows of some primeval fraternity house. The castaways from the big turkey (which was parked at that moment under unfiltered moonbeams, many miles to the east) found it an agreeable resort. Quickly, they began to sink into a kind of sleep, each at the base of a separate tree trunk.

"Good night, Miss Spoon. Good night, Mr. Sock."

"Good night, you two," said Spoon. "I'll be mentioning you both in my prayers."

"Yeah," mumbled Dirty Sock, who was still disgruntled over the lecture he had received on his slang.

Can o' Beans wanted to ask Spoon just to whom she thought she was praying, but he yawned instead and let it slide. He didn't even hear Painted Stick and Conch Shell slip off into the woods in search of a larger clearing, there to communicate with the constellations.

An hour, more or less, had gone by when the bean tin was jolted into consciousness by a horrible screaming.

*   *   *

"Help! Help me! Goddamn! Help me!"

It took a moment for Can o' Beans to recognize the voice as Dirty Sock's—and another moment to actually see the silhouette of the monster.

In the fading moonlight, the creature loomed huge and spiky, like a punk haircut mutated and vitalized in a nuclear accident.

"Help! Get this motherfucker off me!"

"Oh dear! What is it?" asked Spoon.

"It's a porcupine. It's got hold of Mr. Sock."

Indeed, it had. The thirty-pound rodent had the sock in its mouth and was greedily chewing the salt out of its fibers, the salt from Boomer Petway's sweat.

"Let go of me, you evil bastard! Help!"

"Oh, Can o' Beans, do something! Do something, please!"

With all the clumsy force in its newly heightened mobility, the bean can threw itself against the porcupine's left front leg. Startled, the animal wobbled for an instant and ceased to chew. It very nearly dropped the sock. Then, having analyzed, in its rodent fashion, the threat presented by its much smaller attacker, it stepped to the side and whacked Can o' Beans a good one with its tail.

The porcupine was surprised, and even mildly pained, when its quills were repulsed by the metal container. Nevertheless, the whack had sent Can o' Beans tumbling into the shadows, and the intruder returned to its gnawing.

"Help! Hit it again! Hit it again!"

Upright now, his/her Van Camp's label scratched and torn by barbs, Can o' Beans thought it futile to strike again. But he/she had an idea. "Hurry, Miss Spoon. Over here. Lean against this log."

"Oh, dear."

It wasn't really a log, merely a fallen pine branch, but Spoon leaned against it as instructed. "I'll try not to hurt you," said Can o' Beans, nudging a pebble into her ladle. Then he/she struggled up onto the branch, steadied him/herself, sighted the target, and jumped. *Zing!* The pebble was catapulted at the porcupine: direct hit! Unfortunately, because Spoon's ladle was designed to fire nothing of a larger caliber than a candied strawberry (the kind the old bishop loved to gum), the pebble did the porcupine not much more harm than a deerfly. After three or four more missiles were bounced off its quills, however, it grew annoyed and, to the dismay of the bombardiers, lumbered off into the trees, Dirty Sock hanging from its muzzle like . . . like the slipped veil of a copulating harem girl.

"I'll follow them!" shouted Can o' Beans. "You yell for Mr. Stick."

That proved unnecessary. Having heard the commotion, Painted Stick and Conch Shell had interrupted their celestial enterprises and were even then rushing into the little clearing. "What is the trouble here?" asked the shell.

Her soft voice jackhammered with sobs, rubberized with hysteria, Spoon babbled a largely incoherent account of the emergency, but Painted Stick eventually got the picture. He took off in pursuit. Conch Shell and Spoon followed after.

By that time, the porcupine had arrived at the creekbank. It stood there, absentmindedly chewing, too narcotically blissed by the salty delicacy in its chops to invest much effort in either battle or retreat. Can o' Beans caught up with the animal but had no idea what to do next.

End over end, like a Chinese acrobat, Painted Stick flipped furiously along the forest path. He flipped directly up to the porcupine, striking its nose with a resounding *swack*. The animal squealed with pain, dropped the sock, and wheeled dizzily around in two complete circles before scrambling up the trunk of the nearest tall conifer.

"Heeelp!" screamed Dirty Sock, from far away, and to his/her horror, Can o' Beans realized that the porcupine's thrashing tail had swept the sock into the white waters of the stream.

True, Boomer Petway washed his socks infrequently (aristocrats never have shared the bourgeoisie's infatuation with personal hygiene), but Dirty Sock *had* been underwater once or twice. It was preferable to a porcupine's mouth. He didn't panic until he realized that the current was carrying him downstream with such speed that he would be back in Idaho by breakfast.

He struggled to surface; the current held him under. He was out of control. Reality whistles a different tune underwater. Time and space are wadded up like old newspaper. There is light underwater, even at night, but it is a far cry from the lights we all know and love.

The light is green and its shine is mean. Shark light. Fecal light. The light by which the Reaper reads his list. The light our antecedents crawled out of the sloughs to get away from. A light filtered through old cabbage brains.

The torrent spit up Dirty Sock long enough for him to yell for aid, then sucked him down again into its rolling green barrel of funless foam monkeys.

This is it, thought the sock. *My sock life is over. I'll turn into muck at the bottom of this cold damn river and never see that seashell pussy again.* He would have welcomed the funky confines of Boomer Petway's dresser drawer. He would have embraced that odd-angled lump of a foot, shielded it from spilled beer and the stray welding spark. Dry-rotting in the cave with that know-it-all bean can would have been better by a damn sight than this.

Hope springs eternal and all that, yet isn't it a fact that when we give up and quit hoping; genuinely, sincerely quit hoping, things usually change for the better? Zen masters say that when we become convinced that the human situation is hopeless, we approach serenity, the ideal state of mind. Dirty Sock wasn't exactly Zen, there was just too much polyester in him for that, but he had pretty much resigned himself to a watery grave when the rapids temporarily ran out of gradient. His flaccid, battered form was discharged into a quiet pool, where he swirled for a moment, putting the fear of the polymer gods into a couple of trout, before hooking himself on a driftwood snag.

He tried to call out, but nothing escaped him save a bubble.

It took them more than an hour, bumbling along the creekbank, to locate him. Conch Shell swam out to him and revived him with her pink touch but failed to free him from the snag. She swam back to shore, picked up Painted Stick, and ferried him out to the snag. The stick pried the sock loose, and the two of them rode to safety on board the seashell.

Dirty Sock's threads had been bruised and, in some cases, broken by porcupine teeth. Worse, he was sopping wet, far too soaked to walk, and in the predawn chill a brilliant and biting scum of frost was collecting on his fibers.

Rather desperately, they were wondering what to do when Spoon spied a flickering glow off a ways through the trees. Having no better alternative, they made for it, Painted Stick dragging Dirty Sock from his nubs. Within a hundred yards, they came upon a small public campground, where in addition to a teal-colored Volvo sedan and one of those fancy many-zippered tents from the R.E.I. backpackers' boutique in Seattle, they found a cheerful campfire, snapping and smoking in the prime of its life.

Although the fire had been recently kindled, the campers were nowhere to be seen. From inside the tent, however, there issued a murmur of sleepy voices.

"We'll have to risk it," the objects agreed. While Spoon watched the tent, Painted Stick pulled the waterlogged stocking to a flat rock beside the fire and laid it out. It occurred to Can o' Beans that if he/she were to roll upon Dirty Sock, it would press some of the water out of him and permit him to dry faster. Although the sock was less than charmed by the arrangement, it was too weak to protest. Back and forth rolled the bean can, back and forth, while rivulets webbed the rock and the frost on the synthetic fibers turned slowly to steam.

"But hon-eee," whined an ostensibly male voice from inside the tent, "I don't *want* instant coffee, even if it *is* cappuccino."

"Imported. Quite as good as fresh."

"I want, just this once, coffee boiled in the pot over an open fire."

"He-man coffee, Dabney?"

"It needn't have gender."

"Hemingway coffee?"

"Indeed."

The woman's voice was high-pitched, nasal, pinched, as if strained through the eyelets in Jane Austen's corset. "Hemingway would have caught his limit by now."

"Before daybreak? Faddle! Hemingway had excellent values. He believed in the good breakfast. In the good stiff coffee."

"Normally you would pour such coffee down the drain."

"This isn't 'normally,' Heather. This is our adventure."

"Very well. But if your sense of romantic adventure demands that you drink battery acid . . ."

The man sniffed. His sniff fluttered the wall of the tent. "*This* is not battery acid material. *This* is Starbuck's Colombia-New Guinea blend."

"It will be industrial waste when you're through boiling it. By that, I mean if you wish your he-man, fisherman coffee, you are going to have to prepare it yourself."

"Heath-er," the man whined. "*I* built the fire." Even as he protested, however, he was unzipping the tent's front flaps.

By rapping her ornate handle against a metal tent stake, Spoon sounded the alarm. Deftly, like a Pamplona bull hooking a drunken tourist, Painted Stick hooked Dirty Sock and began pulling him toward the bushes. Conch Shell pushed from behind. As for Can o' Beans, he/she had just been rolling off the flattened sock at the instant that the stick jerked it up and away. The sudden yank sent Can o' Beans rolling right off the rock and into the path of the approaching camper.

"Heather! There's something out here!"

"Oh, my God!" gasped the woman. Visions of Ted Bundy, of hairy Charlie Manson, stretched in her mind like blood-drenched elastic.

The man forced a deep chuckle. "It's only animals, dear," he called. "Some small animals attracted to my fire."

"They could be rabid," snapped the woman. Then, abruptly conscious of her hysteria, she added in a steadier tone, "Toss some pebbles at them, dear."

In teal flannel pajamas, over which he had Velcroed a raspberry nylon parka, the man was having a look around. He was not old, probably between thirty-five and forty, yet he hobbled like a nursing-home lecher in his spanking new Timberland brogans. Although chunky spectacles rode his sharp little nose like the wheels of a chariot overrunning an emaciated fourth-century Christian, he still appeared handicapped by myopia. He had the look of a midlevel academic, perhaps one of those literary moles who compound their pallor in stuffy rooms, stroking the musaceous nuances of E. M. Forster; or else the editor of an urban weekly newspaper that fills its pages with wine-shop and gallery advertisements and earnest evaluation of the anal-retentive sawings of European string quartets. Only a day or two before, that same man had glared at Boomer Petway with such haughty disdain, as the Volvo passed by the giant turkey, that Boomer turned to Ellen Cherry and asked, "Do you think there's males that suffer from penis envy?"

"Heather," called the man. His bugged eyes had discovered an artifact in front of the campfire.

"Yes, dear."

"Did you bring pork and beans?"

"What?"

"Pork and beans."

Squinting hard, he squatted in the firelight. The Chinese fingers of dawn, slender and opium stained, were massaging the bruised bottom of the sky, and owl-hoots were beginning to be supplanted by benevolent birdsong and what may have been the sound of the night shift punching off duty at the bugworks. On the sidelines of a planetary routine that seldom has failed to inspire the poets—those among them who'd been awake and sober at that hour—the man made as if to pick up Can o' Beans, then thought better of it and prodded him/her with a length of store-bought kindling.

In the underbrush, Spoon emitted a tiny squeal. "Oh, what can we do?" she asked.

"Do not move," ordered Painted Stick.

The woman emerged from the tent. She looked remarkably like her husband, down to the flannels and the aquarium-weight eyeglasses. She may have been an inch taller than he, which meant that she still would have had to stand on a peach basket to curry the ears of a Shetland pony. Aggressively as a TV cop, she strode up to the helpless bean tin.

"You're asking me if I brought pork and beans? Dabney, I shopped for this excursion for over a week—"

"For *more than* a week."

"Excuse me. *More than* a week. Are you aware of the money I spent?"

"So these aren't *our* pork and beans?"

"Really, Dabney!" The woman looked as if she had just gotten a whiff of a Calcutta latrine. Then, she softened and smirked. "For breakfast I'm preparing orange crepes. With Cointreau. But not until you've had your go at the fish."

"Agreed." He positioned a small log on the fire. "I'll dress and get cracking." As he crawled into the tent, he called, "Oh, honey. You won't forget the linen tablecloth?"

"Have I ever?"

Purposefully, the woman snatched up the tin of beans, subjected it to a rather scatological scrutiny, then, with amazing strength, hurled it against a boulder at the edge of the campsite.

*   *   *

The canning process was invented in 1809 by a French confectioner named Nicolas Appert. *Oui,* the simple proletarian vessel that shepherded our Spam from processing plant to dinner dish emerged in Paris, birthplace of so very much genius, so very much chic. Is it inappropriate, then, that a painter, Andy Warhol, had caused the soup can to be the most recognized image in contemporary art? Is it mere coincidence that the most representative Parisian dance is called the cancan? Or that the famed French film festival is held at a place called Cannes? Yes, of course it is, but no matter: there are more tin cans in the world than there are human beings (a hundred billion new ones are manufactured each year in the U.S. alone), and they trace their beginnings not to some savage simian savanna, as do we, but to the home of Matisse and Baudelaire, of Debussy and Sarah Bernhardt; to the metropole of the muses, the City of Light.

For all of the fizzy artistry that surrounded its birth, however, the can is sturdy, dependable. Incidences of rupture or spoilage are rare. Cans have been opened after five decades to reveal perfectly edible contents, if you fancy potted mutton. If only we could so can our innocence, our sense of wonder, our adolescent libido. Campbell's Cream of Youth. Swanson's Spring Chicken.

Early food cans were handmade from tin and sealed with solder. Today, they're machine-fabricated from pressed steel. The only tin in a modern "tin can" is an internal coating so thin you could read through it. You could read *The Tin Drum* through it, were you bent in that direction. Tin habitually broadcasts extra electrons, and those superfluous particles create a barrier against acids in the foodstuff that would otherwise corrode the can, slowly weakening it from within, the way political convictions weaken morality and religious convictions weaken the mind.

When Can o' Beans was dashed against the rock, the impact naturally dented his/her steel cylinder. That would have been problem enough, since a deep dent couldn't help but impede equilibrium. Alas, it didn't end there. Because the dent occurred directly over the seam, the seam split. There was an inch-long tear in his/her side, out through which tomato sauce was flowing like blood.

Humming a melody from Prokofiev, the man lugged his fishing tackle, price tags still attached, blithely to the stream. With trepidation, the woman paid a reluctant but necessary visit to the campground privy. As soon as the couple was out of sight, Painted Stick and Conch Shell rushed to rescue Can o' Beans. First, they turned him/her so that the wound was topside up. That stemmed the flow of sauce. Next, they pushed the can—rolling was out of the question—into the underbrush.

Reconnaissance by Conch Shell turned up a well-concealed but soon to be sunlit rockpile. Painted Stick dragged the sock there; then, with the shell's assistance, pushed the can there, as well. Painted Stick may have been having second thoughts about his choice of traveling companions. He was a talismanic device, the sanctified awe-detector of a community of ecstatics, not a nursemaid. It was time for an assessment.

Although confused, tired, perhaps in shock, the old purple footsnood was out of danger. The holes in its envelope were minute and manageable. A few hours in direct sunlight would draw out the last of the moisture that plagued it. Cleaner, if none the wiser, the sock would persevere.

The vessel of legumes, on the other hand, was in definite peril. Were it to lie in any but the one position—on its side with the seam on top—its juice would leak. If enough of the sauce bled out, the beans inside would congeal into a hard, dry lump. Eventually, bacteria entering the wound would decompose the lump. The crippled container would be full of rattle and rot. Can o' Beans was incapacitated. Further travel was impossible.

What to do? Dirty Sock did nothing. He lay the entire morning as if in a stupor, soaking up sun like a wage slave on the first day of a cut-rate Hawaiian vacation. Can o' Beans was equally silent and still. Never leaving his/her side, Spoon repeatedly smoothed the can's bedraggled paper jacket, as if mending its tatters with the compulsive caresses of her ladle. Conch Shell cast her pink net of oceanic compassion over the lot of them, not that it did them much good, while Painted Stick, anxious to keep an appointment in far Jerusalem, paced to and fro, his little "horns" twitching like feelers. What to do?

The scene was glum, and boring, too. By midafternoon, Can o' Beans had had enough. "I realize that I'll probably have to be left behind," he/she announced. "I can accept that. It's the breaks of the game, that's all. But I can't let you get away, Miss Shell, Mr. Stick, without at least telling me why I was going to where I'm not going.

I've been just bursting, no joke intended, ha-ha, to learn the purpose of this marathon to Jerusalem, and now. . . . What's your
background? What's your mission? What am I missing? Leave me in
the night but please don't leave me in the dark."

Perhaps they, too, needed a diversion, something to take their
minds off the trouble and delay. At any rate, Conch Shell and
Painted Stick settled in the disorder of broken rock (it was as if the
mountain god had come home drunk and thrown his clothes on the
floor) beside the disabled bean can and addressed its curiosity.

"As previously mentioned, we come originally from Phoenicia, a
great trading center beside the mild blue sea. Phoenicia was blessed
with hills and harbors; a land of lighthouses, cedar groves, and
purple dust on the olive fruit. It was divided into two kingdoms, the
city-states of Sidon and Tyre—"

"You might be interested in knowing," Can o' Beans interrupted,
"that those two cities still exist. They're in a country that's called
Lebanon nowadays."

Spoon regarded Can o' Beans adoringly, as if once more overwhelmed by his/her intelligence.

"Most fucked-up country on earth," mumbled Dirty Sock. "Pardon
my French." He hadn't moved a thread. Nobody realized that he'd
been listening.

"A long civil war's been raging there," Can o' Beans explained.
"Moslems fighting Jews, as usual, but also Moslems fighting Christians. And Moslems fighting Moslems. Everybody fighting everybody,
including themselves. It's crazy. Murderous and crazy."

"That is sometimes the way it is with human beings," Conch Shell
said.

"Absolutely," agreed Can o' Beans. "But human beings in your
neck of the woods seem to have a special gift for it. I'm curious about
why that is."

"Well, the Jews were the first to deny the Goddess," said Conch
Shell.

"And Islam is merely an offshoot of Judaism?" ventured Can o'
Beans.

Was Conch Shell implying that it was her goddess who had put a
curse—*the* curse, the legendary curse—on the Jews? And, by extension, on the whole Middle East? Was there, indeed, a curse at all, or
was it simply a desperate (at times, violent) clinging to narrow, rigid
belief systems that had brought so much suffering to the region, to

the race? Could it be coincidence, a mere accident of geography and history? Or was there yet a different reason for the travail: something fabulous, unexamined, unthinkable, even; some circumstance hidden from human knowledge as if by a . . . a veil?

Phantom swimmers, greased with speculation, took a few bright strokes through the waters of the bean can's intellect, but in its present condition it failed to provide adequate buoyancy, and they rapidly sank into the deep unconscious. When the ripples had subsided, Can o' Beans said, "I regret to inform you that Sidon and Tyre have shrunk in size and importance. They're just backwater burgs these days. But you're not returning to your place of natural origin, anyway. You aren't going to Lebanon, which used to be Phoenicia, you're going to—"

"We are returning to the Holy City for the opening of the Third Temple," said Painted Stick. It was practically the only relevant remark he was to make all afternoon. For Painted Stick, this period of exegesis proved merely an excuse to comment upon the galaxies, which he described as if they were inkwells into which he, like a busy pen, must be regularly dipped.

"Sounds like an event you've been looking forward to."

"Much of the world has been looking forward to it," said Conch Shell.

"How come?"

"Oh, sir/ma'am, don't you know?" blurted Spoon, amazed that there might be a gap in Can o' Beans's erudition. "When the Third Temple is built, it will mean that the Second Coming is here."

Can o' Beans shrugged. "Third Temple. Second Coming. Who's on first?"

"Christians associate the rebuilding of the Temple in Jerusalem with the second appearance on earth of their deity, Jesus Christ," explained Conch Shell. "Jews associate it with the *first* appearance of their long-awaited Messiah, if that is what you intended. In either case, it is supposed to mean the end of the world as we know it."

"What if the Christ *and* the Messiah come, and they're two different guys?" asked Can o' Beans. "Would they debate on television? Would they lead their faithful off to two different rewards; separate, re-stricted heavens? And would Jesus, a pious Jew, really run with the Gentiles? Would there be a war between saviors that would 'save' the world by ending it? You look at the Middle East right now, look at Northern Ireland, at India with its Hindus and Sikhs; it would seem that most of the bloodshed in the world is the result of religious squabbling. Maybe that's why I'm cynical about religion."

"You *are*?" asked Spoon, incredulously. "Why, in your condition . . ."

"It's blasphemy now, is it?" mumbled Dirty Sock.

"Things do not always turn out exactly as humans expect them to," Conch Shell reminded them.

Painted Stick added something amazing and irrelevant about the moons of Saturn.

"You're quite correct," said Can o' Beans. He/she meant that Conch Shell was correct about people's expectations. The remarks of Spoon and Dirty Sock he/she dismissed as misplaced anthropomorphism, and whether or not Painted Stick was correct was anybody's guess. "Jesus, after all, has been away two thousand years. In all that time, he must have changed. As for the Messiah, he's rather a pig in a poke."

Conch Shell laughed. It was a high, musical, merry laugh, like the singing of field mice going forth to gather grain in a land where the hawks are all vegetarians. "Your attitude is probably healthy," said she. "The Third Temple could turn out to be associated with . . . with something quite different."

"Do you and Mr. Stick know what that is?" The can expected to get an earful of the Goddess.

"Considering the past, we certainly think we do. Yet when it comes to final fruit, we may be in for as much a surprise as anybody else."

"But it *will* be a big deal, this new Temple over there in Jerusalem town?"

"We have every reason to expect it to be."

"And you and Mr. Stick—inanimate objects—will have a part in it?"

"We hope so," said Conch Shell. "We were promised that we would. Is it not time that inanimate objects—and plants and animals—resume their rightful place in the affairs of the world? How long can humankind continue to slight these integral pieces of the whole reality?"

A shiver ran along the container's broken seam. It was excited by the implications of that notion, though despite its vantage point as an inanimate object, it did not fully understand them. *Had* it fully understood them, then for it, at least, for that injured can of pork 'n' beans, the second veil already would have fallen.

the
third
veil

Ellen Cherry and Boomer were trying to decide how to celebrate their anniversary. They had been married one week. Although she would have preferred to spend the evening sketching—try as she might, she couldn't think of a single attribute of wedlock that measured up to the bliss of a penciled line snaking across the Eden of a blank sheet of paper—Ellen Cherry suggested that they go dancing. Now Boomer Petway was a dancing fool, but it so happened that the lone floor open for public dancing on a March Wednesday in Livingston, Montana, was an "international" disco that had recently supplanted the country-and-western bar in the Grizzly Bear Hotel. Livingston's famed literary crowd would be there, the couple was assured, as well as every aspiring jet-setter in that part of rural Montana, rising and falling in the glitz spill of chrome and neon like the studiously posed figures in a baroque masterpiece.

"No way, José," said Boomer. "When I turned thirty, I broke off diplomatic relations with the Pepsi generation. Any hip young people want to communicate with me, they have to go through the Swiss."

That attitude doesn't bode well for our art-scene life in New York, thought Ellen Cherry. But then, what did? "As I recall, honey boy, your relations with ranchers and farmers aren't in any détente mode, either, so I guess it's just as well there's not an ounce of excrement being kicked on the dance floors of this burg tonight. It's getting harder and harder to figure out your foreign policy."

"I'm nonaligned."

"But hardly nonaggressive." She touched her hair. It was familiarly stiff and convoluted, and that seemed to calm her. She wound a finger in a taffy coil, then pulled free and felt it spring. "What *would* you like to do this evening?"

Boomer was of the opinion that it would be piercingly romantic to go to a drive-in picture show. There they could relive, within certain parameters, their youthful nights at the Robert E. Lee. As it turned out, the Yellowstone Drive-in had come out of winter mothballs that very week, kicking off the new season with a blockbuster science-fiction triple feature:

2001: A Space Odyssey
2010: The Year We Make Contact
2020: So Who Needs Glasses?

They had to pay for four parking spaces. The roast turkey took up two spaces lengthwise, and one more on either side was blocked by its drumsticks. "Hang the expense!" shouted Boomer. "Nothing's too good for my juicy bride."

Lowering her eyes, Ellen Cherry turned to the ticket seller. "Of one week," she said meekly.

"Of one whole week!" thundered Boomer. "How 'bout a tub of popcorn, darlin'?"

"You're going to spoil me."

Since they had legal and physical access to four speakers, they used them all, receiving the cartoony assault of the snack bar commercial quadrophonically. They also cranked up the Airstream's heating system, for, with the setting of the sun, an icy blue wind had come yowling out of Canada and into the drive-in picture show. The wind filled every available parking space but listened only to itself.

Since he had legal and physical access to what was inside them, Ellen Cherry removed her panties, to save Boomer the trouble, but after kissing her once or twice, he repaired to the Dometic eight-cubit-foot, AC/DC refrigerator, ostensibly for beer, only to surprise her by returning with a reasonably good bottle of French champagne. "The wine steward says this here is the perfect complement to buttered popcorn."

"There's hope for you yet," she said. She herself could not determine whether that flicker of hope caused her cheer or concern. "Happy anniversary." Beneath her skirt, where the panties had come and gone, where there was nothing but hair and nakedness, beneath her skirt (she was a southern woman, still, and refused to go about in jeans or trousers), Ellen Cherry crossed and uncrossed, crossed and uncrossed, her fingers.

"**I** wonder where they are now?" Verlin Charles had a folding map of the United States of America spread out on the coffee table before him. Verlin was looking at the states, which is to say, he was looking at the little variously colored shapes into which the larger shape, the shape representing the nation, was irregularly divided. Verlin's concept of "where they are now" was relative to the state shapes, nothing more, nothing less. People tended to regard those shapes, those comparatively brand-new, arbitrary, political subdivisions as if they were natural facts, ancient and inviolable; as if they were end products of evolution ("No, children, Texas did not evolve from Rhode Island; Texas and Rhode Island evolved from a common ancestor"), or, supposing the people were Bible Belt creationists, as if God had made the states, had sat down at his big cumulous desk with his big titanium pen in his big creative fist and said in his big boom-boom voice, "I think I'll make Louisiana look like a Frankenstein boot." Either way, people got very attached to the imagined physical reality of those states.

Because the map was printed on a flat surface, only four colors were required to separate each and every state shape from its neighbors. On a sphere, a globe, four colors likewise sufficed. Had the map been printed on a torus—a doughnut shape—*seven* colors would have been needed to allow for the state-shape distinctions. There are, of course, additional reasons why one seldom encounters a map of the United States on one's doughnut.

"I wonder where they are now?" said Verlin. He was tracking, after a fashion, the progress of his daughter and son-in-law, subconsciously wishing that it would take them a long, long time to reach the dreaded New York.

"I wonder where *he* is now?" said Patsy. She nodded her exploded cuckoo's nest—the head of hair whose trillion tornado curls had somehow forced their pattern into her chromosomes and been passed along to her daughter—at the Reverend Buddy Winkler.

In the easy chair, where he had dozed off while watching "Jeopardy!" on the Charleses' console, Buddy was writhing in a dream. It didn't appear to be a nightmare: his thin lips were parted in a pious sort of grin. Yet, he twisted and kicked, and he was sweating like an icebox. Patsy was fascinated by the sheen he projected, the way his boils glistened. Patsy switched off the lamp.

"Hey! What're you doing?" complained Verlin. "I'm studyin' this dad-blamed map."

"Sorry, sweet pea. I just wanted to see if you could read by the light of Bud's boils."

The instant she switched the lamp back on, Buddy snapped awake. Once he had gotten his bearings, once he realized that they were into prime time and the game show was over, he turned to Verlin and Patsy and gave them a serious smile. "The Lord has just spoken to me," he said. Effortlessly, he switched into his saxophone voice. "*The Lord* has addressed me in this living room!"

"That's rude. He didn't say beans to me, and it's my house."

"Patsy, now."

"Did you hear the Lord, Verlin? I swear, if I'd known the Lord was gonna show up, I'd of emptied the blessed ashtrays."

Verlin and Buddy in perfect unison: "Patsy!"

"Sorry. I didn't mean any disrespect. It's just so . . . unusual." She looked to Verlin, hoping that he would pick up the ball, but he was as closed as the Kellogg states, those little Plains states on his map that were all shaped like cereal boxes. Patsy jumped back in. "What did the Lord say to you, Bud?" She was sincere. Sincerely sincere.

"The Temple," Buddy answered vaguely. "God said something about rebuildin' the Temple." It was as if the preacher had not heard the Lord too clearly.

"Rebuilding what temple?"

Abruptly, Buddy rose to his feet. "What time is it?"

" 'Bout eight-fifteen," said Verlin.

"Hmmm. Well, too late tonight." Almost affectionately, Buddy stroked the epidermal eruptions about his chin. "First thing tomorrow morning," he announced, "I'm gonna get me a Jew on the phone."

Can o' Beans had feared that when Ellen Cherry married the husky fellow with the thinning black hair, the man called Boomer, he/she might have been emptied out and, along with a whole string of other cans, tied to the bumper of a honeymoon car. As the car drove down the street, trailing paper streamers, inflated condoms, and squiggles of shaving cream, the cans would clatter and clang, proclaiming to one and all in their vulgar clamor that the bashful, nervous innocents who occupied the car were en route from the altar to the bed.

As it turned out, the honeymoon car was the Airstream turkey, and none of Ellen Cherry's friends—the waitresses who wept and then got drunk and wept some more—could muster the courage or whatever it took to decorate the thing. The Airstream turkey just didn't lend itself to decoration. "How about cranberry sauce?" one waitress suggested. "A hundred pounds of it," added another. "Where we gonna put it?" asked a third. "Where we gonna get it?" asked a fourth. A fifth, openly weeping, inquired, "What's cranberry sauce got to do with having a husband to love you forever and ever?" In the end, they hadn't touched the turkey. Perhaps the turkey was a complete statement, a sentence to which no further clause or phrase could logically be appended. Perhaps it was just too weird.

Now, Can o' Beans was thinking that he/she would be satisfied to end up in a wedding procession. If, with the help of Mr. Stick, he/she could make it as far as a church, a little roadside chapel, well, he/she could just lie around in the yard there, drained dry of sauce, and sooner or later some bridesmaid or younger brother would tie him/her to the bumper of a honeymoon car, and *JUST MARRIED JUST MARRIED honk honk honk clatter bangle clink,* he/she would end his/her career, if not in a blaze of glory, at least as a participant in a traditional rite of noisy joy. How much finer that would be than being left on this rockpile for the porcupines to lick and the buzzards of the sky to pee upon.

But, wait. Why was he/she sinking into morbid fantasies? There were a couple of hours left before dusk. With thermonuclear nonchalance, the sun was still cheerfully converting hydrogen into helium at the rate of four million, two-hundred-thousand tons per second, and inside the solar-heated can, the beans were enjoying genetic memories of the photosynthesis that had made them possible. Moreover, Conch Shell had resumed her narration. Can o' Beans shrugged off his/her sense of impending doom and paid attention.

Boomer was disposed to swill the champagne directly from the bottle, a procedure that violated some sense of propriety in his wife. Ellen Cherry was from the South and had good manners. She didn't have panties on, but she had good manners.

Ellen Cherry walked back to the galley and fetched two glasses. They were water tumblers, but they were glasses. "Honey," she said, "I've lost my spoon."

"You were gonna take this champagne by the spoon?"

"Hey, it's good, but it's not *that* good."

"You were gonna eat your popcorn with a spoon, then. A Yankee habit you picked up in Seattle."

"Just shut up, Boomer," she said. The movie had started, and some men in monkey suits were prancing around a huge sculpture of a candy bar. For a second, Ellen Cherry thought it was a wilder version of the snack bar commercial.

"Whaddaya mean you've lost your spoon? You only had *one* spoon?"

"Forget it." On the screen, the apemen were worshipping the great god Hershey. Some sort of primitive chocolate cult. "I've got—*we've* got—a whole blessed set of stainless steel flatware. But I had a special little spoon. It was a silver dessert spoon. I bought it at a Catholic garage sale."

"That spoon meant right smart to you," said Boomer. His mouth was stuffed with popcorn. "And now it's lost."

"You're making fun of me. It's no big deal." She filled their glasses. "For the first three years I lived in Seattle, it was the only spoon I had to my name. I had chopsticks and one spoon. I think I left it in the cave back there."

"You wanna go back and get it?"

"Well, obviously I do!"

Boomer stared at her. "Seriously?"

"No, God, no. Don't be silly."

" 'Cause I'll do it."

"Forget it, Boomer."

"I'd go back and get your spoon. It's hundreds of miles, but I'd go."

"I know you would. Forget it. Let's drink a toast. It was just a dumb little secondhand spoon."

He lifted his glass. There was a spaceship on the screen. "Well, your spoon can just keep my sock company."

They laughed. They toasted their week of marriage, including their hour in the cave. Little did they know.

"**S**o Mr. Stick was made from the wood of a fig tree, a very old fig tree that apparently had some special aura about it, like the locals thought it was enchanted or something. Maybe it had been struck by lightning or there was a spring beneath it. Maybe it was just old. Sometimes, being old is enough. Clearly, I'm not respected because I'm a bean can but rather because I'm old, as bean cans go; I've been around, seen things, learned a thing or two, survived, and that puts me in a separate category, a kind of elder statesman among canned vegetables. It's a common thing with humans. Mr. Petway remarked to Miss Charles that now that he'd reached the age of thirty, he was going to start starching the collars of his Hawaiian shirts. He said, yes, of course, it would chafe his neck but dignity had its price. Droll fellow. Although disagreeably prolific in the production of epidermal foliage. I'm sure happy that inanimate objects have been spared the curse of body hair. Anyway, there was this venerated fig tree in Phoenicia, and Mr. Stick was fashioned from its wood by an equally venerated astronomer."

As Conch Shell and Painted Stick were telling their story (the stick's contribution consisting mainly of irrelevant asides pertaining to what did and did not get caught in the spiderweb of the stars), Can o' Beans retold it to him/herself. That was his/her method of absorbing information. Whatever Can o' Beans heard or overheard, he/she immediately repeated it—or a personalized version of it—to him/herself. That way it stuck. It would be interesting to see if a kid could get through Harvard using a retention technique perfected by a can of pork and beans.

"This revered astronomer maintained an observatory on the Plain of Al Biqā. It's amazing that there were observatories so long ago, nearly a thousand years before Christ, but I guess the ancients paid a lot of attention to the heavens, even though they had no instruments. That is, they had no telescopes. Evidently, Mr. Stick was designed as an astronomical instrument of some sort. He pointed out unusual occurrences in the sky.

"The astronomer cut the stick and walked it to his observatory, where, under a full moon, it was painted by the priestess. The observatory doubled as a special shrine where the more educated Phoenicians would come to adore Astarte. (One of the Goddess's titles was Shepherdess of the Stars.) There was an attractive priestess on duty there, and Mr. Stick is claiming that she would have sex with anyone who made a cash donation to the observatory. A novel means of institutional fund-raising. Wonder if the Smithsonian knows about it?

"Later that same year, a sailor donated Miss Shell to the observatory. The Phoenicians were a seafaring people, famous for their navigation, and this fellow had discovered the conch shell on a deserted beach. In his opinion, she manifested an aspect of Astarte, so he brought her to the astronomer, who'd taught him everything he knew about starlight, and to the priestess, who'd shown him the irrefutable link between pussy and the Pleiades. Carl Sagan, eat your heart out.

"Mr. Stick and Miss Shell hit it off right from the start. Individually, they were fine, but in tandem they were terrific. Like Tracy and Hepburn. Gradually, they acquired a reputation as especially effective talismans. It was partly because of them that King Ethbaal and Queen Acco of Sidon paid a royal visit to the observatory, bringing along their young daughter, Princess Jezebel. The child enjoyed her first spiritual experience there. She realized that there was something larger, more meaningful in life than licking honeycomb and dressing up her pet monkey.

"Several years later, when Jezebel was the blushing bride of King Ahab of Israel, her parents wrote her that the astronomer had died. Jezebel dispatched an agent to Phoenicia to acquire the contents of the observatory reliquary for a shrine she was having built in Samaria, capital of northern Israel. Jerusalem was capital of southern Israel, known then as Judah. Isn't it true that there's always a rivalry between north and south? North and South Korea, North and South Vietnam, Northern and Southern Ireland, Yankees and Rebels, uptown and downtown. Somebody please tell me why that is? Maybe southerners get too much sun, like Mr. Sock over there, frying his threads, and northerners don't get enough (although I hardly think northern Israel a cool spot in the shade), but southern peoples—tropical and downtown types—always seem to lean toward decadence, whereas uptown, in the north, progress is favored. Decadence and progress obviously are at odds. In any case, Israel and Judah were rivals, and it was a peacock feather in Israel's cap, militarily and commercially, when Ahab married Jezebel, cementing close relations with Phoenicia. When Ahab got Jezebel, though, he also got Astarte, which wasn't that bad of a deal since few around him except a bunch of angry old geezers with bad breath and impotence anxiety gave much of a hoot for Yahweh. At least, that's what Miss Shell is reporting."

Midway through *2010: The Year We Make Contact,* Ellen Cherry lost contact. She was tired of bland Right Stuffers, gay computers, and extraterrestrial chocolate bars. ("It's from Jupiter," she said. "It's not even a Mars bar.") Champagne and popcorn were long gone, leaving a greasy bubble in her belly and her mind, and their petting session had petered out; it was tough to snuggle in bucket seats.

Finally, after considerable squirming of buttocks and clearing of throat, Ellen Cherry dared to ask to be excused. "Honey, would you be terribly upset if I went in the back and painted for a while?"

"Do what you have to do."

Pretending not to notice the sudden drop in husbandly temperature, the fidelity with which his tone mimicked the death grunt of a hypothermal polar bear, Ellen Cherry kissed her mate's broad forehead, from which the hairs were retreating like farm boys fleeing the old homestead for the lights of the city, and said, "Thanks, hon. I'll make it up to you on our two-week anniversary."

"We'll be in New York then." He said it as if being in New York was the equivalent of being in some kind of trouble.

"Yeah!" she exclaimed, cheerfully. "The biggest apple in the orchard, and we're going to sauce it." Before he could refute her, she sailed from the cockpit into the cabin, moving with speed and grace, considering that she was dragging a dead skunk of guilt by a logging chain.

As she selected one of several stretched, sized, and primed canvases from the full-length pull-out storage drawer beneath the side lounge sofa, she thought:

I've ruined it for him.

As she set up her easel in the side lounge, she thought:

He wanted me to stay. I wanted to go. Somebody had to lose.

As she mixed her colors, squirting ringlets of paint from the tubes, she thought:

He thinks it's not right that art is the most important thing in my life. But that's why I'm good at what I do.

As she unwrapped her brushes, inspecting each one individually in the ghastly, stale turkey light, she thought:

He says I love my art more than I love him. Well, he's correct. But I also love it more than I love me.

Once she commenced to paint, she ceased to think. That skunk corpse of guilt floated off like a hairball. Soon she was whistling and humming, dancing first on one foot and then the other. She slopped the paint on, and she dabbed it on, she knifed it on thick, and she washed it on thin, she tinted it with white and shaded it with black, she blended it into creamy textures and isolated it in singular, emphatic, commalike brush strokes. When it came to techniques, she was definitely a slut.

On her small canvas, she recreated a section of the Crazy Mountains, the range near Livingston that they had admired earlier that day; that is to say, she recreated the mountains not as she had originally seen them but as she eventually chose to see them, for a person has not only perceptions but a will to perceive, not only a capacity to observe the world but a capacity to alter his or her observation of it—which, in the end, is the capacity to alter the world, itself. Those people who recognize that imagination is reality's master, we call "sages," and those who act upon it, we call "artists."

Or "lunatics." Can o' Beans was correct when he/she linked low-reality orientation to mental illness, but the true idiot is distinguished from the "idiot" sage or "idiot" artist by his or her lack of control. The idiot's twisted perceptions of the world are not voluntarily or imaginatively altered, they are merely faulty. Lunatics are at the mercy of misunderstood and unmanageable perceptions. When it comes to *their* reality, artists call the shots.

Ellen Cherry was calling the shots, turning mountains upside down, changing boulders into willow trees and willows into lemon meringue pie. The canvas vibrated with mad megajoules of natural energy: geology, meteorology, zoology, and botany all mixed together in a slow boiling tribute to nature and paint. Painting, she sang a song of cobalts and oxides, cadmiums and umbers; naming the pigments aloud as a novice in a convent might recite the names of the saints: "Vandyke brown," for example, patron saint of cheap cigars; "rose madder," protector of irate florists.

She sang and whistled and danced; she winked and squinted and stuck out her tongue; she smirked and scowled and scratched her pussy (her panties were still dangling from the cockpit gearshift); she got paint on her elbows and in her hair (where, because it was yellow ochre—patron saint of Tulsa Chinamen—it blended in and went unnoticed for days); she flung, plodded, stabbed, and caressed with loaded brushes, lost in a state of dizzy transcendence, as glad as a hobo on the way out of town.

The finished product? Well, it was neither a harsh slice of reality nor a harmless fluff of fantasy, but something in between. In the unpromising surfaces of bare rock, she had found a bright wheel of capricious emotions, while in cloud puffs that surely must have been burping with innate whimsy, she found such a bleakness as would chill the heart of a commissioner. She wasted little time admiring the finished product, however, but set right to work tidying up after herself. And once disengaged from the act of creation, her guilt came back. In her rush to return to her husband, she committed the cardinal sin of the painter: she inadequately cleaned her brushes.

As far as Boomer was concerned, she needn't have hurried. He was fast asleep, folded over the steering wheel like a bearskin rug. Gently, she shook him. Blinking, bewildered, it appeared as if the act of waking was something foreign to him, as if the very idea of waking was a concept that his mind could not frame.

"Why you waking me up?" he grumbled.

For some reason, she could not tell him the truth: that it was after one in the morning, they were parked in four spaces at a drive-in movie theater in the middle of Montana, the movies were over, the lights were up, the other cars had left, a loud, vulgar wind was spitting snowflakes like seeds from an albino watermelon, the attendants were too intimidated to rap on the window of this grotesque vehicle and were probably debating at that moment whether or not to telephone the sheriff. Ellen Cherry, for some reason, couldn't tell Boomer that. So, she said, "Because you were snoring."

He blinked some more. He couldn't believe his ears. "I wasn't snoring," he said indignantly. "I was on assignment."

When the police cruiser pulled alongside the roast turkey, Ellen Cherry was still turning his words over in her mind, as if, in understanding them, she might learn whether she loved him or whether she did not.

"Phoenicia means 'land of the purple.' Grapes? Wisteria? Diarrhetic prose? A violet haze in the hills? No, Phoenician traders were famous throughout the Mediterranean and beyond for their red-purple dyed goods.

"Believe it or not, the source of the purple dye was the conch, the marine animal that occupied, that constructed, shells such as this one that sits beside me in my hour of need. Phoenicians actively hunted conch for the dye that was in them. In prying loose the animal, its shell was usually damaged, which was why a large, unbroken specimen, such as our friend here, was comparatively rare.

"In a sense, the dye conch symbolized Phoenicia. The Phoenician language was closely related to Hebrew, the language of King Ahab, and there were other cultural bonds, but even so, Jezebel was homesick for her native land. Miss Conch Shell became a comfort to her, serving her emotionally as well as spiritually, representing not only Astarte but placid, palm-lined coastal towns whose buildings, streets, and workers' hands were perpetually permeated with a reddish-purple dye. As far as the queen was concerned, the thoroughly Phoenician Miss Shell was the centerpiece of Samaria's principal goddess shrine. Wrapped in purple papyrus, she was often clutched to the royal bosom.

"Land of the purple. That has a nice ring. O'er the land of the purple and the home of the mauve. Our Mr. Sock is purple, come to think of it, purple like the circles under a Mafia don's eyes, purple like the government inspection stamp on a cut of raw meat. I'm tempted to ask what Mr. Sock might have fetched on the Phoenician market. Ooops! Mustn't laugh. Makes my sauce burble out."

"**M**er-cee," said Patsy. "Bud sure left here in a good mood."

"Why shouldn't he be in a good mood?"

"Not saying he shouldn't. Just saying he was."

"Something happened to him while he dozed off after supper. Something definitely happened. The Lord speaking to him in a dream and all. It may be beyond your and my understanding. God works his wonders in mysterious ways."

"That's a fact," agreed Patsy. She returned to her crocheting, Verlin went back to trying to fold his road map. "You know, though, hon, that rebuilding the Temple business—don't it strike you as being up to something?"

"I don't know a blessed thing about it. What kind of up-to-something?"

"Well, it just seems like so many preachers these days are in it for the fame and fortune."

"Huh! Buddy don't have a pot to whiz in."

"Not yet."

"You casting stones, Patsy?"

She sighed. "Not in any position to, I reckon." She fell silent for a time, reflecting upon her own transgressions, comparing them to those she imagined of Buddy Winkler: the weakness of the flesh versus the hunger of ambition. That, of course, got her nowhere, and eventually she gave up on it. She smiled fatalistically and hid the smile behind her crocheting. *I'd be obliged to say this much*, she concluded. *Of the Seven Deadly Sins, lust is definitely the pick of the litter.*

As the spring afternoon wore on, as noisy birds gargled bug juice and buds struggled to free themselves, layer by layer, from their tight Victorian undergarments, Painted Stick and Conch Shell told how the misogynist Yahweh party relentlessly slandered the reputation of Astarte and her champion in Israel, Queen Jezebel, and how, finally, the widowed Jezebel was murdered by Elisha's Yahwist puppet, Jehu. They told how they were spirited into hiding by brave farmers, who secreted them in grain jars during the cruel purge that followed Jehu's usurpation of power. By the hundreds, priests and priestesses of the goddess were butchered, their holy places leveled. It was 843 B.C. The year the patriarchs won the pennant.

In a matter of months, however, Jezebel's daughter, Athaliah, came out of left field, so to speak, and managed to seat herself on the throne of *southern* Israel, Judah. Painted Stick and Conch Shell found themselves smuggled into Jerusalem, into the Great Temple, itself; the First Temple, Solomon's Temple, so-called; the magnificent Hebrew hobble-gobble, where curtains of Phoenician purple, a kind of lullaby, calmed the strident psalms of agitated gold.

Athaliah lasted six years before a patriarchal assassin took her life. During Athaliah's reign, the goddess once again held Jerusalem on her lap. In the temple that Hiram and his skilled Phoenician artisans had built for Solomon, Painted Stick and Conch Shell lived among loaves of gold and silver, among ten thousand candlesticks that were nightly lit; alongside forty thousand harps, two hundred thousand trumpets; among countless jewel-encrusted censers, cups, and vials; among alabaster jars of anointing oils and, for the bronze altar at which offerings were burned, shovels, basins, snuffers, and tongs, all of the finest brass. Those showy furnishings, ordered by Solomon, had little to do with the Goddess, except that they were decorated everywhere with images of lotus, fig, pomegranate, and what the historian Josephus called "the most curious flowers" (vaginal symbols, each of them); but the stick and the shell were comfortably at home amidst the splendor, for as long as Astarte was honored there, they were considered as valuable as treasure.

In the housecleaning that followed Athaliah's homicide, however, they were shunted to an obscure storeroom, where in the company of various golden calves, sperm boats, maternity funnels, tambourines, donkey masks, dance scrolls, and lazy ivory-inlaid vipers, they collected a century's worth of dust. "We were not put in a trance as we were in the cave back yonder," explained Conch Shell, "so even for the inanimate, time passed slowly." She recalled that in the storeroom there were rosewood vials designed to catch the teardrops of women in childbirth, and how the impatient vials filled to overflowing with their own dusty tears. Yet, the talismans were to return to their high station. For centuries, from the time of its completion (962 B.C.) until its destruction by the Babylonians (586 B.C.), the Great Temple swung like a pendulum, back and forth, between Yahweh and Astarte.

Solomon, himself, consorted with the Goddess, a fact so well documented that even biblical revisionists have dared not attempt a cover-up, although they have blamed his "tolerance of paganism" on the influence of his numerous foreign wives. Solomon was said to know the secrets of the plant and animal worlds and how to cast spells that could exorcise demons and heal the ill. Josephus was told that, actually, the king's wives and concubines performed those deeds in his name. Perhaps the pagan women—there were more than seven hundred of them—were the source of his celebrated wisdom, as well, although the book containing his alleged profundities wasn't written until six hundred years after his death, and many of its ideas can be traced to the early Greek philosophers.

In any case, when King Manasseh was crowned in 693 B.C., the pendulum swung back to the Goddess with such force that Painted Stick and Conch Shell, dusted and polished, were consulted and employed with a regularity and reverence that they hadn't experienced since their heyday in the observatory. Painted Stick not only pulled astronomy duty up on the roof (made of Phoenician cedar plated with gold), but joined Conch Shell in the inner sanctum when the priests deflowered privileged virgins, winners of a series of "Miss Judah" contests.

Spoon was as shocked as she could be by this talk of fornication in the Holy of Holies. Conch Shell explained to her that the First Temple had teemed with sexual activity from the night of its dedication onward, even, to some extent, when under strict Levite (Yahwist) control. A famous pair of phallic pillars guarded its entrance, and, like almost all the temples of the ancient world, it was financially supported by the earnings of holy prostitutes.

"Oh dear, oh my," muttered Spoon. She felt as weak as the stricken bean tin and had to steady herself lest she collapse beside it.

From his/her awkward position, Can o' Beans tried to comfort her. "As near as I can determine, Miss Spoon, this business had nothing in common with some sordid grinding in a cheap motel or drunken octopusing in the backseat of a car, such as you might have heard the Jesuits condemn. Why, it was even more exalted than marital congress. This was sacred sex, conducted with ceremony and in full consciousness, meant to mime the act of original Creation, to celebrate life at its most intense and crucial moment. We're not talking the old in-and-out, slip-slap here, Miss Spoon, we're talking the ignition of the divine spark and . . ." For the first time, Spoon closed her ears (not that she had ears, understand) to the erudition of Can o' Beans, turning away from him/her, offended and disturbed.

Dirty Sock chuckled under his breath (not that he had breath, understand).

Like a neon fox tongue lapping up the powdered bones of space chickens, the rising sun licked away at the light snow that had fallen during the night. Ellen Cherry was already out of bed. She was filling a tray with fried egg sandwiches, chocolate doughnuts, and beer: Boomer's favorite breakfast.

She wasn't kidding herself. She was trying to assuage her guilt, pure and simple. Intellectually, she knew that she had done nothing about which to feel guilty, yet emotionally it was so deeply embedded in her that a woman's job was to tend to her husband that she was compelled to do penance for having allowed the most important thing in her life to momentarily interfere with the trifles of tending. That's just the way it was. No sense fighting it.

"Did I get enough mayonnaise on the bread for you, sweet darlin'?"

"Yes ma'am, and I thank you for that." He licked a squiggle of excess off his upper lip. "I also thank you for talking that cop outta locking me up last night."

"You weren't exactly Miss Manners with him, Boomer. He only wanted you to identify yourself."

"He wanted me to be afraid of him. All cops want that. I'm a terrible disappointment to policemen."

Watching him dunk a doughnut in his beer mug, she said, "You *aren't* a particularly fearful person, are you?"

"Long as you're not afraid, nobody can run your life for you. Remember that. Hell is being scared of things. Heaven is refusing to be scared. I mean that literally." He took a bite of soggy doughnut. "Now you know my religion."

"Yeah, but can people really choose not to be afraid?"

"Damn right." Staring into the nude Buddha colors of his beer, he chewed quietly for several minutes, then abruptly looked up at her. "I'm lying like a dog," he said.

"What do you mean?"

"I am afraid of something. I'm afraid of *you.*"

"Aw, come on." She issued a laugh so dry it was almost a cough. "How could you possibly be afraid of me?"

"You have my heart."

"Honey!" She was astonished to find him blurry-eyed and openmouthed, like a child about to cry. "Why, I would never intentionally do anything to—"

"You have my rough ol' welder's heart, and you have your art. I don't know if you're big enough for both of us."

"Oh, baby, of course . . ." Even as she was protesting, however, she was gazing past him, through an Airstream window, at the sun climbing above the lightly dusted hills, and thinking how she would like to paint it as a neon fox tongue licking up the powdered bones of angels.

"**O**ne of the hills on which Jerusalem sprang up had a threshing floor atop it, a threshing floor being a large flat rock where farmers mugged wheat, beating and shaking down the harvested sheaves until the grain spilled out. Well, the story got around that this particular threshing floor was actually crowning Mount Moriah, the place where in the myth of Abraham and Isaac, the father was ready to slit his son's throat to prove his devotion to Yahweh. Talk about your loyalty oaths. Consequently, by design or arbitrariness, that flat rock became to the Hebrews a sacred spot, a power center—enlarging the folktale, some claimed the rock had come from Eden and that Adam was buried under it—and when Solomon decided to have a great temple built, this alleged Mount Moriah was the site he selected.

"To hold the massive complex that Solomon had in mind—a Superdome of faith—the hill had to be topped, leveled, and terraced. It was time-consuming, and it wasn't cheap, but Solomon, or his harem, was at least wise enough to realize that when you're out to erect the most holy building on earth, a sanctuary that must help you unify and control a large imperial nation of mixed race and religion, you don't just stick it in a handy vacant field like you would a new shopping mall. Your building lot has got to have some magic about it."

(At this point, Can o' Beans, who had been pumping Conch Shell and Painted Stick for background information about the First Temple, would have liked to interrupt their account [and his/her silent reiteration of it] to inquire about the nature of magic—he/she suspected that the shell and the stick, considering their origins in an age when such things were not held up to ridicule, were well versed in the magical arts—but like many a timid or hidebound novelist, he/she dared not still the narrative flow.)

"Once the top of Mount Moriah had been transformed into a wide plateau and its slopes recontoured to accommodate roads and steps, Solomon, through Hiram, got down to the nitty-gritty of erecting his extravaganza. Solomon was the producer, you might say, and Hiram the director. They commanded a cast of thousands. All nonunion. For openers, there were a hundred and fifty thousand Canaanite slaves, laboring to avoid the lash, plus thirty thousand Israelites drafted into the Temple job corps and not even earning *falafel* money. There were three thousand straw bosses barking orders, and probably an equal number of skilled masons, metalworkers, and master carpenters from Hiram's Phoenicia. The Phoenicians dressed in purple and got the pick of the chick-peas from the company store.

"Even with all those grunts and gofers, it took seven years to complete construction—an additional three years had been spent getting the materials together. Ever thus with government projects, I suppose. When it was done, though, it was a sight to behold. With its tiered walls and hierarchical courtyards, one inside the other like Chinese boxes, it covered several acres. As Miss Shell describes it, the outer walls, like the buildings, were made of stone, Israel's lone natural resource. Inside, the stone was planked with good old Phoenician cedar, and then to the cedar they affixed plates of silver and gold, many of them set with gemstones. At today's prices, the Temple's structural precious metal bill alone would run upward of six billion dollars. Makes you appreciate aluminum siding. Wonder what the insurance premium would've run Solomon on a spread like that?

"Of course, vain King Solomon had been dead for more than a century before Miss Shell and Mr. Stick arrived on the scene. They learned about the Temple's construction from the stones themselves. The place was a bit beat-up and stained by the time our friends landed there, but it still was a compound of considerable glory, especially on national holidays, when thousands would stream up its steps, chanting, banging tambourines, grappling with their bleating sacrifices, so blinded by the shine and sparkle of their surroundings that they couldn't look directly at them. Oops. Hold on a minute, bean can. I said Sol had been dead for more than a century. Wrong. Solomon died in 933 B.C., Miss Shell and Mr. Stick were first employed in the Temple in 843 B.C. That's ninety years, not a hundred and ten. This backward counting gets confusing. But think what it must have been like for the folks who were around when Baby Jesus was born. They'd been counting backward all their lives, their ancestors counted backward as far back as anyone could remember; and, *scheeech,* all of a sudden they woke up one morning, skidded to a halt, and had to start counting in the opposite direction. I tell you, that switch from B.C. to A.D. must have driven people nuts. I bet more than a few Israelites missed their dental appointments."

Blue lights flashing like a mutant shoppers' special at a postnuclear K mart, a squad car forced a smoke-spewing, rust-freckled, tailpipe-dragging old Chevy wagon to the curb.

"I'm the Reverend Buddy Winkler," the driver announced hopefully.

"And I'm Officer Dishman. Let me see your driver's license."

Buddy had only been going twenty-nine miles an hour, but the speed limit on the Strip was twenty-five and not an internal combustion more. When the shock of recognition he'd been expecting proved not forthcoming, the preacher pulled out his wallet. An empty gum wrapper came out with it, fluttering like an anorectic moth to the blue-lit pavement at the policeman's feet.

"God spoke to me tonight, officer," said Buddy. "I nodded off after supper, and God come to me and showed me a vision and gave unto me a mission." He was warming up his saxophone. "You can't be completely holden to man's speed limits when you're on a mission for the Lord."

In many cities, he would have been hauled to the station for a Breathalyzer test, but this was Colonial Pines, Virginia. The policeman not only let Buddy drive away without a citation, but he also donated five dollars to the cause. "Remember my little Jimmy in your prayers. He's got allergies right awful."

Oddly elated, Buddy didn't feel like going straight home. He poked the five-dollar bill, which he saw as a sign of blessings to come, into his shirt pocket, and, for some reason, circled back past the Charles house, site of his epiphany. Through the living room window, he glimpsed his cousin and his cousin's wanton wife. Verlin was still trying to fold that blamed road map, but Patsy had finished crocheting her bikini. That hadn't taken long. Of course, the thing was so teeny a couple of silkworms could have knocked it off on their lunch break.

Although by now he had chugged past their house, Buddy pushed down hard on his horn. "Make a joyful noise unto the Lord!" he cried through the worm-eaten crucifixes of his dental Golgotha.

"The pendulum swung yet again. This time a ramrod named Josiah took control, and during the thirty years of his reign, Miss Shell and Mr. Stick had to lay low, shuttled by night between the various clandestine shrines that dotted the desert near the Dead Sea. In human celebrity terms, it was as if they were reduced to playing small suburban clubs after a career of headlining in the likes of the Hollywood Bowl—yet dear Conch Shell and Painted Stick suffered no ego contusions. Oh, to the contrary. The First Temple, after all, served its nation as treasury, academy, seminary, council chamber, and talk-show set, and was so boisterous with political, economic, and theological debate (not to mention sexual shenanigans) that it threatened to engulf the Holy of Holies in institutional jabber. The crude desert shrines, although always in danger of Yahwist attack, provided our shell and stick welcome respite from the plots and intrigues that invariably poison the honey in the hives of the powerful.

"Believe it or not—and this is starting to make me dizzy—the Yahweh-Astarte round-robin *still* wasn't over. After Josiah's death, his successor, King Jehoiakim, immediately undid his reforms (the pull of that old goddess was pretty strong, obviously), and Miss Shell and Mr. Stick, patinaed now by brine and sandstorm and bonfire, were carted out of the boulder-strewn wilderness to be displayed in the Great Temple once again. From 609 until 586 B.C., they sat among priestly paraphernalia, acting as rods that might attract Astarte's capricious lightning, any bolt of which was said to jolt a human psyche temporarily free of the chains that bound it to a mundane life of tears and toil. Then . . .

"One evening, as twilight was buttering the stones of the city, as smoke from the cookfires trailed like the beards of ascending prophets in the dimming sky, Painted Stick was carried to the Temple roof. All Jerusalem lay below him, as much in squalor as in splendor; a thorny, windy, sun-baked hill town, stiff of roofline, elastic of spirit; knocked a little cockeyed by all the comings and goings of armies and superstitions, cults and caravans, plunderers and philosophers, saviors and destroyers; but a *habitat* in spite of everything, a shelter, sinking now into a night of small and simple pleasures: wineskins and pita breads, snores, prayers, and embraces—its stone eyelids already closed to the singular debt that I'm afraid it must someday settle with eternity.

"Beyond the Jaffa Gate, Gaza swallowed the sun like quicksand swallowing a flamingo, and the priests finally turned toward the eastern quadrant, which was now dark enough to entertain a star or two. At once they noticed an unfamiliar dull red glow clinging to the northeast horizon line the way that a stray spark would cling to a woolen cloak, winking, smoldering, unsure of whether to flare or fade. Their eyes automatically fell on Painted Stick, but the stick registered nothing. One of them held the stick aloft, pointing it like an accusing finger at the distant ember. Nothing. They wagged the stick then, coaxing it the way a dowser must sometimes coax a divining fork. Neither a twitch nor a vibration. The instrument was totally unresponsive. The red spot glowed on. Very strange."

There was a famous landscape painter, Russell Chatham, who lived in Livingston, Montana, and Ellen Cherry had hoped to pay him a courtesy call. Under the circumstances, however, she decided against it. No sense slipping another art burr under Boomer's saddle, especially when she couldn't make up her mind whether or not she wanted him bucked off. Surely, there were other women in the world who were confused about their feelings for their husbands. Otherwise, there would be no excuse for Burt Reynolds. The question was, were there other women who were confused about their feelings for their husbands after one week of marriage? She concluded that there must be. Probably some women, maybe a lot of women, walked down the aisle asking themselves, "Who *is* that man in the tuxedo? Why is he looking at me like that? How much better do I really want to know him?" At any rate, Ellen Cherry thought it better that she shove art on the back burner until they reached New York. When the subject did arise, later that same day, it was Boomer who brought it up.

Leaving the last snowfall of spring to melt in the Crazies, leaving the famous landscape painter, Russell Chatham, to go through life without ever meeting his colleague, Ellen Cherry Charles, they goosed the turkey northeastward and late in the afternoon crossed the Missouri River. "You know who loved this here Missouri River?" Boomer asked. "You know who lived along it and loved it well?"

Thomas Hart Benton, thought Ellen Cherry. However, since she didn't want to mention an artist, she answered, "No, hon, I don't."

"The outlaw Jesse James," said Boomer. "That's who." Boomer was quiet for a while, as if the river had taken his tongue and carried it to some faroff place. Then he said, "Jesse James robbed beaucoup banks and near as many trains. He was in shoot-outs, ambushes, what have you, there was a posse big as an army on his tail around the clock, including Christmas. But, you know, ol' Jesse never got a scratch.

One day, though, he turned reckless and went to hang a picture on the wall. He was standing on a chair just hanging and admiring that pretty picture, and Robert Ford snuck up behind him, blew a hole in his skull. So much for art, I reckon."

The sun peeked through the cottonwoods not long after that, and the roast turkey, stuffed with silence, glimpsed its own reflection swimming in the Missouri River.

"**T**he priests sent for the high priestess. 'There's something wrong with your stick,' they told her. 'It won't report on that red glow in the sky.' The high priestess ran a test. 'Nothing's the matter with the stick,' she said. 'That glow happens to be man-made.'

"Come midnight, every priest, priestess, rabbi, sage, and counsel in temple service were up on the roof gazing to the north and the east. By then, there were *three* red glows in the sky.

"The despised old prophet, Jeremiah, was trying to get up onto the roof, as well, but every time his smelly gray beard appeared at the top of the steps, someone swung a fist at him and chased him down again. 'It's the Babylonians!' Jeremiah kept yelling. 'Yahweh has sent the Babylonians as punishment to you who have desecrated his laws.'

"Jeremiah was at least half right, and everybody knew it. At last, they sent a messenger to awaken the king. Just before dawn, the king ascended to the rooftop. He stood there in a robe of Phoenician purple and watched his outlying fortresses burn. 'Surrender! Surrender!' old Jeremiah was screaming. 'Surrender and accept Yahweh's judgment, else Jerusalem be destroyed.' The king ordered somebody to brain Jeremiah with Mr. Stick, but the high priestess, not willing to risk breaking the instrument, threw her sandal at the prophet, instead.

"For most practical purposes, the Babylonians had been running Judea (that's southern Israel, remember) for a decade. Much in the way, I suppose, that the Soviet Union ran Poland or Czechoslovakia.

Babylon was riding tall under its powerful leader, Nebuchadnezzar.
My, oh my, they don't make names like that anymore. Ronald,
George, Gary, Jimmy, just plain Bill: these modern mediocre moni-
kers aren't fit to shine the shoes of Nebuchadnezzar. John is a label.
Nebuchadnezzar is a poem. A monument. A swarm of killer bees let
loose in the halls of the alphabet. Anyway, back to the point,
Nebuchadnezzar and his Babylonians had already invaded Jerusalem
eleven years earlier, but after looting the Temple, filling their gunnysacks with some of those ten thousand candlesticks, two hundred
thousand trumpets, and forty thousand harps, they withdrew. They
informed the city that it could maintain autonomy as long as it
behaved. Ha. Fat chance. Proud little Jerusalem grew increasingly
defiant, and, now, the dreaded Babylonian war machine was lighting up the suburban sky with some very nonentertaining fireworks.

"Jerusalem was destined to lie under siege for many months,
during which time Mr. Stick failed to register a single auspicious
omen in the clouds. As hunger, thirst, and disease overtook even the
priests and priestesses, our stick finally was forgotten, abandoned on
the Temple rooftop where they'd dropped him after one last futile
sweep of the sky."

A San Antonio taxi driver with a degree in ichthyology was spinning green on "Wheel of Fortune," racking up big bucks in every
category, but Buddy Winkler was barely watching. Buddy was reading a book, of all things, a book checked out with no little embarrassment from the Colonial Pines Public Library.

A bible usually lay open in front of him, on the SpaghettiO–
spattered Formica or on the upholstered arm of his favorite easy
chair (worn so thin that puffs of stuffing periodically launched
themselves from it like seeds escaping a milkweed pod). But Buddy
didn't actually read the Bible, not anymore, he consulted it the way
that an actor consults a cue card. He needed merely to glimpse the

words, "And he opened the bottomless pit and there arose a smoke . . ." to be off and running, blowing long-winded tenor riffs on his favorite subject, the End Days, the horrifying, blood-flooded terminus of history, the deluge of boiling guts that many claimed would wash away all sin and sinners and leave the universe squeaky clean forever.

On that March evening, however, the Reverend Buddy Winkler was reading a book. There was, in fact, on the dinette, a stack of books so tall it could have allowed a cat easy entry into any mockingbird nest in the neighborhood. Only one of those books held Buddy in its spell.

Buddy had sometimes suspected that God Almighty didn't quite approve of him, had found his service wanting, and had kumquatted him with boils, wired him with toothaches, to demonstrate his displeasure. But now the Lord had spoken to him, had given unto him a mission. Buddy felt vindicated (even if at that very moment there was in the middle of his chin a furuncle the size and temperature of an oven-baked hors d'oeuvre); felt both humble and heroic, and was more than ready to put his martyrish shoulder to the wheel. Trouble was, the Jews wouldn't cooperate. He had telephoned every rabbi in Richmond and Norfolk (the lone Jew living in Colonial Pines was an army officer stationed at nearby Fort Lee), to no avail. When he explained to them the essence of his mission, they had rudely intimated that he might be a crank. Buddy was as surprised as he was irritated. He thought the Jews wanted to rebuild the Temple. He thought they wanted the Messiah to come. Bloodied but unbowed, he went to the library to pick up some books on Judaism. That's when his eyes fell upon this other book, the one absorbing his evening.

Entitled *Christian Wives: The Women Behind the Evangelists,* it was written by James Schaffer and Colleen Todd. He didn't know why he checked out the blamed thing, let alone why he was reading it. When he read that Tammy Faye Bakker, spouse of superpreacher Jim Bakker, kept her husband's interest up by changing her wigs several times a day, his mouth fell open so wide that that bouchée on his chin gave him a stab of pain. And when he read that Mrs. Bakker kept her marriage exciting by never ever letting the Reverend Bakker see her without makeup, that she routinely wore false eyelashes and earrings to bed, well, he just let "Wheel of Fortune" roll on without him.

"Jezebel business," he kept saying to himself. "That there's flatout Jezebel business." Small wonder, he thought, that Jim Bakker and his associates had fallen from grace. When the most powerful preachers in the land take unto them painted hussies as their lawful wedded wives, then surely the Age of Wickedness is reaching its apogee. Where is the sanctuary that is safe from Satan, Satan in his most insidious form: the Whore of Babylon? Were he, Buddy Winkler, foremost evangelist of the Southern Baptist Voice of the Sparrow Network, were he to take unto him a wife. . . . He caught himself. What was he thinking?

At that instant, there was a rapping at his door. "Damnation!" he swore. "It's Verlin and Patsy." If Patsy caught him reading that book . . . ! Frantically, Buddy shoved *Christian Wives* under the sofa. It was not until he was about to unlatch the screen that he realized that there was bulging in his trousers, the oldest story of man, a tome that would slide beneath no furniture, an opus that he could not hide.

"**N**ebuchadnezzar was a patient man. That much he had in common with inanimate objects. Month after month, he strolled along the rampart with which his troops had encircled Jerusalem, his big Babylonian nose in the air. When the stench from inside the walls became intense enough that he could assume half of the inhabitants must be dead, he ordered his men to erect their breaching engines. They met scant resistance as they battered down the vulnerable northern wall.

"Well, when the breach in the wall was accomplished and the boys from Babylon streamed through the narrow streets, our old hand-painted stick, who'd been watching from the Temple roof, prone upon a sheet of sun-warmed gold, did something that, except under the most rare and surreptitious conditions, no object had done since the evolutionary development of human beings on earth, had not done in more than a million years. He got up and ran.

"The reason behind his radical act, I can only guess. Maybe he was just fed up with all that back and forth nonsense, maybe he didn't see any reason why he had to go down with the ship. It could be there wasn't any logical reason, or if there was, its origins were in the stars. It wasn't a piece of cake, I know that. An enormous amount of effort was required to set forces in motion that had lain dormant for so long. Certain subatomic particles had to be coerced to change direction, to orbit paths previously untraveled. Yet, in barely thirty minutes of human subjective time, Mr. Stick was clattering down the steps toward the Temple's main courtyard.

"Bippity-bopping past the emaciated corpses of priests and priest-esses with whom he'd once shared a mutual dependence, he crossed the vestibule and entered the great hall. As luck would have it, Miss Shell, all wrapped up real pretty in purple linen, rested upon a pedestal of white stone at the far end of the hall. Had she been inside the Holy of Holies, he would have been unable to pry open its heavy gold doors and get to her. Miss Shell isn't going into any detail about this, but somehow Mr. Stick persuaded her to invoke her own powers of mobility and flee with him. He blew in her ear, for all I know.

"Miss Shell put up some initial resistance. Many females do, I'm told. She pointed out that the Babylonians were devout wor-shippers of Ishtar—the goddess Astarte under another name—and that no sanctified relic of the Great Mother religion should have anything to fear from Babylon. Mr. Stick countered that soldiers are soldiers, from any culture, in any age. Soldiers like to hack and break and rape and burn, and when they are in their invasion frenzy, nothing, living or inanimate, is sacred to them. And any-way, it wasn't fear that had caused him to bolt. It was . . . some-thing else.

"She joined him.

"Heading southward, away from the advancing invaders and not really caring, in the exhilaration of flight, that a half-starved Jeremiah had witnessed them and begun jumping up and down, they made their way to the Mount of Olives, and from its summit, in the sketchy shadow of a stripped-bare orchard tree, they looked on as the Temple was first plundered, then battered, then torched. Call it King Solomon's Temple, call it Hiram's Temple, it must have been one magnificent structure, that First Temple; opulent beyond the wildest Beverly Hills daydream; and the very heart and lungs, hub and corolla, anchor and balloon of the fated nation of Israel. The Babylonians fairly quickly reduced it to cinders. Then they trampled the cinders. Not one stone from it has ever been found."

"**S**ome women have bedroom eyes," said Boomer Petway. "My wife has bedroom hair."

Boomer winked at Ellen Cherry. They were moored in a trailer park in North Dakota. A small crowd had gathered to gawk at the Airstream turkey. Some in the crowd had let their attention be diverted by the largely ceremonial gesture of Ellen Cherry running a comb through her curls. Ellen Cherry sat on the Airstream doorstep, sawing and raking with the comb. The comb was bent nearly double from the strain.

"Before it was captured by the Commies," Boomer said to a housewife with mousy bangs, "her hair was as straight as yours. KGB tortured it for days, but it wouldn't tell."

"Wouldn't tell *what?*" asked the woman.

"What happened to *your* hair?" asked her twelve-year-old son.

Boomer actually blushed. His bald spot flared like the head of a match. For a moment, it rivaled the setting sun, reflected now by the turkey's silver fuselage.

Ellen Cherry giggled. "He doesn't like to talk about his war experiences," she said. "But I assure you, his hair didn't spill the beans, either."

Squeezing past her, Boomer went inside. "Getting chilly out here," he said.

"His head gets cold," Ellen Cherry told the boy in a conspiratorial tone. They both laughed, then she followed her husband into the turkey. He was in the galley, rummaging through cupboards.

"What you said about spilling beans gave my stomach ideas," he said, rummaging.

"If you're looking for pork and beans, there's actually some in there," said she.

"Where?"

"They're in there. There's a can of beans that's been sitting on my shelves for years. I swear, I've moved with those beans three different times. Guy in Seattle gave 'em to me when he graduated from the art school. Before that, they sat on his shelf for years. Those poor beans are so old they'll probably give you crude oil instead of gas."

"They're not here."

"Well, I don't . . ."

"I know what happened to 'em. We left 'em in that cave."

"No."

"Yeah, we did."

"Beans, too?"

"Yep."

"Are you sure, Boomer?"

" 'Course, I'm sure. I have a photogenic memory."

Can o' Beans watched the last tangerine peel of dusk swirl down the drain behind the mountains. It was completely dark now. It was time.

When he/she considered that Painted Stick and Conch Shell were the sole surviving oddments from the great Temple of Jerusalem, they seemed all the more precious and wondrous, and he/she felt all the more sorrowful to part company with them. For one thing, there were many questions left unanswered. For another, there was a unique and perhaps momentous adventure under way from which he/she was now excluded. Ah, well . . .

There was plenty still to be thankful for. What was a can of beans but a pawn in the game of consumption? From field to factory, from market to household, from cook pot to lunch plate, the destiny of a can of beans was as sealed as it was simple. Ultimate destination: rust heap and sewage pond. Yet, he/she had managed to escape the norm, to taste a freedom unimagined by others of his/her "lowly" station. Moreover, were the lives of most humans really any better? When humans were young, they were pushed around in strollers. When they were old, they were pushed around in wheelchairs. In between, they were just pushed around.

The thick veil that shields a being from the transformative and tricky light of liberty, from the dizzy incandescence of self-determination, that veil had been briefly parted for Can o' Beans. Obviously, freedom's glare is too bright for many. They panic when any sudden gust lifts the hem of the brocade. Eyes blinking frantically, they'll cling with their last broken nail to the protective folds of social control. A few, among them Can o' Beans, bask in the glow. It warms them in hidden and unexpected places that might have been forever dark and cold.

Of course, like the cliché moth courting the trite candle, the lit-up libertarian runs a constant risk. Is it not finer, however, to sizzle whole in the flame of freedom than to slowly stew to pieces in one's own diminishing juices, constrained and constricted before the veil? Can o' Beans thought so. Out of the sauce pan and into the fire! That was this can's credo. Were it not for the burden that he/she would surely be to the others, he/she would tackle the road to the Middle East *regardless* of his/her handicap! Alas . . .

They made a sled for Can o' Beans out of aspen bark and loops of grass. Painted Stick pulled it. When a rock, log, or steep incline blocked its path, Conch Shell pushed from behind. Lying back, its wound open to the moon, the bean can let itself be dragged, bumpy mile after bumpy mile, until, toward dawn, the band of objects arrived at a weedy churchyard on the outskirts of a small Wyoming town.

"Fare you well, Can o' Beans. Thank you for your sage counsel regarding this bizarre land of yours."

Painted Stick, so charismatic, so primal, so difficult to know. Good-bye.

"The Goddess shall monitor your fortunes, dearest noble vessel."

Conch Shell, lovely siren, still nurturing, charming, offering hope. Good-bye.

"See ya in the funny papers, perfesser."

Not if I see you first, vulgar fellow, but persist in your candor and enthusiasm. Good-bye.

"Boo-hoo-hoo."

Spoon. Brush those sentimental globules from your elegant ladle. Goodbye, Miss Spoon.

Since it was Painted Stick's intention to lead his party beyond the village before daybreak, the good-byes were not drawn out. From the weeds beside the little whitewashed church where they deposited Can o' Beans, he/she watched his/her erstwhile companions bounce, toddle, and scurry along until they disappeared, one by one—Spoon last, looking back through her tears—into a ditch. The ditch was running with snowmelt, littered with filthy newspaper, shreds of tire rubber, and beer cans as empty as the bean can surely would be soon, but the small pilgrims let themselves be swallowed up by it as though it were a glory road. Oh, strange are the routes to Jerusalem!

"We're here about the miracle, Bud," said Verlin.

"Why, bless your souls. Come right in." Buddy Winkler was so flattered that he forgot, as quickly as he had noticed it, his *Christian Wives* hard-on.

"Yes sirree," Patsy chimed in, eyeballing his protruding fly but resisting commentary on it, "I reckon you heard about the miracle?"

Buddy's eyes narrowed with disappointment and suspicion. "Now what is it that y'all are talkin' about? What kind of miracle? Where?"

"A religious visitation," Verlin explained. "Out there on the Chesterfield road somewheres."

Strongly conflicting emotions seized Buddy Winkler. On the one hand, the possibility of a religious miracle right there in the county excited and encouraged him. On the other, he had to worry whether this alleged visitation might not steal the thunder from his own recent vision—and the mission it had generated. He was hoping that Verlin and Patsy, his congregation and, if the Voice of the Sparrow Network approved, his radio audience, would soon be moved to support that mission with their personal checks.

Now, here Verlin and Patsy were telling him that some woman had folks in a tizzy because for the fourth night in a row, her neighbor's porch light was casting the shadow of a bearded man on her standup freezer.

"It's on the local news," Verlin said. "Ever' preacher in the area's been out there. We thought sure they woulda called you."

"Phone's broke," said Buddy. "I think one of them rabbis put a whammy on it."

"That's a crying shame," said Patsy. "We thought you'd of been on this miracle like a hobo on a ham sandwich."

It was nearly ten at night by the time they found the woman's house, but more than sixty people were milling about her carport, which was where the freezer stood.

"It's him," proclaimed somebody in a loud whisper. "It's Jesus!" Buddy, however, was of the opinion that the shadow looked more like Willie Nelson.

"Or else Castro," Verlin suggested. As for Patsy, she said, none too softly, "When the Good Lord shows up, we may rest assured it is not gonna be on a major appliance."

Shortly before eleven o'clock that morning, cars, dozens of cars, began pulling into the churchyard. Can o' Beans was elated. What splendid timing that there would be a wedding on his/her very first day at the church! If his/her luck continued, he/she might be clattering behind a honeymoon car by noon.

With effort, the bean can stood upright. The dent in its side threw it off balance, making walking difficult, but it wobbled toward a more conspicuous spot near the front steps, where it might attract the attention of someone requiring its services in the nuptial parade. *I wonder if they'll have a can opener on them?* thought the container. Never had it imagined that it might form the words "can opener" with such positive anticipation. Fatalistic calm, yes, but hardly glee.

Yet, here it was, practically longing for the singing blade. Now that its fortunes had come to this, now that the greatest opportunity in the history of canned vegetables had been lost, it was anxious to play out its hand, to embrace the fate to which, prior to gaining mobility, it had been equanimously resigned. Can o' Beans turned a complete circle, hoping to get a look at the bride. A thin orange rivulet of sauce, like a thread from a volcano's bloomers, unfurled from the vent in his/her side, alerting the antennae of nearby ants.

It was then that the hearse drove up. Followed by the military Jeep carrying the color guard.

Can o' Beans staggered back into the tall weeds and lay down again. Forty yards away, mourners would be laying down for all eternity, or at least for a sufficiently long time, a local boy who'd let his young body be punctured and splayed by the insatiable can opener of the Middle East.

"**W**e could cross over into Canada," Ellen Cherry proposed, "and come down into New York by way of Montreal."

"Nah," said Boomer. "Them people up there call their cheese *fromage*." He made a poison-bottle face.

"I see your point," she said, humoring him. "*Fromage,* indeed. That's enough to keep *me* away from the snack table."

"Sooner or later," said Boomer, "I'd like to ease this baby into Chicago."

Ellen Cherry glanced out the galley window. It was quite dark now, but several people were still studying the roast turkey. The people wielded flashlights and behaved as if they were inspectors from the Center for Poultry Abuse.

"Why Chicago?" she asked. She knew that it wasn't the Chicago Art Institute that was beckoning him. Ellen Cherry knew that her husband wasn't licking his muscular chops over the Chicago Museum of Contemporary Art.

"Well, I'd kinda like to see where they held the Saint Valentine's Day massacre."

Just look in on any married woman on February fourteenth, she thought. But she said, "What else?"

"The hospital where Dutch Schultz died."

"Oh, right, Dutch Schultz. Wasn't he the boy who saved the community by sticking his finger in the dike?"

Boomer looked at her as if she had referred to their dinner as macaroni-and-*fromage*.

"Sorry, hon. Guess I was thinking of a different story. You're obviously talking about 'Dutch Schultz and the Silver Skates.' "

Boomer took a long, long swallow of beer. *She must be getting her dot,* he thought. Ellen Cherry called her period her "dot." *She gets like this right before her dot.*

For all practical purposes, we're going to leave them now, Boomer Petway and Ellen Cherry Charles, we're going to leave them in a North Dakota trailer park, ringed by overstuffed midwesterners with flashlights; leave them finishing supper at the Airstream dinette, Boomer thinking that if her "dot" was coming on he'd better hurry and sweet-talk her into the sack, since she was protective of the sheets once the monthly pot began to percolate (talk about your Valentine's massacre); Ellen Cherry thinking, wondering, if now that she was married and moving to New York, was she going to suffer more, or less, for her art—and if she suffered less, would she paint less, or more; and if she suffered more, would she paint more, or less; and if she painted less, would she paint better, or worse; and if she painted more, would she paint worse, or better, and did it matter so long as she wasn't waiting tables?

We're going to leave our newlyweds sitting there, thinking their private and, perhaps, all too disparate thoughts, and, except for a brief overview, when we catch up with them again more than a year will have passed, and their lives will have taken unexpected turns.

These pages were never meant to be a chronology of their travels across America, but rather a revelation of their indirect but indisputable link to Jerusalem, old and New, a city far from our shores, far from our life-styles, yet, it could be argued, a city in which each of us psychically dwells: Jerusalem, sacred and terrible, bloody and radiant, the most important town in America.

Suffice to say, their trip afforded them both pleasure and edification. With Boomer at the wheel, they continued to zigzag, to meander, at a pace that allowed them leisure for sexual intercourse with each other (time out for her "dot") and social intercourse with their countrymen. They did, by the way, visit Chicago, where Ellen Cherry executed a tiny painting of the street corner where the gangster John Dillinger was gunned down (Dutch Schultz, it turned out, died in New Jersey) and presented it to Boomer as a wedding gift. He shed a couple of muscular tears. Then he took her dancing.

At journey's completion, in Manhattan, they had telephoned her parents and reported that all across the continent, folks seemed to be talking about just three things: AIDS, the Middle East, and the Final Four. AIDS was a fatal, as yet incurable, disease. The Middle East, although capricious in its daily ups and downs, seemed to be firmly connected somehow in people's minds with "the end of the world." The Final Four was the culminating event of the postseason collegiate basketball tournaments (then under way), and by its very name—it logically might have been dubbed the Top Four or even the First Four—conveyed, not unlike AIDS and the Middle East, a sense of finality, entropy, apocalypse, something forcibly drawing to a close. Thus, the newlyweds concluded, America had termination on the brain like a tumor. Endings, happy or otherwise; exits, dramatically correct or not; climaxes, not to be confused with orgasms, dominated their thoughts. Their minds were on end, so to speak.

"Bud'll be pleased as punch," said Patsy.

Verlin got on the line. "How'd that, what do they call it, Dura-Torque suspension system, hold up?"

"Like ridin' on mashed potatoes," testified Boomer.

"Figures," said Verlin.

Speaking of the roast turkey, wherever they stopped it, coast to coast, onlookers had invariably inquired, "What're you selling?" "Who do you represent?" "What company are you doing this for? Armour's?" "Are we on TV?" It was a sad commentary, but people simply could not accept that the giant entrée was not an advertising gimmick, a promotional stunt.

"They don't get it," complained Boomer. "Can't they comprehend that not ever'thing's done for a paycheck? That sometimes you just make a thing 'cause you wanna see how it'll turn out, 'cause you have a feeling in your gut that it oughta be made?"

Ellen Cherry regarded him then with something barely short of admiration. She regarded him in the cardboard ray of newfound optimism. *This bozo might be capable of understanding art, after all,* thought she.

Forward! *March!* Single file, in step, *hup two three four (five six seven eight nine ten eleven twelve*—each had three pairs of legs), rotating their twitchy feelers like parallel filaments in Salvador Dali light bulbs, a formation of licorice-backed ants (a throbbing artery of blues notes, a line of aardvark cocaine) advanced on leaky Can o' Beans the way that hundreds of columns of warriors, over the years, have advanced on Jerusalem.

Fastened to its rocky hillsides with hooks both physical and abstract, Jerusalem could only stand and fight. Can o' Beans, however, by wobbling a yard in one direction, toddling a yard in another, could manage to evade the regimental ants. *That's the weakness of bureaucrats,* he/she thought, with a grin. *They just can't hit a moving target.*

The ants were dressed in black, like the people inside the church, an irony not wasted on Can o' Beans. In truth, it made him/her a little uneasy, but he/she joked about it. "You don't think ants are stuffy?" he/she asked a nearby brick. "Why, not even William F. Buckley would wear a tuxedo to a picnic." Possessing no more of a sense of humor than the ants, the brick looked blank, and Can o' Beans doddered off a yard to the left. Those evasive tactics interfered but marginally with the fascinated attention he/she paid to the funeral service.

Like a deceased Italian mama damned to make pasta for the demons in hell, the minister's wife pulled strands of death spaghetti from a wheezy old organ. Resisting the temptation to toss in a few brimstone meatballs, the minister wove a tinsel garland from the various bromides of sympathy and laid it upon the bowed heads of the mourners. He used words such as "heroism," "sacrifice," and "eternal reward," while the heads bobbed with sobbing, like corks in a popular fishing hole. Later, they carried the broken skeleton (yearning in its bones for rock 'n' roll) out back to the cemetery, dipped an American flag over it, fired shots in the air (as if it were the clouds' fault the boy had died), and, while a lonely bugle wounded the spring morning with sounds more mournful than a midnight freight, they slipped it below the vegetable layer into the mineral earth, to be compressed into gas for the jets of a future that Wyoming had not imagined yet.

Taking all this in, while dodging the ant advance, Can o' Beans wondered if human animals didn't set themselves up to suffer excruciating grief, most of which could have been avoided with a slight expenditure of imaginative thought. Without quite realizing it (being ignorant of the ramifications of Salome's dance), the bean can had identified the veil of political illusion—and the reluctance of humankind to part it—as the reason behind the morning's sad occasion.

Lost now to family, buddies, girlfriend, rabbit hound, society, and himself, this poor young sailor had fallen—not very many miles from Jerusalem—understanding virtually nothing of the situation in the Middle East. He probably believed it involved a struggle between right and wrong, good and evil, freedom and oppression. That was his second mistake. His third mistake was in trusting that even if *he* didn't understand the situation, his leaders did. His first—and worst—mistake was blindly doing what he was told to do. Without questioning their methods or their motives, he allowed politicians to make the decisions that led to his early demise.

What is politics, after all, but the compulsion to preside over property and make other people's decisions for them? Liberty, the very opposite of ownership and control, cannot, then, result from political action, either at the polls or the barricades, but rather evolves out of attitude. If it results from anything, it may be levity.

Inanimate objects, destined to spend their existence in *outwardly* passive and obedient behavior, understood perhaps more sharply than humans that true freedom was an internal condition not subject to the vagaries of politics. Freedom could not be owned. Therefore, it could not be appropriated. Or controlled. It could, however, be relinquished. The Wyoming sailor had surrendered his soul long before he sacrificed his body. And that inner death—in the eyes of Can o' Beans, at any rate—was more lamentable than the physical death that followed.

In the not too distant future, in some abrupt movement of the dance, the third veil, the veil that permitted political expediencies (usually transitory, often stupid, regularly corrupt) to masquerade as timeless universal expressions of freedom, virtue, and good sense, could conceivably fall away. Young persons, from then on, might be more particular about the "freedoms" they would be willing to defend, thus preserving their souls and—if quick enough of wit and foot—their bodies, as well.

Meanwhile, individuals had to yank at the disguise as best they could; to pull, poke, and peek, and finally, when they had sufficiently penetrated it, to take command of their lot. Assuming responsibility for one's lot was no nap on the beach. Ask Can o' Beans. Tantalized by the leaking sauce, by the sugar and corn syrup in that sauce (perhaps in the same way that industrial nations were tantalized by Middle Eastern oil) the ants were relentless in their pursuit. They were starting to wear the bean can down.

But just as the individual usually can outwit the herd, the bashed-in bean can, in a desperate ploy, suddenly gathered its remaining strength and leapt wildly, clumsily into the middle of a puddle that had formed when the cemetery caretaker, cleaning up after the service, had overwatered the graveside flowers. The lower half of its label was soaked and beginning to become unglued, but what the heck, there were compensations. Frustrated ants lined the shore, cursing the Creator who, in crafting them as the most efficient creatures on earth, had somehow neglected to teach them how to swim.

the fourth veil

This is the room of the wolfmother wallpaper, the room where the black virgin fell down the chimney and burned a hole in the linoleum. Countless are the antelope hooves that have pounded this floor. No wonder the linoleum is worn.

This is the room where the black virgin was kidnapped, later to be caged in the grand mosque at Mecca. After all these years, they are still interrogating her about the location of true north. "Why won't the polestar stand still?" is what they want to know. That and . . . One Other Thing.

In this room, the salamander was squashed between the pages of the rhyming dictionary, thereby changing poetry forever. Here, Salome walked around with a big red fish held high up over her head. Old Father spanked her with a ballet slipper, sending her to bed without milk or honey. Dance was changed in this room, too.

So this, then, is the chamber of the hootchy-kootch. Its bathtub full of orchids. Its closet full of smoke.

And on the wolfmother wallpaper, little beads of dew.

Maybe Ellen Cherry Charles didn't look like a million dollars, but nobody could deny that she looked like the *tax* on a million dollars. Raoul, the doorman, was impressed.

For months, Raoul had observed her moping about the Upper

West Side in sneakers, paint-spattered sweatshirts, and denim skirts, unrouged lips so pendulous in their pout she could have picked pennies off the street without bending over. Yet, here she was on a drizzly autumn afternoon pulling a new red vinyl slicker over a tight-fitting red wool dress, elevated by the sort of heels that Raoul called "follow-me-home-and-fuck-me shoes," her usual frown sweet-talked into an approximation of pleasantness by the hedonistic pigments in her lip gloss and eyeshadow. All that vivid makeup under all those unruly curls would have activated every Jezebel detector in Colonial Pines. Raoul didn't mind one bit, however, although something in his subconscious did provoke him to run a slow thumb over the crucifix he wore. Ellen Cherry, noticing the gesture, actually smiled, mainly because of the *salsa* buildup observable beneath the thumbnail.

"Mmmm, man, you looking so fine, man," said Raoul. "Get you a taxi?"

"No, thanks, Raoul. My boss is sending a car for me."

"Yeah? Didn't know you worked. Where you working, Miz Charl?"

When Raoul opened the door for her, the first thing she noticed was a teal Volvo station wagon hissing by in the wet. Instantly, she was reminded of a similarly colored Volvo, that one a sedan, that the roast turkey had passed eighteen months previously. The driver of that car had annoyed Boomer somehow, and in order to distract him, prevent him from launching into a tirade, she had said, "Volvos are supposed to be the safest cars on the road. Why is that, hon?"

"Damned if I know," Boomer had said, fuming. "There's probably something in the seat covers that draws the toxins outta your body."

Ellen Cherry became lost in memory, and to her face returned a sadness that no eyeshadow could console.

Raoul stood watching her. His baggy raincoat was so dirty a cash crop could have been grown in its folds, but atop his head sat a crisp, expensive, absolutely spotless porkpie hat. Raoul wore the hat every day. "I say, where you going to work, Miz Charl, looking so fine?"

"Huh?" Ellen Cherry snapped back into present time, the time of laying aside grief and art, the time of a new beginning, a fresh opportunity in the food service field. "Oh." She looked at Raoul brightly for a moment. "Jerusalem," she said.

*   *   *

A limousine as sleek and potent as a vitamin capsule stopped in front of the building. Raoul and the driver took turns helping Ellen Cherry into the backseat. A lot of help for a girl that small.

"Jerusalem, shit man, Jerusalem," muttered Raoul as the car pulled away. Raoul wondered if the *blanquita* Jezebel was not woofing him in some way. In Raoul's mind, the name Jerusalem evoked a place vague and sacrosanct, a city on this earth but not of this earth, a place watched over by angels, but where bad things happened, man. Even the Pope didn't go there. Jerusalem was the most holy and spooky place in the world, man. Raoul closed his big brown eyes to picture Jerusalem. He saw rocks and robes and gold domes and donkeys. He didn't see any angels, but he knew they were hanging around. Jerusalem was where it all went down, man. It was connected to heaven like Spanish Harlem was connected to Puerto Rico.

Returning to the lobby of the Ansonia, Raoul removed his porkpie hat and flicked raindrops off it, carefully, one by one. Flicking, he wondered if this "Jerusalem" where Mrs. Charles worked was a club. Maybe it was an art gallery. He remembered that she was an artist. Like her loco husband, before he split. Maybe she worked in a shop that sold religious art. In a dress like that? With an ass like that? No, man. Forget it, man. A P.R. girl would go to church, even, in shoes like hers, but not a *blanquita*. High heels, they put a woman that much closer to heaven, but gringos didn't see it that way. Riding to "Jerusalem" in a limo, man? Bu'shit.

Raoul took a pencil from his filthy raincoat and scribbled on a damp notepad:

> *The Virgin Mary ride on a donkey*
> *Her son Jesus he ride on a cross*
> *Mick Jagger ride on a Concorde jet*
> *And a rolling stone gather no moss*

Maybe he would record a song for Mrs. Charles. Mrs. Charles would hear it on the radio. Then she would fuck him, man.

In the drizzle, the limousine shot through Central Park like a blow dart shooting through Amazon foliage, whooshing toward the haunch of an unsuspecting sloth. It was the first time that Ellen Cherry had ridden in a rubber-tired vehicle since the turkey changed hands.

Tomorrow, she would be once again a subway passenger, but tonight was special, and she labored to feel special about it.

Tonight was the grand opening of Isaac & Ishmael's. Rather, it was the grand reopening. Isaac & Ishmael's originally opened back in June. Within a fortnight, it was firebombed. Now, damage repaired, security improved, it was ready to try again.

Personally, Ellen Cherry wasn't particularly worried about working at the I & I. She would, starting tomorrow, be working day shift. The time-honored safety of lunch. The dinner staff and the cocktail staff were said to be as nervous as a Q's tail in an alphabet stampede. They were reasonably positive that the restaurant would be targeted again.

No less than seven organizations, after all, had claimed responsibility for firebombing the I & I. They included three militant Zionist groups, three outlawed Islamic cults, and a fundamentalist Christian gang known as the Little Matches of Jesus. Taking as their credo these words that Luke (12:49) attributed to Our Savior—"I have come to set fire to the Earth"—the Matches had been sneaking about for a year or more, torching "ungodly" establishments, mainly in Brooklyn and Queens. They were sometimes referred to as the Holy Pyromaniacs or Firebugs for Christ.

In reality, police investigators suspected the I & I firebombing to have been instigated by an eighth organization, a coalition of ultraorthodox Zionists and evangelical Christians incorporated as the Third Temple Platoon, Inc. One of the group's principal spokesmen was the Reverend Buddy Winkler of Colonial Pines, Virginia.

Uncle Buddy had found his Jews.

An Arab and a Jew opened a restaurant together across the street from the United Nations . . .

It sounds like the beginning of an ethnic joke. But Isaac & Ishmael's was no funny story. Oh, it had its humorous aspects, as any worthwhile enterprise probably does, and neither the Arab nor the Jew was a stuffy old toad, yet the I & I was an earnest undertaking, an idealistic undertaking, perhaps a heroic undertaking.

An Arab and a Jew decided to open a restaurant together. It was to be a gesture of unusual cooperation, a symbolic reconciliation, an exemplary statement on behalf of peace—in the Middle East and beyond. If it could be demonstrated on a small scale that traditional, "natural" enemies could join together for a common purpose profitable to both, then might it not inspire adversaries on a global level to look into one another's eyes, to explore avenues of mutually beneficial friendship? That was the rhetoric, that was the hope.

"You're hearing of cosmic love?" asked Spike Cohen, the Jewish partner, the "Isaac" in Isaac & Ishmael's. "Well, between the Jews and the Arabs there's cosmic *hate,* already. So much to hate, the hate has permeated the dust, the hate has risen to the stars what are up above. It's no easy thing to reduce such a hate, but the easy things I have done already. For the sake of humanity, the sake of our grandchildren, my pal Abu and I confront together this most difficult."

"My father used to say," put in Roland Abu Hadee (the I & I's "Ishmael," obviously) "that 'In Allah's garden there grow all kinds of radishes.' Although I myself do not share in my father's concept of Allah, I have always been fond of the saying. In fact, I wanted to call our restaurant Two Radishes, but my friend, Spike, did not think so much of that name. Isaac and Ishmael's was our first compromise. It is a clever one, is it not? You see what can be done?"

Indeed. On the other hand, would eight separate organizations have been interested in firebombing a restaurant named Two Radishes?

Two varieties of radish opened a restaurant together across the street from the United Nations. It was destined to become, on two separate occasions and for two entirely different reasons (neither of them having anything to do with food), the most famous restaurant in New York City. It was called Isaac & Ishmael's.

Why Isaac & Ishmael's instead of Spike & Abu's or Cohen & Hadee's? Mythology. The purple exhaust of myth, through whose plumes events and forces too huge, too complex to easily explain, crystallize into human perspective.

As Brahma, the great father god of India, moved westward with the spice caravans, his name evolved into Abram. Over the generations, he was given skin and teeth and bushy eyebrows, and became known as Abraham. However more corporeal, the Semitic version of Brahma maintained his status as patriarch.

Before he wandered from Mesopotamia, birthplace of our species, into the land of Canaan, looking for the polestar (which had gradually moved out of its usual—many had thought invariable—place in the northern sky), Abraham married his half-sister, Sarai (Sarah). Until the cities of Sodom and Gomorrah carried it to such orgiastic extremes that they lost their federal funding, incest was an acceptable practice in Middle Eastern myth, if not in everyday reality. When a year or more passed and Sarai had not conceived, she presented her husband with a little bundle of a different sort of joy, i.e., her servant girl, Hagar. Abraham took Hagar into his tent, where he wasted no time impregnating her. The son she bore him was dubbed Ishmael.

Sometime later, while in southern Canaan digging wells, Abraham managed finally to knock up Sarai. "Well Diggers Do It Deeper," the bumper sticker read. Sarai's baby boy was Isaac.

Now that she and Abraham had a son of their own, Sarai gave reign to repressed jealousy and kicked Hagar and Ishmael out of camp. The concubine and her tot roved in the wilderness, eventually settling in the desert next to what is now Saudi Arabia. When he came of age, Ishmael was married off by Hagar to an Egyptian girl, and from that union, legend has it, all Arabs are descended.

Isaac, following a narrow brush with the sacrificial knife, went on to wed his cousin Rebekah, and their offspring became known as *Hebrews,* a Semitic word for "wanderers."

Thus were the lines drawn. Isaac and Ishmael, mythic half-brothers, fellow nomads, fathered by the mythic proto-patriarch to beget the Jews and the Arabs, respectively; forever joined with a blood rope of rivalry and loathing; slandering, slighting, and slaughtering one another, century after century, beneath the Middle Eastern sun.

And now, Isaac and Ishmael, pseudonyms for a couple of guys trying to demonstrate that two varieties of the radish family could flourish in a common patch, could even cross-pollinate—if only hot-headed horseradishes would leave them alone.

Regular customers—and during its second period of fame the restaurant did acquire customers—referred to Isaac & Ishmael's as "the I and I." Its staff called it that, as well, except for Ellen Cherry Charles, who usually spoke of her place of employ as "Jerusalem," due to the fact that its proprietors were so in love with that distant town that they were inclined to rhapsodize about it night and day.

In the paeans of Spike Cohen and Roland Abu Hadee, Jerusalem was as dreamlike and inaccessible as it was in the musings of Raoul the doorman, even though Raoul's notion of the Holy City stemmed from lurid and inaccurate illustrations in a Spanish-language edition of the King James Bible, whereas Spike and Abu had not only visited Jerusalem on several occasions, but also had the means to do so again. They might, in fact, have opened their restaurant in the city of their dreamy longing if only the Israeli government had granted permission.

In the end, the gentlemen were pleased with their location. While the site may have been their second choice, its proximity to United Nations Headquarters lent the I & I a semiofficial aura; tying it, symbolically at least, to the center of world aspirations to unity and peace. In addition, their situation in the New York market afforded them far, far more media exposure than they would have received in Jerusalem. They behaved as though the UN neighborhood had been their preference all along.

In no way, however, did that prevent them from mooning about Jerusalem as if Jerusalem were a rich and gorgeous woman who would take them as lovers the minute she recovered from her disease.

Joshua Cohen, who became Spike, was born into a poor, Yiddish-speaking family on Manhattan's Lower East Side. He was twelve years old before he ever saw a human toe other than his mama's or his own. We must now learn why.

In the snowy winter of 1923, his paternal grandparents and their three children had fled Russia on foot, escaping a brief but cruel pogrom organized by Chekists in Kiev. They continued across Poland into Germany, where they had relatives. Grandfather Cohen was a tailor, and his wife had gathered up every scrap of cloth in his shop to sew warm, many-layered coats and caps for the flight. Their shoes, however, were street shoes of the thinnest leather. When the family arrived at last in Germany, their feet were so frostbitten that their toes had to be amputated. Each toe on every Cohen foot. Fifty toes in all, fifty green-sheened ice worms, tossed like fish bait into the garbage pails of a hospital in Berlin.

Berliners called them *Die Krebs Familie,* "the Crab Family," because of the manner in which they walked, scurrying about sideways on the tips of their stubs, sometimes pitching forward onto their faces. Embarrassed by those giant land crabs in their midst, the Cohens' German relatives took up a collection and bought the toeless tribe passage to America.

When the middle child married, and he was the only one of the three to do so, he brought his bride to reside in the tenement above the Orchard Street tailor shop, where, tilting first to one side and then the other (they ambulated more erratically than Can o' Beans), the Cohens daily performed their crab dance of life. As a young boy, Joshua thought his mother's toes, long, rosy, and complete, were the most beautiful things on earth.

Recoiling from the clumsy clubs upon which the rest of the family staggered about, little Joshua gazed at his mother's feet, caressed his mother's feet, as if her feet had been carved from alabaster by a Renaissance genius, whereas in actual fact, they were rather ordinary specimens. As he grew older, his love for his mother's lower appendages expanded to include the feet, the whole, healthy feet, of women in general. Because bare feminine feet were not commonly on display in the Orchard Street ghetto and because outings to Coney Island were few and far between, Joshua's podalic passions gradually were transferred to shoes. Women's shoes.

Showing his heels to the tailor's trade, an adolescent Joshua apprenticed himself to a cobbler. By the time he was twenty-one, he had opened a small shoe store on Delancey. By the time he was thirty-five, he was known as the Shoe King of Long Island, where, distancing himself from the crustaceous scootings on Orchard Street, he owned and operated dozens of footwear boutiques. By the time he was fifty, his chain—Golda Shoes (after his mama)—had spread upstate and into New Jersey and Connecticut.

Joshua Cohen was self-educated. In the area of history, he was quite well read. About midway through his career as a shoe store tycoon, he chanced upon, in a book about modern Japan, a photograph of a mother and daughter whose feet were almost eaten away by radiation sores. They were survivors of the atomic attack on Hiroshima. Joshua stared at the picture in nauseated horror. The picture affected him in two significant ways. To begin with, it awakened in him a feeling of deep sympathy for his father's family. He recognized for the first time that the Cohen land crabs, like the Hiroshima women, were victims of man's inhumanity to man. That, in turn, aroused in him a powerful revulsion toward war, persecution, terrorism, any sort of violence that might maim human flesh and bone, especially the cute flesh, the darling bones of female tootsies.

Consequently, Joshua Cohen became a pacifist, growing increasingly active as the years passed. Having assumed personal responsibility for the world's mutilated and missing toes, he marched, picketed, pamphleteered, and petitioned, protesting military action in Vietnam, in Afghanistan, in Nicaragua, El Salvador, and South Africa. As a Jew, he began to focus more and more on the situation in the Middle East, especially after a particularly enamoring sojourn in Jerusalem.

By the time, at age sixty, that he met Roland Abu Hadee, he was ready to turn over his retail empire to his only son (his wife, uncomfortable with his adoration of her feet, had left him after but ten months of marriage: one month, he was to say, for each of her toes) and devote his life to the cause of Middle Eastern peace.

He gave up his shoe stores, but not his affection for their inventory. At the tennis club or in coffee shops, when he and Abu were dreaming their restaurant; at the reservation desk playing host once the I & I actually opened; on the sidewalk tearfully surveying the burned-out dining room after the bombing; at those moments, as well as at so many others in between, he would find his eyes straying from business at hand to fall upon the shod extremities of a nearby female (most often a stranger in the crowd), absentmindedly identifying designer and manufacturer; then, the mundane dispensed with, visually toying with a strap, say, or a bow, some laces, a tassel, a clasp, some studs; stroking from afar the various textures, slick or grainy, of calfskin, vinyl, or crocodile; finally, as if advancing from foreplay, tracing the lines of the yonic-lipped vessel: soft, fleshy swells, sleek animal musculature, insinuating curve of instep, giddy slope from heel to toe; the exact contours of the supple, rhythmic membrane that separates the exterior infinite from the interior particular, the infinity of movement, that is, from the relative quiescence of an object in space; that separates sweet and sweaty foot-meat from the broken glass and dog turds outside its protective shell.

Shoes, how did Cohen love thee? Let us count the ways.

Flats, heels, high heels, platforms, pumps, toe shoes, slippers, clogs, sling backs, loafers, moccasins, wedgies, oxfords, saddle oxfords, sneakers, sandals, go-go boots, Beatles boots, Birkenstocks, mules, Wallabees, granny boots, thongs, flip-flops, Timberlands, desert boots, Docksiders, cycling shoes, track shoes, huaraches, scuba flippers, wing tips, riding boots, Top-siders, espadrilles, high tops, golf shoes, stilettos, bowling shoes, snowshoes, clown shoes, Capezios, spikes, orthopedics, bucks, wading boots, ballet slippers, harem slippers, Japanese geta, Mary Janes, Hush Puppies, hiking boots, sabots, tap shoes, and galoshes. O shoe, leather ship that sails our cement rivers and woven seas, steering by the star of fashion, circumnavigating hostile reefs of tar and bubble gum; one hour, a tanker ferrying champagne to a playboy's sip; the next, a raft in the slime; bon voyage, bright barge! May you dock in calm closets, safe from the rape of shoe trees.

Caterpillars might sing of the terror of shoes, Spike Cohen sang of their delight. In his memory, his mother's plain black brogans were dessert dishes privileged to display the peach ice cream from which her surprising toes were molded. And, like Cinderella's prince, he instinctively knew the slipper to represent the cave by which the phallic hero enters the uterine underworld. To the boy on Orchard Street, Mercury's magic cobbler had had no monopoly on ankle wings.

If the I & I was dedicated to the preservation of humanity and its achievements, the loveliness of shoes must be counted among those achievements. Thus, Spike felt little or no guilt that his pacifist restaurateuring was subject to distraction by a passing pump. A true friend, Abu Hadee tolerated the distractions, although he couldn't understand them. "To me," Abu confessed, "shoes are no more than tin cans. Shoes are the cans that feet come in."

Spike laughed at that remark. (A certain container of pork and beans might have enjoyed it, as well.) Friends could sneer, wives could flee, the fact remained that shoes were the Poli-grip that anchored the false teeth of his desire.

"**A** shadow does not belong to the object that casts it." That was one of Roland Abu Hadee's favorite quotes. His understanding of it was incomplete. He knew that it had something to do with the fact that shadows were produced by light, not objects; that a shadow lengthened, shortened, or disappeared altogether, relative to availability and position of light, even though the object remained motionless and unchanged. He knew that much, and as far as he was concerned, it was more than enough. The scientific implications—for that matter, the philosophical implications—didn't interest him. What mattered to Abu was the *music* of the sentence. "A shadow does not belong to the object that casts it." To Abu, it was a little poem. And in general, it was the poetics, the music of things that tossed his confetti.

He had been born in a city whose name was a little poem: Dar es Salaam. He grew up in Alexandria, whose vowels rise like yeast on the tongue. The languages the boy Abu spoke were the rather prosaic English and Greek—his father, you see, was an international shipping magnate, and those were the languages of that business—but the script he saw written all about him, on the signposts and facades of Alexandria, was musical, all right. It ran complicated scales on the optic nerve. Everywhere, the Arabic alphabet wiggled and popped, enlivening crumbling architecture with outbursts of linguistic jazz, notations from the DNA songbook, energetic markings as primal as grunts and as modern as the abstract electricity of synthesizer feedback.

Fascinated though he was by the volume, voltage, and velocity of this vermiform verbiage, this symphony of snake eyes, it wasn't until many years later—in Madison, Wisconsin—that he learned to read it particularly well.

Although his father was Syrian, his mother, Egyptian, and both, Moslems; although little Abu was made daily to pray, and to study the Koran, emphasis in the Hadee household was upon success in commerce, and to that purpose was he educated by his father's example, as well as by tutors from Britain and Greece. His childhood circumstances were quite the opposite of Spike Cohen's. Abu, *Roland* Abu, was born with a silver spoon in his mouth (an expression that invariably caused our Miss Spoon to quiver with ill-concealed arousal). "In Alexandria," he liked to say, letting the vowels foam like fizz powder against his palate, "in Alexandria, we lived in the porcine penthouse." High on the hog. An acceptable arrangement, from the pig's point of view, since no Hadee ever sank fangs into ham. Oh, there was a period when a rebellious Abu entertained a diet of convenience-store weenies and Miller beer, but that was in Madison, Wisconsin, when his elevator was no longer stopping on the upper floors of the swine.

At age eighteen, Abu had been packed off to Harvard on an allowance that was probably triple what the college president earned. He fell in with some other well-heeled students, bought a fast car, and soon was spending more time in New York nightclubs than in the classroom. Raised on belly-dancing, it was but a short hop to the hootchy-kootch. He hickied the silhouette of crescent moons on the backsides of shimmy-shammy princesses all over Manhattan. When the dean called him in to inform him that he had flunked out, the tall young Arab was puffing a stogie that cost half as much as the office furniture and weighed more than the phone on the desk.

Duke University gave him a chance. Duke, after all, had gambled on Richard Nixon and Plucky Purcell. Dressing in zoot suits and sporting a mustache as thin as a crack in an espresso cup, Abu played the fool before bemused southerners, who allowed him to ogle their daughters in exchange for the drops of illegal absinthe he squirted into their juleps. Eventually, he squirted a fetus into a debutante, sealing his fate with the same liquid wax. The sheriff who escorted him to the city limits later referred to wild heathen gibberish and savage gnashing of teeth. Actually, it was merely a severely hung-over Abu trying to translate into Greek and faulty Arabic the musical line, the little poem, "Nigger, don't let the sun set on you in Durham County."

Next stop was UCLA, with its proximity to movie-star champagne and swimming pools large enough to drive stolen cattle trucks into, which he did so often he began to list it as a hobby on his resumé. He lasted one quarter at UCLA. Academic responsibilities behind him now, he was at liberty to pursue the course of full-time playboy. Abu and postwar Los Angeles seemed made for each other. One night, in an absinthe, champagne, and cocaine frenzy, he bit the right nipple off a Warner Brothers starlet and spit it into a bowl of blue-cheese chip dip. Even Hollywood was shocked.

The incident made page one of sleazy tabloids the world over. When the news reached Egypt, Hadee senior settled out of court for eighty thousand 1950 dollars, then cabled his errant son that he was disinherited and disowned. Abu scoffed. Convinced that his father would in time relent, he set about turning his bank account into one more phantom in a community of phantoms (phantom fortunes, phantom fame). As the cash ghosted out, his liver solidified. A dawn arrived when, after spraying a pink stucco duplex, six palm trees, and a passing poodle with a Cinerama of all-singing, all-dancing, Technicolor vomit, he hadn't enough money left for Pepto-Bismol.

"Help me," he cried. It was not a musical line, it was no little poem. And nobody paid attention. Not an Arab in Los Angeles would heed his pleas for aid. He had disgraced the race. His collect calls to Arab contacts around America were declined. "Infidel!" they would shout in the poor ears of the operator. Finally, a distant cousin in an outpost known as Madison, Wisconsin, offered him a job in his French restaurant—on condition that he work three years at minimum wage, during which time he must read the Koran for an hour each day and refrain from alcohol, pork, and the company of women. It was an offer he couldn't refuse.

Because he was tall, polished, cosmopolitan, and had studied at Harvard, Abu presumed that he would be made headwaiter or maître d'. He presumed erroneously. Upon arrival (via polished, cosmopolitan thumb) in Madison, he was led through the back door of the restaurant and straight to a mammoth sink full of dirty dishes. "There is a cot in the storeroom," his cousin said. "You can sleep there. Once the kitchen is spotless. And tomorrow, you shave off that stupid mustache."

Water simmered. Drains gurgled. Pipes knocked. Steam rose. Suds bubbled (no elegant Alexandrian vowels these harsh industrial bubbles!). Grease congealed. Scum collected. Islands of lettuce scraps and buoys of duck fat bobbed in the boil. Spatulas were caked with *mousseline de volaille,* whisks were encrusted with *oeufs à la Bourguignonne,* bulb basters were plugged with *beurre d'anchois,* and the dried batters that coated some baking dishes were like hardened deposits of lunar cement. The baking dishes blistered him, skillets blistered the blisters. Poultry shears, cheese graters, broken wine goblets, and metal disks from food mills joined forces with knives of all sizes to hunt down his hands in the murky waters and nick, puncture, scrape, and slice. Should the wounds commence to heal, steel wool and scouring powder ground the lids off of the scabs, exposing pink sores to heat and abrasion. As far up as his biceps, his arms were shiny with grease; his face was steamed as red as a prawn, and his wrinkled fingers that so resembled the foreskins of aged hermits stunk perpetually of residual garlic, rancid oils, and garbage soup. His clothes were soaked with the same smelly brine, and upon any part of his anatomy at any time one was likely to discover soggy warts of cooked stuff, flecks of flora and fauna that no nature goddess would ever bless again.

For many, just to contemplate those torrid waters with their roiling foams, gobs of goop, organic effluvia, and hazardous mines of metal and glass would be the beginning of a descent into hell (a hell devised by Julia Child to punish Colonel Sanders). Indeed, the first few times that Roland Abu Hadee stared into that blowhole of a sink, he saw the pitiless orbs of Satan staring back, and as a sinister shock shook his stomach, he heard asbestos ghouls chuckle and piss. Holding his breath, closing his eyes, he plunged his hands into the mephistophilian broth—and instantly passed out.

It was the most wonderful thing that ever happened to him.

After about a week, when the biliousness and swooning spells subsided, dishwashing began to have a calming effect on him; more than that, a purifying effect; more, even, than that, a transformative effect. It was as if the dishwater, as gray and oily as a mobster's haircut, washed away his arrogant confusion. As he scoured pots, he likewise and unintentionally scoured his conscience, scoured the calluses from it so that he was resensitized to humanity. An alcoholic film dissolved, exposing, first, a layer of guilt, then a layer of dread. The guilt was understandable: nipple-snapping and all that. The dread was a surprise. Until his baptism in the frothy napalm of the sinks, he hadn't realized how terrible had been his dread of walking in his father's footsteps, of wearing the starched smile and octopus arms of an international businessman, of going about with a headful of numbers that neither sang nor scanned.

Slowly, a gentleness, a piety enveloped him. His Madison relatives attributed the change to the Koran, but it was the scalding vats that purged Abu, the sinks seething with submerged cutlery, drowned

cockroaches, and floating boogers of *sauce béarnaise*. Wire brush ritualistically in hand, he would part the soapy veil and enter his
underwater grotto in the manner of a pilgrim entering a sacred river
to bathe. Beside a greasy Ganges of goose gunk, he laid his burdens
down.

Three years passed. His bargain fulfilled, Abu took his leave of the
pots and pans. A monk without a monastery, he wandered Madison,
more than a little lost. In a kind of conditioned reflex of rebellion, he
embarked on a binge of hot dogs and beer, devoting his evenings to
largely unsuccessful pursuit of University of Wisconsin coeds. Six
months of this failed to provide a single hour of satisfaction. His
savings spent, he returned to the restaurant and begged for his job
back. "Fine," his cousin said. "But there are conditions. You must
train in my kitchen as a chef. And you must marry my daughter."

Nabila was no beauty, true, but take a gander at Roland Abu
Hadee. Tall and dark he might be, and he bore himself with quiet
dignity, but his nose. . . ! Steam had permanently reddened his big
Semitic beak until it looked like the prow of the S.S. *Tomato,* like a
stop signal designed in a wind tunnel. How grand a catch was a
bachelor whom the children of Madison had nicknamed "Rudolph!
Rudolph! Rudolph!"? Moreover, what bride longed to be fondled by
fingers so waterlogged they threatened to ooze cold fishy fluids from
a hundred separate crinkles?

Pushed into wedlock, nevertheless, Nabila and Abu grew to like,
and, eventually, to love each other. To become independent of her
father, they saved their dimes and opened a *falafel* stand near the
university campus. Profits were small but steady, the couple lived
simply but happily. The *falafel* stand was a window onto the academic world that Abu had previously scorned. From the undergrad-
uates, graduate students, and young instructors who were his primary
customers, he picked up little poems of science, musical lines of law
and art. In return, he treated them to descriptions, in his own
fashion, of the Middle East, a geographical snapping turtle that even
then had the American brain stem in its bite and would not let go.

"Egypt?" he would say, feeding chick-peas to the grinder. "Egypt is
as hot as a gypsy honeymoon and as dry as scarab breath. Egypt
looks at the world through cat's eyes. Egypt has a heart of green
paste. With crocodile claws and mummy jewelry, Egypt scratched its
name into the foundation stone of history. Before Islam, Egyptians
thought only of immortality. Since Islam, they think only of life after

death. What is the difference? To understand the difference, you must live for many months without moisture. Is the Middle East a matter of climate, then? Perhaps. The moon . . ." With a cucumber the same size but opposite color of his nose, he pointed at the ethnic crescents that decorated his stand. "The moon is no more Islamic than it is Hindu or Eskimo. The lunar mirror simply reflects the hidden poetry in us all. The sun, however, is a Semite."

And so forth and so on.

The *falafel* stand window also provided a close-up view of the antiwar demonstrations that rocked Madison during the 1960s. Watching his student friends brutalized by police and defamed by politicians in the pay of the military-industrial complex, he soon lost his detachment and sided with the forces of brotherly love. He took to closing his stand during demonstrations and joining the pacifists in the streets, a practice that disturbed Nabila because by then they had two babes to feed. As it turned out, he was frequently gassed (the tear gas usually drifted into the stand, anyhow) but seldom clubbed.

The Vietnam War ended. The years falafeled by. The children grew up. Abu kept an ear tuned to the music of things, kept an eye on the scoundrels in high places. He had been demonstrating in favor of a disarmament treaty on the day that an official letter arrived from Alexandria. Unbeknownst to him, his late father's will had set aside six million dollars for Abu, provided that, by age fifty-five, he had settled down and succeeded in business. Relatives contested Abu's right to the bequest. A *falafel* stand! After all! His attorney proved that Abu's stand had made a tiny profit every year since it opened. "Red nose, black ink," said Abu. He got the inheritance.

He took his wife to Jerusalem, the favorite city of his youth. They remained there a month and saw many poetic sights and some acts of violence.

"I will now read books and listen to music," he announced upon their return. "I will learn to play tennis, and I will work for world peace. For my Nabila, I will hire a maid. Two maids. They will vacuum her carpets and make her beds. I, however, I, Roland Abu Hadee, as usual, will wash the dishes."

When the limo deposited Ellen Cherry at Isaac & Ishmael's, Abu was in the kitchen inspecting, for the tenth time that day, the dishwashing equipment. It was Spike who answered her rap at the door. "How's it going, Mr. Cohen?" she asked. "Everything set?" Spike could say nothing. He was too overwhelmed by her shoes.

It was Spike who had hired her. She had arrived for that interview in penny loafers—sensible waitress shoes—and it's difficult to say whether or not footwear influenced his decision. More than likely, it was her politics. Or, rather, her lack of them. After interviewing scores of do-gooders—well-meaning but incompetent liberals who wished to be personally identified with his experiment—Spike was refreshed to speak with an experienced waitress who professed to know next to nothing about the situation in the Middle East.

"I'm an artist," she explained.

"And it's not political, this art you make?"

"A lot of artists don't get it yet, Mr. Cohen, but 'political art' is a contradiction in terms."

"What about this guy, Goya? His famous pictures against war?"

"Goya's work is powerful because his technique was powerful. It was fortuitous. A bad painter painting atrocities is committing atrocities himself, in my opinion. Besides, what about Rubens? His big, rosy, joyful nudes are just as much a statement against war as Goya's mutilated victims. Rubens is saying Yes to life. Way I see it, anything that says Yes to life is automatically saying No to war."

Spike hired her to wait tables. When he told Abu about her, Abu suggested that they promote her to lunch shift maître d'. And they did.

*　　*　　*

Two weeks later, Ellen Cherry was unemployed. On the phone to Colonial Pines, she had said, "If Uncle Buddy's behind this, he owes me bucks."

"Your daddy says no blessed way would Bud go that far," Patsy replied. "Your daddy says terrorists did it."

"What does my mama say?"

"Ha! Don't nobody listen to your mama. 'Less she's offering 'em fried chicken or a piece of you know what."

"Piece of what, mama?"

"Never you mind."

"Piece of what?"

"Hush. I'm not gonna say it."

Ellen Cherry hadn't been overly concerned about being blasted out of a job. That was back in June, when she still believed things would work out with Boomer. Now, with the weasel fart of impending divorce hanging in the air, she needed the income. Boomer promised a generous settlement if his show went well, but she would sell her hair to a museum of natural history before she'd accept a crumb from *that* foul loaf. In her darker moments, she imagined her hair in a display case alongside a woolly mammoth. Schoolchildren on field trips would compare them in essays and scare their little brothers and sisters with slightly exaggerated descriptions. "In the Ice Age, things had to be real hairy," they'd explain, brandishing garish postcards.

She was one of the few employees to return to the I & I for its second incarnation. Most of the others had found work elsewhere or built personal bomb shelters. As the new staff arrived for the grand reopening, Ellen Cherry could tell there wasn't a food-service professional in the lot. Mainly, they were youthful idealists. Some signed on at the I & I because it made them feel important. Others, she suspected, had suicidal tendencies.

"Should I check the setups, Mr. Cohen?"

"No, no, no. Teddy'll take care of that." Teddy was the dinner maître d'. "Relax already. Have a little drink, enjoy."

"I've noticed you looking at my feet, sir. Are these shoes too . . . too loud for here?"

"No, no, no. Very attractive, very nice. Cassini. I hope you got a bargain. You need more Cassini. I get them for you wholesale." Spike handed Ellen Cherry an empty glass and nodded at an ice bucket. "You got to admit, though, those shoes of yours are as bright as Hadee's schnozz."

Ellen Cherry laughed politely. She filled her glass. It was the same brand of champagne with which Boomer had surprised her at the Montana drive-in movie. She winced. Sentimental memories were like sugar-water icicles. Was she to be poked in the heart the rest of her life?

Outside on United Nations Plaza, the water was softer, if more sour. The rain was the color and flavor of toad sweat and had been all day. It vinegared the mobile TV units that were beginning to vie for parking spaces near the corner of Forty-ninth Street.

Media coverage of Isaac & Ishmael's reopening was even more extensive than it had been at the initial debut. A restaurant dedicated to Jewish-Arabic brotherhood might be good feature material, but a restaurant that could be blown to sesame seeds on camera was potentially hard news.

Simultaneously with the newsmen, as if choreographed, protesters arrived: small ragtag groups of extreme Zionists and Palestinians. Police officers made sure they kept well apart, although when the colors began to run on their rain-dampened placards, only by their headgear could you tell which was which. "Notice how similar their shoes," said Spike. "Yes," agreed Abu, who had been drawn out of the kitchen. "To a bird in the air, it's beanies versus dishcloths. To a bug on the street, both groups are the same."

Then, moments before the doors opened at seven o'clock, a chartered bus pulled up and disgorged a well-groomed mixture of Jews and Aryans, mostly in Burberry raincoats. They were equipped with amplified bullhorns, and the "Redemption Now!" banners their members bore were executed in waterproof paints.

Through the fogged windows of the I & I, Ellen Cherry thought she recognized her "uncle" Buddy. The man was ordering people about and chatting it up with the cops. As haggard as a prisoner of war, he was a scarecrow whom no amount of Burberry tailoring could make distinguished. It had to be the Reverend Buddy Winkler. When at last he spoke into his bullhorn, broadcasting his vocal saxophone to the neighborhood and, through network mikes, to the nation, identification was positive. At once brutish and soothing, the heavy-toned chords vibrated slowly, turning over in the rain like an Italian stallion turning over in bed.

Keeping her distance from the doorway, lest Buddy glimpse her, Ellen Cherry, nevertheless, could hear his words. He kept advocating ejection, by force, of Moslems from Jerusalem's Temple Mount so that the Messiah could come. She had only the slimmest notion of what he meant, but his voice made her so horny she could barely keep from squirming, crossing her legs, or hopping about, like a little girl who had to go to the bathroom.

On the subject of Egypt, Ellen Cherry was so vague she thought Ramses II was a jazz piano player. From that, we might conclude that she was equally dumb about jazz. As a matter of fact, she did believe "Birdman of Alcatraz" to be Charlie Parker's nickname in prison. In her favor, it might be reported that, despite similarities in the crowds they flocked with, she did not confuse the Alcatraz Birdman with St. Francis of Assisi.

One of the Egyptian gods had had the head of a bird. With his great scarlet beak, Roland Abu Hadee somewhat resembled him. When Abu came out of the kitchen (the dishwasher had threatened to quit if Abu didn't stop looking over his shoulder) to join Ellen Cherry at a corner table, she was as pleased as a priestess of the Nile might have been had she been visited by the hawk-headed deity. Abu could distract her both from the buzz of her clitoris (an organ unattended for the past six months) and the chaos out on the sidewalk, where the milling mobs of Moslems, Jews, and Christians, shouting slogans and shaking fists, now had been joined by a gentle delegation of New Age doom-sayers who had seized this opportunity to quietly advertise the latest in a chronic if not insipid series of cataclysms (earthquakes, comets, planetary alignments, etc.), which either failed to materialize or to produce the hoped-for alterations in social consciousness.

It was much noisier outside the restaurant than within, for the protesters, prophets, cops, cameramen, reporters, and curiosity-seekers outnumbered diners at least twenty to one. A number of celebrities had been invited to eat free at the grand reopening, but among the notables who had appeared at the original opening, only Norman Mailer had had the guts to return. Mailer and the couple dozen other guests seemed to be shunning their dinners in favor of the Egyptian and Israeli wines, which meant that the food was pretty bad or else they were worried about having to run for cover on a full stomach.

At any rate, Ellen Cherry and Abu had little trouble conversing in a normal tone.

"This dining room strikes me as rather drab," Abu confessed. He gestured at the gold-flecked bamboo matting that covered the walls. "We paid a decorator good money for *this*? There is not a stalk of bamboo in the entire Middle East."

"Maybe he thinks Jerusalem's in Polynesia," she said.

"Jerusalem is everywhere," said Abu, a bit too solemnly. "The aura of it extends around the globe. Jerusalem is everywhere. There is just not enough of it in this room." He thought for a moment. "My dear, you are an artist. Why do we not hang some of your pictures in here?"

When she didn't respond right away, he added, "Naturally, we would have them insured."

Ellen Cherry had to smile. Were her paintings blown up with the I & I, she might realize some financial gain from them. "Well, I showed you slides back in June," she said.

Abu concealed a shudder. He remembered trees that resembled old gay actors trying on kimonos, hills that bounced like red rubber hemorrhoids. Who could eat in such company? Who could meditate on brotherhood or fair Jerusalem? "Yes, dear, but those were done awhile ago, as I recall. When you lived in that place, Seattle. How about something more . . . recent."

"Don't have anything recent. I've not exactly been painting since I've been in New York."

Ellen Cherry was lying. True, after the Airstream turkey had been sold to the Museum of Modern Art (which had outbid a large corporation that wanted to sponsor it in the Macy's Thanksgiving Day parade), she had thrown her brushes and colors into an incinerator. In late summer, however, she started painting again. Almost feverishly. She had enough new canvases to cover every wall in the I & I, including the pantry and the men's room. But she wasn't showing them to anyone, not even her alleged dealer, Ultima Sommervell, who, like Abu, had asked to see new work. It was not Ellen Cherry's intention to ever, ever show them.

Suppose, though, that one moonless night you were to dress in black pajamas (the ninja kind, the cat burglar kind), and, employing spider lines and tree frog cups, you scaled the wedding-cake facade of the Ansonia Hotel at Seventy-third and Broadway, climbing (pity your poor butt if you're afraid of heights) to floor eleven, where you use a short lightweight wrecking bar to pry loose a window frame. Suppose, then, you were to pull yourself in, your ebony Taiwanese sneakers last to slide over the sooty ledge. Discreetly flashing a powerful penlight, suppose you locate the paintings in question, stacked against the apartment wall, their faces resolutely to the plaster. Silently, one by one, you pull them back and inspect them. To your surprise, there's not a landscape in the lot! In many of the pictures, nothing is depicted but a small silver spoon. Others feature a single bedraggled purple sock. And just when you thought pop art had been buried with Andy Warhol, you discover realistic renderings of a can of Van Camp's pork and beans. One after another, spoons, socks, and bean cans, spoons, socks, and bean cans, the sequence broken only occasionally by full-length nude portraits of a man you, as an art lover, recognize as Randolph "Boomer" Petway III. From the single bedroom, you hear the feathery moans of a woman sleeping alone, and as you tiptoe out of this Gallery of the Missing, you recall that someone once said, "The purpose of art is to provide what life does not."

Abu was called up front to pose with Spike again, to grant yet another joint interview. He preferred to chat with Ellen Cherry or to supervise the dishwashing and *falafel*-frying, but when one made a grand public gesture such as Isaac & Ishmael's, one was obliged to meet the press.

While he was away, Ellen Cherry tuned in the demonstrations. She could hear her uncle Buddy's sax crooning to the faithful, crooning them up the slopes of the Temple Mount, crooning the Messiah down from heaven to say hi to them there. Screened by a starched white veil of tablecloth, she touched herself between her legs. It was like stroking a live bee. A bee trapped, tiny wings awhirr, in a puddle of molasses.

When Abu rejoined her, he announced, "I am afraid Spike is permitting the demonstrators to get him upset."

"They don't upset you, Mr. Hadee?" Lifting her errant left hand into the light, she surreptitiously examined it for traces of moisture.

"Of course they do. I am appalled by the fear and ignorance that motivates such behavior. I am concerned about violence. The difference, dear one, is that I am Arab and Spike is a Jew. Oh, yes! To say that Arab and Jew are brothers and sisters is not to say that we are the same. There are racial differences among people, yes? There are cultural differences, sexual differences." (At the mention of the word "sexual," Ellen Cherry involuntarily squirmed.) "In my opinion, those differences can be good. What a dull world this would be were we all alike. What an evolutionary dead end! To be brothers, to live in peace, we do not have to be overly similar. We do not have to admire or even like one another's peculiarities. We need only *respect* those peculiarities—and to be grateful for them. Our similarities provide us with a common ground, but our differences allow us to be fascinated by one another. Differences give human encounters their snap and their fizz and their brew."

Trite or not, Ellen Cherry liked what Abu had to say. If he could say those things in Uncle Buddy's voice, she thought she might follow him anywhere. To her mind, could a man combine Mr. Hadee's content with the Reverend Buddy Winkler's style, he might constitute a reasonable facsimile of that Messiah that the excitables on the street were so ga-ga about. Of course, Ellen Cherry was near to drunk.

"What's your take, then, on the demonstrations?"

"My *take*?"

"Yeah, you know, your . . ." Her train of thought switched to a siding, perhaps to try to balance its effervescent load. Abu's flowery freight, however, stayed right on track.

"There are differences among Jews," he said. "Jews are not cut from whole cloth, do not imagine they are. Their so-called clannishness, their solidarity, has many exceptions. Yet, a candle burns in their blood, and as different as their lives outwardly may be, each from the other, every Jew reads his or her life story by the light of that same candle. It hurts Spike Cohen when he is attacked so bitterly by other Jews. He may deny it, our Spike the Shoe Wolf, but you can tell the attacks wound him. The Arab, he is used to that. We have been fighting among ourselves as long as grains of sand can remember. Vendettas, raids, bloody feuds, they are more common among Arabs than oil wells or dromedaries. Arabs have injured one another more than they have injured Jews. I am not surprised that there are Arabs out there on UN Plaza who would make me into a lollipop. You understand? My head on a stick."

Abu paused. He and Ellen Cherry exchanged furtive glances, both of them laboring in vain to keep from picturing his dark head impaled like a toasted marshmallow.

Eventually, he continued. "You are an artist . . ."

He's changing the subject now, she thought. *He's back to decorating. Well, I can't help him there. He wouldn't understand what I'm painting these days. I barely understand it myself.*

"*You* are an artist. You know that big picture at the museum midtown, that picture by that fellow Rousseau, it is called *The Sleeping Gypsy?*"

"Yeah. Sure. That's a very famous painting."

"It ought to be called *The Sleeping Arab,* that picture. An Arab lies in the desert, sleeping under the crazy-faced moon. A lion sniffs at the Arab, the Arab is unafraid. The Arab dreams·on. The river in the background, I think the river is the Arab's dream. Perhaps the lion is also dreamed: you notice it has left no paw prints in the sand. In any case, that picture, my dear, is the definitive portrait of the Arab character. Fierce and free, sleeping fearlessly beneath the wild night stars. But dreaming. Dreaming always of water. Dreaming of danger when real danger is absent, in order to demonstrate bravado. Arabs live in their fantasies. We are not a practical people like the Jews are. The Jew gets things accomplished. The Arab dreams—and converses with the moon.

"But, dear Ellen Cherry, what else is in that beautiful picture by Rousseau? Tell me?"

"What else? What else is in the painting? Let me see. Uh, well, I think there's a jug of some sort. . . ."

"Yes. Yes. A water jar. What else?"

"Uh . . ."

"A musical instrument. Correct? Kind of a mandolin or what in Greece they call a bouzouki. And that tells you something further about the Arab. Another side of him. We love music. Arabs love the music of the stars. But also the arithmetic of the stars. Both are Arabic inventions. Did you know that? Oh, yes, in the arts and sciences, the Arabs were once masters. Our architecture was original and powerful. We invented astronomy, modern mathematics, map-making, shipbuilding, perfumery. I could go on. We have an ancient literary heritage. In the eighth, ninth, and tenth centuries, while Europe wallowed in its Dark Ages, while Europe was ignorant and impoverished and altogether barbarous, there was enlightenment in the Arab lands. The Arab world was cultured then, rich, educated, and, in its fierce, dreamy way, refined. Mathematicians strolled in rose gardens. Poets rode stallions.

"So what happened? Why, my dear, the Crusaders paid us a little visit. The Crusaders came. Christian knights from Europe. And they massacred men, women, and children—Jew as well as Arab, it should be told: all who were non-Christian. The Crusaders destroyed the intellectual and scientific life of western Asia and northern Africa. They burned the largest, most complete library in the world, the great library of Tripoli, and they reduced to rubble *scores* of scientific and artistic centers. Such a tragedy. Such a waste."

Abu leaned across the table, leaned across the bamboo place mats, bamboo napkin rings, and lotus-patterned linen napkins that had prompted Spike to wonder why the decorator hadn't supplied the I & I with chopsticks, already; leaned toward Ellen Cherry until his rosy proboscis, the flesh incarnate of Painted Stick, was only millimeters from rubbing against her own dwarfed nose, and as the metronome inside her panties suddenly amplified its tick, marking time, marking estrogen time, marking an insect rhythm of feminine heat, he parted his lips. Ellen Cherry fully expected him to bark or growl or hiss. Instead, he spoke in his customary mild tone.

"Noble Crusaders. *Holy* Crusaders. They pulled the Arab lands down into the muck pit with Europe. And the Arab lands have never recovered. No amount of oil profit can buy back their enlightenment. How different conditions would be today in the Middle East, how much saner and safer the entire earth might be, had those Christians not defiled a civilization too advanced for their arrogant little minds to understand. Did they teach you these things in your Jesus school, pretty Cherry?"

Before Ellen Cherry could respond, one of the protest groups, it was difficult to identify which one, attempted to invade the restaurant, creating a huge commotion as police beat them back at the door. Clubs swung, blood drops flew, cameras flashed, and diners, spilling wine and sputtering lentils, stampeded in the direction of the kitchen. Both her clitoral hum and her champagne static drowned out now by spurting adrenaline, Ellen Cherry made as if to rise, but Abu just sat there. "The Crusaders wanted Jerusalem," he said placidly. "Jerusalem was their prize. I suppose we cannot fault them for that."

It was a long, troubled evening, but the I & I survived. The only damage it sustained was wine stains on its ubiquitous bamboo. Moreover, the media exposure had been terrific.

On the way home, alone, in the limo, its backseat so spacious, the city it purred through so threatening and unknowable, Ellen Cherry felt like a small child. She pulled her feet, red spikes and all, up onto the seat and hugged her knees. But that made her feel even smaller. In order to grow big again, she began to think about whom she was going to sleep with.

Obviously, she was going to sleep with somebody soon. It didn't take Nostradamus to forecast that. But who?

Boomer would have been first on her list. Fat chance. It almost made her laugh. Eighteen months earlier, when they were crossing the country in the honeymoon turkey, she entertained a scenario: in New York, sooner or later, she was bound to fall in love with a fellow artist, a successful painter, probably; a man who really understood her, her work, her creative needs; and she would have to leave Boomer for him, she would have to break ol' Boomer's heart. It seemed so inevitable that she went so far as to rehearse her speech, the sincerely weepy one in which she would tell Boomer she wanted a divorce. (They were in Minnesota then, mind you, Minnesota and Wisconsin, stray grains of wedding rice still sparkling here and there on the Airstream carpet.) What a presumption that turned out to be. What a joke.

Boomer had left *her*. And she had yet to meet a New York painter she would allow in her mind *or* her pants. Granted, she hadn't met very many.

As for other men, the bachelors she had encountered at clubs and bars and parties, well, most appeared to have one thing in common: having been hurt at Point A, they insured themselves against being hurt again at Point C by becoming assholes at Point B. In all fairness, that was true of the single women over thirty, as well.

One-night stands were out, anyway. Fear of AIDS.

Could she sleep with Mr. Hadee or Mr. Cohen? Yes, indeed, she could. Mr. Hadee was so gracious and sweet, Mr. Cohen so dynamic and handsome. It might be nice to take an older lover. Sleeping with one's boss had obvious advantages, although it always seemed to backfire on the waitresses she had known who'd done it. Alas, Mr. Hadee was happily married. And Mr. Cohen, well, it made her somehow uneasy the way he stared at her feet. What had Mr. Hadee called him? Shoe Wolf.

One older man who definitely was *not* a candidate for her favors was Buddy Winkler, no matter if his voice did carbonate her fluids.

Thus far, her daddy had concealed from Buddy that she had gone back to work for the Arab and the Jew. Bud had learned, however, that she and Boomer were estranged, and since he assumed automatically that it was her fault, he'd expressed interest in counseling her. God, she hoped he didn't drop in on her in her weakened condition! Of course, Buddy would have been happy to call her "Jezebel" as often as she wished. What exactly did go on in bed with a preacher? she wondered. Patsy would know.

At the Ansonia, Raoul met the car. The rain had stopped, and he wore a tight tan uniform with plastic "brass" buttons. Were it not for his porkpie hat, he might have been an officer in a banana republic air force. As he helped her from the limo, he squeezed her wrist. "Didn't stay long over dare in Jerusalem, Miz Charl." The thing about Raoul was his availability. She could have him *now*! That was a solid inducement. Her knees turned into chewing gum imagining it. But she resisted. No more Latin lovers: a pledge she would stick to like Scotch tape to a Chihuahua.

Raoul seemed to sense that he had been considered and rejected. However, instead of pouting when Mrs. Charles entered the elevator without glancing back, he scribbled in his notebook:

> *Muddy Waters he play in the river*
> *Joan Rivers she play in the mud*
> *Swami guru play in a big salad bowl*
> *Counting lettuce and chewing his cud*

The day would come, man, when every *blanquita* in New York would want Raoul Ritz, man. Raoul was born to star.

At the bathroom mirror, removing her makeup and wondering in amazement—as she had virtually every day for twenty years—at the epic scope of her hair, Ellen Cherry inquired of her reflection, "You know who I'd like to sleep with? Who I'd really like to sleep with?" She giggled. "I'd like to sleep with the only real artist in New York City. I'm talking 'bout Turn Around Norman."

She wasn't referring to Norman Mailer, the novelist who had looked her over—approvingly or disapprovingly, she could not determine—at the I & I party. No, she referred to a certain street performer, who . . . well, never mind. Turn Around Norman's turn will come. Let's allow Ellen Cherry to sleep this off.

*　　*　　*

Knock knock knock! Something was knocking like the pistons on Satan's Nash Rambler. Ellen Cherry actually couldn't tell whether the sound was external or internal, whether it was a visitor rapping at her door or her hangover trying to hang a picture on the wall of her skull. A picture of *The Massacre of the Innocents* painted on black velvet by a hydrocephalic baboon.

She sat up in bed and opened her eyes. She opened her eyes carefully so that they wouldn't break. Her eyes seemed to be playing the eye game without her. The room was so out of focus she was afraid to breathe until she made absolutely certain she wasn't underwater. She could hear better with her eyes open, however. Most people could. *Knock knock!* It was the door.

"Who is it?" she called—and instantly winced.

"Me!"

"Who?"

"Me! Open up! I used to live here! Wahoo!"

Why now, dear God? Why now? She hadn't seen the fool in more than a month, and he shows up when she was undressed, hung over, and doubtlessly looking like *The Massacre of the Innocents* painted on black velvet by a hydrocephalic baboon. The fact that he'd seen her a hundred times first thing in the morning after a hard night didn't mean a thing. That was then and this was now. She sprang from bed. "Give me five minutes," she called, knowing full well that it would take longer than that just to peel the wallpaper off her tongue.

The fact that she didn't have to brush her hair—what difference would it have made?—cut down on her repair time. In eight minutes, exactly, the mirror showed her only marginally below the summit of her potential. Of course, she hadn't bathed, but a splash or two of Jungle Desire cologne would take care of that. She splashed, then went to the door.

"Sugar britches."

"Yeah, Boomer?"

He was wearing one of his old faded Hawaiian shirts and, were she not mistaken, the same steel-toed work shoes he'd been married in, but his leather pants were new and expensive. A beret as red as a mosquito's belch reduced the amount of scalp revealed by his receding hairline to an area just slightly too small to invite spray-can graffiti. The beret was nothing new, however. He had taken to wearing it the day that he discovered that he was an artist.

She found him a beer in the fridge, a Pabst Blue Ribbon that he'd left behind. There wasn't a slice of cold pizza on the premises, but he didn't suffer, having consumed three that morning already.

"I was in the neighborhood . . ."

"Yeah. Right. Well, then, how're you doing, Boomer?"

"Got my nose to the grindstone."

"Good."

"My shoulder to the wheel."

"Fine."

"My ear to the cauliflower."

"Uh-huh."

"My cheeks to the halibut."

"You're certainly flip these days."

"My lip to the flipper."

"Is that what she calls it?"

"Be nice."

"How *is* ol' Ultima, anyway?"

"Ellen Cherry, I don't hardly ever see Ultima. I don't see her that much. She wants to see you, though. I told her I thought you were painting again."

"Well, I'm not."

"Whadda ya call *them*?" He nodded, beret and all, toward the twenty or more canvases stacked against the wall.

"Experiments."

"I don't see why—"

"No! Don't you touch those paintings!"

"I thought they weren't paintings."

They sat for a time in silence. Boomer gulped his beer. She didn't offer another. He crushed the empty can in his big welder's fist, then began twisting the aluminum into some form or other. She wondered if he would include it in his exhibition.

After a while, he asked, "You doing okay?"

"Indisputably. I'm gainfully employed. I've got my health. Except I *have* been having psychic problems lately. I keep channeling Janis Joplin."

"Huh?"

She commenced to sing. "I'm gonna wash that man right outta my hair, I'm gonna wash that man right outta my hair . . ."

"Ellen Cherry."

". . . and send him on his way-ay."

"Ellen Cherry, now."

"Sorry. I've got no control over it. Sometimes she just takes over my body."

Nervously, Boomer scratched his thick neck. "Yeah, well, that was some kind of Broadway show tune you were singing. Janis Joplin never sung any song like that. She was rock 'n' roll."

"She's dead, Boomer. In death, a singer can expand her repertoire."

"And I don't buy that bull about washing a man outta your hair, neither. That hair of yours? Man get caught in there, you could shampoo forever and not set him loose."

"Well, that sure wouldn't be any problem for you. Exactly how many hairs do you have left now? Under that corny damn beret?"

That was the way it went, sparring, beating around their respective bushes, neither of them saying what was really on his or her mind, until Ellen Cherry glanced at the clock and realized that she had to be at the I & I in twenty-four minutes. He offered her a ride, and because she was late, she accepted. She made him wait in the hall while she changed, not so much out of modesty as fear that as soon as her back was turned, he would sneak a look at her paintings.

Descending in the elevator, she primed herself for some industrial-strength flirting with Raoul. She wanted Boomer to have a good look at how much that young stud wanted her. Raoul wasn't manning the door, though. She'd forgotten that he didn't come on duty until four in the afternoon. *He's probably home balling his sister,* she thought. *Or brushing his hat. Maybe both at the same time.*

Ellen Cherry was wrong. Raoul was in a recording studio spending his Ansonia earnings to lay down a track.

> *Pigeon she strut on the rooftop*
> *Cockroach he strut on the sink*
> *My baby strut down to Jerusalem*
> *Where blood is the favorite drink*

"*Leban zabadi.* That's the creamy Egyptian yogurt. *Turshi.* Uh, *turshi* is the . . . the mixed vegetables in . . . a spicy sauce. *Dajaj mashwi.* That's the half-chicken marinated in lemon, oregano, garlic, pepper, and olive oil. Why did the half-chicken cross the road, Boomer?"

"Which half was it?"

"Either half. Take your pick."

"Well, if it was split down the middle, it'd be a half-assed chicken. I'd have to be pretty hungry to order that."

"*Shawarma*. That's the thinly sliced beef with Middle Eastern spices. *Majadra* is the rice cooked with lentils and flavored with fried onions. *Roz bel khalta. Roz bel khalta.* Now what the heck is *roz bel khalta*?"

"Yiddish for Mrs. Jimmy Carter?"

"Sounds more like a stripper to me. Roz Bel Khalta, the Gypsy Rose Lee of the Middle East. But we've got no strippers at the I and I." (Maybe not yet, Ellen Cherry. But a time is coming. Oh, yes! A time is surely coming.)

"*Shish kabob.* Everybody knows *shish kabob. Shish tawook.* Same thing, only chicken. Funny name, though. Mr. Hadee likes the name, *shish tawook.* Musical name, he says. Like a little poem."

Boomer shook his head until his beret slipped askew. "Right out of Robert Frost," he said.

Riding to the restaurant in Boomer's brand-new Ford van, Ellen Cherry was going over the menu in her head. She had to know it intimately so that she could monitor the waiters and waitresses. It was her job to scold them should they misinform a diner or mix up an order. Neither extensive nor, in her opinion, particularly appetizing, the menu was a challenge, nonetheless.

"*Baba ghanoug.* I ought to know that one. *Baba ghanoug . . .*"

"That's the name Richard Alpert took when he got back from India. Or else it's what that Walters woman drinks at Christmas time."

He dropped her off on the corner of Forty-ninth and United Nations Plaza at precisely 10:00 A.M. He blew her a big welder's kiss as he sped away. Outwardly, she scowled, but her insides turned into *leban zabadi.*

Since this was a shakedown lunch, the first lunch of the I & I renaissance, Spike and Abu were on hand. In the future, they would be present only in the evenings. They would spend most of their days playing tennis.

They had met at a senior citizens tennis camp in Florida. Fate threw them together as doubles partners. The best duo in camp, they were well on their way to winning the camp doubles trophy when

Spike announced that he wouldn't be available for the championship match. To Spike's surprise, Abu said that he couldn't participate, either.

The next morning, at the scheduled time of their forfeited match, there was a modest peace rally in Miami Beach. Spike and Abu bumped into each other outside the Fontainebleu Hotel, where a jingoistic presidential candidate was ranting about the need to reduce Soviet influence in the Middle East. Spike stared at Abu's placard. Abu stared at Spike's. They laughed. After that, they were partners off court and on.

Ellen Cherry's title was maître d', but technically she was day manager. Her duties included captaining the reservations desk, orchestrating time slots and table configurations, making up work schedules, assigning sections, finding replacements for ill or hooky-playing employees, receiving deliveries, ascertaining that tables were set correctly, that ice bins were full and the bar stocked, and generally overseeing service. She wasn't required to keep books, but she did have to inspect waitpersons for dirty nails, unusual odors, and flamboyant hickeys, and she had to be vigilant against cockroach appendages in the *baba ghanoug.*

As did most other Manhattan restaurateurs, Spike and Abu bribed the health inspectors. Still, a skinny little leg draped over a chickpea, like a bathing beauty's gam encircling a beach ball, was considered bad for business.

"What business?" one might fairly ask, since the dining room was no more than a quarter full for that first lunch, and those diners—unsuspecting tourists in the neighborhood to visit UN Headquarters—were evacuated in a hurry when a bomb threat was phoned in a few minutes past noon.

Standing on the sidewalk waiting for the bomb squad to complete its search, Spike asked Ellen Cherry if the caller had mentioned his affiliation.

"No, he didn't," she said. "He had a foreign accent, but I couldn't tell if it was Arab or Jewish."

"In many parts of the Middle East, they sound alike," said Spike. "People ask, what's your menu, Palestinian or Israeli? So, what's the difference? I ask back. In Jerusalem, all peoples are eating basically the same. One time down the street there at the United Nations, no kidding, the PLO officially complained that the Israelis had stolen their national dish, *falafel*. Ha! The Israelis laughed and kept munching already. You know what science says: you are what you eat."

"Are you implying that Arabs and Jews are a whole lot alike? Mr. Hadee thinks otherwise."

"Alike or different is not the problem. The problem is that they *think* they're so different. Each one thinks they're superior. Their religions teach them they're superior. I love my people. In modern times, at least, we have been a smart, industrious people, and a caring people. A kind and humorous people. But to say that we're God's 'chosen' people, the ones what are favored above all the others, hoo boy! that's tempting fate. That's begging for trouble. And trouble we got already. Jerusalem is the trouble capital of the world. For thousands of years, Jerusalem is the capital of trouble and death."

"Then why do you and Mr. Hadee love it so much?"

There was a long and dramatic pause. The pause was almost as long as the East River, that scruffy orphan of the ocean that ran like a gutter of snot at their backs. The pause was nearly as dramatic as the UN Headquarters building, that modern Tower of Babel, tower of ego, cipher, hope, and suspicion, that rose into the brittle sky a block to the south. There was a long, dramatic pause, during which Ellen Cherry suspected that Spike was leering at her slippers.

Spike Cohen was considerably shorter than Roland Abu Hadee. He was stockier, and usually more animated. Whereas Abu was as placid as the eye of a storm, Spike was a funnel of worry twisting around and around that eye. His hair was as silver as a royal tea tray. He oiled it lightly and combed it straight back. It resembled the moonlit surf on a chrome beach, a wave breaking over a tropical Detroit. His features were as finely formed as those on a poster in a Greek delicatessen, but his eyes were anything but classical. They were ray-shooting emeralds that might have been scooped from the sockets of a jaguar idol. Indeed, there was something feline about him; Shoe Lion rather than Shoe Wolf. Abu—who had walked up in the middle of the long pause—had taken, as he matured, to wearing dark, heavy clothing, but Spike wore the orange sports jackets and chartreuse ties of a man who dressed to impress racehorses.

Abu had just begun to comment on the mess the bomb squad
was making inside the restaurant, when Spike terminated his
pause. "What I love most about Jerusalem is that it's not about
money."

"Pardon?"

"New York here is a city about money. L.A.'s about money. Las
Vegas is about money. Dallas the same. Tokyo and London, Milan,
Zurich, Singapore, the whole reason for them is money. Tel Aviv's
about money. But Jerusalem, it's not about money."

"He is absolutely right," put in Abu. "Jerusalem is about . . .
something else."

The bomb squad proclaimed the area safe, questioned Ellen Cherry
briefly, and then departed. Surveying the disorder, Spike commented
that the I & I might have sustained less damage had there actually
been an explosion. Chick-peas rolled hazardously beneath their feet,
and loosened bamboo matting hung from the walls like the baggy
folds of elephants. "How much liquor did they steal?" Spike asked
the bartender.

"About twelve bottles."

"Oy! With our best brandy they wash down their doughnuts."

"If there is another bomb scare, we should let our own security
guards handle it," proposed Abu.

"What you mean *if?*"

It took the three of them and the lunch staff most of the afternoon
to get the place in shape for dinner. Around five o'clock, the cooks
and waitpersons were sent home, and Ellen Cherry sat down with
Spike and Abu for a glass of tea. Spike had a shot of rum in his. "Hoo
boy!" he said.

When Ellen Cherry expressed her condolences for the external
problems besetting the I & I, Abu advised her not to fret. "It is quite
flattering," he said. "There are so many people, many of them
powerful, who object to a peaceful settlement in the Middle East. It is
encouraging that they think our little restaurant could make a difference. Let them protest. Let them bomb. I am flattered."

"Not me," said Spike. "I am heartsick already that there are Jews in
this hanky-pank. I got heartbreak even though I know that in ancient
times there were Jews behaving worse, that biblical Jew behavior set a

bad example for the Christians what followed. All that 'smite smite smite,' 'slew slew slew.' "

Wondering aloud how there possibly could be people who didn't want peace in the Middle East, Ellen Cherry realized instantly that she should have kept her mouth shut. Abu and Spike, each in his distinct fashion, were all too willing to fill her in. Their explanations might have been instructive had they the virtues of simplicity or logic, but apparently such assets were entirely missing from any accurate Middle Eastern account.

Until quite recently, if Ellen Cherry had been asked what was the first thing she thought about when she heard the words "Middle East," she would have answered, "Rugs."

She had never paid much attention to the Middle Eastern situation, per se, and now she knew why. It was an overload of craziness. It was a seventy-piece orchestra rehearsing a funeral dirge and a wedding march simultaneously in a broom closet. It was a firebug convention in a straw hotel.

Since her association with the I & I, she'd learned about the various kinds of Arabs: Druse, Shiites, Sunnis, Hijazi, Bedouins, Sufis, Wahhabis, Arab Christians—and the Palestinians, who didn't really consider themselves to be Arabs and who were contemptuous of the nomadic traditions of their "Sleeping Gypsy" cousins. Jesus! The Middle East had more kinds of Arabs than Cartier had pillboxes. Apparently, it was about as bad with the Jews. Hardly a monolith, Jews ranged over a wide, politically diverse spectrum; instead of one Jewish point of view, there were dozens, angrily divided along ethnic, class, and religious lines.

As for who was legitimately entitled to Jerusalem and the land surrounding it—entitled to Palestine or Israel or whatever it ought to be called—forget it! You could make a perfectly just case for either side; in fact, you could make a different just case for either side every fifteen minutes from now until bulldogs barked for bean sprouts. And then you'd have to factor in the Christians.

It's too complex, too confusing, she thought. *Nobody'll ever straighten this damn mess out.* From that afternoon on, when anyone mentioned the Middle East, she went back to thinking *rugs.* Give her an Oriental carpet, opulent and jazzy, comforting yet intense, like an overtuned eye game flattened and spread out on the floor. Give her pattern and color, give her a map of the higher mind, a map woven from dreams and hair and dyed with spices and wine. Give her beauty, in other words. Give her humanity's best shot. Give her art.

She kissed Abu and Spike on their sad, spunky foreheads, untangled herself from their wild weave, and walked what remained of her hangover hurriedly up to Fifth Avenue, hoping that she wasn't too late to catch Turn Around Norman at work.

There was a full hour of daylight left, but it was the lame-duck daylight of autumnal afternoons, a daylight that already had been defeated by night. Long brown shadows sepia-toned the streets, and the chill that was settling upon Manhattan felt as invigoratingly decadent as the breath of a jack-o'-lantern. Indeed, the watered-down morbidity of Halloween trappings haunted the windows of the recherché brownstones along East Forty-ninth Street. There was actually a paper skeleton dancing in the doorway of the Mel Davis Dog Boutique, where Ellen Cherry paused ever so briefly to gaze in a kind of pre-Halloween horror at a prissy hound being anointed with oils. She wondered why Mel didn't paste a *dog* skeleton on his door glass, little that poodles understood about the Way of the Dead, although all dogs, including barbered poochie-woochies, had a nose for invisible paths.

The street was lined with trees, many, one supposed, that poodles had peed upon. Businessmen swinging attaché cases plodded homeward through fallen leaves. From time to time, an executive would intentionally kick up a brass geyser of leaves, then glance around sheepishly as if he might be cited for a violation of adulthood.

Every time she passed a Japanese restaurant, which on East Forty-ninth was about every twenty seconds, Ellen Cherry thought, *The bamboo was intended for this place, they delivered it to our Jerusalem by mistake.* When, on the corner of Third Avenue, she passed Wollensky's, a well-known hangout for politicians, she wondered how many inside secretly opposed peace in the Middle East. Then she thought, *rugs.* Then she kicked up a brass geyser of leaves, glancing around brazenly as if to say, "I'm twenty-four, jilted, and work in food service; I'm free to be as free as I please." It occurred to her that despite the failure of her marriage, the failure of her career, despite her hangover and chronic horniness, she suddenly was feeling rather light and giddy. She couldn't understand it. Was she simply too shallow to suffer indefinitely, or was she too wise to become attached to her suffering, too feisty to permit it to rule her life? She voted for wise and feisty, and walked on, kicking leaves.

By Lexington Avenue, the trees had thinned out. The noble old brownstones had given way to glassy apartment towers and classy hotels. Sidewalks had widened, stretched by the muscular fingers of money, and the pour of office workers had curdled into a cyclonic multitude, well-dressed, cologned, and silently pouting because the limousines double-parked along each and every curb were not idling obediently for *it*. Crossing Lexington, she trod on the grates over the Grand Central underground tracks. As every child in New York was aware, there was another city down there in the tunnels, populated by fugitives, hermits, gypsies, mad scientists, albino alligators, giant mutated roaches, sorcerers, sages, and surviving members of the lost tribe of Manhattan (clothed in twenty-four dollars' worth of blankets and beads).

Ellen Cherry entertained the notion that Turn Around Norman resided in that subterranean milieu. If he didn't live for free in the tunnels, where could he live? The donation box that he set out at his performances seldom had more than a few dimes in it. Airheads who played wooden flutes out of tune in Times Square attracted larger donations than he did. Aromatic winos with pus in their eyes earned more from intimidation than Turn Around Norman earned from his artistry. Either he slept in the streets or he had a patron. Ellen Cherry imagined a beautiful Barnard girl sacrificing her clothing allowance in order to provide Turn Around Norman a warm place to come home to. Grazed by a bullet of jealousy, she vowed to toss ten bucks into his box that day.

At Park Avenue, there were banks on all four corners. Money in every direction. Bank of the West, Bank of the North, Bank of the East, Bank of the South. Bank of Fire, Bank of Air, Bank of Earth, Bank of Water. Spike was right about New York, it existed for moola. But how was Jerusalem any different? Wasn't one of the main attractions of the New Jerusalem (heaven, if you will), to be streets that were paved with gold? At that moment, she noticed that there also were hot dog vendors on all four corners. Carts reeking of sauerkraut and farty sausages. Strangely, that seemed to balance things out—as far as New York was concerned. As for Jerusalem, she was positive that whatever it was that it was about, it was not about food. It was no accident, surely, that the Bible never mentioned cuisine in its descriptions of the City of Heaven. How many people would forgo cheating on their taxes or their spouses if they knew that their eternal reward included a steady diet of *baba ghanoug*? In the twelfth

century, there was a thoroughfare in Jerusalem named the Street of
Bad Cooking, a fact that for better or for worse had failed to deter
Spike Cohen or Roland Abu Hadee in his culinary selection.

Jostled past the Waldorf-Astoria and several more Japanese restaurants (this neighborhood reminded Ellen Cherry of a petri dish in
which sushi bars and tourists multiplied like bacteria), she finally
reached Fifth Avenue, turned uptown past Saks, and came to rest on
the steps of St. Patrick's Cathedral. Was she the least aware, during
her trek, of how often New York and Jerusalem had interfaced,
interpenetrated in her consciousness? Probably not. In any case, it
didn't matter now. There before the massive bronze doors of America's most famous monument to Jerusalem's most famous former
resident, her attention was nailed, as if to a cross, to the talents of Turn
Around Norman.

Turn Around Norman always performed in the same spot: on the
sidewalk just to the south of the cathedral steps. As near as Ellen
Cherry could determine, he was at his post from morning until dusk,
daily with the exception of Wednesdays. For some reason, Turn
Around Norman didn't work on Wednesday afternoons. He took
Wednesday afternoons off, the way doctors did. What did Turn
Around Norman do on Wednesday afternoons? Ellen Cherry tried to
picture him playing golf with dermatologists from Yonkers, proctolo-
gists from White Plains.

The steps of St. Patrick's were comparatively short, but Ellen
Cherry was able to attain an elevation that afforded a satisfactory
view of the performance space. She was settling onto her step like a
dowager settling into her box at the opera, when a hand landed as
softly as a dove on her shoulder and a familiar voice flared like a
match near her ear.

"As I live and breathe! Bless my sinful soul! It's my little doll
baby."

And there was the Reverend Buddy Winkler, in all his seedy glory,
smiling at her through a bonfire of new gold fillings.

"Uncle Buddy. What a surprise. Wow! They could pave the streets
of heaven with your teeth."

"And they could paint the gates of hell with your lipstick. But,
darlin', lemme tell you, it's right nice to hear you speakin' of heaven

and to find you in such close proximity to a house of God—even if it's a corrupted house. You weren't headin' into this papist monstrosity, were you now?"

Both Ellen Cherry and Buddy surveyed St. Patrick's, their gazes slowly climbing the three hundred and thirty feet to the tips of its twin spires, then parachuting to the steps again.

"No. I may be a Jezebel, Uncle Buddy, but I'm a Protestant Jezebel."

"You got a tongue like your mama's, girl." Ellen Cherry grinned in a sassy, knowing way, causing Buddy to blush uncomfortably, as if some memory of Patsy's tongue shamed or inflamed him. When he regained composure, he asked, "Well, what *are* you doin' here? In front of the doors through which passeth the richest mackerel-snappers in New York City? Some of whom, I might add, give generously to my cause. All hush-hush, of course." He ran a hand over his cheek, over lacunae that all the bullion in Fort Knox could not plug. "My associates and me got us an office right up the street there. In the Bank of Austria. They're better to us than our own countrymen."

They were nice to Hitler, too, she thought, but she said, "I'm waiting for somebody." Surreptitiously, she glanced at Turn Around Norman, irritated that this chance encounter with Buddy was making her miss the subtleties of his work. One had to watch Turn Around Norman very, very closely.

"Not waitin' for our boy, Boomer, I needn't expect. Naturally, I heard 'bout the separation and have been sorely distressed. Sorely distressed. I yearn to be the instrument through which God reunites you screwballs."

"Well, you'll have to speak with ol' Boomer about that."

"I have spoke with Boomer."

"You have?"

"Yes, indeed. Your hubby bulled into my office only this mornin', claimin' he was goin' to bust my born-again choppers if a hair offen your head was to be harmed at that satanic café where, I'm sorrowed to learn, you've once agin taken up employ. We need to chat 'bout that, too."

Ellen Cherry wasn't interested in chatting about the I & I. For the moment, she wasn't even interested in watching Turn Around Norman. She just kept thinking about Boomer coming to her defense, trying to protect her. "Boomer did that? He *did*?" Suddenly, inexplicably, her heart was full of something, she did not know what.

*   *   *

The Reverend Buddy Winkler was sheathed in a mustard-colored sharkskin suit that fit him so tightly one was moved to take up a collection to send his crotch on vacation. His starched white shirt was stiff to the point of being bulletproof, and at its collar, a gray knit tie was knotted in one of those dated Windsor lumps that made him look as though he were plagued by a particularly hideous goiter. His shoes were black loafers that appeared to have been chewed by wolves. Ah, but his smile was golden now, and his voice had lost not a calorie of its old blue heat.

"Naturally, naturally, Boomer is concerned with the welfare of his little wife. As am I. What'd you do to that boy, doll baby? That fop French thing he's totin' around on his head. And his 'art.' I understand he's having an exhibition. That boy used to do an honest day's work. Did you have to go and turn him into an artist?"

"I didn't have a blessed thing to do with it. He turned himself into . . . whatever he is."

Once more, Buddy lay a surprisingly light hand on her shoulder. "When you was just a youngun, knee-high to a wiggly worm, you used to stare at your dish of Jell-O—raspberry Jell-O, usually, with cream on top—and see Santy Claus in it. 'Santy's in my Jell-O,' you'd say. You'd see pictures in your food. We figgered way back then that you was goin' to be somethin' different, somethin' special. It didn't fool nobody when you went in for art. But Boomer Petway . . . that boy ain't no artist."

"You said it, not I."

"But you do agree?"

"Did little Boomer boy ever see Santa Claus in his Jell-O?"

"Hell—heck no! He'd gobble up his dessert so fast there wasn't *time* to see no pictures in it."

"I rest my case," said Ellen Cherry. A darkening sky was sucking up daylight like a sump pump siphoning milk gravy. Turn Around Norman would be quitting soon. She tried to concentrate on him, hoping to detect some nuance of great purity or grace, but the Reverend Buddy Winkler was practically standing in her shoes.

"Who's that?"

"Who's what?"

"That sorry fool over there that you been pretendin' not to gawk at."

"Oh, him."

"He hasn't moved a muscle since I been here. Standin' there blank-faced like a cigar-store Indian. He afflicted, or what?"

"He's a street performer."

"Well, when's he gonna perform?"

"He *is* performing."

Buddy tightened his grip on her shoulder. He even shook her, ever so slightly. "Darlin', he's paralyzed, for God's sake! That's his act? Paralysis? This is what show business has come to? No wonder the Good Lord called Ed Sullivan home."

"But he does move," objected Ellen Cherry, tumbling into a discussion she had sworn to avoid. "That's the point. He turns around. Completely around. But he turns so slowly you can't see him do it. If you watch him long enough, you'll notice that he'll be facing in a different direction than he was when you started watching. Over a period of a couple of hours, he'll turn three hundred and sixty degrees. Only you'll never see him move, no matter how hard you look. That's what's exciting about him."

Buddy let his hand slide off her. He issued a grunt of astonishment, followed by a sigh of exasperation. "Excitin'," he mumbled. "Excitin'. If you wasn't my own flesh and blood. . . . Let me ask you somethin'. How often you come here and eyeball this poor petrified simpleton?"

"Now that I'm working within easy walking distance—" Oops. She hadn't intended to admit to that. "Oh, I don't know. I come here fairly often, I guess. He's a source of comfort and inspiration to me, Uncle Bud. I suppose you'd have to say—you won't like this—he's my church."

"Humph! Some church. He don't have diddly-squat in his collection plate."

St. Patrick's cornerstone was laid in 1858, at a time when New York was starting to strut its stuff and Jerusalem (under the Turks) was up to its ears in woe and ashes. The age of Ellen Cherry's "church" could not have been easily guessed. Turn Around Norman was one of those creatures of indeterminate years; he might have been any age between his late twenties and early forties. His poundage, too, was ambiguous, for while almost any observer would have classified him as overweight, nobody would have thought to call him fat. Just a bit rosy, just a bit round, he was molded like a healthy cherub. But, oh, his face was fastened to his large head with hellish hinges. His screaming blue eyes, his deeply furrowed brow, his mad poet's mouth (poised to suck the marrow out of the bird bones of beauty), his nose so perfect it might have ridden into town on a swan; those features combined to create a countenance of the most serene intensity, a mixture of the tranquil and the tragic that could have fired the hearts and dampened the underpants of half the city's women, had they paid him the smallest attention as he stood silently and ostensibly inert on the crowded street in a brown bag of a suit, soiled sneakers, and a colorless sweatshirt bearing the phrase *Aplodontia rufas,* which, research taught Ellen Cherry, was the Latin for a species of mountain beaver.

For the moment, Turn Around Norman was facing downtown, so they saw him in profile. Apparently, in his present position he couldn't see *them* at all, which suited Ellen Cherry fine. She didn't relish her "church," her "art museum," her "ballet hall," noticing that she kept company with the pushy evangelist of another faith. She hoped that Buddy would go away while there was still time to tap the quiet ecstasy of the performer's relentlessly regulated passion, but Buddy stood there in the sad titillation of the autumnal chill, gawking at Turn Around Norman like a farm boy examining a runover snake.

"Now don't that beat all," he marveled. "An able-bodied male spendin' his life on the public sidewalk doin' nothin' but turnin' around all day, and doin' *that* so slow you can't see him do it. Haw! Then expectin' on top of it to be paid for what we don't know he's really doin' in the first place."

"Another way in which he's like the church, I guess. I hadn't thought of it till now."

Buddy's hidden saxophone emitted a soft indigo honk. "Girl, I'd warn you that God Almighty's goin' to strike you dead, exceptin' I been warnin' your mama that for years, and he in his infinite mercy has so far seen fit to withhold his lightnin'."

"You'd be sorry if Patsy got zapped. You and half the men in Colonial Pines."

Now Buddy placed both hands on her shoulders. He got as close to her face as her hair would allow. "You know 'bout your mama's flirtations?" he whispered.

"I knew about them back when I was seeing elves in my pablum. But that's in the past, I reckon, and I don't want to gab about the past."

"Me neither. Let's us gab 'bout the present."

"Uncle Buddy, I don't have time to gab." Anxiously, she surveyed the failing light. Another five minutes and Turn Around Norman would be history. Or, more accurately, geology. "But next time we run into each other, you can explain to me why you object to peace in the Middle East."

"I'll explain right now."

"No. Please."

"I'll explain here and now. If you'd been readin' your Scripture, you'd have knowed the answer. It's not God's plan for there to be peace in the Middle East. Not yet, it ain't. First, we'll be witness to an impressive scene. Yea, I say unto you . . ."

Oh, shit, she thought. The sax was out of its case.

". . . the awfulness of the impending judgment will be unequaled on the earth! The Holy Land, your so-called Middle East, is prophesied to be the scene of the ultimate world war. Combatants will be lured to the area by demons sent by Satan to assemble the armies of the world to challenge the armies of heaven. Up and down the Holy Land, they'll battle. On the very day of the return of Christ, there'll be house-to-house fighting in Jerusalem itself, the homes ransacked and the women raped. Zechariah, fourteen, two."

"Bud, really . . ."

"This is to be the last war, darlin'. The wicked will be destroyed once and for all, whereupon the righteous will dwell with Christ in the New Jerusalem for—"

"Bud!"

"Come on now, let me answer your question. It's not a matter of us Christians not wantin' peace, it's a matter of the time not bein' ripe for peace. First, our Messiah must return. Then, the fightin' in the Holy Land must begin in earnest. These bleedin' hearts who're clamoring for peace in the Middle East understand not what they do. They're uninformed troublemakers, interferin' with—and slowin' down—the natural chain of events that'll fulfill God's promise and make the world sweet as pie for eternity."

Turn Around Norman was about to break his concentration. Ellen Cherry recognized the signs: a fluttering of his girlish lashes, a relaxing of the origami creases in his forehead. Still, she was unable to refrain from blurting, "Is that why you picket and bomb Isaac and Ishmael's? Because their concern for brotherhood and love is screwing up some alleged timetable for destruction?"

"Hush, now. We might picket, my associates and me might, but we don't bomb. You and Boomer and the damn Yankee *po*-lice are jumpin' to conclusions." He flashed his gold teeth, teeth anxious to sink into afterlife pie. "That café is small fry. Small fry. When the Third Temple Platoon throws our dynamite, it'll hit a right more important target than that grubby little restaurant, I promise you."

"Oh? And what target would that be?"

"Hush. I've said too much already. But lemme set you straight on somethin'. The Arab and the Jew that runs that peacenik greasy spoon, it's their own people that wants it shut down the most. Their own kind."

Ellen Cherry had to admit that that seemed the case. "But why?" she asked.

"Because they are not real Arabs and Jews, them two. They are not religious! That Arab, Hadee, he's well-known as an infidel, a livin' insult to the teachings of Islam. They wouldn't let him touch Mecca with a ten-foot pole. And that ol' Jewboy, Cohen, when was the last time he set foot in a synagogue? He sports a Yid accent that'd curdle a bowl of schmaltz, but I understand that in private he can spout English as pretty as you or me. How can they pass themselves off as representatives of their people when neither one of 'em subscribes to the deepest beliefs of their people?"

"They're kind, decent, compassionate—"

"Kind and decent got nothin' to do with it! In the End Times, there're to be many false prophets and false religions. You, little lady, your false religion is art. Verlin, I often suspect, his religion is football. He ain't alone in that one, lemme tell you. Patsy's religion I don't want to speculate on. But the most insidious and dangerous of false religions is secular humanism. It's so crafty, so sneaky, with its kindness and its decency, that only Satan hisself could've come up with it. Well, that's precisely what them two old peaceniks practice, and that's precisely why they're so offensive to the truly devout, includin' the Moslems and the Jews. I told Boomer and I'm tellin' you, I want you to pull outta that heathen café, git back in holy matrimony where you belong, 'cause *I* can't be responsible for your safety there."

Early religions were like muddy ponds with lots of foliage. Concealed there, the fish of the soul could splash and feed. Eventually, however, religions became aquariums. Then, hatcheries. From farm fingerling to frozen fish stick is a short swim.

The Reverend Buddy Winkler was correct about Spike Cohen and Roland Abu Hadee: they did not glide in numb circles inside a glass box of religion. In fact, they, Spike and Abu, wouldn't hesitate to directly attribute the success of their relationship to their lack of formal religion. Were either of them actively religious, it would have been impossible for them to be partners or pals. Dogma and tradition would have overruled any natural instinct for brotherhood.

It was as if Spike and Abu had been granted a sneak preview behind the veil, a glimpse in which it was revealed that organized religion was a major obstacle to peace and understanding. If so, it was a gradual revelation, for it unfolded slowly and separately, a barely conscious outgrowth of each man's devotion to humanity and rejection of doctrine.

At best, perhaps, when the fourth veil does slip aside, Spike and Abu will be better prepared than most to withstand the shock of this tough truth: religion is a paramount contributor to human misery. It is not merely the opium of the masses, it is the cyanide.

Of course, religion's omnipresent defenders are swift to point out the *comfort* it provides for the sick, the weary, and the disappointed. Yes, true enough. But the Deity does not dawdle in the comfort zone! If one yearns to see the face of the Divine, one must break out of the aquarium, escape the fish farm, to go swim up wild cataracts, dive in deep fjords. One must explore the labyrinth of the reef, the shadows of lily pads. How limiting, how insulting to think of God as a benevolent warden, an absentee hatchery manager who imprisons us in the "comfort" of artificial pools, where intermediaries sprinkle our restrictive waters with sanitized flakes of processed nutriment.

A longing for the Divine is intrinsic in *Homo sapiens*. (For all we know, it is innate in squirrels, dandelions, and diamond rings, as well.) We approach the Divine by enlarging our souls and lighting up our brains. To expedite those two things may be the mission of our existence.

Well and good. But such activity runs counter to the aspirations of commerce and politics. Politics is the science of domination, and persons in the process of enlargement and illumination are notoriously difficult to control. Therefore, to protect its vested interests, politics usurped religion a very long time ago. Kings bought off priests with land and adornments. Together, they drained the shady ponds and replaced them with fish tanks. The walls of the tanks were constructed of ignorance and superstition, held together with fear. They called the tanks "synagogues" or "churches" or "mosques."

After the tanks were in place, nobody talked much about *soul* anymore. Instead, they talked about *spirit*. Soul is hot and heavy. Spirit is cool, abstract, detached. Soul is connected to the earth and its waters. Spirit is connected to the sky and its gases. Out of the gases springs fire. Firepower. It has been observed that the logical extension of all politics is war. Once religion became political, the exercise of it, too, could be said to lead sooner or later to war. "War is hell." Thus, religious belief propels us straight to hell. History unwaveringly supports this view. (Each modern religion has boasted that it and it alone is on speaking terms with the Deity, and its adherents have been quite willing to die—or kill—to support its presumptuous claims.)

Not every silty bayou could be drained, of course. The soulfish that bubbled and snapped in the few remaining ponds were tagged "mystics." They were regarded as mavericks, exotic and inferior. If they splashed too high, they were thought to be threatening and in need of extermination. The fearful flounders in the tanks, now psychologically dependent upon addictive spirit flakes, had forgotten that once upon a time they, too, had been mystical.

Religion is nothing but institutionalized mysticism. The catch is, *mysticism does not lend itself to institutionalization*. The moment we attempt to organize mysticism, we destroy its essence. Religion, then, is mysticism in which the mystical has been killed. Or, at least diminished.

Those who witness the dropping of the fourth veil might see clearly what Spike Cohen and Roland Abu Hadee dimly suspected: that not only is religion divisive and oppressive, it is also a denial of all that is divine in people; it is a suffocation of the soul.

As night buttoned the spires of St. Patrick's in its blouse, Buddy Winkler gave Ellen Cherry a hard, nervous hug. "I'll be prayin' for you, doll baby," he called, hurrying off to a meeting with some of his Jews. "And I'll be in touch. You git yourself straightened out, you heah?"

She waved meekly. When she turned back in the direction of downtown, Turn Around Norman was gone. He was slow to rotate, fast to fly. She hadn't even had an opportunity to throw a donation in his box.

Well, she'd be sure to return the following day. *Tomorrow, I'll slip him a twenty,* she thought. Extravagant, maybe, but she felt a responsibility to encourage him. After all, he was one of a kind—and as far as she could tell, there was no one else who so much as acknowledged his existence.

As far as she could tell. The fact was, there had been five pairs of eyes on Turn Around Norman all day. Perhaps "eyes" was not quite the right word. From a grate over a shaft that led into the basement of the cathedral, Turn Around Norman's performance had been watched at length and with interest by an odd quintet of inanimate objects, hiding there in the cellar.

There was a voluptuous seashell watching Turn Around Norman. There was a decorated stick. There was a little silver spoon, a man's frazzled stocking, and a battered lump of tin from which hung scraps of paper that once had proclaimed the lump to be a can of pork and beans.

the fifth veil

Once upon a time, the wolfmother went to market and picked out wallpaper. It was patterned in spirals and molecular chains. It was bordered with electrons and well-gnawed bones. The wolfmother licked the tip of the salesman's shoelace and turned it into jade. That was her down payment.

Once upon a time, a painted stick and a conch shell arrived in New York City. The shell was warm, heavy, and wet, like the earth, the sea. The stick pointed at the sky. On its tip, it balanced configurations of gases. Although they had traveled long and far, the painted stick and the conch shell were not welcome in New York City. Accustomed to the protection of holy places, they hid in the cellar of a midtown cathedral. It was just a place to rest while they figured out a way to cross the Atlantic Ocean. Nevertheless, they were compelled to remark on how much its ambiance might have been improved by the right kind of wallpaper.

There were two more bomb scares at the I & I that week. Both occurred during dinner, so Ellen Cherry was not directly affected. The publicity reached her, though. Coming or going, she had to wade through the cameras of the curious. Like a reclusive movie actress, she donned a scarf and dark glasses, and studied her walking feet as if she had a research grant from the Stubbed Toe Foundation. Her fear was that she would encounter Buddy on the picket line. Or that he would recognize her in a media picture. Family trouble was the worst kind. Some families ran their own little versions of the Middle East. Come to think of it, what was the Middle Eastern situation but a family squabble that had gotten out of hand? *Isaac* v. *Ishmael*.

Her parents phoned her at work. "I'm busy," she lied. The only customers in the most famous restaurant in New York were two tables of Japanese tourists, drinking green Egyptian beer and giggling uncontrollably at the *baba ghanoug*.

"How many eating places in New York City? Ten thousand? Twenty thousand? More? Your mama says 'more.' And you gotta hook up with the only blessed one that's—"

"Relax, Daddy, the worst is over. There're not going to be any further explosions."

Indeed, the week passed without violence, and as a result, onlookers thinned out considerably, another example of the teeny-weeniness of the metropolitan attention span. But there was an explosion. It happened in the safety of Ellen Cherry's own apartment, and while it had been expected, still, it nearly blew her into backward somersaults. The "bomb" was an invitation to Boomer Petway's one-man show at the Ultima Sommervell Gallery.

The day they arrived in New York, they had aimed the Airstream directly for Seventy-third and Broadway, where a one-bedroom apartment awaited them in the orchidaceous Ansonia Hotel. They were subletting from a sculptor who had moved to Florence for three years and who, in turn, was subletting from the new curator of contemporary art at the Seattle Art Museum, a man who admired Ellen Cherry's talent. This curator also had provided a letter of introduction to the prominent dealer, Ultima Sommervell.

As quickly as they were settled, as quickly as they had made the bed, scoured the bathtub, and stocked the kitchenette shelves with *ramen,* pizza mix, Pabst Blue Ribbon beer, and six brands of roach killer, Ellen Cherry had fetched her slides to the Sommervell Gallery. Ultima didn't exactly fall out of her Josef Hoffman "Sitzmaschine" chair, but she was interested enough to promise to come up to the Ansonia and examine the paintings themselves. Three days later, she came.

For his part, Boomer had found that welding shops were located mainly in the outer boroughs. Holding out for a job in Manhattan, he was lying around the apartment reading an espionage novel when Ultima showed up. She was so breathless that they thought she must have climbed the stairs. It turned out that she had chanced upon the big roast turkey in a nearby parking lot and suffered a cultural experience of the brightest magnitude.

"Why, ol' Boomer made that," said Ellen Cherry, innocently, pointing to the husky fellow lounging on the sofa in a T-shirt, Colonial Pines High School track shorts, and one purple sock.

"Really? Really, darling? Oh, *magnifique!*"

Ultima Sommervell was tall, dark, and jumpy, somewhere on the dry side of thirty. Her face was shaped like a strawberry and colored like an olive, simultaneously soft and tart. She was simply but elegantly attired and coiffured, the kind of woman who might have been designed by a Bauhaus architect, except for her bosom, whose free-flowing volume all but contradicted the severe planes of the rest of her body, impeding her balance, creating such a clashing contrast that, speaking strictly aesthetically, she might have benefited from a double mastectomy. It was as if Gropius had created her, then allowed Gaudi to add the boobs. In a spitty British accent, which reminded Ellen Cherry of a schoolgirl trying to mimic Alfred Hitchcock, she continually interrupted her self-assured appraisals of Ellen Cherry's canvases to query Boomer about the drivable bird.

"What I find in your pictures finally is an awkward dichotomy between illusion and abstraction. Energetic, yes; charming, yes; but as I said, awkward. They typify the unlovable nuttiness of modern art before it finally matured and developed a social conscience." She turned to Boomer. "What are you saying with your *enormous* silver turkey, Mr.—ah—Boomer? It seems fraught, simply fraught, with commentary."

Professing that the market was running rather thin for what she termed "socially insignificant picture-making," Ultima nevertheless

agreed to represent Ellen Cherry on a limited basis. She selected
three paintings, requesting that they be delivered to her gallery. Her
uptown gallery, not the SoHo branch where, Ellen Cherry knew, all
the action was. Then she asked Boomer if she might have a tour of
his "monstre sacré."

Wriggling into his jeans, Boomer seemed eager to accommodate
her.

When they had gone, Ellen Cherry didn't know whether to be
glad, mad, or sad. She'd gotten a foot in the door of a major gallery,
no mean accomplishment for an unknown artist fresh from the ferns.
It ought to have been New Year's Eve squared in her heart. But she
wasn't happy with the way Ultima had carried on about that dumb
turkey. She wasn't happy with the way Boomer had stared at Ultima's tits.

"Really, darling?" she found herself muttering, after Boomer and
Ultima disappeared into the elevator. "Oh *magnifuckingfique*."

The first ax hit the persimmon tree when Boomer informed his wife
that Ultima was going to sell the turkey for him.

"I thought it was *my* turkey. I thought it was my wedding present."

"Yeah, but you don't get the picture, honey sugar. This isn't no
used-car deal. Ultima wants to sell it as *art*. And I'm the artist. I
made the fool thing."

Wasn't that cute? It was art and he made it. Well, okay, let him
enjoy his delusion. Ellen Cherry had to confess that the turkey was a
novel idea, and she was all too aware that it was costing a small
fortune to park it in the neighborhood. Whereas, should it sell, she
would share in the proceeds and could replenish her materials. She
decided to be pleased.

But further chips flew when Boomer commenced to accompany
Ultima to the "presentations." She was pitching the Airstream two or
three times a week, Boomer at her side. *At her front is more like it,*
thought Ellen Cherry, examining her own petite protrusions in the
bathroom mirror. Suspecting that cookies were being eaten behind
her back, she began to test Boomer in bed. Either his relationship
with Ultima was strictly business or he was, indeed, a biological marvel.

But there was a rain of green persimmons on their coital parade
following the eventual purchase of the rolling roast by the Museum

of Modern Art. Ellen Cherry had thought that the sale would be the end of it, that Boomer would use his half of the profits to set up his own welding shop and they would return to the life they had plotted and planned. But no, according to Ultima, Boomer was in demand. His turkey was a smash, and he was constantly being invited to parties and gallery openings. For a while, Ellen Cherry went along. She was even grateful at first for this backdoor entry into the New York art scene, although rather quickly she came to think of it as entering a peacock through its rectum. She withdrew.

"In the old days," she complained, "and it wasn't that long ago, artists had the best parties in the world. They had wild and imaginative parties. There was romance, there was colorful behavior and brilliant conversation. Look at these posing contests we're being dragged to! Look at these artists we're being bored by! They're vain as fashion models and shallow as real-estate developers. All they talk about is money. Careers. And will any single one of them look you in the eye? No sirree. They're too busy looking over your shoulder so that if something new should pop up on the horizon, they'll be sure to notice it—and exploit it—before you do."

"I guess that's what I like about 'em," said Boomer. "They aren't these great soaring eagles of genius like I imagined famous artists would be. They're just as petty as everybody else."

"They weren't always. Artists used to be special. A breed apart. It wasn't that long ago."

While Ellen Cherry was genuinely disappointed by her introduction to the New York art world, by the revelation that it was just like Seattle's, only bigger, part of her dissatisfaction may be attributed to the fact that her husband was lionized at the parties, was treated as if he were the creative one, while she, except by the occasional lecher or fancier of ungovernable hairdos, was largely ignored.

Boomer continued to go out. *Vanity Fair* reported that he was "Ultima Sommervell's favorite escort." The art world took to Boomer Petway. He was a welcome shot of gamma globulin in its jaundiced system. People who ought to know better were delighted with his upbeat redneck manners, his muscles, his aloha shirts and new red beret. When he and Ultima performed the tango at their favorite club, Boomer adding bizarre little variations due to his lame foot, Liberty's torch wasn't good enough to light his cheap cheroots.

Ellen Cherry sat at the Ansonia, wrapped in her belief in the unique and the beautiful, solaced by her eye game, and further comforted by the knowledge that, (1) a check soon would be arriving from the Museum of Modern Art, and, (2) Boomer would ball her with bravura once he got home—although the hour of his homecomings seemed to be inching steadily in the direction of sunrise.

The chain saw didn't run amok in their persimmon grove until that dawn when Boomer, instead of making love to her, wanted to talk about art.

"At least six Palestinian youths were killed by Israeli army gunfire yesterday as demonstrations, strikes, and protests erupted anew in the occupied West Bank and Gaza Strip after a month-long lull in the uprising.

"The casualty toll for twenty months of strife includes at least four hundred Palestinians dead and about a thousand wounded, according to official figures. Palestinian sources said there were six hundred additional dead and thousands more injured."

Ellen Cherry had programmed the clock-radio to wake her at three in the morning so that she might get up and brush her teeth, thus presenting Boomer with a fresh, minty mouth to kiss when he got home. Instead of music, however, the radio punctured her sleep with the foregoing report from a news service correspondent in Jerusalem.

For some reason, she started wondering what time it was in Jerusalem, if there were wives there concerned about oral freshness, and whether Israelis and Palestinians used separate brands of toothpaste. She wondered if Jezebel had brushed her teeth on that fatal day when she "painted her face and tired her head" before going to the window. Ellen Cherry lay there wondering these things for a full half hour, but time proved to be of no essence because Boomer didn't show up until quarter past five. By then, bacteria had returned to her scrubbed gums like bathers returning to the beach after a summer storm and were holding sour picnics there and fetid games of volleyball.

Boomer came through the door like *The Thinker* on ice skates, moving fast, fairly gliding, yet pensive, distracted. Ellen Cherry, reawakened, was set to give her mouth another brushing (bikini-clad microbes could hear the rumble of distant thunder) but changed her mind when Boomer slid into bed with his jeans on.

Optimistic, nonetheless, she snuggled up to him and ran her fingers through his chest hair. As she scratched his pelt, it gave off fumes of stale tobacco smoke so concentrated that they would have asphyxiated the Marlboro Man; but at least, thought she, he didn't reek of Ultima Sommervell. Ellen Cherry had commenced to unbutton his fly when, staring at the ceiling, he asked, "How do people go about making pieces of art?"

"What do you mean?"

"Just what I said. How do you make art?"

"You ought to know. Didn't you make that 'significant' turkey some famous museum bought and hasn't paid for yet?"

"You know as well as me that I didn't start out to make anything significant."

"Artists hardly ever start out to make significant art. And if they do, it's usually a flop. Help me with these buttons, hon."

"I don't get it."

"And you're not going to get it if we don't take your pants off."

"If artists don't set out to make significant art, what do they do?"

"Oh, Boomer." She sighed, and abandoned his fly. "Maybe they do set out to make something significant, in a roundabout sort of way, but it's not like setting out to make something practical or useful. For one thing, it's more like play than work. On the other hand, they don't have a whole lot of choice in the matter. The good ones make art because they *have* to make it—even though they probably won't understand why until after it's already made."

"But how do they know what to make?"

"That's dictated by their vision."

"You mean it comes to 'em like in a dream?"

"No, no, it's seldom that dramatic. Listen, it's really pretty simple. If there's a thing, a scene, maybe, an image that you want to see real bad, that you need to see but it doesn't exist in the world around you, at least not in the form that you envision, then you create it so that you can look at it and have it around, or show it to other people who wouldn't have imagined it because they perceive reality in a more narrow, predictable way. And that's it. That's all an artist does."

"You paint landscapes . . ."

"Right, but they don't look like the landscapes that nature provides, and hopefully they don't look like landscapes that any other painter has ever provided. If they looked like either one, then there would be no excuse for me painting them—except maybe to earn money or call attention to myself, and those are low motives that lead to low art. Not that artists can't use money. Not that we couldn't use a little around here. What did Ultima say about why that check didn't come?"

Boomer was quiet for such a long time that she thought he must have fallen asleep, but when she regarded his face in the dawn's dairy light, she saw that his eyes were as wide as pinballs. "What are you thinking?" she asked.

"Just studying on what it is that I'd like a gander at but can't see because the world don't have it in stock."

A sudden icy wind razored through the persimmon branches. Elsewhere, they might call the wind Mariah, but here its name was Something Fishy.

"*Why*, Boomer?"

By the time he got around to confessing that Ultima wanted to market further examples of his art, half of Manhattan was at breakfast, and a persimmon famine was abroad in the land.

Summer and the check for the turkey arrived on the same day, although in separate envelopes. The check so distracted the Petways that they momentarily forgot to sweat.

(That same sweltering mid-June Friday had found the five pilgrims—who'd scooted, toddled, and bounced across the Rockies at the pokey pace of 4.2 miles per night—stuffed into a prairie-dog hole, taking shelter from a line of tornadoes that was coiled on the horizon like the bedsprings of Bluebeard. When an impatient Painted Stick ventured out to investigate, a twister snatched him up, lifting him more than a thousand feet in the air. According to Conch Shell, who had peeked at the whole thing, the stick beat the lightning right out of the funnel, poked the cyclone in the ribs so hard that it set him down not an arm's length from where it had picked him up. "Goodness! If that had been Mr. Sock," said a flabbergasted Can o' Beans, "he would've blown all the way to Panama." "How the hell do you know?" asked Dirty Sock.)

The turkey had sold for two hundred and fifty thousand dollars. Ultima Sommervell scooped off exactly half of that (dealers had come to regularly charge artists commissions of fifty percent). Of Boomer's half, the gallery withheld nearly forty percent for state and federal taxes. That left seventy-five grand. Boomer's mother needed to be placed in a nursing home, so he contributed twenty thousand toward that. Over Ellen Cherry's strenuous objections, he donated five thousand to the Reverend Buddy Winkler for some religious project that had yet to be adequately defined. He paid nine months' rent in advance at the Ansonia, for the security that was in it: that amounted to eighteen thousand. He handed Ellen Cherry five hundred for art supplies and five hundred for new clothes. The remaining thirty-six thousand was deposited with Manufacturers Hanover Trust in a joint account. Most of it was slated for Boomer's welding shop.

By the end of June, every artist who could afford to, which is to say, every artist who mattered, had left town for Woodstock, Provincetown, or the shores of Maine. The dealers went to the Hamptons. The collectors went to Europe. There were no arty parties, no gallery openings. Artless, or at least, artistless, New York itself went on display, a kinetic sculpture fashioned from taxicabs, steam, and garbage. As the summer wore on, garbage climbing to the sun, steam wisping from each and every armpit, it became increasingly difficult to distinguish homeless mental patients from ordinary citizens driven by stench and humidity to howl in the streets. In the Ansonia apartment, the air conditioner raged like the ghost of Admiral Byrd, but Ellen Cherry hung limp and was often close to whimpering.

One morning Boomer had gone out, ostensibly to check on some shop space that was for rent, only to return within the hour carrying a secondhand trench coat, a couple of yards of nondescript fabric, and a small bag of needles and thread.

"I'm gonna make something," he'd announced. "I'm not saying it's art, but it's something I've always had a hankering to see."

He worked daily, he worked diligently, he worked merrily, whistling as he worked, the way Ellen Cherry used to do. *Used* to do. For now she found that she could not work at all. The more involved Boomer became with his project, his stupid sewing, the more alienated she became from her brushes. And from him.

"What exactly's eatin' you, honey?" Patsy asked her.

Ellen Cherry sighed into the heat-sticky phone. "I don't know, mama. I can't paint and I can't fuck and I'm angry all the time. Now I know how a critic must feel."

While Ellen Cherry stewed, Boomer sewed. He sewed through the day, and he sewed through the night. He sewed through July, and he sewed through August. He sewed five hundred secret pockets into that trench coat, and in each pocket he hid a message, each message encoded in a different code of his own invention. It was the spy coat to end all spy coats, and when it was done, his grin was so wide he could have swallowed a Robert Ludlum paperback without bruising his palate.

Ultima Sommervell returned to Manhattan shortly after Labor Day, whereupon Boomer showed her his spy coat with its five hundred secret pockets with their five hundred cryptic messages in five hundred different codes. Ultima found the spy coat fraught, simply fraught, with social significance. She found it a witty and ingenious commentary on the dangerous schoolboy shenanigans of superpower gamesmanship. She locked the coat in her vault and offered Boomer a one-man show the following autumn. The show would be mounted in her SoHo gallery, where all the action was.

Ellen Cherry took the big news gracelessly. She, in fact, spun on her heel and fled the apartment. She walked to the bank, withdrew a thousand dollars, and flew, without toothbrush or a change of underpants, to Virginia. For two days, she cried on her mother's shoulder. Then, fortified with Patsy-wisdom, she flew back to New York, prepared not only to accept Boomer's success (as unfair as it might be) but also to assist him in every way possible during the year that he'd been allotted to prepare for his (undeserved) exhibition.

In her hasty exodus, she had neglected to take a key. When there was no response to her knock, she had to get Raoul to let her into the apartment. Raoul was aware that Boomer had decamped, but he didn't let on. Keeping time with his fingers to some inaudible rhythm, Raoul just looked at Ellen Cherry as if he could tell that her panties were dirty.

There was no note, no forwarding address, no nothing. Nearly a month went by before she learned that Boomer had rented a loft in the Bowery and purchased a new Ford van. It didn't take her anywhere near that long to learn that their bank account had been closed.

When at last he turned up at the Ansonia, he was neither sheepish nor defiant. In even tones, and with no more than two or three tugs at his beret, he told her that he was sorry but that her good ol' welder had found him some other fish that he must fry and that the aroma of their frying obviously had been making her sick. She could only agree, but suggested that she might grow accustomed to the smell and that she probably could be of service to him in filleting the fish. "Even if one of 'em is Ultima?" he asked. She bit her lip and shook her head no, but inquired if there might also be room in the pan for her. "If you shear off some of that hair," he joked. She smiled, but she was still biting her lip.

In the seasons that followed, they made several tenuous attempts at reconciliation. Over the winter and into spring, they "dated," enjoying each other's physical presence on the dance floor and in bed but rarely focusing on their problem. Perhaps Ellen Cherry was just too ashamed of her feelings to air them. As for Boomer, well, he had a new life—a life that was supposed to have been *hers*—and he was as protective of it as she was resentful. In their superficial conversations, the subject of art was strictly taboo, and when once they did broach it, in early May, the result was a bitter quarrel that put an end to the dating, sending Ellen Cherry to Isaac & Ishmael's in search of a job and Boomer back to his Bowery loft in pursuit of something that scared him (or puzzled him) so badly he simply had to lock horns with it. And never, not once, did he reveal to her that the five hundred messages in the five hundred secret pockets all said the exact same thing in five hundred separate codes. They said, "Randolph Petway III loves Ellen Cherry Charles."

Six months later . . .

The invitation to Boomer Petway's one-man show Ellen Cherry ripped into tiny pieces, which she let sift into a pile on the coffee table. When she threw herself upon the sofa to have a good cry, half of the pieces in the pile turned into snowflakes, half turned into sparks. The sparks melted the snowflakes, the snowflakes extinguished the sparks—and in the dynamics of their interaction, in the dialogue between snowflake and spark, in the exchange of energy between melt and extinguish, a scrap of wolfmother wallpaper was formed.

The scrap was as silver-white as birch bark, it was tattered and curled at its ends like birch bark, and when a sudden draft blew through the tatters and curls, it made a sound like a war canoe moving downstream, like kites fighting, like shadow puppets mating, like a magician's sleeve disgorging live doves and aces, like a pregnant scarecrow dragging her dugs through the corn, or more exactly, like veils being stripped from the gyrating body of a dancing girl and flung with studied abandon to the temple floor.

Because of her bitter sobbing, Ellen Cherry heard none of this, and by the time she got things out of her system and extricated herself from her sofa of silly sorrow, the noisy scraps had turned back into pieces of shredded invitation. These she scooped up and carried to the garbage bag beneath the sink, where, without looking, she sent them fluttering down upon a surprised creature at the bottom of the sack, as if she had unintentionally sponsored a ticker tape parade to honor a cockroach astronaut: "One small step for a man, one giant leap for mankind, eight itty-bitty speedy little steps for the first stowaway to the moon."

At work the next morning, Ellen Cherry seemed to be walking around with her head in a cud of licorice gum. So dark and sticky was her mood that Abu and Spike postponed their tennis date in order to keep watch on her. They sat at the corner table sipping sugary tea and conversing about Jerusalem, but their habitually vigilant eyes, different in magnitude and hue, monitored her every move— not that she had to make that many moves to oversee a luncheon crowd that could have fit into a rubber life raft and still have left room for the suppressed flatulence of a diplomat.

It had been a fairly rough week in the environs of Jerusalem, a city that never has been a tub of laughs, a rough week for Arabs and Jews alike. When Israeli troops used excessive force to break up a nationalistic demonstration at a West Bank university, a Palestinian student retaliated by lobbing a fire bomb at a passing car, killing a woman passenger and critically burning her husband and three young children. Jewish settlers in the area responded with a vandalizing rampage through a Palestinian refugee camp that was already up to its brown eyes in misery.

"I'm thinking it's the stones," said Spike. "So many stones in the Middle East, already! When you got that many rocks, it's too easy to pick one up and throw it at your neighbor. In olden times, everybody bounced rocks off other people's noodles. Nowadays, Molotov cocktails they throw. Throw, throw, throw. It's a tradition, this throwing."

"From stones to Molotov cocktails to nuclear missiles. Yes," agreed Abu, "it is a sad but logical progression. You know, the Jews' most sacred place in Jerusalem was erected upon the Moriah *rock*. Today, we Arabs' most sacred place is called 'the Dome of the *Rock*.' And Jesus reportedly said of Peter, 'Upon this *rock* I will build my church.' Could we say that in matters of religion we all have rocks in our heads?"

"Hoo boy. By me you could say that."

"Do you ever wonder how the history of the region might have differed if its hills had been forested and green? With time and effort, a man can fashion a weapon from the wood of a tree, but a rock is a weapon to begin with. Palestine is nature's own arsenal. No, Jerusalem is not caught between a rock and a hard place. Jerusalem *is* a rock and a hard place."

"Jerusalem is getting it in the neck from geology, okay. But, Abu, you tell me: there is a more beautiful city somewhere? You tell me you wouldn't be full from joy what if this morning you could walk down its streets? Ha!"

Spike received no argument there. "The light, Spike, remember the light?" Unconsciously, Abu tapped his radiant nose. "We can complain about rocks until the sheep come home, but it is the golden light of Jerusalem that holds us, that draws us back. Ah, to live in that glow is a religious experience all by itself. No wonder our brothers go crazy there. Even you and I have been made a little crazed by it. It is almost too intense for the soul to bear."

While the proprietors of the I & I were thus engaged, Ellen Cherry went about her duties in a solitary gloom. Every droop, every quiver, every scowl, every silent sigh of hers was registered by the two men, and when at last her shift was complete, they summoned her to their table.

"Do you hear, darlink, what the new dishwasher wants to be called? An 'underwater ceramics engineer,' already! Abu doesn't believe his ears. He doesn't realize what a big shot he used to be in the kitchen. Ha!"

Ellen Cherry tried to laugh, but her chuckle was as thin as the cream on powdered milk. They sat her down, poured her a glass of Kuwaiti wine, and insisted that she explain why her aura looked like the ring around a coal miner's collar. She told them everything.

Without hesitation, Spike Cohen assumed personal responsibility for her suffering. He patted her hand, patted her shoulder, reached down where her legs were crossed and patted the shoe upon the foot that she was dangling. "Now that you tell me the reason behind your sourpuss, I'm going to be bringing the smiles to you, darlink. Plain talk: friends in the art business you need, friends in the art business I got! Okay? We're talking wholesale, we're talking retail. I'm getting for you your own gallery in what to be showing your nice pictures."

Abu Hadee was slower to respond. When he did, he said, "My dear, I think that you are looking at this all wrong. In regard to your estranged husband's exhibition, you really ought to be more positive."

"But, Mr. Hadee, it isn't fair!"

"And who ever said the world was fair, little lady? Maybe death is fair, but certainly not life. We must accept unfairness as proof of the sublime flux of existence, the capricious music of the universe—and go on about our tasks. . . ."

"Abu, you know from nothing. Such injustice—"

"Quiet, Spike. What does Boomer's success, or lack of it, have to do with Ellen Cherry's art? Forgive me, but she reminds me of those crybabies—professional athletes and entertainers are the worst—who are always whining because somebody else in the same position is earning more money than they are. Greed compounded by egomania. It should not concern us what rewards others may reap."

"Okay, but it isn't a question of Boomer getting more recognition or a better show than me. I haven't got recognition or a show at all."

"Only last week you informed me that you have hardly painted since you arrived in New York. Perhaps you need to pay less attention to Boomer's business and concentrate on your own. Rejoice that someone about whom you care has done well. If his work is inferior and undeserving, then let that inspire you to do even better. Take it as a challenge, not an insult. As my father used to say, 'Do not turn slights into bedsores.' A little poem, eh? Rejoice! Paint pictures! Paint, perhaps, something to cover this affliction of bamboo that causes our Middle Eastern restaurant to resemble the hut where Confucius composed fortune cookies. Scenes of Jerusalem would fit the bill."

Between the sympathy of Cohen and the exhortations of Hadee, Ellen Cherry gathered enough traction to spin her tires out of the mud. She thanked her employers, squeezed them, and then set a course for Fifth Avenue, where she suspected the example of Turn Around Norman might give a jet assist to her creakily rising mood. Could she have imagined what other examples were lurking there, there's no predicting at what speeds or in what directions her mood might have spun.

As it was, passing the Japanese restaurants along East Forty-ninth Street, she was reminded that disposable diapers had been invented by Eskimos. It was true. They made them out of seaweed. *Someone with a good seaweed supplier ought to open a combination diaper service and sushi bar,* she thought. *It would be only appropriate for the menu to stress bottom fish, but good taste might preclude the listing of yellowtail.*

Spoon was the first to recognize her. "Look!" she squealed. "Look there! It's *her*."

"Look where, Miss Spoon?" asked Can o' Beans. "To whom are you referring?"

The stocking saw her next. "Well, hang me by the chimney with care!" it exclaimed. "Damned if it ain't. I'd recognize that haystack anywheres."

"Haystack?" asked Can o' Beans. Then he/she spotted a careless harvest of hair-sheaves bobbing in the crowd along Fifth Avenue, and immediately understood. "Amazing!" he/she marveled. "My Miss

Charles! Imagine seeing her again! Seeing her in the swarm of New York City! Do you know how long I sat on her shelves?"

The three objects pressed closer to the grid of the grate.

"She's stopping," said Spoon. "I think she's watching our gentleman."

"I'd better notify the leaders," said Can o' Beans, and he/she dropped down from the window grate and wobbled away into the half-lit gloom of the cathedral cellar.

As dusty as it was dark, the sub-basement of St. Patrick's was littered with cardboard boxes, carpet ends, coal buckets, snow shovels, flower baskets, discarded hymnals, blown fuses, and broken sections of pews. To the mobile inanimates, it offered a profusion of hiding places in the event that a custodian or somebody should come snooping around, but so far no one ever had. All in all, it constituted a much safer refuge than most of the barns, silos, junkyards, burnt-out warehouses, pigsties, toolsheds, cemeteries, abandoned cars, freeway ramps, groves, thickets, culverts, and swamps where the quintet had rested days during its eighteen-month march from the Far West to the Atlantic.

Their trek had been long, slow, and perilous, and had taken its toll on each of them. Driven by a mutually held vision of their destiny in the Third Temple of Jerusalem, Conch Shell and Painted Stick had never wavered. Simple curiosity had kept the banged-up bean can going. Dirty Sock, frayed and burr infested, persisted because he thought it would have been sissy to give up. "A winner never quits and a quitter never wins," he reminded himself on those many occasions when he felt like jumping into a Salvation Army clothing bin and forgetting it all, although he lacked any clear notion of what it was that he might be winning. As for Spoon, her delicate features tarnished and scratched, her impetus resulted in large measure from the gratitude she felt to the Virgin Mary for having answered her prayers and saving Can o' Beans.

To the secularly inclined, it was Dirty Sock who deserved credit for that rescue. It was the sock, after all, that had noticed the welding shop on the outskirts of that little Wyoming town on whose opposite side they had said good-bye to the bean tin. And it was the sock that had rather casually suggested that it had learned enough about welding during its time with Boomer Petway to seal the can's split seam, if only there was a way to physically manipulate the equipment.

Throughout the day, concealed in a deserted chicken coop (a place that still stank not only of old hen droppings but of the incessant imbecilic cluck-cluck platitudinizing that would make chickens the perfect constituency for any number of aspiring demagogues), the objects mulled it over. That night, instead of continuing eastward, they backtracked to the churchyard, where, to Spoon's overflowing joy, they found Can o' Beans present and reasonably intact, although industriously beset by a determined battalion of ants. Talk about a work ethic! Ants don't even sleep, perchance to dream. They are the original workaholics. An eminent social scientist has offered a ten-thousand-dollar reward to anyone who will bring him a lazy, laid-back ant. It would be worth every penny, for it would demonstrate that in our unspoken but desperate competition with insects, there is still hope for the human race, especially the Japanese.

At any rate, Conch Shell splashed puddle water on the ants, and Painted Stick dragged Can o' Beans away. They maneuvered him/her through the dark village streets to the welding shop, which they entered by smashing a window.

From the igniting of the oxyacetylene torch to the puddling of the filler rod, from the tacking of the can's separated sides to the forming of a lap joint, Boomer's lost sock knew exactly what needed to be done—and under its expert direction, Painted Stick proved dexterous enough (just barely) to do it.

Once the metal was fused, the seam in the can was actually stronger than when it had come fresh from the factory. Dirty Sock, having absorbed some of Boomer's pride along with his proficiency, insisted that they dress the weld, smoothing down the nicks, burrs, and blisters with a disk sander-grinder. That operation was soon aborted, however, for the sander-grinder threw off a shower of sparks and debris that frightened Spoon, threatened to set Dirty Sock afire, and caused Conch Shell to worry that they might attract attention from passing motorists.

So, Can o' Beans went out into the world with a rough, high-relief scar running from his/her top to his/her bottom. Along with the deep dimpling dents and the shambles of what had been a label, the can was not a pretty sight. But it was safe, healthy, free—and back with its comrades on the road to Jerusalem. If happiness was daylight saving time, Can o' Beans would have been the twenty-first of June.

"Mr. Sock, dear Mr. Sock, how can I ever thank you?"

"Ferget it, perfesser. Now we're even."

From the very first moment that the inanimates had looked through the street-level grate of their new refuge and spotted Turn Around Norman, he had held a maximum of fascination for them. Of all the human beings that they, singularly or together, had ever encountered, he was the most like them. Heretofore, they had neither known nor imagined a human animal who operated on something so similar to object time. Maybe the man or woman in the street could not register his movements, his glacial rotations, but to the five inanimates, they were overt, familiar, and up to speed.

His movements may have conveyed a shock of recognition, but the street performer himself was a novelty to them. He caught their fancy for the inverse reasons that the animated cookie jar in the first Disney cartoons had caught the fancy of human moviegoers. It was anthropomorphism in reverse. And it was refreshing.

Having met not a single priest nor priestess of the Goddess during their cross-country odyssey, having observed but a mere handful of people who openly expressed the values of the Great Mother—who demonstrated affection, respect, or concern for forests, rivers, deserts, marshes, and the moon—Conch Shell and, especially, Painted Stick had lost much faith in the American race. So, although Turn Around Norman in no apparent way embodied the wild old ways, still he was such an exception to what they perceived as the contemporary human rule that shell and stick both paid him the compliment of daily attention. As for the others, they were just about ga-ga: ready to line up for him like pimpled schoolgirls lining up for a rock star.

Beyond identity and entertainment, there was also a practical interest in Norman. The objects had reached the edge of the continent. Between them and Jerusalem were over five thousand miles of open sea. They could not envision how they might escape the crush of New York City (where even midnight had wide eyes) and conquer the broad Atlantic without aid. Painted Stick and Conch Shell had grown used to human assistance in the past, had come to rely on it just as many in the priesthood had come to rely on them, and despite their disappointment in modern Americans, they maintained an inclination to seek some kind of human help. This strange fellow, who looked like a cross between a cherub and a fiend, and who behaved like a cross between a stone idol and a teapot, was a long shot, but he was all they had.

Then, Ellen Cherry Charles appeared.

In the dimmest corner of the dim sub-basement of St. Patrick's Cathedral, in the darkest grotto to be found within that granite and marble reef, that atoll exuded by the affluently pious and in whose crust so many guilts and longings lay embedded; in a snuggery so somber and deep that no ray of prayer had ever penetrated to it nor any nun come there to secretly dance the boogaloo; in soft, safe shadow insured by obscurity against the knife edges of votive candle flames and the artillery of flashbulbs that fired when newly wed or newly dead celebrities made their exits through the God-size doors; down there where God's little vermin, excluded by force from the congregation, partook of his dank hospitality; there in a homogeneous, socialistic blackness that suppressed the rights of individual colors for "the greater good," there Painted Stick and Conch Shell huddled together in conference or embrace.

"What do you suppose them two do when they slip off like that?" Dirty Sock had once inquired. "They up to something *cee*-lestial, as they call it, or is it"—he grinned at Spoon—"s-e-x?"

"What's the difference?" Can o' Beans had asked.

"Probably none where you're concerned. You don't even know which sex you are."

"I happen to be both. Which, I daresay, is two more than you. Besides," he/she huffed, "gender is not the same thing as sex."

"Yes, Sock," the spoon had chimed in. "Just because technically you once had a mate doesn't mean you've had experience in carnal matters."

"And I suppose you have?" He had leered at her fiercely.

"Certainly not!" she protested, and if any memory of jelly—the way that jelly jiggled or the way that jelly teased—was aroused in her, she promptly purged it of possible erotic connotation by announcing that she served the Blessed Virgin and would likely choose celibacy even were she of that animate nature where such a choice would have been more than academic.

As for Can o' Beans, he/she, at that point, might have accused Dirty Sock of being jealous of Painted Stick, but he/she was reminded of his/her eternal debt to the foul footwear and had backed off. "Mr. Sock is less mean than grumpy," he/she told him/herself, "and while meanness is a function of the insensitive, grumpiness is merely a function of the dissatisfied."

In any case, returning to the moment, whatever it was that the ancient fetishes were doing there in the lightless corner, sheltered by the splayed dog leg of a long-cold furnace, Can o' Beans interrupted them. Too excited to be discreet, he/she blurted out the news of the sighting of Miss Charles and bade them return to the grate at once.

"Is she still there?" the can called as it doddered near.

"Oh, yes," answered Spoon. "She's watching him. She seems entranced."

"That's her," said Can o' Beans, nodding, with a mashed and scalloped rim, toward Ellen Cherry. "She knew all three of us. Miss Spoon, she knew intimately. And she's an artist, not your usual, orthodox young woman. If we're really going to dare to risk human contact, I couldn't imagine a more likely candidate than she. I mean, what do we know, really, about that strange fellow out there?"

"That is her on the steps? The pretty one with the unfortunate hair?"

"Exactly. We've got to do something. We've got to act." Sauce gurgling, Can o' Beans was uncharacteristically bouncing up and down. "We can't just let her walk away."

"Calm down, dear friend. That woman will return. She has been here almost every day."

"She has?"

"Really and truly?"

"No shit?"

Conch Shell laughed. "You three have been so intent upon our semianimate gentleman that you have completely overlooked your old mistress. She comes here of an afternoon, late, about this time. She stands there and fixes upon him almost as steadfastly as you."

"There exists a connection 'twixt those two," said Painted Stick. "I cannot suppose what it is; it may be no more than the force that pulls a planet into the path of a star. Yet, where our future voyage is concerned, I take it as an omen most fair."

"And I," said Conch Shell. "The fact that she has such interest in *him* could mean that she may be capable of accepting *us*. In any case, she will be back on the morrow, never fear. And the morrow after. We have ample time to meditate on her potential service to us."

The lot of them nodded in harmony. They grew quiet, pressed to the sooty, rusty grate, watching Ellen Cherry watching Turn Around Norman.

"You know," Spoon whispered after a while, "she doesn't seem as merry as she used to be."

Conch Shell was wrong. Ellen Cherry failed to reappear on the morrow—or the morrow after. The bean can and the spoon panicked and had to be assured over and over by Conch Shell that their erstwhile mistress would, indeed, return. Dirty Sock didn't seem to care. "I don't know where you birds get the notion that that woman's some kinda fairy godmother that's gonna whisk us off first-class to Jerusalem. Personally, I think she's damn near a bimbo."

"Sock!"

"Now, Mr. Stocking . . ."

"Hey, she took off and left us in that killer cave. If it wasn't for the luck of the draw, I'd be right now up to my ass in dry rot. And don't forget, little Spoonzie, what she was doing in that cave."

"She's a married woman."

"Uh-huh." Dirty Sock broke into an artificial falsetto. "Call me Jezebel! Oh, please, *please* call me Jezebel."

"That's unfair." The bean can drew up its contents with indignation. "Jezebel was an honorable woman."

"So? What's that gotta do with it? And if Miz Charles is so all-fired married, what's she doing here every day, making eyes at that ol' boy on the street? Where's Boomer Petway, that's what I'd like to know."

Like the mother of a bratty brood, Conch Shell scolded, separated, and soothed. She promised them that they might expect Miss Charles's imminent encore. And she hinted that Painted Stick and she were formulating a plan that would utilize their past relationship with the woman to their best advantage. "Now, be good and watch the grate," she said.

Not surprisingly, Ellen Cherry did turn up at St. Patrick's again, although it was not for several days. Her previous visit had seen her sail a twenty-dollar bill into Turn Around Norman's donation box, only to sense immediate disapproval. Norman said nothing, naturally, nor did he make any gesture, yet from his eyes he projected rebuke, projected it so strongly that Ellen Cherry felt it like an actual slap on the wrist. *Maybe I've been hanging around too long and tipping too much,* she thought. *Maybe he's worried that he's got himself a groupie.* She was pleased, though, that he'd become aware of her. She doubted that he had taken particular notice of her before.

A second factor in her decision to boycott Fifth Avenue for a while was the apprehension that she might bump into Buddy again. The preacher had been on TV recently, saying spooky biblical things about the latest bloodshed in Israel, saying those things with a kind of smugness, trying to make the shooting and beating of Palestinian teenagers sound peachy, unavoidable, and right as rain. The idea that some holy prophecy was being fulfilled and that true Christians should be jubilant about it, she found repulsive, and she dreaded having to face the so-called kinsman of hers who was perpetuating that idea.

Thus, for a couple of reasons, she thought it would behoove her to curtail her trips up Forty-ninth Street for at least a week, and she made a vow to that effect. In four days, however, she was back on the cathedral steps. It happened to be the evening that Boomer's show was to open at the Sommervell Gallery, and if she couldn't rely on Turn Around Norman for distraction, for comfort, there was no telling what she might do. She might even get drunk and go to the opening.

Braced against the November chill, hands in coat pockets, legs apart, Ellen Cherry found herself turning with Turn Around Norman, very gradually altering her position so that his back was always toward her. *It may be best that he doesn't see me,* she thought. *I wouldn't want to make him self-conscious.* Deprived of the ambivalent allure of his face—that plowed moon sewn with seeds of nettle and narcissus, that pink grapefruit carved with an assassin's dagger—she was free now to concentrate on his feet, and she focused on his grubby Converses, sometimes separately, sometimes both together, alert to their position vis-à-vis one another, vis-à-vis a crack in the pavement. Yet, even as those positions shifted, she was unable to intercept a single signal from brain to muscle or to detect the slightest violation of skeletal freeze. They were like potentates of dirty ice, his sneakers, borne in a circle upon the backs of heated molecules, passengers aboard an imperceptible subhuman squirm.

As incredible as it was, one wouldn't think it exactly compelling entertainment for a girl who'd grown up watching action-packed spectacles on screens large and small—not even for a girl who had transformed each and every show with her eye game and made it her own. In truth, it wasn't what Norman did that bewitched her, but rather that he bothered to do it at all. Certainly, there was no demand for what he did, less demand than for her paintings. On those rare occasions when it dawned on passersby that Norman was performing, they shook their heads, muttered, and walked away, frowning or smiling, according to their character. Should anyone linger, it usually was to ridicule. The black youths who danced for coins in the area had taken to taunting him ("Why you dance so slow, fat boy? Where you music?"), sometimes poking him painfully in the ribs and stomach with fingers or unopened switchblades. Maybe they wanted his place on the street, maybe they simply didn't know how else to respond to an exhibition that pure, that unmotivated by any ambition that they could share or comprehend. One tended to lose one's bearings in the presence of willful and persistent acts of craziness, and the more gentle the act, the crazier it seemed, as if rage and violence, being closer to the norm, were easier to accommodate.

But was he actually crazy? Ellen Cherry was in no hurry to find out. For now, she was content with the inspiration that he provided, and the oblique solace. *This,* she told herself, *this, and not what's happening tonight at Ultima Sommervell's gallery, or any other gallery, this lonely, uncompromising, obsessive tug-of-war with presumed reality, this is what art is all about.*

The bustle of shoppers and tourists sometimes threatened to knock her off the steps and sweep her away into the jaws of this or that commercial transaction; and when the bustle finished with her, the bluster took over, for November had invaded Manhattan with troops of whirling crystal. Still, she stood there, hands in coat pockets, feet wide apart, until she sensed that the performance was abating, at which point she left abruptly, choosing, for once, not to make a donation. If she had offended him with her previous largess, she wished now to draw the sting out of the offense. Moreover, with no financial help from Boomer, who had sunk everything into his loft and his show, and with tips at the I & I almost as scarce as pearls in Cracker Jacks, she really couldn't afford to be generous.

Departing, she fretted for a moment about his health (he wore a scarf, now, and woolen mittens, but no sweater or overcoat), then reasoned that he must have been on the street long before she knew of him and that it was highly presumptuous to assume that his survival in any way depended upon her. She crossed Fifth Avenue, heading for the Seventh Avenue IRT station at Fiftieth Street, and did not look back.

When she had disappeared into the grit and crystal that seemed to be grating against each other in the wind, Spoon and Can o' Beans became mildly distressed. "Do not worry," urged Conch Shell. "Patience, please."

"Yes, Can o' Beans," said Spoon, "we really should be patient. What's our rush? We're objects, don't forget. Besides, even if Miss Charles can help us get to Jerusalem, the last news we overheard from there had it torn by strife."

"That was weeks ago. When we were in the suburbs. The radios that pass by here play nothing but rap music. Sounds like somebody feeding a rhyming dictionary to a popcorn popper."

"While shoving 'em both up a guard dog's ass," put in Dirty Sock.

In spite of him/herself, Can o' Beans had to chuckle.

Spoon ignored the indelicacy. "Well, I'm sure conditions are still hazardous in Israel. I, for one, don't relish getting caught in one of those violent demonstrations. I can wait. We've come a long, long way, and as our leaders say, we can use a good rest. You, especially, ma'am/sir."

"Doubtlessly, you're correct, Miss Spoon. Every indication is that the Third Temple is not yet on the drawing board, that it may be years, even decades away. Were it built and were we there, what would our role be, anyhow? We're just along for the ride, you and Mr. Sock and I. Still, I'd hate to miss that ride."

"We won't miss a thing, silly. Trust our leaders. And relax."

"You have my word," said the bean can. Then, it pushed its misshapen bulk to the grate and looked anxiously, wistfully at the congested, cacophonous avenue where Ellen Cherry had vanished in the dusk.

Can o' Beans knew something that Spoon did not. He/she knew that if worse came to worst, Conch Shell was capable of swimming the Atlantic Ocean; was capable, too, of towing her navigator behind her. She could tow Painted Stick, but not the rest of them. Therefore, it was the rest of them, the American objects, that were in danger of holding up progress. Since there was surely a limit to how long the stick might endure delay, there was a definite possibility that sooner or later the three of them might have to be left behind in New York. Can o' Beans had been left once. He/she didn't want to chew on that cold bone again. That was why he/she was anxious.

It's a foolish being, a being without vision, who has not formulated a contingency plan, however, and Can o' Beans's contingency plan was this: should they fail to secure the aid they needed to cross the sea, should he/she be deprived of Jerusalem and the momentous events that were promised there, then as second choice, as compensation, and for whatever motive, he/she intended somehow, some way, to get back into the life of Ellen Cherry Charles. That was why he/she was wistful.

The subway spat out Ellen Cherry onto the cement welcome mat of a neighborhood bar. Not wishing to insult Fate, which obviously had orchestrated the scene, directing the flow of the crowd to deposit her at that particular place and none other, she went dutifully inside and ordered a shot of Wild Turkey. That's a good girl.

In the time that it took to sip that lone jigger, three different men tried to pick her up. Although she spurned their advances, she was grateful for them. They took her mind off the opening at the Sommervell Gallery, nudging it onto a sidetrack that was slightly less hazardous. Slightly.

Winking at her rejected suitors, she paid up and left without escort. She stopped off at a certain shop on Broadway and made a certain purchase. Five minutes later, carrying a small, plain brown paper bag, she entered the lobby of the Ansonia.

Raoul greeted her. "Hey, Miz Charl! You home from Jerusalem?" He grinned and tipped his immaculate hat.

Ellen Cherry paused and looked him over. Raoul was cultivating a mustache. Wispy little whiskers, as skinny and forlorn as African cattle, wandered the plain beneath his nose. She imagined how they might graze her lips, her nipples, her ticklish belly; how they might assemble at the salt lick that she could offer them. Before she knew it, she was undressing him with her eyes. She didn't intend it, yet she couldn't stop. And when, in her mind, she freed the skimpy Fruta del Telar briefs from the erection upon which they were snagged like a dishtowel caught on a railroad spike, she actually feared that she might swoon. She was so wet she felt as if she had sat on a tomato.

She was virtually at the point of reaching out for him, plastic "brass" buttons, porkpie hat and all, when he said, "Hey, I'm jealous, man."

Startled from reverie, she asked weakly, "What'd you say?"

"Some rich movie star sending you flowers, man. This your birthday?" From behind the desk, he retrieved a long, green floral delivery box, bound with green twine. "You know this Romeo? Man, I'm so jealous."

Ellen Cherry accepted the box. Barely locomoting, locomoting at a speed slightly faster than Turn Around Norman's rate but slightly slower than Painted Stick's, she moved across the black and white checkerboard tiles toward the elevator, opening a tiny envelope as she walked. The card read, "To our most favorite artist," and was signed, "Spike Cohen and Roland Abu Hadee."

Oh, well. She glanced over her shoulder at Raoul. "Thanks," she called. Then, patting her brand-new vibrator, sleek and subservient in its protective sack, she boarded the car—leaving Raoul on the verge of composing one of those trite romantic lyrics that, lacking the ivory flame of great poetry, nevertheless stay with a person forever, like a scar, a tattoo, or third-grade arithmetic.

The next morning started up like a fine German car. It was Ellen Cherry's day off, and she slumbered late. When, at last, she was fully awake, motor purring, she wiped the vibrator with a damp cloth, kissed it, and secreted it in a drawer where cotton underpants lived simply but proudly, without envy of satin or lace. *"Merci, mon capitaine,"* she said to the vibrator. "Thanks for a lovely evening."

She prepared an authentic breakfast, the kind God intended for mortals to eat: eggs and bacon and grits and toast. Gone now were the chocolate doughnuts and cold pizza of breakfasts past, gone to the Bowery, where decadence could always find a parking place. Gone, too, the *leban zabadi,* the creamy Egyptian yogurt of recent morns—but the fact that she'd skipped *leban zabadi* at breakfast meant that she would likely have to eat it for lunch. Leftovers from the I & I were proving essential to her survival. Once, she'd even brought home *baba ghanoug.*

It was time to bathe, and she seriously considered inviting Captain Vibrator to bathe with her. "Maybe I should wait until I know him better," she said to the vase of roses on the breakfast table, the roses that Spike and Abu had sent. She bathed with the roses, instead. They floated in the water around her, all one dozen of them, rubbing velvet faces against her, sometimes pricking her with their tiny thorns. "Acupuncture," she said. "I needed that." Petals came loose like pages from a magazine about aphid life-styles, only to be trapped in webs spun by spiders of soap. Ellen Cherry pasted wet rose petals on her nipples, plastered one under her nose like a comedian's mustache. *"Springtime for Hitler,"* she said. Outside, it was November, and the margarita glasses of the skyscrapers were salted with frost.

Sanitary now, and most casually attired, she wrapped the drowned roses in newspaper and laid them with the garbage. "They wouldn't have lasted anyway," she told herself, drying her hands on her sweatshirt. "Not for long. They were grown in a hothouse. Hothouse flowers wither fast, just like hothouse art." She was referring to the art that was grown under the artificial lights of fad and fashion, overly fertilized with personal ambition and deprived of those weathers that evolve strong systems in the slow, hard garden of belief. Perhaps she was referring to the kind of art on display at that moment at Ultima Sommervell's gallery. She didn't expound. Rather, she shut the door on the roses, consigning them to oblivion beneath the sink, and set up her easel. Mr. Hadee was right: it was time to stop hurting and start painting.

Since moving to New York, she had been gradually abandoning her old ideas about the nobility of suffering. The more suffering she witnessed—and the New York art world was wormy with it—the less she subscribed to it. Some pain came with the territory, of course, but most suffering artists were narcissists, she was starting to believe. Narcissistic artists seemed attached to agony, to the writhe and the whine, to the yowl, the howl, and the botched suicide; their fits of despair (preferably in public) carefully timed to impress the serious-ness of their aesthetic upon critics and collectors. In the past, she'd embraced the suffering artist image, she supposed, but in her heart she had always considered artisthood more of a privilege than a curse, and those to whom the creative life brought only misery, she now invited to go into food service. The world could always use another waitress, another fry cook.

Upon the easel, she set the last canvas that she had completed, a reasonably realistic portrait of Boomer Petway, executed from mem-ory two weeks earlier. Impulsively, with a loaded brush, she gave him the long, coiled tongue of a frog. She stepped back and squinted. And she saw that it was good.

In addition to the frog tongue, in whose banderole she painted a fly, Ellen Cherry gave Boomer the black, bumpy tongue of a chow dog. Then she rooted in his mouth the soda-straw tongue of a butterfly and the Y-flick tongue of a boa. She gave him a woodpecker's tongue, arrowheaded and barbed; an ox tongue, muscular, broad, and hung with drool; and, finally, the shy, happy tongue that the porpoise employs to push the waves to shore. After the seventh tongue, she rested. Then she began to work on his ears.

There was nothing disrespectful in her alteration of the portrait. The tongues lacked any psychological or symbolic significance. It was a painterly act, a purely visual experiment. "Don't take it personally," she said to Boomer's picture. "I'm just having fun."

"Why didn't you come to my opening last night?" Boomer's pic-ture said back to her.

Obviously, the picture didn't speak. Even with seven tongues, it was mute, as all pictures are. However, so certain was Ellen Cherry that Boomer would be confronting her with that very question, perhaps before the day was through, that her unconscious mind forced the words from the picture's mouth.

The words had an accusatory tone. After she heard them, after she *imagined* that she heard them, she couldn't paint anymore. She laid down her brushes. A lot of *leban zabadi* would run under the bridge before she would pick them up again.

In the lobby of the Ansonia, there was a public telephone. To demonstrate her independence from Patsy, the newlywed Ellen Cherry had elected not to install a phone when she and her groom had moved into the apartment, and now she didn't think that she could afford one. So, it was to the pay phone that she descended, bearing the coin of the realm. She was in her painting clothes, spattered and baggy. *Thank Jesus Raoul isn't on duty yet,* she thought.

Boomer sounded sleepy. He must have been still a-bed. It was half past noon, but, then, he would have had a big night. She wondered if Ultima was lying there beside him.

"It's me," she said. "I just wanted to say I'm sorry I didn't get to your opening."

"No problem," he said. "I didn't really expect you."

"You didn't?"

"Nope."

"Why not?"

"Well . . . let's just not talk about it."

He sounds strange, she thought. *Strange and cold. Beyond hangover.* Had his show been a total fiasco? It wouldn't have surprised her. He was in way over his head, and no beret could hide it. "Why can't we talk about it?"

"Why should we talk about anything important? Spoil our perfect record."

She was taken aback. "You're kidding. We've always talked."

"Horseshit, Ellen Cherry. We never talked. We traded wisecracks. Wisecracking is not talking."

She started to refute him, but couldn't muster any ready evidence to support her objection. While she was trying to remember the last time they'd had a heart-to-heart, he broke the silence with an outburst. "You know how come we never talked? 'Cause you never believed I *could* talk. Not on your level. I couldn't talk about art. I didn't understand art. I didn't, in fact, give a big rat's ass about art. And in your opinion, that made me inferior, you know; some kind of second-class citizen like all those other clods in Colonial Pines. . . ."

"No! You were different. And I loved you."

"You never loved me. You never. You loved to the left of me and to the right of me, maybe. You loved above me and underneath and in back of me somewheres. But you didn't love *me*. You loved my biceps and my big ol' welder's cock, and the way I danced and the way I was looser and more free than you. That's what the hell you loved. It turned you on that I could be uninhibited, because the only place *you're* free is on a piece of canvas. In art, you can break loose of your restraints. Otherwise, you're tight as the peel on a turnip."

"Hey! Hold on, buster. I don't know that you're so uninhibited. Lot of things you wouldn't do. It was you who wouldn't call me 'Jezebel.' "

Boomer paused. He lowered his voice. "That's another story, that is."

"Yes, isn't it?"

"Yeah, it is."

"Another story entirely."

"You can say that again."

But she didn't say it again. She didn't say anything for a while, and neither did he. Then they spoke out at the same time, in ironic unison.

"The trouble with you—" she began.

"The trouble with you—" he started. His voice, being the stronger of the two, won the right to proceed. "Is that the only way you can communicate is through art. You've never learned to communicate your feelings to a man. You don't even *want* to communicate in a relationship. You think if you open up to love, you'll lose your independence or your self-expression or creativity or whatever you call all that passionate, wonderful stuff that makes you feel alive inside. Patsy warned me that you'd never wanna have kids, 'cause raising babies would siphon off that juice that makes your paintings go—"

"My mama never—"

"Oh, yeah, she did! You say you love me, and maybe in a peculiar way you do, but you don't love me for myself. You never have. When I was just a welder, you looked down on me. You didn't really want me till you thought you couldn't have me, till you saw me climbing that ladder you thought was up against *your* wall. If I was to go back to being a welder, Ellen Cherry, if I was to come back uptown to you, you wouldn't be thrilled with it for more than about two days. 'Cause after you got through having orgasms, you'd have to have a relationship, and that's a sideline you don't care to more than dabble in. You can't be married to a man 'cause you're already married to your art."

It was her turn, but she hadn't the belly for major counterattack. Softly, but with practiced conviction, she said, "Art is the only place a person can win."

"It may be the only place *you* can win. I believe we can win any damn place we try."

"The trouble with you, Boomer—"

"Yeah, go ahead now, tell me the trouble with me."

"You think the world is a piñata. You think if you keep hitting it and hitting it, smacking it and banging it, one day it'll bust open and all the prizes will fall out at your feet."

He considered that analogy for a moment. Then he said, "Well, I didn't do that bad last night."

"Oh?"

"Sold every damn piece but one. And if I care to travel with it, that one's sold, too."

Ellen Cherry was gelatinous with shock. She had to steady herself against the lobby wall. "Why . . . why, that's incredible, Boomer. That must have been . . . incredible . . . for you."

"It was right nice. Not all that sensational, really. It woulda been better if you'd showed up. I mean, I kinda thought you might. I appreciate how envious and bitter you are, and I don't blame you. You know a trillion times more about art than me. But I've learned that it isn't necessary to know all that much. You just make what you wanna see, right? It's a game, right? It's like being paid for dreaming." He laughed. "I feel like an undercover agent. A mole in the house of art. Anyhow, Ellen Cherry, I started out doing it 'cause I wanted to understand you and earn your respect. Then, I reckon, I wanted to show you up, 'cause you've always acted so goddamned *superior* about it. Now, I don't know. It's gotten out of hand. Maybe I'm hooked on it, although I feel guilty sometimes. Guilty about you—and guilty about people taking a fool like me so seriously, and guilty 'cause it's so much fun, in a real nerve-racking, useless sort of way. But that don't matter. I was heartsick that you didn't come to the opening. I reckon that's why I'm pitching a tizzy this morning. Is it still morning?"

They were silent for several literal minutes. A recorded voice came on the line and instructed Ellen Cherry to deposit additional coins.

After the last nickel dropped, with a hollow yet musical clink, like a robot passing a kidney stone, Boomer asked, "What're you thinking?"

"I don't know. What are *you* thinking?"

"Oh, well, I was thinking that what was said just now probably needed to be said, but after saying it, I'm starting to think that maybe wisecracking is not so bad, after all."

She smiled in such a way that down in the Bowery, on the other end of the line, he could tell that she was smiling. There are smiles that actually travel along telephone wires, although no engineer at Bell Laboratories could explain how it works.

Boomer answered the smile. "Folks take art too seriously. Did I say that already? But, you know, they take their relationships too seriously, too. I sure used to. Then, you did. This morning, I reckon we both are."

"Seems like I used to know that, but then I forgot. Like a strong swimmer who one day just up and drowns."

"You cramp and you sink. It can happen to anybody. You let love lay too heavy in your stomach . . ."

"People tend to take *everything* too seriously. Especially themselves."

"Yep. And that's probably what makes 'em scared and hurt so much of the time. Life is too serious to take that seriously."

Another smile ran along the wires on its badly bowed legs. "I want to see your show. I do. I will. Soon as I whip up the nerve. Then, maybe sometime we could get together and wisecrack a bit."

"All right," he said. "Let's us do that. I'll be in touch. Right after I get back from Jerusalem."

Jerusalem. Jeru Salaam. "City of Peace." The only humorous thing about it was its name. Thirty-seven wars (not battles but wars) fought over it. Reduced to ashes seventeen times by seventeen different conquerors. Each time rebuilt—and each time coveted anew.

Jerusalem. A dry and hilly provincial pit stop on the windy road to nowhere. Lacking a port, lacking strategic fortress sites, lacking fertile fields around it. No trees to cut, no fish to net, no ore to mine, little but thistles for its flocks to chew. A location with almost nothing to offer, yet desired by everyone. Desired for three thousand years.

Jerusalem. Jeru Salaam. Shaped out of pure spirit, irrigated with spurting gore. Incessantly blackened by arson and blood, only to be polished to a golden shine again by prayerful knees and unwinding scrolls of dreamlike prophecy. Jerusalem. When they could no longer bear to hear its children screaming, stones went deaf all over the world.

Jerusalem. A mystical metropolis with seven magic gates. Entered by few, forgotten by none. Simultaneously the capital of death and the seat of immortality. Hub of the wheel of pilgrimage. Focal point of all received starlight. Fly-specked mirror of heaven on earth. Jumping-off place to eternity. The town that logic could not shut down. That city, among all cities, into which both the Second Coming and the Redemption have been booked and to where both the Christ and the Messiah are said to be holding tickets. Jeru Salaam.

As far as Boomer Petway was concerned, Jerusalem was founded in Sunday school and developed on the six o'clock news. It was not a place that anyone actually visited. It wasn't even a place one discussed, unless one was a religious or political nut (which was getting to be the same thing). Yet, now he heard himself saying that he was going there, and although such a journey seemed even less real to him than his rise in the art world, he conceded that it was probably true.

Throughout his adult life, Boomer had saved the cardboard tubes out of toilet tissue rolls. He wasn't sure why. He had been given the little cylinders to play with when he was a tot, and some affinity for them had likely carried over into his manhood. In any case, he had more than a decade's worth of toilet tissue rolls stored in the attic of his Colonial Pines bungalow, and when he commenced to make art, he drove his van down to Virginia and loaded them up. Hundreds of them. He sprayed them with black acrylic, and when they were dry, he employed them like Lincoln Logs to construct a sort of hut, five feet wide and seven feet high. Inside the structure, he released a live crow. The crow was provided with a perch made of bathroom tissue rolls (black, like the others), as well as a black plastic water dish and a black ceramic bowl that was kept filled with a dark variety of sunflower seeds. This piece was mounted in his one-man show under the title of *Ministry of Covert Operations.*

A curator from the Israel Museum in West Jerusalem's Givat Ram was sufficiently attracted to the piece to make an offer. The Israeli would purchase it on condition that Boomer accompany it to Jerusalem and personally reassemble it in time to be included in an exhibition dealing with issues of national security as seen through the eyes of artists. That exhibition was set to open in less than two weeks.

Ultima thought it a good idea, even though it would mean removing the piece from her gallery ahead of schedule. Boomer, who wasn't completely convinced that Jerusalem existed, said that he'd think it over. It wasn't until he heard himself informing Ellen Cherry of his departure that he realized that he had already decided to escape the pressures of his estranged wife, his dealer, and his sudden fame, and jet off with a cargo of toilet paper rolls and a cantankerous pet crow to that puzzling city that has been variously described as the *Eye,* the *Navel,* the *Song,* and the *Hemorrhage* of the world.

Boomer flew out of JFK in mid-November, expecting to be back in Manhattan for Thanksgiving. Sardined into his carelessly packed satchel, among the jeans, boxer shorts, aloha shirts, and compatible couples of socks, was a single purple stocking that, except for some dubious sentimental value, would have been ash-canned ages ago. Yes, as the ever perverse proclivities of Fate would have it, Clean Sock—Clean Sock!—was winging to Jerusalem.

Were the unsuspecting and fortuitous traveler's long-lost twin apprised of the situation, profane oaths would have popped like corks in the basement of St. Patrick's Cathedral, and it would have kicked itself from one end to the other of that environment that, to its thinking, was only slightly less dreary and confining than the inside of any sock drawer.

So, it was just as well that Dirty Sock did not know. He lay, curled and otiose, in front of the grate, innocently awaiting the appearance of Turn Around Norman, paying only a modicum of notice to Can o' Beans as he/she, in his/her way, speculated to Spoon about the possible size, shape, and significance of the Third Temple of Jerusalem.

*   *   *

Of the Seven Dwarfs, the only one who shaved was Dopey. That should tell us something about the wisdom of shaving.

If Can o' Beans were a man, it's probable that he/she would be bearded. Some, at least, could imagine the bean can sporting a neatly trimmed vandyke, or else something Lincolnesque; dressed, maybe, in a white suit, frayed of cuff and buttercupped with age; and supported by an eagle-headed cane; imagine the can pensively twirling a snifter of cognac as it pontificated before a library fire at the Explorers Club.

Perhaps that projection is far too narrow, far too simplistic to do justice to a complex figure, but no matter. As it was, facial hair and the dopey removal thereof was no issue for the tin of beans. It simply did its dignified best to protect what was left of its label as, misshapen and scarred, it squatted atop a soot-powdered hymnal, which in turn lay atop an overturned coal bucket, straining to make itself heard above the mad waltz of traffic whose goosey crescendos honked and hissed through the grate. Nevertheless, the dessert spoon that sat at its feet could not have been more attentive had it raised a hand from time to time to stroke a pedagogish tassel of whiskers.

For Spoon's benefit, Can o' Beans had reviewed the information about the First Temple—Solomon's (or Hiram's) Temple—that had been imparted upon that shaky, pessimistic day in the aftermath of their ordeals in the Wyoming mountains. Now, he/she was reviewing aloud what they had learned of the Second Temple—Herod's Temple—from accounts provided, at Can o' Beans's prodding, during a siesta in a fossil bed in northwestern Nebraska.

"I suppose we ought to keep the dates straight," said Can o' Beans. "Solomon's Temple was destroyed in 586 B.C. Right? The Second Temple, its low-rent replacement, was knocked together in 515 B.C. That would mean that for, let's see, seventy-one years, Jerusalem had no temple at all. Of course, most of the Jews were in exile in Babylon during that period, so there would've been no reason for a temple in Jerusalem town. But by 515—aren't you glad, Miss Spoon, that inanimate objects don't live in history? At least, not in one that requires us to memorize dates. We're luckier than we admit. No historical dates, no common cold, no income tax, no toe jam, toothaches, dandruff, herpes, halitosis, heartburn, or body hair. Especially body hair. Ugh! Although a smart goatee might be agreeable."

"Dry rot," growled Dirty Sock.

"Begging your pardon?"

"At least humans don't dry rot. Or rust."

"Oh, I'm not so sure," Can o' Beans disagreed. "Remember those old Republicans we saw at that rally in Iowa?" Spoon tittered. "But, say, Mr. Sock," the can went on, "do you happen to recall the date when King Herod is said to have renovated the Second Temple?"

"Sure do. It was back in the year twenty-one afore Christ that the ol' boy come across that fixer-upper." Dirty Sock rolled over and turned his full attention to the street, leaving Can o' Beans and Spoon to gape at each other in mild amazement.

It was during the Babylonian exile that the patriarchs finally got their monotheistic ducks in a row. In the tens of centuries that had rolled by since the tribe of Abraham made the political decision to promote its local tribal deity, Yahweh, as the one and only god in the cosmos, worship of the Great Mother had continued in Judea and Israel. Ancient Jews loved the Goddess, loved her wisely and well, and even when they came to accept Yahweh, they kept a shrine for her—in their temples and in their hearts. Astarte, or Ashtoreth, as they called her, reigned in the First Temple of Jerusalem alongside Yahweh and, periodically, in place of him, a state of affairs that rankled the right-wing misogynists of the Yahwehistic extreme.

In exile, however, the Jews were unified as they never could have been at home. Oppression and homesickness strengthened their common bond. The more the Babylonians mocked the macho Yahweh, the tighter the Hebrews clung to him as a unique, indigenous cultural icon. Spurred by the prophet Ezekiel, the patriarchal priests hastened to take advantage of the situation.

It was in Babylon that the heretofore multitudinous, unmanageable laws and rituals of Judaism were edited and codified. New traditions, such as the synagogue, were established. And a stern, broad, inspiring dogma was hammered out of the ancient desert ores that they had hoarded and slowly refined in the fire of their longing. From that time on, a shield of dogmatic brass would deflect every tendered kiss of the Mother. So great was the patriarchs' hatred and fear of her that she was left unnamed in their transcriptions. When referred to at all, it was as some vague, unspeakable, whorish pagan evil.

By 538 B.C., when the jubilant exiles were permitted to return to a desolated Judea (it had been leveled in the Babylonian invasion, remember), nearly a half-century of reprogramming would have purged them of their matriarchal affection. It was for the glory of Yahweh and Yahweh alone that they rebuilt their nation, their capital, and their Temple. The Second Temple, although as large as the First, was simple and plain; an odd, impoverished, jerry-built, unembellished religious blockhouse erected upon a pile of rubble. Neither the Goddess nor Conch Shell and Painted Stick would ever see the inside of that particular version—but their days and nights on the Temple Mount were not yet done.

"Yes, my goodness, yes," said Spoon, "it's coming back to me now. We were in that place with all the old petrified creepy-crawly things, and you were under the impression that Conch Shell and Painted Stick had been subjected to some kind of exile of their own, but Conch Shell explained that once they had escaped the rampage of the Babylonian troops, it had been business as usual, as far as their lives were concerned. Wasn't that the story, ma'am/sir?"

"Correct. Under cover of darkness, as the expression goes, Mr. Stick and Miss Shell stole down from the Mount of Olives and made their way by starlight to a village, I forget its name, where they knew their goddess to be adored, and there they laid themselves on the doorstep of a priestess. In the morning, they were taken in, no questions asked, dusted off, kissed, and placed immediately upon an altar. Because the Babylonians were lovers of Ishtar, the occupation wasn't hostile to those activities that Mr. Stick and Miss Shell were employed in. Judea was bread-and-water poor then, I guess; populated by a scattering of downtrodden shepherds, and it surely was a far cry from their glory days in Temple Number One, but our friends apparently were busy and content. As Mr. Stick put it, human folly does not impede the turning of the stars. During the exile, they were at work, never more than a few miles from Jerusalem. What was left of Jerusalem."

"But after the Jews returned . . ."

"Ah, after the return it was a different ball game. Idolatry was no longer tolerated."

"As well it shouldn't be," said Spoon, with a squeaky firmness. She rotated her dainty stem toward the far corner where the shell and the stick were conferring. "No offense intended."

"My dear," said Can o' Beans, "don't you see that an 'idol,' so-called, is usually just a derogatory name for the other fellow's god. To a non-Christian, a statue of Jesus could be considered an idol."

"Blasphemy! There's only one god."

"And who is that, Miss Spoon? That silversmith in Philadelphia who made you?"

"You know very well who I mean."

"I could take a wild guess. As an object, however, I confess to being bewildered by the whole rigamarole of religion. And I'm convinced that the way Mr. Stick and Miss Shell are involved in it is not at all the same as the way humans are involved. In the Bible, an 'idol' is any deity other than Yahweh. But there's a second definition of 'idol' that describes it as an object that humans worship. An object, Miss Spoon. One of us. Why, you or I could be 'idols,' if only someone cared enough. Can you imagine Spoonism? Or the Bean Can Cult? The Church of the Dirty Sock? No, I can see that you can't. No matter. You would have fit in quite well in post-exile Jerusalem, although I daresay there was precious little crème caramel being spooned thereabouts. But our friends didn't fit in anymore. And after several decades underground, so to speak, they were smothered inside a basket of wool and secreted to Phoenicia on the rump of a camel."

"Scary."

"Exciting."

"A tribulation."

"Or an adventure. Depending on your outlook. In any case, they remained in Phoenicia for a very long time. After the Greeks took over Judea, I believe that was around three hundred thirty-something B.C., wasn't it, Mr. Sock—oh, he's not listening—they very well could have come back—the Greeks loved beautiful things and were pagan to the tips of their sandals—but our stick and shell were suitably occupied in their native Phoenicia, apparently, and happy to be there."

"But separated."

"Well, yes, Miss Shell was serving in a splendid temple in Sidon, Jezebel's old hometown, and Mr. Stick was at sea a lot. On long voyages, Phoenician ships often had priests aboard, and they found a use for Mr. Stick. A combination of scientific and spiritual duties, it sounds like."

"They were separated."

"No, in ancient times, the scientific and the spiritual were virtually synonymous. At the higher levels, they still are."

"I'm not talking about that, you big silly. I mean Conch Shell and Painted Stick were separated. How sad."

"Do you really think they were sad about it? Maybe they were. At any rate, they got back together eventually. Reunited in Herod's Temple. Just like a Hollywood movie."

"Sigh."

Herod was a Semite, half-Hebrew, in fact, and king of Judea, but he had "Property of the Roman Empire" stamped on his backside, and nobody would let him forget it. He stood on his head and spit shekels in an attempt to win favor with the Jews, but liking Herod was harder than trying to explain quantum radiation on a Mexican postcard. The pillaging, the rape, the torture, humiliation, and butchery visited upon Jerusalem's Jews over the centuries by various foreign contingents were simply too great and too horrendous to ever, ever be forgotten. Herod could part his hair like a Jew, shine his shoes like a Jew, trim his wick like a Jew, and spit in the whiskers of every pig he passed, but having received half of his chromosomes from Edom, and his throne (and license to tax) from Rome, he was considered an opportunistic foreigner who could not, would not be trusted.

During the thirty-three years of his reign, Herod did everything but wiggle his ears to wow Jerusalem, including restoring its architecture and religion (the buildings that originally had replaced those demolished by the Babylonians were functional, at best, and the practice of Judaism had been brutally restricted toward the end of the Greek occupation). Although Herod's friendly overtures were appreciated, even applauded, he remained personally unpopular until that time when, in a final magnanimous gesture, he set about to renovate and glorify the Second Temple.

Unattractive to begin with, the Second Temple had been reduced to practically a burnt-out shell by Hellenistic antagonists. Nevertheless, it had stood for four centuries, and the rituals performed therein had so impressed a visiting Alexander the Great that he consented to leave it standing. Everyone was excited, if suspicious, when Herod whipped out the hammer and the paintbrush. But Herod did it up right.

To assuage the fears of his subjects that he would pull down the existing temple and then be unable or unwilling to complete his grand design, Herod spent eight years gathering materials and selecting and training a work force. The inner buildings were built by a crew of one thousand Hebrew priests, laying every stone according to some arcane religious law.

The overall structure, with its retaining walls, cloisters, massive pillars, and courtyards within courtyards, covering thirty-six acres, was virtually a carbon copy of the First Temple, which is to say, ironically, it was an ancient and thoroughly pagan Phoenician or Canaanite design. (As Can o' Beans had learned that day in the fossil bed, Phoenicians and Canaanites were really the same people, their chief difference being that the branch of the race called Phoenicians were coastal dwellers and seafarers, while Canaanites lived inland in the deserts and hills. Incidentally, Canaan meant "land of the purple" in a Near Eastern dialect, precisely what Phoenicia meant in Greek, so both branches were indelibly colored by the royal dye of the conch.)

Herod's embellishments turned out to be every bit as lavish as Solomon's. The Temple and its enclosures were covered with plates of silver and gold, so much gold that Josephus claimed that men literally went blind from temple-gazing on sunny summer days. From a distance, it shone like the sun itself.

Perhaps unconsciously, certain pagan compounds were stirred into the mixture. Josephus mentioned that the Temple roofs were "adorned with cedar, curiously graven," and surrounding the inner buildings were rich spoils that Herod's armies had pillaged from Arab countries. The lintel above the entrance to the Temple proper was "adorned with embroidered veils, with flowers of purple." Purple, mind you. And from the crownwork hung carved vines of purple grapes, clusters "as tall as a man." At the back of the foyer, giant gold-plated doors were concealed by what was described as "a Babylonian curtain . . . of fine linen . . . in scarlet and purple," and "embroidered upon it all that was mystical in the heavens excepting that of the twelve signs." While the priests may have sought to avoid depicting the animalistic aspects of astrology, they didn't hesitate to include celestial symbols: the first enclosed section of the Temple contained a candlestick with seven branches for the seven planets that were known, and a table upon which rested "shew-bread—twelve loaves representing the circle of the zodiac." And wittingly or not, they paid tribute to the most intimate feature of the Goddess, when to the ceremonial garments of the high priests they attached sweet little vaginal pomegranates of solid gold.

So overshadowed were these vestiges of nearly forgotten paganism by the trappings and rituals of Yahwehistic Judaism that even purists glossed them over. Yahweh would be honored in those halls more exclusively and magnificently than he had ever been honored before.

Alas, just when Herod had the Jews in his debt, had them trusting enough to buy a used chariot from him, he blew it. As the Temple was about to be dedicated, following eleven years of planning and perspiration, he had to go and stick a huge Roman eagle over its main entrance. That act infuriated the Hebrews, not only by its arrogant, insensitive tribute to hated foreign overlords, but by its signal—to those aware enough to interpret it—that paganism once again would be allowed to infiltrate and pollute Yahweh's central authority. Indeed, not many years passed before first Conch Shell and then Painted Stick were quietly reinstated in the Temple household.

The autumn moon is the color of nectarines and iron.
It is swollen and dizzy, like a hashish dumpling.
After it sets, all the gold in the Temple sighs with relief.
But its colors linger on in the grapes that pout on the vine.
The priest awakes before dawn. He puts his pomegranates on.
And he walks on down the hill.
He comes to a pure little spring, below the Temple walls.
He dips a conch shell in the gurgling waters.
And he walks back up the slope.

Pomegranates jingling like sheep bells, the priest carries the shellful of water to the sacred enclosure.

The area is illuminated by thousands of candles.

Each candle is meant to be a star.

Slowly, slowly now, the priest pours the water onto the ground.

A conch tongue of clear water licks the old stone pulse.

While a candle galaxy bristles with secrets of the night.

Over and over, the priest makes the journey. Sky to water. Water to earth. Earth to sky.

Until the sun rises and gives the gold something new to fret about.

Thus, for the last part of its five-hundred-year life, the Second Temple integrated the old religion into the new. Married spirit to soul. Provided a functional metaphor for transcendence. Drew human individuals into the cosmic cycles in a real and personal way.

Conch Shell served as a chalice to cup the juices of existence. Painted Stick was a rod for psychic lightning, a post to which the Milky Way was moored.

Passing under the hated Roman eagle, ignoring its military talons the way the other pilgrims did, young Jesus would have witnessed those ceremonies. In contrast to the hypocrisy, doctrinairism, and corruption that was becoming rampant among the Temple hierarchy (and that would soon incite him to open revolt), Jesus must have found the rituals nourishing. On the other hand, they may have made him uncomfortable. Certainly, those who were to establish a religion in his name were uncomfortable with them. For those who would pray but not dance, fast but not feast, baptize but not splash, flog but not fuck, for those who would buy spirit but sell soul, crown Father but deceive Mother, those men found Herod's Temple a threatening place at vernal equinox and under a harvest moon.

As Can o' Beans recounted the rites, all that he/she had learned about them from the reticent stick and shell, Spoon felt a teensy bit uncomfortable, herself. There was a beauty and grace in them that appealed to her refined sensibility, but they made her queasy, none-theless. The part that really made her squirm, however, was the part about Salome. How the teenage Salome had driven her stepfather, poor beleaguered King Herod, over the brink of sanity the night she danced the Dance of the Seven Veils, skinny legs and all.

"That must have been some dance," said Can o' Beans. "Herod never got over it."

"Oh, but ma'am/sir, it wasn't just that lewd hootchey-kootch that sickened Herod. He was already suffering from melancholy and rejection. Why, to entice Salome to dance, he had to promise to behead John the Baptist. Served up the head on a silver platter. Ooo, isn't that just too gross! A human head on a dish like a pot roast. I can't bear to think about it."

"It was Herod's wife, supposedly, Salome's mother, who wanted John the Baptist killed."

"No matter. Herod agreed to it. Just to get a good look at that young girl. Kiddie porn, they call it nowadays. . . ."

"She was sixteen. In that era, a sixteen-year-old was in every respect a woman."

"Not the point, begging your pardon. The point is that it was Herod's own accumulated wickedness that drove him crazy, not some shameful feminine display."

"Perhaps you're right, Miss Spoon. Who knows what causes the human brain to split its britches. It would seem that the brain hangs so many curtains between itself and the true universe that eventually light can no longer reach it, and it molds and rots and festers in the dark. In any event, the king of Judea had a lot of spit in his harmonica. By the time Salome's dance was done, he was playing a feeble tune, indeed. Defiant Jews cut down the Roman eagle from the Temple while he was still alive, slobbering and raving on his couch."

"Good for them. Finally, he was too drunk and depraved to stop them from cleansing God's house."

"Well, the eagle was gone, but the Temple didn't change all that much. Miss Conch still poured at festival times, and Mr. Stick was always on hand if some priest should take a notion to stir the stew of sex and stars. He'd become their compass needle, in a sense, pointing to the north from where their Messiah was prophesied to come. And there was plenty of commercialism, plenty of corruption left in the Temple, as well. Remember how Jesus was said to have grabbed an ox whip and driven the money changers out?"

"Herod had passed away by then."

"Yes, he died while Jesus was a child. Miss Shell and Mr. Stick, by the way, have no recollection of this Jesus fellow at all. According to them, he had precious little impact on Jerusalem until four decades after he was crucified. But I know you don't want to talk about that. The thing to bear in mind is that the situation got generally worse for the Jews after Herod expired. Rome clamped down. The Jews resisted. Clamp. Resist. Clamp. Resist. Until finally the Romans got fed up with the constant hassle and, in 70 A.D., razed Jerusalem yet again. Again! Can you imagine? Just obliterated it. Killed a million people. General named Titus plundered the Temple, stripped it bare, and sailed for Italy with all of its treasures. The spoils were put on public view in a place called the Temple of Peace. From the City of Peace—Jerusalem—to the Temple of Peace in imperial Rome. Humans tend to use the word *peace* rather loosely, don't you agree? That disregard for the true meaning of words may be one of the main reasons their brains go bad. Did I ever elucidate my theory—"

"Indeed, you did, ma'am/sir," Spoon hastened to inform the can. "Quite adequately. Sticking to the subject, if you don't mind: Conch Shell and Painted Stick, they weren't abducted to Rome."

"They were the type of booty that a military mind such as Titus would be inclined to overlook."

"Somebody thought enough of them to save them."

"Fortunately. Some Phoenician slave. Stole them out of the Temple ruins and hightailed into the wilderness. Miss Shell contends that there're always a few enlightened human beings around who have need for her. Even today. Maybe more today than there's been in a long, long while. That's why she and Mr. Stick are active again. I don't know, Miss Spoon, it smacks of wishful thinking to me. Magic and enlightenment at the end of the twentieth century? This wild idea of a Third Temple?"

"Oh, goody, the Third Temple," chirped Spoon, relieved that the history lesson was over. She adored to hear Can o' Beans expound, but the version of biblical events that the tin had garnered from the stick and shell was most unsettling. "You did set out, you know, to tell me what you imagine the Third Temple will be like."

"If there ever *is* a Third Temple," said Can o' Beans.

Out on Fifth Avenue, in the pitch of urbanity and the roar of ritz, the Reverend Buddy Winkler and two kosher-looking gentlemen had stopped at a hot dog cart. As the others watched, the preacher sank his new gold fangs into a frank. "I shouldn't oughtta be eatin' this," he announced, wiping meat juice from his lips with a tissue napkin the size of a playing card. "Had a pound of pig barbecue for supper last night. It was so greasy my arteries took on a life of their own. Woke up this morning and they was already up, reading the newspaper. 'Fuck you,' they said to me. 'We don't need you.' Then they turned to the financial page and commenced checkin' out the latest listing on pork bellies."

The two rabbis regarded him with disbelief. Dirty Sock regarded him, too. The sock thought Buddy looked familiar. Before it could satisfactorily link the face to Colonial Pines or Boomer Petway, however, the preacher and his associates shot off down the chilly avenue, random projectiles in that long vomit of cashmere and fur that the electric muscles of the metropolis—"Stop! Go! Wait! Walk!"— expelled or contracted, in rhythm with their engineered pathology.

Turning his attention to Turn Around Norman, who, like a frozen planet, had just begun his slow diurnal revolution around a tar sun on the sidewalk, Dirty Sock called, "Hey! The ol' boy's at it! Showtime!"

His comrades failed to respond. Can o' Beans was still garrulously speculating about a Third Temple in Jerusalem, and Spoon was too intrigued, or too timid, to cut him/her off.

"Well, now, it's correct that the First and Second Temples were physical twins almost, or duplicates, to speak more precisely, and therefore more sanely, but I can't for the starch of me imagine Jews today, as much as they might cherish tradition, building anything closely resembling the first two. Not with all the advances in modern architecture. Not with wiring and sewer codes. Obviously, they're not going to plate a large complex with silver and gold, not at what precious metals are going for. And think of the kidding they'd get if they erected phallic pillars or covered the doorways with carved fruit. It's a different world we live in, wholly different, different right down to its molecules; even for fundamentalists, it's different.

"In the Second Temple, for example, females were prohibited from entering the inner court. They were restricted to an enclosure within the secondary courtyard, and when they were, excuse the expression, menstruating, they weren't allowed in at all. Can you picture contemporary women sitting still for that? Ho-ho! Of course, there persists to be ultra-orthodox cults and sects in which the wives shave their heads and dress in gunnysacks in order, I suppose, not to pose any threats to their sexually insecure husbands. The fly in that ointment, as I view it, is that once potential fornicators get used to seeing women that way, pretty soon it won't repulse them anymore. There'll be men who get *aroused* by bald women. I mean, there could be magazines with shaved-head, gunnysack centerfolds."

"Please, ma'am/sir, you're digressing."

"Oh. Right. I am," conceded Can o' Beans. "Sorry." But before he/she could get back on track, Painted Stick and Conch Shell approached them.

"Good morning," said the container. "Greetings. Are you going to catch a bit of Turn Around Norman? Mr. Sock reports he's spinning like a top."

The ancient relics hadn't come over to enjoy the inimitable Norman, however, nor had they arrived to add to or subtract from the bean can's rehashings and conjectures. Rather, they had come to announce that a decision had been reached, a decision so unexpected that it tore Dirty Sock away from the grate—and sent the dumbfounded little Spoon into a convulsive clatter.

It wasn't complicated. The talismans had decided that one of their group must leave the cathedral, leave the hiding place and venture into the city. Specifically, one of them must link up with Turn Around Norman, must follow him home, observe him and his life-style at close range; offstage, as it were; and report back, if possible, the following day. Obviously, it was a dangerous ploy, but it was the only way the objects might accurately ascertain whether or not the street performer was capable of playing an active role in getting them out of New York and across the sea to Jerusalem.

To minimalize the risk of discovery, the object selected for the mission would of necessity be the smallest among them, the least conspicuous. And that would be, of course, poor Spoon.

A week before Thanksgiving, Ellen Cherry had a waitress dream. She had *the* waitress dream. She had the Nightmare of the Mixed-Up Orders. In that notorious dream, the waitress (in this case, Ellen Cherry) delivers the blood sausages to a table of Buddhists and serves the vampire party the garlic soup.

She awoke with beads of sweat the size of popcorn above her upper lip and doming her nipples. And she didn't feel a whole lot better after turning on the lamp because she knew that this dream was standing with one leg in reality.

In the week since her conversation, her confrontation, with Boomer, she had been twisting in a cyclone of introspection. She'd gone from hurt to hope and back again; she'd endured pang, then numbness, and, finally, self-examination. She'd gone through her soul like a street thief going through a drunk's pockets. And what she had found, along with enough emotional loose change to feed every vending machine in the Institute of Pop Psychology, was a snapshot of herself taken before she had declared herself an artist. The picture was so old and faded and crinkled that she couldn't tell what she looked like in it.

Maybe Boomer's right, she thought. *Right not only about me not really loving him—God knows I've never been willing to bet the farm on the steadfastness of my devotion—but right also about me being so lost in my identity as an artist that I couldn't find my heart with a map and a flashlight. Certainly, he's right about me being married to art, I've never denied that, but what I've got to consider, for the first time in my life, is whether maybe it isn't a bad marriage. Whether I didn't marry art when I*

was so young that I missed out on a lot of other things, things that might
have taken me places and shown me stuff and made me whole and happy
in ways I can't even guess. If I had waited, maybe I would've ended up
just dating art instead of marrying it, or maybe I would have had no
truck with art at all.

When she had forsaken painting the previous year, it was because
she was disillusioned with the New York art world and devastated by
Boomer's conquest of it. It had been a negative reaction. Now she
thought she would like to attempt a positive withdrawal. She decided
to see what it would feel like not to merely give up art but to give up
being an artist. To honestly, completely give it up. To be something
else for a change. And since, for the time being, there was only one
other thing she was qualified to be, she wrote "I am a waitress" five
hundred times on the blackboard of her consciousness. Not "I am an
artist/waitress" or "I am an artist temporarily working as a waitress,"
but "I am a waitress."

Perhaps after Thanksgiving, after he had returned from Jerusalem,
she would try out her new identity on Boomer. Tomorrow, she'd
disclose it to Spike and Mr. Hadee. That night, however, she set
Popeye's spinach down in front of Wimpy, and, tossing and moaning, dreamed away any chance of a tip.

To tone her waitress muscles—the *extensor hallucis,* the *tendo calcaneus,*
the *tibialis anterior*—Ellen Cherry walked to work the next morning.
Along the frosty trek downtown, her nose parting lace curtain after
lace curtain of her own exhalations, she passed countless kiosks and
newsstands, each, it seemed, festooned with the same inky banners
announcing further violence in Israel. In cries or whispers, depending upon their style, the public journals told of curfews and road-
blocks, flaming tires and bulldozed kitchens, bridal veils of tear gas
and sweaters of blood; told of leaders with tongues of stale lightning,
cradles filled with stones, and young girls who danced with live
ammunition when they should have been dancing with their fathers
(too young were they to dance with boys); told of the old primate
grab-and-hold—the berserk baboon dance that anthropologists call
"territorial imperative" and politicians call "national interest"; told of
the gash that four thousand years had not sewn shut, the lunatic
legacy of Isaac and Ishmael.

Ellen Cherry's shift, the one she hoped would be her last as maître d', ended at three o'clock, but she waited around for Spike and Abu, who generally returned from tennis at quarter past four. She intended to ask them for a demotion. It was silly, in the first place, to have a day captain on duty in a restaurant whose lunch crowd would fit comfortably into a hermit's rec room. As well-to-do as Spike and Abu might be, they couldn't continue to lose money indefinitely. If they agreed to let her wait tables, they would save her salary plus the wages of the waitpersons whom she'd replace. The I & I's staff consisted mostly of earnest but errant young liberals killing time until they could be readmitted to law schools, and she was confident that she could do the work of two of them. Possibly three. For a lunch crowd of a dozen, what was there to do?

When her employers did arrive, Spike's feline eyes searching the room at shoe-level, Abu's nose flaming more red than usual (whether from the cold or the tennis, she could not tell), it was obvious by their manner that they, too, had tasted the latest toxic headlines from Israel.

Normally, the owners refrained from overt political discussion inside the I & I. Their running commentary on the Holy City was more in the order of a paean to its loveliness, its passion, its mysterious hold on the hearts of men. Or bemused puzzling over such questions as, why, always, in the hills of Jerusalem did the rocks look like sheep and the sheep like rocks? Today, however, the harsh pepper that sifted from the media's grinders was stinging their throats and inciting them to speak out in strained voices.

"The suffering of the Jews, everyone knows already," said Spike. He, Abu, and Ellen Cherry were sitting in the empty bar, staring at empty glasses, as if expecting them to fill spontaneously. For the moment, not one of them was sufficiently motivated to stand up and play bartender. "Much more on the subject of our persecution we don't need. You don't have the Jews on your conscience today already, you're not going to have them next Tuesday. What needs to be said is that we're dishing it out as well as taking it."

"Ah, but there is no comparison," Abu objected. "The Israeli army uses excessive force in quelling protests on the West Bank, true enough, and sometimes sadistic and cruel force, but even though it is racially motivated, and directed against my cousins, I must regard it an insignificant trifle compared to the Holocaust—"

"Hold on, my friend," said Spike. "For one minute, hold on. Holocaust? We Jews perpetrated our own holocaust, I'm telling you.

When? Who against? Over three thousand years ago against the Canaanites, that's when and who. How is the Land of Canaan turning suddenly into the Land of Israel? By what sale, what deal, eh; what magic trick? By a holocaust. The Hebrews escaping from Egypt invaded Canaan and killed everybody, the whole country, old men, women, children, little babies what were in arms. A million, we butchered. Look it up. In history, maybe the first recorded act of genocide. The only Canaanites left alive were a few what were good for slave labor."

"Wow!" said Ellen Cherry. "That's pretty heavy. But that was a very long time ago. And, anyway, weren't the Jews just taking back their homeland; you know, fighting to recover their promised land from these Canaanites?"

"Ha! So who is telling you this? The ghost of Moses, maybe? A homeland the Hebrews have never had. We're nomads, already. Our tribes shlepped through this Canaan, lived there among its inhabitants for a while. Then, most of them moved on into Egypt. So, a long time passed, and then the Hebrews were slaves of the pharaoh, too bad for us, and this guy Moses told them, 'Hey, we're getting out of this mess, we're going to escape.' And the Jews said, 'Okay, but where's it to that we're escaping, already?' 'To Canaan,' Moses said. 'Canaan is our rightful home in case you've forgotten it. God spoke to Abraham personally and said, "I promise you the Land of Canaan. You are my number one people what I've chosen, and Canaan is the place I've set aside for you, for your own forever." ' Good. Only nobody read the fine print, which said that to move into our new home, we had to slaughter hundreds of thousands of human beings what were living there at the time."

"You're not exaggerating, Mr. Cohen? Wasn't Canaan kind of a wilderness area that was open for settlement?"

"Hoo boy! You young people today, you're knowing nothing very much. An advanced civilization, we're talking about here. Already two thousand years old when the Hebrews invaded it. A lot of our culture comes from Canaan. You believe, darlink, that God told Moses go invade an advanced civilization, pilfer its territory, and kill all its people? Suppose in Westchester you had a nice house, and I stayed there the weekend as your guest, and then years pass and one day I come back and say, 'God promised me your house.' You would believe such a cockamamie story? No, you would not. So, okay, I murder you and your kids and your grandmother what's in a wheelchair and your cat and your dog and your three goldfishes. And I say to the neighbors, 'It's my house now, don't be peeing on my lawn.' Hoo boy!"

"I guess we got America the same way," ventured Ellen Cherry. "From the Indians."

Spike ran his index finger, stubby and liver spotted, along the rim of his dry glass. "Okay, yes," he said, "but at least John Wayne never said that God promised it to him. He honestly stole it."

He paused. "I can tell you something?" He paused again, and Ellen Cherry could detect tearwater magnifying the green gooseberries of his eyes. "I can tell you something? Why I changed my birth name? Abu knows this, but no other body. I quote to you from the Old Testament. Joshua 'carried off all the livestock of these cities,' meaning the cities of Canaan, 'but all the people he put to the sword, not sparing anyone who breathed.' Joshua 'plundered,' Joshua 'burned,' Joshua 'massacred,' Joshua 'wiped them out,' Joshua 'put to death,' Joshua 'turned his forces,' 'all were taken by storm . . . annihilated without mercy and utterly destroyed,' Joshua 'subdued,' Joshua 'slew,' Joshua 'left no survivors.' In your Christian Bible you will find this nice story of this nice guy Joshua. You think I could go on living when I wear the name of such a man?"

Ellen Cherry was both touched and embarrassed. She reached out and patted the cuff of his canary-and-catsup plaid sport coat.

Abu came on line. "Aside from the Joshua business, my friend, which I think you are ridiculous to take personally, I can appreciate what you are saying. You are wondering if in the Middle East it wasn't the Jews who started the bloody ball rolling. Maybe, maybe not. And you are asking, where does the Israeli get the chutzpah to be so self-righteously possessive about territory his ancestors acquired in such barbaric fashion? Fair enough. For that matter, the West Bank, itself, was taken by force in fairly recent times. But, Spike, I wish to point out to you yet again that these so-called Palestinians who contest the Jews for this territory have little or no legitimate title to it."

"They don't?" asked Ellen Cherry. The question slipped out before she could harness it. She bit her tongue, too late, and thought, *rugs.*

"No," said Abu. "They are not descended from the Canaanites. Nor from the Phoenicians, who were the only Canaanite people to survive Joshua's rampage. What's more, the disputed territory has not been

2 2 3

their home since time immemorial, as they contend. Very few of
them have lived in the area for more than fifty years."

"Rugs."

"It is true. Jews did not displace Arabs in Palestine. Quite the
reverse. Most of the Arabs there have foreign roots. They migrated
and immigrated into areas settled by Jews in pre-Israel Palestine. In
the nineteen-forties. I said 'migrated and immigrated,' but what really
happened is that they were trucked in from all over the Arab world
by the British. The Brits resettled them there in a land that was new
to them."

"Beautiful rugs."

"With American compliance, I am sure, the British actively imported Arabs in great numbers when it became obvious that the UN
was going to establish the state of Israel once World War Two was
over. So, I am always reminding Spike that no matter how brutally
and unfairly they are being treated, the Palestinians have even less
claim to the territory than the Jews.

"But you may be wondering," Abu went on, "why the British, with
American compliance, I am sure, bothered to resettle foreign Arabs
in Palestine."

"Hand-tied, vegetable-dyed rugs."

"It was a deliberate trick to lock the Jews in a pressure cooker and
keep them there. To place them in such a permanently volatile
situation that it would severely restrict any financial or cultural
influence they could exert on the rest of the world. It was a huge,
cynical deception. Spike understandably cannot face up to this, but
to my mind, if Hitler's Holocaust was the greatest anti-Semitic act in
history, the creation of the state of Israel was the second greatest. A
monstrous Anglo-American trap."

In Ellen Cherry's mind, flying carpets of exquisite weaves were
buzzing the control towers of various airports. When eventually
it dawned on her that both of her employers had fallen silent, she
arose and filled their glasses, Spike's with rum and Coke, Abu's with
tea.

"You are having nothing, darlink?" asked Spike.

It was then that she entered her plea for demotion, assuring them
that they would not only save money but would also acquire the
services of a waitress totally absorbed in and dedicated to her profession.

"But, my dear, you are an artist," said Abu.

"Patience. A nice gallery for you I'm getting," said Spike.

When she persisted, they asked if they might discuss the matter privately. She consented to take a walk and return for their decision in an hour.

As she was leaving the restaurant, carrying a doggie bag of leftover *shish tawook,* she overheard Abu ask, "Why do you suppose she kept mumbling about rugs?"

In her last Seattle apartment, the landlord had provided Ellen Cherry with a Coldspot stove and a Hotpoint refrigerator. Can o' Beans, from his/her perch in the kitchen cupboard, was both amused and dismayed by the titular contradiction, by the imprecise language. As for Ellen Cherry, she said once to Boomer, over the phone, "I've got a cold spot and a hot point."

"You and every other woman I've tangled with," said Boomer.

Ellen Cherry recalled that exchange as she walked up Forty-ninth Street. She had intended to stroll along the East River, but the breeze was too fresh, and besides, there was a demonstration in progress in front of the UN Headquarters building. Arab-Americans, joined by a surprising number of Jews, were protesting the viciousness with which Israel was maintaining authority in its occupied territories. So, she had elected to make a quick jaunt up to Fifth Avenue to catch the last few increments of Turn Around Norman's protracted swivel. As she half-jogged along the familiar route, doggie bag swinging in the chill, she was thinking that never in her twenty-five years had her cold spot been colder or her hot point hotter.

When, passing the Mel Davis Dog Boutique, she noticed a cardboard roast turkey on its door glass (evidently, Thanksgiving was for poodles, too), she was not amazed to find herself growing simultaneously more icy and more ablaze.

Neither extreme of her psychological climate was visible to the objects in the cellar. In fact, they barely registered her presence on the cathedral steps. On that day, at that moment, their attention elsewhere was fixed.

"Would that I could go in your place, Miss Spoon," Can o' Beans said consolingly.

"Would that I couldn't," said Dirty Sock. "But, hey, sugar, you'll do okay. You're too little to scoop shit and too big to scoop cocaine. Nobody in New York'll wanna fuss with you. Just go on out there and win one for the Gipper. Make the world safe for democracy. Remember the Alamo. Damn the torpedoes. Yours is not to question why, yours is but to do or . . ."

Painted Stick barked something in Phoenician that the sock couldn't possibly translate, but it got the drift and shut up.

Spoon was already mute. She hadn't uttered a sound in hours. She just stood there by the grate, looking as glazed as if she'd spent all day in a plate of Patsy's jellied chicken salad.

The plan was relatively simple. As the sun sank, as St. Patrick's umbra turned a half-block of Fifth Avenue into a coalfield, immediately before Turn Around Norman, to zero applause, brought his geologic pivot to a screechless halt, Spoon was to slip through the grate (parting, like veils, the candy wrappers and wadded-up Scientology leaflets that the wind pressed against its bars), slither as quietly and quickly as possible along the five yards of sidewalk between grate and Norman, and dive into the performer's donation box right before he bent to snatch it up.

As in most things, it was the timing that mattered.

Like Ellen Cherry, the objects had become so familiar with Norman's routine that they could predict with exactitude the moment when he would close the show and take off with the receipts. Now, as his doll-baby lashes commenced to flutter like those of a windup Jezebel; as his screw-top brow relaxed, assuming some of the placidity of cork; as his lips unpuckered and his violently blue orbs shifted focus, Painted Stick gave Spoon a nudge, Conch Shell gave her a blessing, and *clink tink,* she was suddenly through the grid and shooting down the sidewalk like a stubby silver arrow released from a toy bow.

"Bon voyage," whispered Can o' Beans.

"See ya later, alligator," called Dirty Sock.

Spoon didn't hear them. More terrified than she had been in her life, she heard only the *clink tink dink* of her body against cement, and the noise was so exaggerated by fear and excitement that she imagined that it could be heard above the rush-hour parrot-thunder of midtown traffic. "Oh, dear! O Blessed Mother, Mary of God!"

Clink tink. There were only two more yards to go, but she felt footfalls so close behind her that she was certain she was about to be stepped on. She glanced behind her—just for a second—but in so doing she angled inches off course and sideswiped the rise of the first step of the cathedral, which sent her flying out of control.

"What's that *thing*?" she heard (or thought she heard) a human squeal. A shadow fell over her (though she was already in shadow), and she could sense (or believed she could sense) a rough, inquisitive hand reaching to yank her from the pavement.

In full panic now, unable to reason or breathe, she took a desperate flying leap into the nearest enclosure, which happened to be the partially open doggie bag that was at Ellen Cherry's feet.

And as Turn Around Norman gathered up his meager earnings and melted into the crowd, Spoon lay in darkness, next to a foil-wrapped serving of *shish tawook,* and shook so hard that a passerby might have surmised the bag to be full of mice.

It was after six now, and the zillions of tiny particles that comprised Manhattan's atmosphere had slipped out of their loud sport clothes and donned tuxedos. As she returned to Isaac & Ishmael's, hopeful for demotion, Ellen Cherry walked inside a bag of night nearly as black as the one in which Spoon trembled. Only the discreet neon of the sushi bars or the flashing headlights of taxicabs clipped random bow ties of brightness and color to the formal collars of evening's molecules. Spoon had calmed down enough to comprehend her general whereabouts, and although still rather terrified, she was comforted by the realization that it was to Ellen Cherry Charles and not some stranger that her fate was wed.

Back at St. Patrick's, Dirty Sock was groaning. "She blew it. Oh, man, she flat out blew it. I knowed I shoulda done the job myself."

Can o' Beans, on the other hand, was unperturbed. He/she explained to the stick and the shell that Spoon, in her panic, may have made a fortuitous choice. "As far as I'm concerned," he/she said, "the little dear's better off with Miss Charles than with Turn Around Norman. Just because our mysterious Mr. Norman has discovered the welding defect in humanity's ironclad notion of progress doesn't mean he's ready to actively participate in the schemes of the inanimate. True, Miss Charles may drop dead at the prospect herself, but unless she's changed, we do know that she's compassionate and eccentric—an excellent combination in a human being; we know that she kept me for four years without opening me up; we know she was fond of Miss Spoon and of your beloved Jezebel; and I feel we may be able to squeeze some valuable assistance from her without directly revealing ourselves to her. You know what I mean? A modicum of subtle manipulation. Harmless, of course."

Conch Shell nodded, while Painted Stick stared off into space, perhaps reminiscing about a time when the gulf between animate and inanimate was not quite so wide.

"Anyhow," the bean can continued, "Miss Charles shows up here in front of the cathedral almost as regularly as Mr. Turn Around. If Spoon uses her wits and follows your instructions, she'll be back with us tomorrow or the day after. And with any luck, we'll be better informed about our chances for Jerusalem."

Alas, Can o' Beans would have been less optimistic, Spoon less brave, were either of them privy to Ellen Cherry's private thoughts. As she trod back down East Forty-ninth Street, wagging the doggie bag in the frigid ebony air (the added weight of the dessert spoon going unnoticed), Ellen Cherry was deciding that since she was forsaking her personal artisthood, she must also forsake art over all. In general. Period. Otherwise, it would be akin to divorcing a man about whom she still cared, then hanging around to watch how he got along with his new wife. Could she not be a participant, she damn sure wasn't going to be a spectator.

But if her vow of rejection would end her dilemma about whether or not to attend Boomer's show (the exhibition had her both itching with curiosity and recoiling with distaste), it would likewise end her cultural pilgrimages to Fifth Avenue, her repetitive homages to "the only real artist in New York." By the time that she reached the Mel Davis Dog Boutique, its turkey cutout now a nostalgic silhouette in the night, she promised herself that she had been to see Turn Around Norman for the very last time.

Clearly, Ellen Cherry was going to miss the street performer. What was less clear was *why*.

Earlier, she had told herself that she was drawn to him for the same reason that Spike Cohen was drawn to Jerusalem: Turn Around Norman was not about money.

But was it entirely accurate to claim he was not about money? And if so, what was the big appeal of that?

Turn Around Norman didn't turn around for free. Nearly, but not quite. One could watch him for hours, weeks, and not pay a penny. On the other hand, his donation box—a cardboard container in which a child's jigsaw puzzle had once been packaged—was invariably in plain view, and there existed no overt prohibition against monetary contributions of Rockefellerian scope. Still, he was fortunate if he collected three bucks a day. Thus, while he seemed willing, even mildly eager, to accept a cash offering as an expression of appreciation for his work, his art, his turning around slowly on the street, he obviously had motives beyond the financial. Or else he was shooting without film in his camera.

To Ellen Cherry's mind, the fact that Turn Around Norman was dedicated to a rigorously controlled minimal act to the extent that he performed it relentlessly, day after day (except Wednesday afternoons), in sweet or murderous weather, before oblivious and occasionally abusive audiences, regardless of negligible material reward, all of that signified that he believed in something. No doubt, Jerusalem believed in something, as well. She didn't know what. For that matter, she had only a hunch about Norman's beliefs. Apparently, he believed in turning around.

"The trouble with these new New York artists," she had once complained to Boomer, "aside from the fact that they're busy stealing from the dead and each other—if that's not redundant—is that they're only in it for fame and fortune, they don't *believe* in anything."

"Yes, they do," argued Boomer. "They believe in fame and fortune."

So. Were there qualitative differences in believing in turning around slowly, very slowly, on the street and believing in fame and fortune? Was an obsession with money a slimy, shameful, rodent-lipped thing compared to an obsession with art?

Being two months behind on her rent at the Ansonia and facing a self-imposed reduction in wages, Ellen Cherry was in the uncomfortable position of having to consider a settlement from Boomer, of having to ask to be cut in on the earnings from his show at the Sommervell Gallery, a show she had just made up her mind to boycott. In order to maintain her current standard of living, she would have to be subsidized by sales of artworks created by a man who she knew didn't believe in anything, which is to say, who believed neither in his work nor hers. She had never objected to trading paintings for dollars. In fact, there was a time when she, Ellen Cherry, had maintained a salivary hankering for fortune and fame. It was not so long ago. But something had changed. . . .

Observing it at close range, artistic success, in socioeconomic terms, proved more of a demon than she had bargained for. Gradually, she found herself repulsed by the realization that her lifelong eye game (her private amusement and personal salvation) could be reduced to a commodity, like soda pop, jeans, TV Christianity, or Preparation H. The relationship between art and money was incomprehensible to her. It was as complicated as the Middle East, and not a rug in sight.

Money itself was incomprehensible. Almost from its inception, it had perplexed and befuddled those in whose lives it had appeared, and although modern people were used to it, although they dealt with it on a daily, if not hourly basis, and although it worked in their every thought the way that yeast worked in bread, they were no closer to understanding it than they had been at the beginning. Preoccupied with it, dominated—and ultimately bewildered—by it, introspective men and women finally had to confess that it clouded their vision of the world like . . . yes, you guessed it, like a veil.

When the fifth veil falls, and with it the illusion of financial worth, individuals might recognize themselves again, might find themselves standing, as if naked, among ancient values in a long-lost landscape.

Meanwhile, it can be stated with some validity that for all of the clamorings and phobias that it generates, money barely exists. An abstraction, a symbol, an act of faith, an IOU backed only by a banker's word, money is first and foremost a substitute. The funny part is that it's a substitute for things that often do not exist.

Within the framework of its temporal unfolding, however, turning around on the street is real.

Both money and art, powdered as they are with the romance and poetry of the age, are magic. Rather, money is *magic*, art is *magik*. Money is stagecraft, sleight of hand, a bag of clever tricks. Art is a plexus of forces and influences that act upon the senses by means of practical yet permanently inexplicable secret links. Admittedly, the line between the two can be as thin as a dime. What's more, the magicians of capitalism strengthen their hold on their audience through the manipulation of artistic images.

Long before the veil of commerce drooped down over the eyes of art, it had impaired the sight of religion. Ancient temples, pagan or otherwise, almost always doubled as treasuries and mints. The Temple of Jerusalem was no exception. The First Temple and both versions of the Second had served as financial centers for the state of Judah/Judea. Ellen Cherry wasn't aware of that. The Reverend Buddy Winkler probably was, but the light in which Buddy had seriously examined religion's ties with wealth was understandably dim. Can o' Beans was definitely aware of it, yet in his/her speculations on what the Third Temple might resemble, he/she had avoided any conjecture on if and how it might interface with the Bank of Israel. Even the fearless intellect of the bean tin found the subject forbidding.

What is plain is that neither money nor the love of it is the root of all evil. Evil's roots run deeper than that. Anyway, money is not a root. Money is a leaf. Trillions of leaves, actually; dense, bushy, dollar-green, obscuring the stars of reality with their false canopy. Who says that money doesn't grow on trees?

The introduction of money, with its seductive, if largely ambiguous promises, added a fresh measure of zip to the sport of life, but the zip turned to zap when the players, stupefied by ever-shifting intangibles, began to confuse the markers with the game.

So, even for those of us who can't personally witness Salome's dance, the fifth veil surely will fall. It will fall at the moment of our death. As we lie there, helpless, beyond distraction, electricity stealing out of our brains like a con man stealing out of a sucker's neighborhood, it will occur to many of us that everything we ever did, we did for money. And at that instant, right before the stars blink off, we will, according to what else we may have learned in life, burn with an unendurable regret—or have us a good silent laugh at our own expense.

This is the room of the wolfmother wallpaper. The room where the lobster tore the pillowcase, mistaking it for. . . . Whoops! Hold on. Speaking of mistakes, this is actually a far cry from the boudoir the wolfmother papered. This is not a room at all. This happens to be the intersection of East Forty-ninth Street and United Nations Plaza, where an abrupt, unexpected flurry of snow, propelled by a gust from the river, whipped Ellen Cherry's chapped face, driving all thoughts of money and art from her cerebrum, causing ice crystals to collect in the badly sprung honeycomb of her hair, and momentarily precipitating a hallucination of crustaceans and bed sheets, a flashback, perhaps, to a room in which her neurons may have strayed off course a forgotten dream ago.

Shaking off the image, the snow, the gust, the dip in temperature, she rounded the corner onto UN Plaza, only to witness in front of the I & I yet another scene that might have spun from a dream. There was a murmuring crowd. A hysteria of flashing red lights. A harsh arrival of men costumed for emergency.

At first, Ellen Cherry surmised it to be a spillover from the earlier demonstration at the UN building down the street, but as she drew nearer, she saw that the crowd was gathered passively about two lone men lying on the sidewalk in separate echo circles of blood. One of the men, who was being covered with a sheet, was Sylvester, a security guard in the restaurant's employ. The other, attended by medics, was Spike Cohen.

Ellen Cherry dropped the doggie bag on the pavement (within minutes, the bag—Spoon and all—was cordoned off by police, and the NYPD bomb squad was on its way to investigate it). She pushed her way to Spike and fell on her knees at his side. Blood was spurting from his head like rotgut from a wineskin. His eyes were wide, and he gasped as if trying to swallow all the air in the world.

Her stalled heart began to thump again when she realized that he was alive. But at that same hopeful moment, a voice of premonition rang in her ears. She didn't know from where it came or whose voice it was. It startled her to the extent that she stood up halfway and looked around. The voice said, "Boomer Petway won't be coming home from Jerusalem."

Why not? And what did that have to do with what was going on here?

She felt Abu's hand on her shoulder.

She overheard a snatch of song from an unseen boom box:

My heart is a Third World country
And your love is a tourist from Switzerland

She had never heard it before, yet it was eerily familiar. (A day would come when she would recognize it as Raoul Ritz's first recording.)

When she returned her attention to Spike, she fully expected him to be dead. However, the medics had capped the spurt, and there was a kind of weak grin on his face. From his vantage point down on the blood-warmed cement, he could inspect at his leisure every shoe in the crowd.

the
sixth
veil

The cold spell snapped in mid-December. Christmas shoppers went about in their shirt-sleeves. Poinsettias could have grown along Fifth Avenue, the days were so balmy and grand. The waxing moon was a winter moon, typically high and pasty, but the nights in which it swelled were as mild as baby oil. By Christmas Eve, the moon was full. It rolled in the sky like a spook wheel, a hoop of grainy ghost cheese. Despite the fact that it was the brighter of the two, the Christmas star kept its distance from that moon.

Midnight mass at St. Patrick's drew a capacity crowd. The archbishop spoke in a long-dead language about a long-dead carpenter. Nevertheless, an air of solemn gaiety prevailed. Down in the sub-basement, the choir barely audible to them, the inanimates lounged in the moonlight that streamed through the grate.

"It's a crying shame little Spoonzie ain't here," said Dirty Sock. "She'd enjoy the puddin' outta these carols and hymns."

"Indeed, she would," Can o' Beans agreed. "Indeed, she would. Personally, I prefer carols to rap tunes, but not by a wide margin. The carol radiates hope, the rap radiates aggression, but both are rooted in humanity's overwhelming feeling of helplessness."

"Stow it, perfesser. Give us a friggin' break. It's Christmas Eve!"

"And what might that occasion have to do with you, my polyester pal?"

In an attempt to head off a tiff, Conch Shell treated the can and the sock to a description of the winter festivals that had been held at that time of year on Jerusalem's Temple Mount. Evidently, the service under way upstairs was rather pale in comparison, although even Painted Stick, taking time out from his contemplation of that point where the beam of the moon intersected light from the star, had to admit that the pipe organ provided musical possibilities unimagined by drum or tambourine.

"Music has changed," said Painted Stick. "But the star in the East is the same."

Outside, in the newspaper delivery trucks that were making their early rounds, the headlines read: "Troops Ring Bethlehem as Tense Pilgrims Flock."

And in the men's toilet at Isaac & Ishmael's restaurant, over on United Nations Plaza, Verlin Charles stared through a tiny window at the Christmas star as he stood with his hand on his fly.

Verlin and Patsy had expected Ellen Cherry home for Thanksgiving, but she stood them up. At the last minute, she realized that she couldn't face the prospect of looking down the long oak table at a roast turkey, what with Boomer not yet back from Jerusalem. Her parents were disappointed but accepted her promise to spend Christmas in Colonial Pines. When Boomer's return was further delayed, she had backed out on Christmas as well.

"Fine and dandy," said Patsy. "If she won't come to us, we'll go to her."

"Hold your horses, woman," said Verlin. "Are you talkin' New York City? Christmas? Us?"

"All of the above. It'll be family. And it'll be romantic."

"It'll be a blessed nightmare. Of all the places to have Christmas . . ."

"Bud'll be there."

"I don't care."

"And I'll be there."

Verlin sputtered. He could tell that she was serious. Dad blast it! She had him over a barrel. He could celebrate the holiday alone—alone!—in Colonial Pines, or celebrate it with conniving wife and errant daughter in a hellish heathen cesspool where their lives wouldn't be worth two cents, not even on Jesus' birthday. And no telling how much postseason football he'd miss.

Now, on Christmas Eve, his bladder falling all over itself in its eagerness to expel the glass of Jewish wine that he had consumed just to be polite, Verlin stood at the urinal in a restaurant that could be blown sky-high at any second, afraid to pull the zipper and expose his tremulous member to the diseases that common sense told him would be lying in wait, grinning like skulls, smirking like queers, in a squalid place such as this.

When he glimpsed the star through the dirty little window above his head, he took momentary heart. Reminding himself that the love and protection of the Christ Child was everywhere, even in this sitting target on this terrible night, he grabbed hold of Baby Jesus' coattails and rode them to a calmer state of mind. Standing as far back from the urinal as the trajectory of his stream would allow, he went cautiously about his business, convinced that within the hour the worst Christmas Eve of his life would be over and he and Patsy would be nestled all snug in their bed in the comparative safety of the Waldorf-Astoria Hotel.

No sense acting sissy about this, he thought. He sighed and permitted his sphincter to uncoil. At that instant, however, the star disappeared, obscured by a strange face pressed suddenly against the windowpane, a dark Semitic face that glowered maliciously beneath a tattered white headdress. Verlin stepped backward, spraying a bamboo wall with his water. "Terrorist!" he screamed, and then fainted dead away.

Nobody heard Verlin's cry. Roland Abu Hadee and his wife, Nabila, were in the kitchen, the one washing dinner dishes, the other preparing coffee and dessert. At a dining room table, Patsy and Ellen Cherry were lost in conversation, this being their first opportunity to speak in private. Their day had been given over to shopping, Verlin and his credit cards in tow, and after baths and naps in their respective quarters, the long dinner party had begun.

The dinner celebration had more excuses than Buddy Winkler had boils. For openers, Christmas and Hanukkah were upon the land. Then, there was the occasion of it being Verlin and Patsy's first visit to New York. Next, there was the recently received letter from the chief of police that granted the I & I the right to reopen for business; it had been ordered closed following the drive-by shootings in November. Last but not least, Spike Cohen had been released from the hospital on the previous day. It was expected, in fact, that Spike

would join them at some point during dinner. He had been scheduled to spend the early half of the evening at a Hanukkah observance
with his son, then catch a taxi to the I & I. However, midnight had
arrived, and Spike had not. The consensus was that the Hanukkah
fete must have worn him out and he'd been put to bed. They hoped
he hadn't hurt himself.

Spike's shooting, in particular, and violence, in general, had dominated dinner conversation—Verlin was full of paranoid questions, to
which Abu supplied philosophical replies—but now that mother and
daughter were alone, the subject shifted quickly to romance.

"Okay," said Ellen Cherry, "this is Boomer's first letter." She
removed a page or two of childish pencil scrawls from a flimsy
air-mail envelope. "He's talking mostly about Jerusalem. He says
here, 'It's a city built upon cities, with one yet to come, the final one,
as Buddy claims, the New Jerusalem. Jerusalem throws you from one
culture into another and back again. You've got throbbing cultures
bumping into each other on every corner. Israel has got the best
people and the worst people in the world. Tough cowboy lunatics
toting Uzis, wall-to-wall fanatics of many persuasions. Folks so sweet
and compassionate they make you want to cry, and folks that's got
that mean streak that seems to always run through those with a
narrow focus.'

"He goes on to say, 'At first glance, you'd swear folks here are
living very close to the earth, which I like, but somehow they aren't
really attached to the earth, even when they work it. In their minds
and hearts, they're up in the sky somewheres. Buddy claims that one
day soon Jerusalem is going to rise into the heavens. If you ask me,
the whole damn city lives up in the clouds already.'

"Let's see. . . . Well, he goes on like that for a while. Then he talks
about how good the museum project is going. And right here he
throws me a crumb about how much he's looking forward to us
getting together. Although now, he says, it might not be until after
Thanksgiving. That's it. That's the first letter." Ellen Cherry looked to
her mother for a reaction, but Patsy just smiled and shrugged.

"All right, then. This is the next one." She opened a second
envelope. "Mama, wouldn't you like another quick glass of wine?
Daddy won't know."

"Lord, no, honey. I'm not used to alcohol. It'd make me plumb
silly."

"Suit yourself. Anyway, this one begins, 'Dear Sugar Booger.' Have you ever? I mean, who else but Boomer Petway? 'Dear Sugar Booger. The craziness of this place has put me under a spell. At times it fascinates me, and at times it makes me want to puke. One minute you're feeling inspired and pure and the next you're feeling like you laid down in shit. And it's all because Jerusalem is so all-fired *holy*. Looks to me like living in a sacred town can make folks extra ugly and hateful just as easy as making them extra nice. Some of the religious types here are downright scary. There's something scary about Jerusalem, on the whole, as beautiful as it is, and you remember how I react to things that scare me. I have to deal with them.'

"Yeah, well, I'll comment on that later. I'm going to skip some stuff here because Daddy'll be back in a second, and besides, Boomer's handwriting is a trial. He goes on to say that he met an Israeli sculptor whose work is included in the museum show, the same show that Boomer's in, and that this sculptor lives on a kibbutz right outside Jerusalem, a kind of kibbutz for artists, where there's a foundry and a metal fabrication shop, and that they're really hurting for an expert welder, because the one they had got called back into the army. Naturally, ol' Boomer volunteered to lend a hand."

"Well, that was right charitable of him."

"Maybe. In case you didn't notice, he neglected to mention whether his sculptor friend was male or female."

"Oh, honey!"

"Okay, so I'm being silly. But listen to this. 'Helping out on the kibbutz'—he spells it *k-e-b-o-o-t-s*—'will delay my getting back to New York for a month or two, but it was fixing to get delayed anyhow. Buddy wired me a considerable amount of money a couple of days ago and asked me to do him a favor and stay on in Jerusalem for a bit as he had a secret mission he wanted to assign me to.'"

Ellen Cherry slammed down the letter on her bamboo place mat. "Now what do you suppose that's all about?"

"I wouldn't have a notion in this world," Patsy said. "Bud's always jawing about how him and his Jews are gonna get Armageddon rolling, but, Lord, I don't know. I'll certainly ask him when we see him tomorrow."

"Uncle Buddy is manipulating Boomer. He knows just how to do it. 'Secret mission'! Boomer's a sucker for that 'secret mission' baloney."

"Yes, he likes his spy stories."

"Anyhow, mama, what do you think? He indicates he wants to stay and 'deal' with Jerusalem because he has to come to terms with the things in life that frighten him; which, I admit, are precious few. But he's deceiving himself if that's his reason, because, I assure you, coming back to New York and dealing with me and Ultima Sommervell and his new big art career is what he's really afraid of. It's scaring his britches off."

With her Miami-pink nails—Verlin had fumed and called her "Jezebel" when she painted them prior to dinner—Patsy scratched at the yellow stains that *tahini* had left on the tablecloth. "If you ask me, and you did ask me, please remember, Boomer's problem is mainly this: he loves you but he doesn't like you. He likes that Ultima woman but he doesn't love her. And he feels like a fake as an artist. The boy's so blessed confused he probably fits right in in the Middle East."

"All artists feel like imposters, except maybe the ones who really are. Even I used to, sometimes. Nowadays, I feel like I'm posing as a waitress, which is less of an offense. Anyway . . . mama, do you really think Boomer doesn't like me?"

Before Patsy could respond, the kitchen door was flung violently open, and out rushed Roland Abu Hadee, followed by an agitated man in a white headdress.

"Cherry!" shouted Abu. "Do you know the location of your father? Spike saw a man collapse on the toilet floor."

"Mr. Cohen?! What?!"

The whole party rushed to the men's room. They found Verlin on his feet again, although ashen and dazed; his fly open to the four winds, the seven seas, the twelve apostles, and ninety-nine bottles of beer on the wall.

After a protracted explanation, followed by a protracted apology, during which time Nabila let the *dondurma* melt and the coffee boil down into tractor fuel, what had transpired was perfectly clear.

Spike Cohen, his head heavily bandaged from the most recent surgery he had undergone to repair his gunshot wounds, had come with a special Christmas gift for the I & I. To enhance the surprise, Spike, with the assistance of his son and two of his son's friends, planned to sneak the present in through the kitchen. They had lugged it to the rear courtyard that the I & I shared with the East Indian restaurant next door. Because there were no windows in the kitchen, Spike had had his son boost him up to the toilet window, from whose perspective he hoped he might get a fix on Abu's whereabouts. It was pretty simple really. Hardly worth the lump on Verlin's head or the Pleistocene ooze at the bottom of the coffeepot.

Spike pumped Verlin's hand and handled Patsy's pumps: "Darlink, where have you found such a chic shoe down in Dixieland, already?" Then, he went out to the courtyard and directed his helpers to tote in the surprise. It proved to be a very large, very advanced, very expensive, state-of-the-art television set. Its screen ran six feet on the diagonal, and it operated with a revolutionary new picture tube, rather than a projector, providing the highest possible video resolution. Spike had had it flown in from Tokyo, and there wasn't a TV in New York that could match it.

"Hot damn!" exclaimed Verlin, coming rapidly out of shock. "You could count the individual beads of sweat flying off a blindsided quarterback on this baby. Heck, you might even be able to see Tom Landry's teeth."

It took nearly an hour to hook the TV up, and might have taken longer without Verlin's expertise. The engineer was put in charge of the project, and he responded with enthusiastic efficiency. When it was perfectly balanced and adjusted, they all settled back and watched the last half of *It's a Wonderful Life*. There wasn't a dry eye in the restaurant.

Although Isaac & Ishmael's dining room had remained virtually vacant throughout the autumn, its bar gradually had begun to attract a small, regular clientele, consisting mostly of bachelors or bored husbands who worked at the UN Headquarters. They filtered in late at night to sip Maccabee beer and munch Abu's *falafel*. The shooting had put an end to that, but Spike hoped that the giant TV would bring the fellows back, and others with them. Could he have guessed the extreme to which the TV would eventually affect their lives, albeit indirectly, he might have wept that night for reasons other than Jimmy Stewart's epiphany.

It was well past two in the morning, and one of those yawn epidemics was gathering momentum, when the diners donned their lightweight coats and exchanged their Merry Christmases and good-byes. As he embraced Ellen Cherry, something jostled Abu's memory. "Oh, yes. I almost forgot. Your spoon."

"What?"

"Your spoon. The one that was in your doggie bag. The police left it."

"I don't know what you're talking about, Mr. Hadee. I never had any spoon in any doggie bag."

"The night of the shootings. Remember? You dropped a bag out front, and the entire police department ducked for cover. It must have been your own spoon in the bag, it was too fine and too tarnished to be one of ours. In any case, I finally got around to restoring it for you. For shame, Patsy. Did you neglect to introduce your daughter to the virtues of silver polish?"

Abu turned and went to the kitchen. Ellen Cherry looked as blank as a paraplegic's dance card. "I don't have a clue what he's talking about," she said, as she hugged and kissed Spike Cohen. She whispered in Spike's ear, "Your big TV made my daddy's day. Only thing he's seen in New York that hasn't disgusted him."

"Always show respect to your papa," Spike cautioned her. He pinned her with the glint in his emerald eyes. They seemed all the more green now, next to the white bandages. "After New Year's I get for you a nice gallery, little artist lady."

"Waitress," she corrected him. "Little waitress lady."

From the kitchen, Abu fetched a petite and gleaming dessert spoon. Ellen Cherry examined it, her mouth opening wider and wider. Her life flashed before her, and her goose bumps hatched gosling bumps. "How in the world . . . ?" The hair on her head would have stood up if only it could have gotten itself untangled.

For her part, Spoon felt greatly relieved by the reunion. But, then, she was already in a state of bliss as a result of Abu's ministrations. The caring professionalism with which he had soaped and rinsed and polished her, oh dear, oh goodness, she thought she'd died and gone to heaven.

At the Radio City Music Hall Christmas Extravaganza the next afternoon, Ellen Cherry might just as well have been blindfolded. Oblivious to the prancing Rockettes in their skimpy Santa suits, she was preoccupied with the same thoughts that had kept her awake most of the night.

She *could* have been mistaken about leaving the spoon in that cave, she supposed, yet, had it remained in her possession, how could it have gone unnoticed for the past twenty months? It could not. Unless Boomer had been concealing it for some demented reason, some kind of lamebrained joke. Boomer was capable of such things, though he plainly wasn't capable of planting the spoon in her doggie bag from his kibbutz near Jerusalem. Had some kind of spooky parapsychological phenomenon occurred? Or was she losing her young mind?

Her parents thought that she was overreacting. They were sure that there was a logical explanation and that it would come to her in time.

"You're making a mountain out of a molehill," said Verlin. "That's what art's done to you."

"Relax, hon," Patsy advised. "Miracles do not occur around secondhand silverware."

After the show, they caught a cab to the Ansonia, where, in Ellen Cherry's apartment, they were to open gifts and share Christmas dinner. During the taxi ride, Patsy was virtually as distracted as her daughter. To nobody in particular, she said, with a sigh, "If I'd of stuck to my dancing, that could've been me up there."

Resisting the urge to question her morals on Christmas Day, Verlin glared at her and shook his head. "You're way too short," he said.

Raoul Ritz opened the door for them, a sprig of mistletoe clipped to his porkpie hat. Ellen Cherry didn't hesitate. She kissed him square on the mouth, going so far as to slide in a length of tongue. The lightning bolt that zigzagged up her thighs must have melted her underpants. She could feel them starting to drip. Without question, she would have invited Raoul to drop by that evening when his shift was through, had not the mystery of the prodigal utensil suddenly interjected itself. She gathered her composure and pushed her parents toward the elevator. She had to find out if the spoon was still there.

"*Felices Navidades,* Miz Charl," called Raoul, running a guitar-callused, nicotine-brightened finger along his freshly kissed lips. "You hear my song, man?"

"What song?" Ellen Cherry inquired, but, alas, the elevator door closed on his reply.

"*He's* cute," said Patsy.

Verlin glowered.

Ellen Cherry's hand was actually trembling as she pulled open the cabinet drawer. But there the spoon was, looking as mundane and lifeless as the stainless steel flatware beside it, although, thanks to Roland Abu Hadee (or so thought Ellen Cherry), generating a sparkle that put the other utensils to shame. *Daddy's right, I'm just being dumb,* she thought. Nevertheless, she was in the process of removing the spoon and transferring it to the mantel of the no longer functional fireplace when the Reverend Buddy Winkler buzzed from the lobby.

"Let him in quick," said Verlin. "It's time we put some Christ and some football back in this Christmas."

Like an ear of corn with a diamond in its lapel, Buddy looked prosperous, in a seedy sort of way. His blue Armani suit was neither baggy nor wrinkled, but his white shirt was so stiff with starch it could have been used to board up a window, and his tie was badly knotted and two inches too wide. Worse, it was brown. With Day-Glo pheasants on it. Ellen Cherry had seen Buddy on television recently, wearing a tie that was embroidered with the words, "Jesus Is Lord." She was glad, upon reflection, that today he had selected game birds.

The Reverend Buddy Winkler still didn't have a TV ministry of his own. For that matter, nearly a third of the radio stations affiliated with the Southern Baptist Voice of the Sparrow Network had dropped his Sunday morning sermons as he became increasingly militant in his political views, especially in regard to the Middle East. The stations didn't necessarily reject his views, but his graphic descriptions of the horror of the End Days, combined with the power of his vocal saxophone and the obvious delight he took in forecasting carnage, had been spoiling a lot of breakfasts. Nevertheless, his fame had spread. He seemed forever to be turning up as guest minister on some other evangelist's broadcast, and the media had come to count on him for hair-raising sound bites. Thanks largely to Buddy, the Third Temple Platoon had gained some credibility, especially among Christian fundamentalists. Buddy's skill at extracting cash from right-wing *goyim* earned him the gratitude of ultra-Zionists, who scarcely minded that he spent portions of the contributions on gold teeth and Italian suits.

Intimidated by Patsy, perhaps, Buddy kept a fairly low profile at table that day. True, his blessing ran on so long the gravy started to clot. And at one point, his saxophone bell muffled by candied yams with marshmallows, he commenced to catalog the various sinful activities of contemporary humanity, leaning heavily on those transgressions involving sex, alcohol, drugs, and socialism. The Lord was sorely vexed, according to Bud. "Well, what does he expect?" said Patsy. "He hasn't made a house call in two thousand years. When the cat's away, the mice will play."

Mostly, however, the feast went smoothly. Ellen Cherry focused on her mother's cooking, although she stole occasional glances at the spoon on the mantelpiece, and, once or twice, closed her eyes and envisioned Raoul. *If the end of the world really is right around the corner,* she thought, *I ought to be having some fun.*

After pumpkin pie, mincemeat pie, and fruitcake, everybody pushed away from the table. They didn't push far. What with all the canvases stacked against the walls, there was hardly an excess of space in which four abundantly fed people might mingle.

"Why don't you show us your new pictures, hon?" Patsy requested.

"These are old ones, mama. I told you I haven't painted since back in the fall."

"They're new to us."

Ellen Cherry wavered. "No-ooo. I don't think so."

"Come on, now. We're family, and we're interested in what you do. Verlin, pry yourself loose from that blessed ball game and appreciate your daughter's talent."

"Oh, mama!"

Buddy stroked his chin. His boils were not quite red enough to actually enhance a Christmas setting. "Yes, doll baby, let's have us a gander at how you're using God's gifts."

Against her better judgment, Ellen Cherry began turning paintings around, careful not to expose any of the full-length Boomer nudes.

"Hmmm," said Verlin.

"My, my," said Buddy.

"Very good, dear," said Patsy.

Privately, each of them was thinking something along the lines of, *At least they're not a jumble and a mishmash like she did before. At least she's got the right colors on things. But why in the world would anybody . . . ?*

The family was unimpressed. And a trifle concerned. But as each fresh larger-than-life rendering of bean can, dining implement, or rumpled sock—*Why in the world . . . ?*—was revealed, Spoon, upon her mantel perch, could barely refrain from leaping into the room and dancing herself all around.

Verlin locked in again on the flying footballs discernible among the flashes, pops, and flickers of the tiny, tinny, black-and-white portable that, at his urging, Buddy had consented to fetch to the Ansonia. It was a close game, a bowl game, and to watch it on the magnificent screen at the I & I, to watch it unveiled by this spray of electric blue eel spit, might possibly have been worth the risk to life and limb. Were it the Super Bowl, there was no question but that he'd chance it. *Christmas is Christmas,* Verlin thought, *but the Super Bowl is something, by golly, a man can sink his fangs in.*

When Patsy began to clear the dishes, Ellen Cherry arose to assist her. She froze in her tracks, however, when the preacher walked up to the canvases still facing the wall and made to turn one of them around.

"No, Uncle Buddy! Don't!"

Too late. He reversed the painting and stepped back a pace or two to regard it. Fortunately, it proved not to be one of those studies of Boomer in which his glorified penis hung like an upside down ice-cream cone (sometimes a scoop of raspberry, sometimes a dip of grape), but, rather, her very last painting, the portrait with the redundancy of tongues.

"My, my," said Buddy. "What have we here? Uh-huh. If this don't broach the Satanic, I'll eat my hat."

"Bud," said Patsy, "you just had dinner."

"Cute remarks ain't gonna get you through Saint Peter's radar, Patsy Charles, and they don't cut ice with me, neither. Instead of tryin' to lighten the air with your smart-ass brand of humor, better you should join me in contemplatin' why your daughter, who looks so much like you, right down to the Jezebel goo on your eyelids, why your daughter has gone and depicted her husband, the man who she's united with in the holy sight of God, as some kinda demon. Yea, as the very Beast!"

"I thought the Beast was a woman," said Ellen Cherry.

"Bud, it's Christmas," said Verlin.

"Oh, let him rant," said Patsy. "He'll give himself a case of heartburn that'll have him praying for mercy."

"Patsy, now . . ."

"Besides, I find the subject interesting. Bud, as you surely are aware, it was Mr. Boomer Petway who went off and left my Ellen Cherry."

"Frankly, I'm not surprised."

"And he's over there in Is-ra-el, as you call it. Now, let us put aside, for the moment, the possibility that a woman who's been deserted, deceived—"

"Mama!"

"—and had her poor heart broken, might be inclined to portray the rascal in an unflattering manner. I want to put that aside and ask you a theological question. You said that Ellen Cherry and Boomer were eternally united. Now, I'm wondering, what if ol' Boomer was to get himself killed over there in Is-ra-el? Wouldn't it be permissible, in God's sight and your own, for Ellen Cherry to then take herself another husband?"

"Last thing *I'd* want," muttered Ellen Cherry.

"Bud?"

Suspicious, Buddy was slow to reply. He thought it might be a trick question. "I can't see what you're aimin' at, but, yes, it's perfectly righteous for a widow-woman to remarry."

"Well, then, when that widow-woman dies and goes to heaven, who does she bed down with there, hubby number one or hubby number two?"

Verlin, who'd turned from the game to shush Patsy, stopped in mid-shush. By golly, that *was* an interesting question.

"People do not 'bed down' in heaven," said Buddy, with a slather of contempt.

"No? They don't? Folks don't never get to recline and rest in heaven? An ol' widow-woman is expected to be on her feet twenty-four hours a day?"

"You weren't talkin' 'bout *rest*."

"I wasn't? What was I talking 'bout, Bud?"

"Patsy, dad blast it!" swore Verlin. "Let him be. Forget that fool picture, Bud, and watch this drive. Washington's getting ready to score."

"All right," said Patsy. "I'm sorry. I guess that's not the kinda question a serious theologian would want to waste his brains on. It was silly. I mean, first off, Boomer is not gonna get killed in Jerusalem." She paused. And smiled so sweetly that the resident roaches, already in a state of high excitement due to the aroma of pies and candied yams, peered out from the plumbing to see where such sweetness was coming from. "Unless you *get* him killed," she said.

"What the hell do you mean?"

"That's what I'd like to know! What I wanna know, what Boomer's little wife here has every right to know, is what kinda monkey business you fixin' to get that ol' boy involved in over there?"

Buddy tugged at the knot in his tie. He looked around the apartment. All eyes were on him, including his cousin's. Washington would have to cross the goal line without Verlin Charles.

This is the room of the wolfmother wallpaper. The room where the giant moth beat its papery scales against the jeweled lampshade. The room where Jezebel beat her kohl-encrusted lashes against the window glass. Where the pinwheel beat her dizzy children for confusing the north wind with Santa Claus.

Few inanimate objects believed in Saint Nick. And who besides they were in a better position to know? Should an old fatso in a red suit free-fall down the chimney in the middle of the night, the family and its pets might sleep through it, but every object in the parlor would a witness be. Certainly, the objects that occupied the cathedral basement hadn't swallowed the Santa story, no matter how often the merchants had told it. They were up and about early on Christmas morning, but not to look for treats or consumer goods. Rather, they were curious to see if Turn Around Norman would report to his station on the holiday.

To their surprise, he did appear. And although Fifth Avenue was deserted, except for the occasional wino or homeless lunatic, he remained there throughout the day, like a hive of hard rubber turning on an axis of bees. Never had the objects seen him turn with greater delicacy, greater intensity. Extending and contracting himself impossibly, like butter that melts and then congeals, like musical butter, a butter pat with harmonica stops, making the trip from skillet to refrigerator and back again several times a second. He stepped out of time, as if time were a pair of pants. He folded time over the back of a chair and paraded around it, trouserless and unashamed, sniffing at the rose that never fades. He turned like a radioactive worm in amber, like a bushel of phosphorescent plankton turning in the colon of a constipated sea serpent.

Had they hands, the objects would have applauded. "That there's good stuff," Dirty Sock proclaimed, and the rest of them concurred.

They conjectured that it might have been the peace and quiet that inspired this extraordinary display, that allowed Turn Around Norman to transcend his limits and turn as they had never seen him turn before, turn more slowly, yet with more fire. Without the squeeze of crowds, the jibes of detractors, the mad mephitic mafficking of traffic, perhaps he was both more focused and less restrained. Then, they noticed something else. On that day, for the first time, Norman was working without a donation box.

"It's Christmas," said Can o' Beans. "It's Christmas, so he's performing for free."

"Yes," put in Conch Shell. "It is as if this performance is a gift the fellow is offering. Although to whom he is offering it we cannot know."

"I only wish Miss Charles were here to enjoy it," the bean can said.

"I wish to hell Miz Charles was here, too," said Dirty Sock. "Maybe the wild-haired bimbo wouldda brought Spoonzie back."

As one, their thoughts all switched to Spoon. Where and how was Spoon spending this Christmas Day? If any inanimate object did believe in Santa Claus, it probably was Spoon.

Spoon was thinking of them, as well. It seemed that in order to justify why he had encouraged Boomer to linger in Jerusalem, why he'd handed him a "secret assignment," Buddy found it necessary to go into a long spiel about the Dome of the Rock. "So that's what the Temple Mount is like these days," said Spoon to a completely bewildered ashtray. "Just wait until I inform my friends."

"Y'all know what the Dome of the Rock is?" Buddy asked.

Patsy rotated her curls in the negative direction.

"A covered stadium on Gibraltar," ventured Verlin. "Where they play the Mediterranean Super Bowl."

"I've heard Mr. Hadee speak of it," said Ellen Cherry. "Must be connected in some way with Jerusalem."

"Well, yes indeedy, it's the blessed *centerpiece* of Jerusalem," Buddy informed them. "It's up there on the Temple Mount, where the Hebrew temples of Solomon and Herod stood, where our young Lord Jesus outfoxed the rabbis, and so forth. In the seventh century, your wily A-rab was running the show in that part of the world, and he built a very expensive mosque on the ruins of Herod's Temple, built two mosques, actually, and the biggest one, the one all covered with beautiful blue tiles and sportin' a bodacious big golden dome, he called the Dome of the Rock. It's the first blessed thing a body lays eyes on when he gets near Jerusalem.

"This here Dome of the Rock is the third most sacred place in the Islamic religion. Why? Because ol' Mohammed swore up and down that God took him for a horseback ride to heaven from the Temple Mount. Rode him around for a spell, introduced him to Moses and Jesus, then dropped him off agin right where he started. How's that for a fish story?

"Well, you can burn your A-rab for a fool, but you won't git no ashes. Mohammed's whopper gave the Moslems claim to the Temple Mount as a place of major importance in their own religion, cuttin' in on the legitimate claims of your Christian and your Jew, and his followers went on to build these ritzy mosques up there. Jerusalem's back in Jewish hands at last, but your A-rab is sittin' tight on the Temple Mount, and he's got the Jew and the Christian by the balls. Pardon me, ladies. Pardon me, please."

"But what's all the fuss about the Arabs having it?" asked Patsy.

"Yeah," said Verlin. "I can't figure out what all that's got to do with us Christians. Or how you, and now Boomer, fit into it."

Ellen Cherry was silent. She leaned back on the sofa, rubbed her full tummy, and thought, *Middle East. Rugs. Boomer. Rugs. Boomerrugs.*

"Prophecy!" It was a saxophone honk of the most forceful urgency. "Prophecy!" A wild, primitive, blue-rimmed blare such as might have issued from the gullet of a marsh stork whose eggs were threatened by predators. "Don't you know your prophecy? To know God's prophetic word is to know the future. The Bible is better than a crystal ball. God's *tole* us ever'thing that's to come to pass. Verlin, you've read your Scriptures."

"All right, I have. But I don't recall any mention of this Dome of the Rock. . . ."

"Well, of *course,* the Scriptures don't mention it by name. The blamed thing wasn't built yet when the Scriptures was written."

"But, Bud," said Patsy, "you just said that God told us everything that was to happen."

The sax emitted a disgusted grunt. "Not by name. God didn't mention things by *name.* Modern names of things didn't mean diddly-squat to the prophets of old. They went by description, which is more lasting and accurate than names. And this is what they conveyed to us concerning the subject in question. Listen up."

"I hope this is leading to Boomer Petway," said Patsy.

"Amen," said Ellen Cherry, which, for better or for worse, was the only religious word she'd uttered all Christmas.

"First," said Buddy, "the first stage of God's program is that your Jew would return to Israel." He paused and cleared his throat. "Is-ra-el. After the Romans destroyed Herod's Temple, the Jews scattered like buckshot, lit out for here, there, and ever'where, this ghetto and that med school, but Jehovah promised that someday they'd regroup and git their milk and honey back, and, now, for a fact, they got it. Second stage was that Jerusalem would once agin be a Jewish city. Well, sure as shootin', in nineteen hundred and sixty-seven, that come to pass, prophecy fulfilled. The third and final stage is that the Temple shall be rebuilt. That's next in line. Then—bingo! Armageddon and Redemption."

"So, why don't they just rebuild the thing?" asked Patsy.

"How can they rebuild it when the dad-gummed Dome of the Rock is sittin' smack dab on their building site? That's the problem, children. Our Lord can't come back till the Third Temple is built, and the Temple can't be built as long as the Dome of the Rock is there. Are you catchin' on?"

"Well, if the Lord said it would get rebuilt, it'll get rebuilt."

"Dang right it will, Patsy. We're gonna make sure of that."

"How?"

"By levelin' them A-rab mosques and recapturin' the Temple Mount."

"You're planning to destroy the Dome of the Rock? You and your buddies?"

"Me and my yeshivas. Yes, you might say that."

"So that the Messiah will come?"

"After the Temple is rebuilt, he'll *have* to come."

"Hold on just one minute, Bud. Sounds to me like you're trying to force the Messiah's hand. To *force* the Second Coming into happening."

The Reverend Buddy Winkler shrugged. He picked a crumb of pie crust from the table and consigned it to the snap and grind of golden choppers, one less midnight snack to which the roaches might look forward. "How long we supposed to wait?" he asked.

"Why, we're supposed to wait until the Lord is good and ready, that's how long."

"Patsy's right," said Verlin. "Doesn't seem right to be messin' with Jesus Christ's timetable. To try to hurry him into something. Doesn't that trouble you?"

"Used to. Then I remembered the words, 'God helps them what helps themselves.' Maybe that's why Christ has been takin' so blamed long. He's been waitin' and waitin' for us to git up offen our fat fannies and seize the initiative. After all, the Jew helped hisself to Jerusalem. It wasn't handed to him on no silver platter. That, as you're aware, was way back in sixty-seven. Time to git on with it!"

Verlin shook his head. "I don't know, Bud . . ."

"Well, I know. It come to me in a vision. Loud and bright. Right in your own living room. Which is the only reason I'm lettin' you in on our plans. 'Course, I can't tell you ever'thing." He fired a glance at Ellen Cherry. "I shouldn't be saying *nothin'* in front of our little painted-up doll baby here. Not with the company she keeps."

"Oh, take a hike, Uncle Bud."

"We met that Spike and Abu last night," said Patsy. "They were right nice gentlemen."

"Right nice tools of Satan."

Verlin spoke. "They weren't all that bad, Bud."

"Oh, no? Well, lemme tell you . . ."

"Just shut up about them! You've got a hell of a nerve criticizing them and anything they do, you and your screwball schemes. Demolishing a mosque somewhere to make Jesus come back. What a fairy tale! They ought to lock you away before you hurt somebody."

"Ellen Cherry, now," said Verlin.

"Oh, a lot of folks are gonna git hurt," said Buddy, grinning. "Make no mistake 'bout that."

"And is one of those folks Boomer Petway?" asked Patsy. "You getting him involved in blowing up that Dome of the Rock?"

"Nobody, I don't believe, said nothin' 'bout blowing nothin' up. And, no, Boomer ain't gonna git hurt. Unless the Devil hurts him. Which he can't iffen he's satisfactorily repentant. I just needed a man in Jerusalem is all. My yeshivas are dedicated, but they're, you know, not like us. They're what you might call exotic. Esoteric. We got us good solid Christians in Jerusalem, but I feel they sometimes let themselves git bamboozled by the Jews. I jest needed a man of my own over there, somebody I could trust, in case I ever have an errand or two to run that I don't necessarily want none of them others to know about."

"So Boomer's your errand boy?"

"Boomer ain't nothin', Patsy. He ain't nothin', and he don't know nothin'. He's just there in case the Lord and I have need of him."

"You better be careful what you get him into."

"Oh, I will. I will."

"Why don't we please change the subject?" Verlin suggested. "The dang game's in halftime. Here, we got us some presents to unwrap." From beneath Ellen Cherry's scraggly but artistically decorated tree, he removed a large package, wrapped in white paper with a green and red holly pattern. "Here, Bud. I do believe Santy left this one for you."

"Why, thank you," said Buddy. "Thank y'all." He pulled at the green bow. "Lemme see what's in here."

"Hope it fits," said Verlin.

"It will," said Ellen Cherry. "It's a straitjacket."

The minister didn't respond. Very slowly, very carefully, he loosened the wrapping, exhibiting a bit more patience with his Christmas surprise than he had for the end of the world. Restless, Verlin stole glances at the halftime show, and Patsy sponged a smear of yam from the tabletop. Under the sink, the cockroaches monitored Patsy's action with exasperation, as if the cockroaches were a needy institution and Patsy one of those coy philanthropists who never give their money away.

The family gathering dissolved about ten-thirty. Alone, Ellen Cherry's thoughts returned again and again to Raoul. She had all but decided to invite him up, but when she went to the toilet to take a pee, she discovered that she'd gotten her "dot."

Oh, well. She sighed. And while begrudgingly inserting a tampon, sang three complete verses of "Jingle Bells."

On the day after Christmas, Verlin and Patsy went to the Museum of Modern Art to have a look at the Airstream turkey. It was Patsy's idea. "I've seen the fool thing for nothin'," complained Verlin. "Why do I have to pay some Yankee good money to see it again?"

They went in a taxi, its windows rolled down to receive the unseasonable warmth. The chaos and din of Day After shoppers flooded in with the weather. "It's like Asia," said Patsy, marveling at the multitudes, their gaily colored burdens, their amplified murmur. "It's like—" said Verlin, unable to conceive of a continent, a country, any community of humans with which to compare this parcel-packing, fume-inhaling, elbow-throwing, traffic-dodging throng. "It's like the coronation of the locust queen," said Verlin finally. Patsy didn't understand, and Verlin wasn't sure that he did, either, although his cerebrum supported the frail memory of a plague documented on a wildlife show.

Understandably, Ellen Cherry had scant desire to see the turkey again, especially now that it was surrounded by art. Surrounded by art? The turkey *was* art. The art cardinals had ordained it so. Well, she would wager that it was the only work in the Modern Museum in which a couple had enjoyed a honeymoon, although, on second thought, there were several paintings in the collection that looked as if they'd been fucked over.

When they stopped by the Ansonia on the way to the airport— Patsy had to pick up her pie plates—her parents had little to say about the motorized turkey except that it looked "different, really different" parked inside a big, grand room. They did, however, chatter about another piece of Boomer's, something the museum apparently had purchased out of the Sommervell show. It was, as they described it, a huge, welded steel coathanger, maybe six feet long. Folded over its bar was a flat, deflated skyscraper, sewn out of canvas, its windows, entranceways, and other architectural features painted on. The piece was hanging from the ceiling, and there was a card on the wall that listed Boomer's name, the materials he had used, and the title. The title was *Donald Trump's Pants Come Back From the Cleaners.*

"Obviously," said Ellen Cherry, in a mock Ultima accent, "it's fraught, simply fraught, with significance."

Verlin was perplexed. "I see that stuff of Boomer's on display in a famous museum, and I see them pictures of ol' socks and cans and spoons that you're making . . ."

"I'm still freaked out about that spoon," said Ellen Cherry, glancing at the mantelpiece.

"Oh, honey, it's not exactly in the poltergeist class," said Patsy.

". . . and I wonder who all's crazy in this world and who's sane."

"Well, Daddy, I used to believe that artists went crazy in the process of creating the beautiful works of art that kept society sane. Nowadays, though, artists make intentionally ugly art that's only supposed to reflect society rather than inspire it. So I guess we're all loony together now, loony rats in the shithouse of commercialism."

"That's pretty language from a young lady."

"I will say this, though: the looniest artist I ever met was normal as white bread beside Buddy Winkler."

"You take your uncle Bud too serious. He's mainly just talk. And some of that talk we sinners would do well to heed."

"I hope for his sake it's just talk, because if I ever find out he had anything to do with shooting Mr. Cohen . . ."

"Hush, girl! Don't you be insinuatin' stuff like that."

"Okay, but . . ."

Ellen Cherry accompanied them to the sidewalk, where Pepe whistled them a cab. Raoul wasn't on duty yet. After Patsy and Verlin had driven away to La Guardia, she went back upstairs, lay down on the sofa, and attempted to nap. Every time she started to doze off, however, she experienced the sensation that the spoon on the mantelpiece was watching her.

Eventually, although she felt ridiculous in doing so, she got up and stuck the spoon in her underwear drawer. Next to her vibrator. It would have been humanly impossible for her to imagine the conversations that were to ensue from that meeting.

After New Year's (a toxically lonely New Year's, on the eve of which she'd gone searching for Raoul, her diaphragm already in place, only to be informed by Pepe that Raoul and "his band" had up and split to Los Angeles, man), Ellen Cherry was switched to the dinner shift at Isaac & Ishmael's. She had become, for all practical purposes, a cocktail waitress, since business at the I & I was largely confined to the bar.

The important thing was that there *was* business. When word of the huge, high-definition television spread through the neighborhood, men dropped in out of curiosity and stayed to drink, snack, chat, and watch sporting events. Many foreigners who were connected to the United Nations had developed a taste for American sports. To watch the contests on a mammoth screen while washing down familiar Mediterranean treats with their native beers, wines, thick coffees, or teas was an enticement hard to resist. Only a few complained about the bamboo. Some even brought their wives. On Super Bowl Sunday, when the bar was packed to overflowing, Greeks actually sat down next to Turks, Arabs next to Jews.

A Super Bowl kicker could have placed a field goal inside the smile of Roland Abu Hadee. Spike Cohen wore a satisfied smile, as well, although his green eyes, greener than the Egyptian beer freighted by the waitpersons, greener than the cucumber slices that garnished the dishes of *baba ghanoug,* eyes hooded now by a crooked arch of scar tissue; Spike's eyes turned frequently to survey the street—and the nondescript black shoes of the two security guards, marching on the frosty sidewalk, to and fro, to and fro.

When Ellen Cherry and Boomer were turkeying across America, they frequently found themselves looking at the rear end of vehicles upon which bumper stickers or license-plate holders proclaimed publicly and rather plaintively, "I'd Rather Be Skiing." Or, "I'd Rather Be

Golfing." Some of the discontented motorists would rather have been hang gliding, while others wanted everyone on the road to be advised that they would have preferred to have been spiking a volleyball, climbing a mountain, sailing a boat, riding a mule, picking wild mushrooms, playing bridge, square dancing, or building the Eiffel Tower out of toothpicks.

"I wonder what *my* sticker would say?" Ellen Cherry had mused. "I reckon it'd be, 'I'd Rather Be Painting.' " She took a long pull from a can of diet Pepsi. "How about you, hon? What would your sticker say?"

She suspected that he'd insist on "I'd Rather Be Engaged in Cunnilingus," although she knew, and believed that deep inside *he* knew, that his proclamations of ungovernable sexual appetite were, like most males', somewhat exaggerated. She wasn't positive that he'd even heard her, for he had been scanning the roadside, counting cows, mentally welding broken hay balers, or something equally absorbing. Yet, Boomer hadn't hesitated. He'd made a frown so sad and wide that it was reflected on the side of her athletically sweating Pepsi. And he'd said:

"They're a right sorry admission of defeat, them signs are. If my life was that compromised, I sure wouldn't advertise it. My sign would say, 'If There Was Something Else I'd Rather Be Doing, I'd Damn Well Be Doing It.' "

Ellen Cherry recalled that exchange as she subwayed to work. By the time she walked from the station to the I & I, the Super Bowl would be over, thank goodness, but there was bound to be a lot of cleaning up to do. She didn't dread it, exactly. In fact, she was ambivalent to a degree that made her wonder how her bumper sticker would have read had one been affixed to her buttocks on that nippy January afternoon. Her life seemed deflated, vacuous, pointless, like Colonial Pines personified. But she couldn't think of a single other thing that she'd rather be doing. At least nothing to which she was willing to admit.

Several blocks away, the objects were lined up at the window grate, wondering where everybody was. It wasn't unusual for them to puzzle over the whereabouts of Ellen Cherry and Spoon. The objects—the can and the sock, at any rate—thought about Ellen Cherry and Spoon as frequently as a reformed cigarette smoker thinks about his little lost friends. Today, however, the population of Manhattan seemed to have disappeared as completely as their comrade and their potential benefactor. There was nothing moving on Fifth Avenue except Turn Around Norman, and he looked like the last strand of spaghetti to twirl out of Pompeii.

The congregation at mass that noon had been untypically small, consisting primarily of elderly women, held upright by mahogany canes and the galvanizing glare of their diamonds. The few men among them had bolted the instant the service ended. Even the archbishop beat a hasty retreat, diving into his waiting limo and lashing his chauffeur with his rosary beads, like a jockey whipping a mount. What was the hurry? Where could everyone else be? Conch Shell tried to reassure Painted Stick that nothing momentous had transpired in Jerusalem. "The age that is to come has not yet come," she said, but she wasn't totally convincing. Those two had never heard of the Super Bowl, naturally, and the other two had forgot.

Eventually, an old sedan rattled up to the crosswalk, full of music, smoke, and rust. When the light changed, it pooted and tooted off in the direction of New Jersey, but not before the objects noted a sticker on its bumper that announced, "I'd Rather Be Partying." Can o' Beans imagined it an infraction of taste, if not of grammar, declaring, "You should never trust anyone who uses 'party' as a verb." He/she felt appropriately chastised, however, when Dirty Sock growled and shot back, "Uh-huh, and don't trust anybody who'd rather be grammatically correct than have a good time."

"Touché," said the bean can. "Although in the age that is to come, the two needn't be mutually exclusive."

Some of the Super Bowl fans stayed on for dinner. Alcohol must have made them very hungry or else very brave. Spike Cohen alone seemed to remember how dangerous the I & I could be. From his post behind the cash register, he kept one eye on the street, as if the street were a crocodile-skin shoe that might at any moment revert to its original state of being. When, around the corner on First Avenue, a truck backfired, thin electrical noises came out of his windpipe.

Spike's jitters were for naught. Except for the fact that they ran out of chick-peas, the evening produced scant catastrophe. The next evening was positively humdrum. And the one after that was as bereft of disorder as a Heidelburg symposium on anal retention. In truth, the entire winter passed as peacefully and leisurely as a python digesting a Valium addict. The many enemies of the restaurant and its politics either shifted their attention to targets closer to the Middle East or else decided that the intractable Cohen and Hadee simply weren't worth the trouble. In any case, Isaac & Ishmael's first stint as the most famous restaurant in New York definitely was over.

Relatively speaking, Ellen Cherry Charles likewise spent an uneventful winter. About the only time that the needle bounced on her seismograph was when Boomer informed her, at the close of one of his increasingly infrequent letters, that if she would drop by the Sommervell Gallery, she could pick up a check.

It seemed that Boomer had been booted off the kibbutz for making what he called "an improper suggestion" (she had to grin as she wondered what the fool might have recommended), but he and his sculptor friend (still no mention of the sculptor's gender: it could only be female) were "sharing a space" in West Jerusalem, where they were collaborating on a project of apparently monumental scale. "This here is a real sculpture," he wrote. "Even you'd have to say so."

Soon after Christmas, she had written and asked him point-blank about what duties he was performing for Buddy Winkler, and now in early February he wrote:

The only single thing I've done for Bud is buy some welding supplies and deliver them to a basement over near East Jerusalem. It was a right weird scene. There were three or four rabbis in long black coats, black hats, and woolly black beards sitting there in a cellar so dark you couldn't read Braille with a blowtorch, and these old boys were knitting. Knitting away with them long clickety needles, just like your mama. I asked them if they was getting ready for a baby shower, but they couldn't speaka the English, and the fellow who let me in explained they were the sacred knitters knitting the sacred garments that the high priests would wear once the Temple was rebuilt and open for business. I asked him when that might be and he patted me on the shoulder and said I understand you weld, and I said yeah, for a price. He smiled and showed me to the door and that was that. Bud ain't said boo to me since.

I guess you been hearing about how bad things are on the West Bank and Gaza Strip. It's a sorry situation. Kids shot or beat up every day. Palestinians setting fire to the orchards. Jerusalem is as jumpy as a jitterbug in a blender. The word you hear most here is revenge. Arabs talking revenge, Jews talking revenge; old people, young people, everybody's set on some kind of vengeance. I swear, they'd rather have them a mess of revenge than a big juicy steak and a roll in silk sheets with a movie star. Crazy folks, crazy town, but highly interesting. Wonderful amount of secrecy and intrigue. I feel like I'm somewhere being here. You know what I mean? Lot of places you go to, when you get there you feel like you didn't really go anywhere, but not Jerusalem, not for a minute. There's honeysuckle here, too, same as Virginia. Smells like the City of Heaven, all right. And the rent's cheap. Which reminds me, I know the Ansonia's a burden on you. If you'll drop by Ultima's, she'll help you out with a check.

Love always,
Boomer

I'd rather drink parasite soup than drop by Ultima's, thought Ellen Cherry, but eviction was staring her in the face like a deviate on the subway, so on her next day off she braced herself and walked down to Fifty-seventh Street in the snow. There were as many art galleries on East Fifty-seventh as there were sushi bars on East Forty-ninth, but she tried not to notice. She hadn't been eyeball to pigment since before Thanksgiving, unless you could count the paintings that leaned against every wall of her apartment, flaunting their blank backsides as if mooning David Hockney. Nor had she paid a visit to Turn Around Norman, an omission painfully clear to the objects beneath St. Patrick's. Whether or not Norman was aware of her absence was anybody's guess.

She expected Ultima to keep her waiting—gallery dealers made a practice of that in order to make themselves seem as busy as doctors and as important as lawyers—but the snowmelt had not completely evaporated from Ellen Cherry's red vinyl boots when she was summoned. As she followed the saleswoman to Ultima's office, she shielded her eyes against the Leon Golub lithographs on the walls. Artburn. She forgot the perils of art, however, when confronted by the perils of dog. Three dogs to be exact, three beribboned, perfumed, but untamed little hellhounds that came shooting across the room, howling, leaping, and baring their fangs. Ultima appeared in a cloud of silk and chic, and shooed two of them away. The third continued to snap at Ellen Cherry's heel. She found herself thinking of Jezebel and protecting every part of herself except her skull, her feet, and the palms of her hands.

"Baby Butts!" called Ultima in a stern but affectionate tone. "Naughty doggy!"

"Homicidal doggy," said Ellen Cherry under her breath. She could swear she detected morbid suds in the corners of the doggy's mouth.

Ultima squatted on the polished hardwood floor. The disproportionate weight of her bosom caused her to tilt forward, but she righted herself before she, too, took a bite out of Ellen Cherry's boot. "Come on, Baby Butts, upsy me," crooned Ultima, and the pooch, still frothing and snarling, leapt into her arms. "Give mums a smooch."

Jesus weeping Christ! thought Ellen Cherry. *Do you suppose Boomer kissed the mouth that licks that mad dog's chops?*

Although she was chilled from the long walk, Ellen Cherry refused coffee, tea, or sherry. She was cordial about it, but she obviously wanted to pick up her money and get out of there. Ultima obliged her. Cuddling Baby Butts while the other dogs tussled beneath the Frank Lloyd Wright desk, she pulled a check from a metal box and passed it to Ellen Cherry, who managed to snatch it away without losing any flesh. She did, however, lose color.

"Is something unsatisfactory?"

"Uh, well, aside from the fact that Baby Butts drooled on it, I guess I was expecting more."

"More than seven thou?"

"The show sold out. It must've grossed a hundred grand."

"In excess of a hundred. But then there were deductions."

"Your commission."

"The gallery's commission, yes. State and federal taxes. And Mr. Petway has had needs. I gather that steel is quite dear in Palestine. He's making—"

"A big sculpture. Yeah, I know." *Does she think Boomer doesn't write to me?*

The women stared at each other for so long and with such will that Baby Butts began to whimper. He seemed surprised and hurt to learn that he hadn't a monopoly on power in the room. Eventually, Ultima smiled and produced a second check. "Congratulations," she said.

"What's this?" Ellen Cherry took the bank draft slowly, deliberately, daring the pup to interfere. It was in the amount of eighteen hundred dollars.

"Two of your works sold," said Ultima. "As you're well aware, there's been a rekindling of interest in the pictorial landscape. I mean, there's so little of it left *outdoors*. Collectors have preferred, of course, naturalistic pictures, but the supply of first-rate *oeuvre* is running thin. In any case, I showed your paintings to a couple from Rochester who didn't seem in the least put off by your, ah, excesses. So, congratulations, my dear, on your first New York sale. Perhaps you should fetch in several more."

"Thanks," said Ellen Cherry. "Thanks. Maybe I will." Not wishing Ultima to be further entertained by how stunned she was, she excused herself and sailed for the door.

Trudging home in the snow, a check in each fist like Chinese hand warmers, she could only think, *Now I have an excuse for Mr. Cohen why I can't put any work in Ye Olde Art Shoppe in Westchester.*

Ellen Cherry didn't take any more paintings to the gallery, not even one of the Boomer nudes (oh, how she would have loved to see the look on Ultima's face!), but she stewed about it for weeks. She lay awake nights debating the pros and cons of it.

Should she resume her identity as an artist? Could a person choose to be or not to be an artist? Once certain childhood forces were set in motion, you either were an artist or you weren't, and if you were, you might choose not to exhibit, you might even choose not to produce; you might, in other words, reject an art career, an art life, but you were still an artist. Right? Or was that just semantics? According to egalitarians, everybody had artistic talent. On a hobby level, that was possibly true. So what? It struck her that while a great many people wanted to want to be artists, they didn't actually want to be. A girlfriend in Seattle once said to her, "I'd give everything if I could paint like you," and Ellen Cherry had replied, with only a trace of pomposity, "I *did* give everything."

Talent was merely the underpinnings. To be an artist, you also had to have nerve. And to maintain nerve, you had to have drive. Apparently, she had lost her drive. Yet if she'd truly lost it, why was she fretting this way? Furthermore, if it was impossible to shed her art skin, no matter how she might twist or squirm, wouldn't it be only sensible to take financial advantage of her lot, to relax and enjoy some modest success? Or was it the "modest" part (in light of Boomer's triumph) that galled her?

On and on she would stew, until, in desperation, she'd reach for her vibrator so that she might distract herself.

To a lesser extent, she stewed over Buddy Winkler. Shortly after the holidays, she had taken Roland Abu Hadee aside and asked him what would happen should zealots attack and destroy the Dome of the Rock.

"War," replied Abu, matter-of-factly. "War would happen."

"You mean the Muslims would retaliate against synagogues and stuff?"

"No," said Abu. "I mean war. Syria, Libya, Iran, Lebanon, probably Jordan and Egypt and Saudi Arabia, perhaps nations as far away as Pakistan and Indonesia would declare war, jihad, holy war, against Israel. That is how strongly Muslims feel about the Dome of the Rock. They are prepared one and all to die for this. The Israelis would be so outnumbered that they would be forced to resort to nuclear weapons. In which case, the Soviet Union would probably be obliged to supply Islam with nuclear warheads. And that most certainly would draw America into it. Oh, yes, were the mosques on the Temple Mount destroyed, there would be a great thunderclap. Both polar caps would rattle like saucers, babies would be born smelling of sulfur. The terror within would then be without. The egg of fire would finally hatch. Armageddon. World War Three, if you prefer."

As soon as Abu left the kitchen, Ellen Cherry went directly to the wall phone and dialed Buddy. Normally, she might not have had the stomach, but she was disturbed, and it didn't matter to her that it was after midnight.

"Ummm."

"Hello. Uncle Buddy?"

"Doll baby. I was jes' dreamin' 'bout you. Or some little play-pretty equally as sweet."

"Listen up, Uncle Bud. Do you know what'd happen if the Dome of the Rock was destroyed?"

Buddy Winkler knew, all right. He might be in pajamas, a night-mask of ointment on his boils, an anchovy paste of sleep in his eyes, but he knew. "It'd precipitate the ultimate struggle between good and evil that's prophesied to precede the Second Coming and the redemption of man. Hallelujah. Amen. What time is it, anyways?"

"It could start World War Three."

"Dang tootin' it could. That's the whole point of it."

"You mean to tell me you're willing to gamble with the lives of innocent people, billions of innocent people, risk the lives of everybody on earth, animals, trees, little children, have them roast in fire storms, have them covered with sores and burns, dying of radiation sickness, all that horrible, horrible pain and suffering—"

"Hold on. You jes' hold on now, little miss bleedin' heart. It ain't a gamble. The word of God is not no lottery ticket. It *shall* come to pass. Shall! His admonitions are as plain as the nose on your painted face. And sure it's gonna be horrible. The Lord God designed it to be horrible. But the righteous'll come out of it jes' fine, thank you. Jesus'll gather unto him the faithful to his breast, and they'll enjoy sweet everlastin' life. Them burns will heal, and them sores will vanish away. As for your careless and wicked, they'll jes' be gittin' what's due to 'em. They've had their fair chance, they'll burn by their own iniquity. So let the war trumpets sound. Let the missiles rain. It's God's will, and *he'll* decide who's innocent and who ain't, not you or the ACLU."

Ellen Cherry was incredulous. "You're so damn sure of yourself that you're willing to take a chance on starting World War Three. You'll put that weight on your shoulders?"

"You got a hearing problem? I already explained to you that—
Never mind. Your heart is hardened. I don't know where you're at at
this ungodly hour, but I beseech you to get yourself home and read
your Scriptures and kneel beside the bed outta which you've driven
your lawful husband, and pray. 'Repent ye therefore and be converted, that your sins may be blotted out when the times of refreshing shall come, from the presence of the Lord; and he shall send
Jesus.' *Acts*, three, nineteen."

" 'The time of refreshing' they call it?"

"Yes, indeedy. Refreshing as a Co'-Cola."

"I have a good mind to tell the cops what you're up to."

Buddy chuckled. "What cops? The *po*-lice here got no authority
over it, and the *po*-lice in Israel are, most of 'em, on my side. Your
righteous Jew wants this as bad as your Christian. 'Course, after the
Second Coming, them Jews that are worthy will be forcibly converted. We'll all of us be Christians in the New Jerusalem."

"How about the Muslims? Or the Buddhists and Hindus?"

"Fried meat."

Ellen Cherry slammed down the receiver. She stewed about Buddy
throughout the night and for many nights thereafter, when she
wasn't stewing about artisthood. What with Buddy's shenanigans,
what with the I & I's raison d'être, what with Boomer's dallying over
there doing who knew what, it was getting harder and harder to
carpet-tack the Middle East to the living room floor of her mind.

In all the years that Ellen Cherry had known Buddy Winkler, she
had never heard him utter a sentence that didn't amount to a cliché.
She concluded that that was what organized religion did to people. It
limited them to thinking secondhand thoughts. It caused them to
live secondhand lives. Wasn't that what religion had in common with
totalitarian politics? Nazi Germany, the Inquisition, Stalinism, the
Crusades, these were what happened when reality was allowed to
give way to cliché.

Behind the sixth veil, like a pearl behind cheesecloth, was the
realization that "the end of the world" was the most dangerous cliché
of all. Incapable of penetrating the veil, unaware of the veil's existence, Ellen Cherry could only stew—and wonder why Buddy had
such a hankering for apocalypse.

1. Because it would mean that his side had finally won?
2. Because the messy, unpredictable imperfection of life/life would solidify once and for all into the perfectly ordered, totally controlled, solid-gold monolith of death/life?
3. Because he was lonely?

If Bud was prepared to act out some reckless biblical fantasy in order to alleviate an unbearable dissatisfaction and loneliness, then there was something that she could do about it. No, no, not even were it that simple, not even were she as versed in dissatisfaction and loneliness as she believed, could she spread herself out on an altar such as that. Impossible. Ridiculous.

The next morning, as soon as she had replaced the vibrator in her underwear drawer, the panties ceased their girlish gossiping and began to chirp, "Who? Who? Who?" Who had it been this time? Whose name had she called aloud when she straddled the white pony of orgasm? Norman? Raoul? Was it Boomer again? "Who, Daruma, tell us who?"

The vibrator would reveal nothing until the panties settled down. He lay there beside a mortified Spoon, chanting Japanese syllables over and over in a low, deep monotone: *"Wooga go nami ne, Wooga go nami ne."* When at last the drawer was still, he said, "A single cloud floating in midday sky contain no duck sauce." He waited to see if the panties would protest, and when they did not, he said, "Good. Name my mistress call aloud was . . . ."

Spoon hummed a tune to herself, hoping to drown out the name, but despite her efforts, she heard it anyway.

"Buddy," said the vibrator. "She call out 'Uncca Bud.' "

Spoon, too, spent much of her time in a stew. A metaphoric stew. She hadn't been eaten with in so long it made her heartsick. Whatever else happened when they reached Jerusalem, she would be eaten with there. Yes! She would see to it. Upon entering the Third Temple, Spoon would go directly to the cafeteria. Interject herself between a priest and his pudding. Now that she was shiny and silvery again, perhaps the Messiah himself. . . . She could not entertain the sacrilege of crossing the Messiah's lips, but she could imagine being cradled in his big healing hand of hide and satin. The

Messiah was feeding fish soup to the blind. Ice cream to starving orphans. The Messiah used her to draw a magic circle in the honey pot. "There," he told his apostles. "That will keep the flies away."

The dreaming was pleasant, but the stewing was not. Objects don't swim in history the way humanity does. Even those rare objects who've recaptured the power of locomotion possess an innate patience to which no human saint could reasonably aspire. Nevertheless, Spoon fretted for reunion. She was anxious to tell her traveling companions about the Dome of the Rock, about Mr. Petway being in Jerusalem, about, most especially, the paintings of Miss Charles. The fact that Miss Charles had painted dozens of portraits of them—of *them*: Dirty Sock, Can o' Beans, and Spoon—could only mean that she was their God-given champion.

And yet, Spoon stewed, *if she cherishes me so much, why has she sentenced me to the perpetual company of shallow, chatty undergarments and her Oriental instrument of debauchery?* Can o' Beans had advised her that one could learn from foreigners, but when it came to Phoenician sticks and Japanese dildos, one hardly could make a drop of sense of anything they said. If anything, the vibrator was more obscurant than Painted Stick.

"Where do you come from, sir?" Spoon had asked when they met.

"Same place guano came from that unseen bird drop into misty sea."

"That's nice," said Spoon, trying to be polite. She wasn't yet aware of the fellow's obscene function, believing him to be a curling iron.

"Three pound of flax," said the vibrator.

The underpants didn't understand him, either, but they acted as if he were as wise as Solomon. (Had Solomon actually been wise, that is.) They bowed to him and called him "Master" or "Daruma," and, as difficult as it was for them to smother their giggles, they chanted with him for two hours every day. *"Wooga go nami ne, Wooga go nami ne."*

"This would give me a headache," complained Spoon. "If I had a head."

"Ah! Headless headache!" the vibrator exclaimed, delighted. "Good. There hope for you, yet."

Left to their own devices, the panties would spend their time jabbering about fashion, fad diets, celebrity life-styles, and popular music. Even when they were meditating under Daruma's supervision, Spoon could sometimes hear them whispering about the weight this actress had lost or that one gained. They also loved to engage in relentless and often highly speculative gossip about Ellen Cherry Charles. They maintained a near obsession with Miss Charles's sex life, which Spoon attributed to the fact that they, singularly and in rotation, were usually in close proximity to the, uh, hub of that presumed activity.

As a defense against their vulgar and embarrassing chitchat, Spoon began to relate her adventures to them: where she'd been and where she was going, under what circumstances and in whose company. Easily entertained, the underpants listened attentively. They appreciated a good story. Not for a millisecond, however, did they believe that she had attained a state of locomotion. To them, it was just a tall tale. Insulted that the panties would question her veracity, Spoon executed a couple of feeble cartwheels and a clumsy pirouette. Don't think that that didn't snap their elastic! From then on, they were twice as attentive. Under his reserved exterior, even Daruma was impressed.

Considering that she could locomote, the panties couldn't understand why Spoon lay around stewing in a dresser drawer. Why didn't she light out for St. Patrick's and rejoin her interesting friends?

"First of all, I don't know the way," said Spoon.

"Way that is true Way cannot be known," countered the vibrator.

"Secondly, the very idea of it gives me a fright."

"Those who would travel must learn to like dust," said Daruma.

"Most important, though, is that we inanimate objects have an ethical responsibility not to shatter the prevailing reality of human beings. Conch Shell was adamant about that. If a man saw me locomoting, why he'd think he'd gone insane or else witnessed a miracle. Can o' Beans says that people are too fragile for miracles."

"*Honto des'*," the vibrator said, sagely. "Is true. Two thousand year ago, virgin give birth. People still not get over it. Ha-ha-ha."

"I've never considered the Immaculate Conception in those terms," said Spoon, "and I fail to find humor in it. But I suppose you could be right. Maybe that's why God had to suspend the miraculous."

Content to listen to Spoon's stories, the panties seldom asked questions. In his own cool way, however, Daruma exhibited an abiding curiosity. "The more talking and thinking, the farther from the truth," he was fond of saying, yet he queried Spoon persistently about such matters as how the decorated stick and the seashell managed to get from Jerusalem to a cave in Utah (or was it Wyoming?). There had been a time when Spoon had puzzled over that, as well. Now, though, she had the answer at hand.

"The Phoenicians took them. You probably think Columbus discovered America. No, he didn't. He was a good, brave Catholic, and I'd like to believe he was first, but he wasn't. The Phoenicians had wonderful sailing ships, and they sailed all over the world. Well, probably not the Pacific, but the other oceans. They knew about America many centuries before Columbus. Many, many centuries. Isn't that amazing? After the Romans destroyed Herod's Temple in—" Spoon had to stop and visualize numerals. She could see a seven, standing tall with its right arm outstretched, like a safety patrol boy at a school crossing, but she couldn't conjure up a clear picture of the number to its left. Somehow five didn't look right, rocking on its brontosaurus tail, nor did the hydrocephalic nine.

"Seventy something. A.D. You know what A.D. means?"

"Oh, yeah," said a pair of cotton briefs. "That's like the current that makes Master vibrate when he's like operating on batteries."

"*All* vibrators operate on batteries," corrected a slightly older pair, bleached as blue as moonlight on snow. "You think a lady would wanna like fuck herself with something plugged into the wall?"

A tittering circulated in the drawer like birdsong in a box hedge. Spoon palpitated, coughed, and elected to press on. "After Jerusalem was destroyed again in seventy something, Painted Stick and Conch Shell ended up back with the Phoenicians. There were powerful priestesses who supposedly could read the future. Phoenicia was by then part of the Roman Empire, the Roman province of Syria. It continued to prosper economically, but the priestesses convinced a lot of people that their culture and religion were doomed. Which proved to be the case. Thanks to them, they began to take measures to try to insure survival, or, rather, reemergence at a later date."

"When people say 'take measures,' I always think like, you know, see how tall or wide something is," said a sweet, young voice from the undie pile. "Forty inches. Fifty inches."

"Like you mean Liz Taylor's hips?"

Again the drawer filled up with titters. Spoon turned to the vibrator, who sympathized but offered little help. "Greedy for bait, fish soon caught. You have only to open mouth, your life lost."

Spoon decided to cut it short. "A priestess carried Conch Shell and Painted Stick aboard a big ship, and they crossed the Atlantic and sailed as far as they could up the St. Lawrence river system. Then a party carried them overland for a long ways until the priestess found just the right hiding place. It was a small cave. The cave had a niche in it, and the priestess hid our shell and stick in the niche, but first she rubbed them in a particular way that put them into a trance. They were programmed not to wake up until they felt a certain familiar energy. That would be the signal that the era of Rome was finished and the earth was returning to its senses. I realize that it sounds ever so frightfully pagan, but that's the way it was explained to me."

"Ah, so," said Daruma the O-maker.

Months earlier, even before Boomer got his lame foot stuck in one of the seven mystical doors of Jerusalem, Ellen Cherry had transferred her wedding band from her left hand to her right, a sign that she was widowed or divorced, although neither was technically the case. Every time that the underwear drawer opened, a burst of light, solar or incandescent, would rush in, followed fairly quickly by a muscular, machine-tooled load of hydrocarbon-laden New York air, and then by Ellen Cherry's right hand, readily identifiable by its Jezebel-colored nails (long and sharp as the wrought-iron spikes around an embassy) and its simple ring of gold.

Each and every time the hand entered drawer space, Spoon hoped with all her might that it was reaching for her. Alas, were it morning, the hand selected the pantie of the day (Ellen Cherry owned few brassieres, as her lumps lacked sufficient mass to fully occupy a harness); were it night, the hand, always a bit hesitantly, withdrew Daruma. Alas.

One afternoon toward late February, when she had stayed home from work with a beefy cold, Ellen Cherry did remove Spoon from the drawer. What a hopeful moment for the stranded utensil! In the end, however, it was Ellen Cherry who benefited from the encounter.

She laid the spoon on the bed while she blew her nose. Then she picked it up and examined it, as if for a clue, previously overlooked, that finally might explain its queer reappearance. When that proved futile, Ellen Cherry held the dainty object about six inches from her face and initiated the eye game. She hadn't played the eye game in what Patsy would characterize as "a coon's age," but she slid readily into it, aided, perhaps, by the film of tearwater excreted by her head in its attempt to flush alien bacteria.

The scalloped edges of the spoon's handle began to flutter like a paper clam shell, to spiral as if they were streams of some Botticelli bouillabaisse, a salty, rococo broth from which the emancipated souls of expiring sea snails rose to mingle in the spray with the flying locks of nymphs. The hollow ladle flattened, spread, and thinned in her vision until it resembled the Springmaid armpit of a ghost, and the shimmering silver of its surface manifested itself as a luminous brand of haywire energy. The deeper the penetration of Ellen Cherry's eye, the greater the loss or breakdown of that energy, and for that very reason it became necessary for her to penetrate more deeply yet, so that she might get in front of, outdistance, the dissolution. With something akin to the visual equivalent of a sprinter's finish-line kick, she did at last propel herself ahead of dissipation and found herself embedded in a continuous solid reef of what she could only describe as "information."

For one giddy moment she felt that she had oriented herself at the interface of the visible and invisible worlds, that she was contemplating wholeness, an ultimate state in which all forms and motions were imminent but protected by physical or metaphysical law from the process of selection or favoritism that would compromise them.

The sensation was short-lived, but while it lasted, Ellen Cherry seemed to hold something slippery by its tail. Slippery and altogether crucial. She couldn't quite identify it. She definitely couldn't analyze it. Instinctively, she realized that analysis would negate it. It seemed to be a kind of rapture, a rapturous essence that was available in all things if only one regarded them in a particular light. On a rational level, it made about as much sense as a whole deck of aces, yet it provided her with a fleeting joy so intense that the memory of it would comfort her for months to come and would drive from consideration any possibility of retreat or surrender.

The moment itself had passed, however. She needed to blow her nose again and swill another swig of cough syrup. She thought about using the spoon to take the medicine, but decided against it. Returning to normal focus, she opened the drawer and laid a sadly disappointed Spoon down among unworthy companions; "unworthy" not because they lacked the mysterious essence but because they were so ignorant they believed Phoenicians to be the people who modernized window coverings. As in, "If it weren't for Phoenician blinds, it'd be curtains for all of us."

Within a week, her immune system had washed her cold out to sea, and Ellen Cherry returned to the I & I to find a change in the situation there. Since there were fewer televised sporting events on weekend nights, the nights when UN employees, like workers everywhere, were most inclined to go out, Spike and Abu decided to experiment with live music in the bar. They lugged a wad of bills to city hall, greased palms left and right, and obtained a cabaret license. Then they auditioned musicians.

After overturning every stone in New York's ethnic music underground, they located a young Yemenite man who could and would sing both Arabic and Israeli folk songs. Bareheaded and wearing a baby blue dinner jacket so as to appear impartial, the fellow performed on Sundays, accompanied by his eleven-year-old brother on bass and his grandfather on clay drums. His guitar and voice had a melancholy cast, no matter what the tempo, and the tunes in his repertoire featured lines such as, "Yesterday I cleaned my rifle while my girlfriend slept and the almond trees wept with infinite joy." Business on Sunday nights did not increase dramatically.

For the entertainment of Friday and Saturday night customers, an East Jerusalem nightclub band was hired. "Why not? Israeli Jews like this music, too," Spike explained. "It's Oriental music. They don't believe this very much in Westchester, but Israel is basically an Oriental country, already."

The musicians in the band were a mixed bag of Palestinians, Egyptians, and Lebanese. Every one of them was older than sixty (sometimes the Yemenite grandfather sat in), but they played with ecstasy and zeal. When they got going, they jiggled the building with shrill desert gusts and tumbling layers of complex thunder. The dissonant melodies of ancient lutes rolled with the rapid-fire punches thrown by the drums, while snake-charmer reeds wrapped themselves sinuously around the ankles of every beat and note.

Indeed, the band did attract patrons, although not in such numbers as to justify the additional expense. It didn't take long for Spike and Abu to realize that live entertainment was a losing proposition, but they personally liked the music so much that they hesitated to terminate it.

"It's a marvelous orchestra," said Spike, "though I regret that they aren't employing a tambourine."

"I miss the tambourine, as well," said Abu. For Ellen Cherry's benefit, he elaborated. "In the Middle East, tambourines are the expressions of both mourning and mirth. Centuries ago, they were the only instruments played at funerals and at wedding feasts. They make the quintessential music of Jerusalem because Jerusalem is simultaneously a funeral and a celebration. Spike, I will inquire of the bandleader if they might add a tambourine."

Several days later, Abu reported on the conversation he'd had with the toothless old Lebanese who led the band. "That gentleman tells me they have no tambourine because they have no woman with the orchestra. He tells me that the tambourine is the sole feminine instrument of the Middle East. Before Mohammed came, it was associated with Astarte, the Goddess. Is that not interesting? One of the other musicians said that the tambourine is a female due to the fact that it makes a pretty jingle and is designed to be spanked. That is the more recent, patriarchal attitude, I suppose. At any rate, I inquired if they knew of a woman who might perform on the tambourine with them some evening. They claimed they did not, but when I hinted that it could prolong their engagement here, they agreed to check into it."

Spike nodded in appreciation. "That's very nice," he said. "Last time I'm in Jerusalem, I got to hear a very nice tambourine being played by a belly-dancer woman wearing no shoes on her feet. This was in the nightclub called the Milk and Honey. No shoes, I'm telling you. . . ."

"Milk and honey," said Abu. "That has become a hackneyed phrase, yet it remains viscerally appealing. Milk and honey. For some strange reason, a little poem."

The two men babbled away, unaware of the difference that their taste for tambourine music was going to make in their lives.

Ellen Cherry didn't care much for the band. Its high-pitched nasal buzz reminded her of a prehistoric busy signal. The Yemenite folk singer also failed to set her music gland to pumping, although she evidently stimulated something in *him*, as he was forever giving her long, smoldering looks. When he asked her for a date, she was tempted to accept. He was broodingly handsome, and as suspect as youthful melancholia always is, it's nonetheless superficially attractive. *Yeah, but I know those Arabic types,* she thought. *He wouldn't be content to be my lover. After three dates he'd want to marry me and whisk me off to the Old Country, hide me behind a veil, make me eat the eyes of sheep.*

After she turned him down, the gloom of his performances darkened by several shades. Lines such as, "Before I depart for battle, please allow me to wipe my sobbing eyes on your embroidered sleeve," didn't have to be in English to cast their pall. Eventually, Spike and Abu let him go.

By April, they were on the verge of firing the band, as well, when the toothless geezer informed them that on the following Friday they would be joined by a "mostly very much beautiful" belly dancer who was "mostly very much excellently skilled" on the tambourine.

While an excited Spike was asking the old musician whether the woman would be shod or in bare feet, Abu, equally pleased if more subdued, fed Ellen Cherry a tidbit about how, during a period of musical inactivity enforced in the seventh century by Mohammed, approval was given only to the *ghirbal* and the tambourine, the latter without jingles, since the instrument with jingles was forbidden. "That is what the new religion did to Arabic culture," said Abu. "It left the drumbeats but took away our jingles."

"We Baptists don't jingle much, either," Ellen Cherry confided. "Except when we're passing the collection plate."

It's the third Friday in April. Spring lies on New York like an odalisque on a harem sofa. Like an AIDS baby on a Harlem sofa. A big moon is rising. Like the odalisque, the moon seems filled to overflowing with sweetmeats and sperm, but the haze through which it rises is emaciated, phlegm-choked, and dappled with sores that almost certainly are malignant. Everywhere, softness snuggles up to hardness. Hardness shrugs, says, "So what?"—rakes in a scum of dollars, jams foot-long needles into its vein. Tender green leaves are unfurling on thousands of soot-encrusted limbs. The acrid, Mephistophelian odor of vehicular exhaust stands out sharply against the chlorophyll. When a person breathes, one nostril sucks in a witchy waft of poisons, the other the syrup-scented push of plant life. In the mingle of moonlight and headlamps, neon and leaf-glow, the skyscrapers are as beautiful as a procession of Hindu saints. Bubbling, winking, and crawling with light, they seem as full of sap as the maples in the park.

Spilling from tenements and condominiums, from boutiques and bodegas, the anxious multitudes have found a new tempo, a pace in between the windup-toy frenzy of winter and the deep-sea diver drag of the humid summer to come. Crushing Styrofoam burger cartons, condom packs, hypodermic syringes, and graffiti-spewing spray cans underfoot, they almost dance as they walk, an unconscious rite of spring in their steps, a forgotten memory of sod and seed and lamb and ring-around-the-rosy. The unfinished and unfinishable symphony to which they move is composed of salsa, rap, and funk from boom boxes, strains of Vivaldi sifting out in a silvery drizzle from fine restaurants and limousines, the sophisticated rhythms produced by Cole Porter's phantom cigarette holder tapping upon the vertebrae of tourists and businessmen in hotel lobbies throughout midtown, fey techno-rock in SoHo bars and art lofts, drum solos banged out on plastic pails and refrigerator trays by brilliant buskers, androgynous anchorpersons announcing the "news," a loud screeching of truck and bus wheels, an interminable red bawling of sirens, the tooting of taxis, an occasional gunshot or scream, girlish laughter, boyish boasts, barking dogs, the whine of aggressive beggars, the yowls of the unsheltered insane, and, on many a street corner, the greased-lung exhortations of evangelists, ordained or self-proclaimed, warning all who pass that this could be the last April that God will ever grant, as if April were a kitten and God an angry farmer with a sack.

By July, the air in New York will be pumped up on steroids: brutish biceps will flex in the lungs of everyone who inhales it, and against the cheeks of the sensitive it will rake like stubble. On this April evening, however, the atmosphere is plainly feminine. The smog wears lace, the breeze is wrapped in maternity cottons, and the jaded urbanites, winked at and cooed to, have let their defenses down. Just before dusk, a slide rule of Canadian geese engineers over Manhattan, giving traffic a honking lesson that nearly drains its batteries. The necks of millions crane as one to follow the flight of the geese, and when the flock fades into the haze, an ancient intoxication seizes the collective brain. Everyone now is mildly drunk on wild goose wine.

Ellen Cherry senses the feminine wildness in the streets even before she leaves her apartment. From the eleventh floor of the Ansonia, neon signs look like smears of wet lipstick, and the jumbled noise that bounces up from Broadway has an underlying purr. Into the usual Friday night mix of commerce and culture, romance and crime, luxury and filth, there's been stirred bud nectar, moon malt, and goose grog: Ellen Cherry can taste it when she cracks the window. She opens the window wider and takes a larger gulp. It's a night of promise, a night when something delirious could happen, and suddenly she can't wait to get out into it.

"New York's swallowed a tambourine," she says. She knows nothing about tambourines beyond what she's recently been told, but she's aware that this untamed female music box is scheduled to ring out tonight at Isaac & Ishmael's, where she'll be working the late shift, nine until three. As it turns out, her metaphor is apt, though she has forgotten it completely by the time she returns to the entryway closet to hang up the coat that she's decided she won't be needing (the extent to which the release from bulky winter clothing has contributed to the city's light new mood should not be underestimated).

The instant that Ellen Cherry leaves the room, there's unprece-
dented movement in the underwear drawer. The drawer is slightly
ajar, and Spoon, too, has felt the tug and promise of the April night.

Daruma watches her. She's shaking like a coke addict at a job
interview. Upright, balanced on the tip of her handle, she periodically leaps in the air to a height where she can peer briefly over the
lip of the drawer. She leaps, hesitates, trembles. Leaps, hesitates,
trembles.

"Kamikaze," whispers the vibrator.

"Kamikaze?"

"Divine wind."

She leaps, hesitates, trembles. "Divine wind?"

"Go," he says. "Go with wind. Go for broke. Nothing to lose. Go!"

Spoon goes.

Soundlessly, she lands on the bedroom rug. Rolls over. Looks
around. Bounds toward the purse that Ellen Cherry has left on the
floor by the door.

The last thing she hears as she dives down deep among the keys
and change, Kleenex and Boomer letters, post-Jezebelian cosmetics
and tattered old magazine photographs of Georgia O'Keeffe, is the
joyful lunatic laughter of the heathen dildo.

The average woman's purse weighs approximately one kilo. The
average woman's heart weighs nine ounces. The weight of a tambourine falls somewhere in between, a little closer to the heart than the
handbag.

When Ellen Cherry returns to the bedroom, she snatches up her
purse and rummages in it. Several times her right hand, the hand
with the exiled wedding band, brushes against the spoon or pushes
the spoon aside, without taking notice of it. Can a woman who does
not know the contents of her handbag know the contents of her
heart?

Ellen Cherry removes her keys, two subway tokens, and a vial
of lip gloss. She secures these items in the flap pocket of her
yellow jersey dress, the Betsey Johnson dress with the outsize

zipper, and drops the purse on the bed. She is going to travel light on this spring-drunk night. Apparently, Spoon won't be traveling at all.

Spoon waits in the purse until she's positive that Ellen Cherry is out of the building. Then she squirms free, much to the envy of a plastic rain cap that's been pining away for years in the bottom of the bag. "She'll never w-wear me," sobs the rain cap. "I won't f-fit over all that h-hair."

"Patience, dear," Spoon counsels. "As my friend Can o' Beans says, 'the world is a very strange place, and the dice are always rolling.' "

After quoting the bean can, she would feel like a hypocrite climbing back in the underwear drawer. In truth, she feels hypocritical anyhow, advising patience at a time when she has lost much of hers. *As the millennium winds down, are certain inanimate objects growing increasingly and uncharacteristically impatient?* she wonders. *And if so, is it a religious thing, or is it secular?*

Spoon surveys the room. Moonrays are driving through the window like a fleet of white Cadillacs. Impulsively, she hops from the bed to the windowsill. "Oh my. Oh dear," she gasps. She's equally enchanted and terrified. Below her, far, far below her, the hard streets, surprised by April, are pulsating in a seizure of color and sound. The warm air washes over her like luxurious dishwaters she has known. The lights of the city ripple over her as well, enlivening her classic contours, giving her a different sort of bath. The cacophony disorients her. The height makes her freeze. She's a motionless star in a spinning sky.

"Kamikaze!"

"Pardon, sir?"

Spoon turns to hear what the vibrator is calling to her from the drawer and, in so doing, slips and goes sliding off the ledge into the vast, noisy void.

Does an object's life flash before it as it falls? Had not Galileo been an animate chauvinist, he might have addressed that question in his experiments at Pisa. On the other hand, it may be absurd to suggest that something inanimate, inorganic, has a "life" to flash. But what is it, then, that Spoon is seeing as she hurtles toward the pavement?

She falls past rough bowls carved from the wood of fever trees and decorated with images of pregnant beasts; past saucers of tortoise-shell, and *compotiers* fashioned from maidens' skulls with alphabets hidden in their cheeks. Most assuredly, Spoon has never dipped custards from vessels such as these.

She falls past a black rooster tied to a bedpost, past a lizard and a robin drinking from the same ancient puddle, past brightly painted acorns, peyote furniture, and chandeliers dripping with the fat of igloo candles. In all of her travels from coast to coast, Spoon had never seen those things.

She is falling not through her own brain, as humans do, but through the room of the wolfmother wallpaper, and shreds of the wallpaper flap against her as she plunges. From a great distance, she thinks she can hear Conch Shell trumpeting her name. Then, it's over. . . .

When she lands, it's not with the hideous clang she expects but with a thunk. She bounces off something comparatively soft, puts a dent in it, makes an arc, and smacks the sidewalk at less than half the speed she was previously traveling. Several drops of blood land beside her.

Had Raoul Ritz been wearing his porkpie hat, it would have ab-sorbed much of the blow. His manager in Los Angeles considers the hat a dorky item, however, and has talked him into forsaking it, at least in public. When he approaches the Ansonia, intent on inform-ing Ellen Cherry that the song he'd written for her (and which had enjoyed limited airplay on a couple of New York stations) is about to be released nationally, his bean is unfortunately bare.

Gripping his head with both hands, Raoul circles himself errati-cally, like a bat with jammed sonar, caroms off a corner of the Ansonia, and collapses. Pepe, the new doorman, comes out to see what's going on, finds Raoul unconscious on the sidewalk, and dials 911. Spoon's instincts are to scoot for cover, but a small crowd has gathered.

By the time an ambulance and a patrol car arrive, Raoul's lights are back on, and he's sitting upright. There's a detective in the patrol car, being driven from a homicide scene. "What hit him?" Detective Shaftoe asks.

"Spoon," replies a witness. "This spoon here fell down on him."

"No kidding?" Shaftoe takes the utensil from the witness, examines it. It's solid silver, heavy for its size. "Fell or was thrown?"

The witness shrugs. Shaftoe steps out in the street where he can see all the way to the top of the Ansonia. Only one window is open on that side of the building. The detective counts the window rows to determine the floor. He's a short, muscular man, black of skin and white of hair, with falcon eyes and a nose that's been broken more often than a seducer's promises. He's played his share of football, though at considerable distance from the Super Bowl. "Who lives in that apartment?" he asks Pepe, pointing to the open window.

"Not sure. I think it be Miz Charl."

"Miz Charl," repeats Raoul. They're the first words he's spoken, and they sound as if they've been strained through an old nun's bloomers. The medics try to convince Raoul to go to the hospital for an examination, but he argues against it. The police are consulted.

"He's a tough mother," says Shaftoe. "Let him be. You want to waste Bellevue's time and taxpayers' money photographing the inside of that head? Besides, he don't want word to get around he's been knocked on his ass by a itty-bitty spoon." Shaftoe grins, and so do some of the bystanders.

"You got a key to that unit?" Shaftoe asks Pepe. "Good. I'm going up." He turns to Raoul, who's now on his feet. "You want to come along?"

Raoul nods his headache. "Yeah, man, I better go wit' you. Miz Charl so mad I go to L.A. and not fuck her, she throw her kitchen stuff at me, man."

"That a fact?" asks Shaftoe.

"I don't think she home," says Pepe. "She go to work twenty minute ago."

"You sure it was twenty?"

Pepe is right, nobody's in the apartment. "It didn't have to come from this unit," says Shaftoe. "They could've shut their window." Raoul seems disappointed, especially after the detective checks the kitchen drawers and finds no silverware that matches the piece that hit him.

They're about to leave when Shaftoe, who paints on Sundays in Central Park, turns one of Ellen Cherry's canvases around. He wants to see how her work compares. When a portrait of a spoon—a spoon identical to the one in his hand—is exposed, he emits a long, dry whistle and helps himself to a seat on the sofa.

On the way to Isaac & Ishmael's, the patrolman at the wheel says, "I don't get it. Guy gets clipped with a teaspoon, don't even require stitches, and you're conducting an investigation."

"Something . . . unusual here," says Shaftoe. "Something weird."

"Hey, this is New York, sergeant, not some jerkwater Ohio. Besides, everything's got a simple explanation, even in this town. Broad leaves a spoon on a windowsill, it slips off, clips a guy. So she and the guy know each other? Coincidence."

"What about all the paintings of this baby?" asks Shaftoe, waving the spoon. "And what about the paintings of bean cans? What if some guy gets brained with a bean can next? Some guy she's pissed at 'cause he didn't ball her? Right, buddy?"

In the backseat, Raoul shrugs, touches his head tenderly.

"Yeah, well, there was socks, too," says the cop. "She can't brain nobody with no sock. Anyway, she was at work."

"And where is it the lady works? The most dangerous restaurant in New York. Joint that's mixed up in all kinds of heavy Middle Eastern political shit. No, I tell you, there's big . . . unusualness here. There's something in the air."

"Spring," says the cop.

Shaftoe says nothing, he just keeps rubbing his fingers over the spoon. Were a genie to pop out of it, his first wish would be to know the spoon's story. No, no, he isn't *that* much of a detective. His first wish would be to play ball again. Second wish: maybe world peace, maybe a cure for AIDS. Third . . . aw, it doesn't matter. He glances over his shoulder. "This lady, Miss Charles, what's she like?"

"She a artist, man," says Raoul.

"No shit."

In front of the I & I, the driver lets the detective and Raoul out of the car. "You wearing a vest?" he asks.

"Naw," says Shaftoe, tapping his shirtfront. "I'll have to dodge 'em. I hear the food sucks, too."

Entering Isaac & Ishmael's, the bar is to the left, dining area to the right. They're separated by a low, bamboo-covered partition, maybe a yard high. The bandstand, as it were, is at the rear of the barroom but is completely visible—and audible—to those in the dining room. Teddy, the maître d', seats Detective Sergeant Shaftoe and Raoul Ritz in the dining area since it's practically empty while the less spacious bar is nearly full. Ellen Cherry's section is toward the front of the bar, so not only does she not wait on Shaftoe and Raoul, but they have to turn their heads in order to see her.

"Man, she looking fine," says Raoul.

"That's some kind of hair," marvels Shaftoe.

Their attention is directed to the bandstand, upon which a very young woman has just received a curt, perfunctory introduction from the bandleader. When the band strikes up again, the girl administers her tambourine a resounding whack and begins to dance. Instantly, Shaftoe knows what his third wish would be. Raoul's headache leaves through his mouth, which has fallen open. Every conversation in the I & I ceases, many in midsentence. The audience is transfixed. Some men raise a hand to clutch at their hearts, but most are paralyzed, pinned like butterflies to a wall of passion. Cooks and dishwashers are drawn out of the kitchen, security guards desert their posts on the sidewalk. The tambourine bangs, the tambourine jingles; the girl—awkwardly, self-consciously—dances, and the audience senses the weight, the weave, the odor of an ancient blanket that has been thrown over it, perhaps the blanket upon which Abraham spread the legs of Sarai and Hagar.

The night has cooled, as April nights will, but by the time the dance is done, the I & I is awash in sweat. Men applaud, pause to wipe their brows, applaud some more. They whistle and stamp their feet. It's been awhile since Shaftoe has experienced such a quickening of the loins. Raoul is muttering aloud in Spanish, something to the effect of, "I write a song for her, man. I write *ten* songs." Raoul has forgotten all about Ellen Cherry. So have the Greeks and Syrians, the Turks and Algerians, the Cypriots, Kuwaitis, and Israelis who've been flirting with her for months, and from among whom she's been expecting, despite her ethnic prejudices, to choose a lover in the near future.

Ellen Cherry must intuit her abandonment, for when a sweat-soaked Abu and a wild-eyed Spike ask her, in breathless succession, "What do you think of that tambourine girl?" and "So what're you thinking of our little Salome?", she pokes out her lower lip so far she could set a potted plant on it and replies, "Her legs are skinny. For a belly dancer, she's sure got skinny legs."

*   *   *

In a minute or two, the music starts up again, and once more the I & I is transformed into a savage sexual steam bath by the bashful young dancer, skinny legs and all. Absentmindedly, Shaftoe removes the spoon from the pocket of his K mart sport coat and drums out a rhythm with it on a bamboo place mat. Spoon is mortified. So shamed is she by the indecent display that she fails to recognize the room as the place where she and Ellen Cherry were reunited five months prior, and she finds herself wishing she had been broken to bits by the fall from the window ledge. She's taken the advice of a depraved, heathenish instrument of onanistic pleasure, and this is where it's led her. The dancer, abdomen jiggling, buttocks rotating, executes a leaf shimmy followed by a double hip bump. Shaftoe rat-a-tats Spoon against his beer glass. "Oh, dear!" she cries. "Mother Mary, release me."

Spoon's prayer is answered. The patrolman enters the I & I, pushes Teddy aside, and strides up to Shaftoe. He speaks into the detective's cauliflower ear. "Captain wants you uptown fast as you can get there." Shaftoe grumbles, slaps five dollars on the table, and backs out of the restaurant, his eyes pasted to Salome. He hasn't wasted any breath offering Raoul a lift.

Once outside, the patrolman says, "When I told the captain where you was, he like to had a stroke. When I told him what you was doing in there, I could hear the dispatcher giving him CPR."

Shaftoe spits. "Motherfucker see what I've seen tonight, it'd take more than CPR to revive his ass."

Reluctantly, Shaftoe turns his back on the I & I, follows his driver around the corner to Forty-ninth, where their car is parked. He pauses at a litter basket. Pensively, he looks from the spoon to the basket and back again. He shakes his head, shoves the spoon in his pocket. He's walked only a couple of steps, however, when he stops again, removes the household article, inspects it one more time in the moonshine. When he sighs, it's as if he's been taken out of another game, as if something in his sighing mechanism remembers the fumble that ended his tryout with the Buffalo Bills. He tosses Spoon in the trash.

The cop has watched all this. "Forget about it, sergeant," he says. "There's a million stories in the Naked City."

*   *   *

It's the third Friday in April, and the moon is setting. When the moon goes, the odalisque goes with it. They take their minty ambrosias, their odes, their hormones, their honker chardonnay. (Soon, present tense will follow them.) They leave the AIDS baby to shiver in the hard, sharp air. The buds on the trees, the vagabonds and cripples in the streets shiver, too.

Salome quits dancing at midnight. "She is just sixteen," the bandleader explains. Spike offers to drive her home, but she's already left, by the way of the rear courtyard that the I & I shares with the East Indian restaurant next door. The band plays on until two, although long before then the crowd dwindles to practically nothing.

"You see?" says Abu. "Everybody prefers the tambourine."

"Right," says Ellen Cherry. "Tambourine." She, too, departs via the courtyard, thus missing Raoul, who, having failed to locate Salome outside, returns to the restaurant to at last inform Ellen Cherry of his song, his desire, the lump on his head.

It doesn't take Ellen Cherry long to regret her coatless condition. Deciding that the night is too chilly and too dark for her to walk to the subway station, she hails a taxi. As the cab pulls away, Raoul staggers out of the I & I. "The little tambourine lady will be back here tomorrow night," Abu calls after him.

Raoul spins to glare at the tall, distinguished Arab. "Man, I'll be in fucking L.A., man," he says, with considerable irritation.

At the Ansonia, Pepe has gone off duty, leaving Ellen Cherry no word of the early evening's excitement and how it involved her apartment. Therefore, she's astonished, and a trifle frightened, when she enters to find most of her paintings staring her right in the eye. For some reason, perhaps having to do with the promise of spring, she suspects that it is Boomer who's been in her apartment. There's nothing vandalized or missing, and who except Boomer, or maybe Ultima Sommervell, is curious about her work?

She's wrong, of course, about there being nothing missing. After she's decided that even if Boomer has come home unexpectedly from Jerusalem, even if he's been by to spy on her art, she isn't likely to be seeing him that night; after she's showered off the smoke and grease from the I & I and applied moisturizing lotion to her face and body, she opens the top drawer of her dresser and reaches for her vibrator. *All that horniness at the I & I tonight must have rubbed off on me,* she thinks.

When she notices that the spoon is not where she left it, where she saw it only hours before, her spinal column draws as tight as Euclid's jockstrap, and a tropical hotel could cool its rooms with her blood.

It has been estimated that during the course of a lifetime, a person spends one year searching for lost objects. Ellen Cherry suspected that she could use up her allotted year and still not find that spoon, but she looked anyway. In a state of near panic, she didn't know what else to do. It took so little time to ransack the apartment that she ransacked it twice.

She struggled into a silk kimono—her goose bumps were so huge that the kimono barely covered them—and took the elevator to the lobby, glancing over her shoulder all the while and jumping at every sound and shadow. She dialed a number that she'd sworn she would never call, and experienced nausea when she heard it ringing in Ultima Sommervell's townhouse.

"Yes?" In the background, faint barking noises could be detected.

"Sorry. This is Ellen Cherry Charles. Can you just tell me if Boomer's back in town?"

"My dear, it's four bloody A.M. You must have had an upsetting dream. No, no, unfortunately he's not. As a matter of fact, I'm flying to Israel on Monday to persuade him to return. He's becoming another Jean-Michel Basquiat, foolishly sabotaging his own success."

"He's not back?"

"You don't sound well. Perhaps you should take something."

"Thanks. Sorry." She hung up and immediately phoned Spike Cohen. "So sorry to bother you at this hour, Mr. Cohen. This will probably sound silly to you, but there's been somebody in my apartment and . . ."

As the story spaghettied out of her, it did, indeed, strike Spike as rather silly. Nevertheless, he was quick to comfort and humor her. "Don't worry, darlink. Right away I'll be there. If it's a dybbuk what is haunting you, I know what can chase it out."

By the time Ellen Cherry found *dybbuk* in the dictionary—she wasted ten minutes looking under the *di*'s—Spike arrived at the Ansonia bearing a copy of the Ninety-first Psalm and a quart of rum. She had already admitted him when she realized that she was wearing her thin, flowered kimono and nothing else except a rapidly evaporating layer of moisturizer. She tried to appear nonchalant, he tried not to stare.

"To get rid of your demon I have to read aloud the Ninety-first Psalm. If that doesn't do the trick, then I got to blow the shofar, the ram's horn. The shofar works every time. Oy! Too bad a shofar I don't have, so I'm bringing a bottle of rum instead."

"Mr. Cohen, you don't really think there's a dybbuk involved. . . ."

He smiled. His teeth were even, and as white as laundry flakes. "No, no," he said. "Of course not. No self-respecting dybbuk would bother a *shiksa*. But it's a lovely psalm, and the rum is also nice."

Spike poured them each three fingers of dark Bacardi. "Now," he said, sitting down opposite her, "you tell me about this spoon what is going and coming, going and coming."

As Ellen Cherry was relating the facts of the matter, Spoon, herself, was gathering the courage to peer out from the sheet of dirty newsprint in which she had concealed herself. It happened to be the editorial page of a New York newspaper. The lead editorial defended the stockpiling of poison gas, chemical bombs, and long-range missiles by both sides in the Middle Eastern conflict on the grounds that if the arsenals were equal in size and capability, they would cancel each other out. It went so far as to quote the unforgettable logic of Henry Kissinger: "We have to have more missiles in order to get rid of missiles." Spoon wasn't cognizant of the paper's content. She was too occupied with hiding under it to read it (even if she could read), just as none but the most conscionable human beings ever question the true nature of the institutions that are theoretically protecting them.

Ascertaining that Forty-ninth Street was empty, she squirmed to the top of the trash basket and leaned against its rim. Up and down the street she gazed, wondering in what direction St. Patrick's lay and at what distance. It was awhile before she realized that she was chanting in the manner of that unspeakable device and his lingerie disciples, except that instead of "Wooga go nami ne," Spoon was endlessly repeating, "Oh dear oh dear oh dear oh dear." She hushed herself—and then immediately cried, "Oh dear." What was that coming down the street?

It resembled a wheel, turning so rapidly that it was no more than a rolling blur. As it whirled closer, Spoon could make out that which an organic eye was probably incapable of perceiving: the blur was Painted Stick.

Had the intoxicant vagrancies of the spring night aggravated the stick's restlessness and lured it, at no slight risk, out of hiding and into the streets? Spoon had been gone for five months, and while in ordinary object time that span was the briefest of moments, neither these objects nor their circumstances were ordinary. It was well known among them that Painted Stick was anxious to strike out for Jerusalem by whatever means. He was contemptuous of this land, America; convinced that not one of its citizens, with the possible exception of Turn Around Norman, was wise enough in the ways of the universe to facilitate his return to Jerusalem. How could they be when they were stupefied by a violent fear of Yahweh and corrupted by a violent love of money? If Conch Shell was more tolerant, more resigned than he, it was the shell, nonetheless, that, in league with the full moon, had influenced his flight from the cathedral.

Conch Shell had spent that third Friday in April—the day that spring tickled New York with the hardest of feathers—lying on her side on the ledge gazing through the grate. Long after Norman had completed his last revolution, she continued to gaze. Or, maybe she wasn't gazing at all. The conch shell is the bride of Taurus, the sea-bull who surfaces each and every April to water the earth with his translucent semen; she is the bull's herald, trumpeting his arrival, softening and arousing the land so that it might open up and receive his vital emissions. It's conceivable, then, that Conch Shell was in direct communication with something in the season that New Yorkers vaguely sensed but couldn't begin to identify. Certainly, the aura she broadcast was both wider and pinker than Can o' Beans had seen it in a great while. "Miss Shell seems to be in deep longing," he/she commented to Dirty Sock. "Poignant reverie."

"So that's what they call it at Bean Can College," said the sock. "Do tell? What do you smarty-pants call what's bugging our buddy here? If he weren't a stick his own self, I'd say he had a stick up his butt."

The sock's ill-bred diagnosis was accurate to the extent that Painted Stick seemed more rigid than usual. For long periods, he would stand upright, perfectly still, on the basement floor below Conch Shell, looking up at her. That would be followed by equally long periods during which he would march to and fro, like a military commander awaiting news from the front. It went on in that fashion for hours, until, late in the night, or more precisely, early in the morning after the moon had set and human activity had flagged, the stick hopped up on the ledge beside the gastropodous undine and announced that he was going to the sea. Before Conch Shell's protests could fully form, he was past her, forcing his way through the grate. A tight squeeze, the maneuver cost him a third of his remaining paint. Tiny shavings, colored by hands that had been dead three thousand years, peeled away and joined the soot and grit on the city sidewalk. Painted Stick took no notice, but moved brazenly to the curb and made a fix on the stars. When he was satisfied as to the location of the ocean, he set out for it at once, turning end over end at a speed that he hoped might render him barely visible to the human eye. When he had traveled several blocks without detection, a familiar, exultant power gripped him, and he wondered why he hadn't attempted this before.

Painted Stick didn't make it to the sea. The East River got in his way. For more than an hour, he perched on the revetment, about a hundred and fifty yards from Isaac & Ishmael's, studying the current of the river and the shipping upon it. There would be a harbor downstream, obviously, and the open Atlantic beyond, but how far he couldn't reckon. Still, it was in reach, and he was determined to lead his group there in the hope that they might stow away on a ship bound for Israel. Those modern vessels passing in the night were massive compared to the Phoenician boat in which he'd been transported to America, although they seemed slower in the water and not nearly as beautiful. The good news was, there would surely be places aboard to hide.

Shortly after four in the morning, the stick, turning like a vertical propeller, began retracing its route. It was only a short way up the street numbered forty-nine when it "heard" the timid, breathy "voice" of the American spoon "calling" its name. Painted Stick didn't show surprise, he wasn't the type, but Spoon could discern his excitement by all of the questions that he asked. She had never known him to be this effusive.

"Oh, sir, just help me get back to the cathedral," she pleaded. "There'll be plenty time for explanation. Are the others still there? Can o' Beans?"

Painted Stick sent her on ahead. "You locomote slowly and can be easily intercepted. Just proceed at the supreme limits of your speed, stay in the gutter close to the curb, and know that I shall be guarding your flank."

Indeed, that is the manner in which they ventured forth: Spoon scuttling along in the gutter between parked cars and the curb, Painted Stick half a block behind, on the sidewalk, whirling rapidly for the invisibility that was in it, but holding his forward progress in check. It seemed a workable system, but they hadn't gotten far before there was a crisis.

The door of the Mel Davis Dog Boutique flew open, and a man in a T-shirt and jeans ran out. He was laden with dog collars, some studded with diamonds, others with rubies that glowed red under the streetlamp like the hypodermic wounds in his arms. He dashed to the curb as if to meet an accomplice in a vehicle and instantly spotted Spoon scurrying by. Instinctively, he squatted for a closer look, visions of an expensive remote-control toy in his mind. Spoon scuttled on. The burglar sought to pin her down by placing his foot on her. A torn, dirty sneaker was in the process of pressing her to the pavement when Painted Stick whirled up, rammed the fellow force-fully in the groin, then, as he doubled over in pain, poked him in both eyes. He toppled and rolled into the gutter, bejeweled dog collars strewn about him like trinkets about a pharoah's mummy.

Never before had Painted Stick struck a human being. No other inanimate object, to the best of his knowledge, had, deliberately and of its own volition, struck a man. He felt as if he had committed a grave transgression, had violated fundamental rules of separation and domain, and that there might be dire consequences. What if a precedent had been established? What if he had rent somehow the fabric of universal order? At the same time that he, in dread and guilt, questioned the ethics of his rash deed, he felt empowered by it. He realized now that no person could safely impede his progress were he to lead his comrades to the sea.

It was a troubled but confident stick and a hysterically jittery spoon that continued down East Forty-ninth Street. But though the crossing of Lexington Avenue proved tricky—and nearly calamitous—they reached St. Patrick's ahead of the dawn.

*"Surely he shall deliver thee from the fowler's snare
and from the deadly pestilence.
He shall cover thee with his feathers,
and under his wings shalt thou find refuge;"*

The Ninety-first Psalm was dramatic and long, and Spike Cohen read it with quiet majesty. Ellen Cherry found herself thinking of how Buddy Winkler would have hammed it up. By the third verse, however, she had ceased to listen. Maybe it was the rum, maybe it was the hour, but she drifted into an involuntary eye game, optically mixing the patterns and hues of Spike's clothing—the salad-green V-neck sweater, the violet and white polka-dotted shirt, the plum and olive windowpane plaid suit—until she felt as if she were being pistol-whipped with a kaleidoscope. As she continued to play, she remembered a previous game, the one that her eyes had played with the spoon, and how it had made her aware of another level of reality, a level, a layer that consensual reality veiled. That experience had had the effect of making the world seem larger to her. Yet, simultaneously more private.

In general, this whole business with the spoon had provided her with a secret point of reference outside the everyday order of things. It was like Turn Around Norman had been, only more personal. Spike had spent a quarter hour sweetly assuring her that there was a rational, simple explanation for the spoon's appearance and disappearance, and that someday that which had seemed mysterious would wax mundane. Now, it occurred to her, in that event, she would feel cheated. Wasn't there a surplus in life of the boring, the repetitive, the mediocre, and the tame? Shouldn't she be glad, *grateful* for this intrusion of the unexpected and unexplained? And if she never understood it, why, so much the better. The surprise and shock of the extraordinary, even when embodied in so small a happening as the riddle around the spoon, could be a tonic, a syrup of wahoo, and

she found herself wishing a dose—dangerous side effects be damned—
for everyone she knew.

> *"With long life shall I satisfy him*
> *and show him my salvation."*

Finished, Spike looked up from the page to see a grin cross Ellen
Cherry's face like the chicken crossing the road, although the grin
more closely resembled the fireman's red suspenders. "Hoo boy," he
said. "Maybe a dybbuk I've chased out of you, after all. Didn't I tell
you it's a swell psalm?" He emptied his glass of its rum. "And the
surrogate shofar what I brought is useful also, ha?"

Ellen Cherry consulted her glass, and giggled.

"So, you relax now, ha? You can be getting some sleep. Dream of
beautiful things, except no wandering silverware, okay? What is this
spoon, Jewish or something?" Spike got up from his chair, as if to
exit. He glanced around the room. "Some other day maybe you can
show me these pictures what some *gonif* is stealing into your apartment to monkey with."

"Okay, maybe someday I will." She felt a tad guilty that she
hadn't at least shown him the paintings of the spoon, since they
apparently were involved in some way with the utensil's departure.
Holding her kimono closed around her, she, too, arose. "Right now,
though," she said, a whoopee cushion of mischief in her tone, "I
think I'd rather show you some shoes."

"Shoes?" Spike asked innocently, as if the subject of footwear was an
alien motif.

"Uh-huh. I always wear flats to work, you've hardly ever seen my
prime-time heels. I mean, hey, I'm no Imelda, but I've got three or
four pair that could loot the treasury of a Third World country and
make the natives say thank you. My hot pink Kenneth Cole ribbon
pumps could fleece Manila in an hour."

Taken unawares, Spike didn't quite know how to respond. "I recall
some red Cassinis what you wore to our reopening," he said. His
tone and manner were meek.

"Right. Those shoes could burn, but they couldn't pillage. Let me
show you a pair that takes no prisoners." Ellen Cherry knocked back
a slug of rum and vanished into her bedroom closet. When she

reappeared, she was holding out in front of her, as if they were twin holy grails, a pair of pumps that seemed to have been fashioned from passion fruit and monkey entrails knotted together in posh bows; with cut-out insteps, ribbon ties, and spool heels, wider at the ends than in the middle. "Ta-da," she said, softly and without emphasis. "Now aren't these the shoes estrogen would wear if estrogen had feet? I call the color 'neon fox tongue,' but that's another story."

"*Oy,* such a show! Very girly, very— I got friends, to be honest, what would complain these shoes are *ongepotchket:* overdone, garish, a mish-mosh, but me I like them." Spike stepped back a step or two. "Yah, I think they suit you. They got . . . Hard to tell when you're just holding them up. Can you . . ." He hesitated, and there was a subtle but discernible increase in the volume and velocity of his breath. "Can you maybe try them on?"

She smiled again and looked him over. She had acquaintances (at that point in her life she really had no friends) who would complain that he was *ongepotchket,* if they could define or pronounce it, but the artist in her approved of sartorial excess, and the woman in her saw past it. Still smiling, she said, "I'll be right back."

In her closet, she put on the shoes. And took off the kimono.

Her worry that Spike might be flustered, shocked, even repulsed, proved groundless. In the thirty years since his wife had decamped, he'd lain only with prostitutes, Upper West Side call girls, to be exact, so when Ellen Cherry appeared in the bedroom doorway naked—"nekkid," rather—except for the Kenneth Cole shoes, he responded in a direct, systematic, and no-nonsense manner. Well, there was some nonsense, but it came later. And for the moment, she was completely content to dispense with conversation and foreplay. They just weren't necessary.

With the same fluid motions with which he was said by Abu to serve a tennis ball and then backhand its return, Spike removed his clothing, every last *ongepotchket* of it. Then he led her to the bed, laid her down, spread her legs (to which the pink pumps were still affixed), and gracefully mounted her.

The cries of her initial orgasm resounded in the room almost immediately. In her underwear drawer, the panties tittered knowingly and teased Master Daruma, who rejoined with sagacity, "On hairy caterpillar there are *many* beads of dew."

In the comparative lull that followed her second climax, a time when he was stoking her with slow but by no means dispassionate efficiency, and when, coasting, she was studying the dawn light reflected in the perspiration on his seesawing shoulder blades, she experienced a jab of guilt. Considering events of the past two years, it was absurdly irrational; yet there it was, a southern feminine conditioned reflex, handicapping her emotions and tarnishing the shine of her physical joy. Ah, but then she happened to remember that Ultima was flying to Jerusalem on Monday, and she returned to the fuck with renewed zeal.

She clasped his buttocks in her hands and pushed against him, not to force him into her more deeply—he was already in so deep she could almost taste him—but to give him more of *her,* to grant him as much of her pussy as was anatomically possible, without reservation, privacy, or shame. Great sea mammal sounds began to issue from them both: a groaning against the heavy pressure of the ocean, a squirty opening of mollusk shells, a slapping of wet flippers, an exhalation of salty and humid vapors, a blubberous explosion of moby dick.

Did she recoil when he withdrew to rub himself against her feet? *Au contraire.* Nor did she flinch when she felt the hot trickle between her toes or complain that he had transformed one of her chic new shoes into a gravy boat. No, Ellen Cherry in time would have some unusual requirements of her own, and she could tell that dear Spike Cohen was just the man to fulfill them.

She awoke at noon feeling that her luck had changed. Undoubtedly, it was a matter of attitude. When a person accepts a broader definition of reality, a broader net is cast upon the waters of fortune.

Sure enough, around one that afternoon, after she and Spike had taken another dolphin ride, the day doorman came to her apartment with an envelope that had been delivered by messenger. There was a check inside, and a note scribbled on rose paper with violet ink:

Forgot to mention last night (rather, this morning) that your remaining picture sold. To a Corning collector this time. My dear, they love you in the provinces! Upon my return from ghastly Jerusalem, you simply must fetch me over some new work.

"Maybe I will, Ultima baby," said Ellen Cherry, scratching her bottom with simian luxury. "Maybe I will."

Spike departed to meet Abu for tennis, whistling like a parakeet in a marijuana field, and she fell back asleep to dream of whitecapped waves. Probably they were sexual rather than creative waves, but later she recalled that just before she woke, a brush in her brain added a touch of naples yellow (patron saint of Neapolitan chain-smokers) to keep the whites from being stark.

Serpent à sonnettes. Rattelslang. Culebra de cascabel. Skallerorm. Klapperschlange. Rattlesnake.

Walking past the makeshift bandstand on her way to the kitchen to hang up her light jacket (she wasn't about to repeat the chilly mistake of the previous night), Ellen Cherry's foot accidentally brushed against Salome's tambourine. It jingled and whirred, causing her instinctively to jump to one side, as if she had transgressed upon one of those vipers that vibrate their tails when disturbed. Abu witnessed this and laughed aloud.

> *Serpent à sonnettes*
> *Rattelslang*
> *Culebra de cascabel*
> *Skallerorm*
> *Klapperschlange*
> Rattlesnake

Separately or all together: musical. A little poem.

By mutual consent, Ellen Cherry and Spike intended to conceal the fresh facet that the diamond cutters of destiny had cleaved into their relationship. They studiously avoided giving each other meaningful glances, nor did they touch or smile when they passed. To further avert suspicion, Ellen Cherry planned to pay extra attention to Abu that evening whenever opportunity allowed. The attack by the tambourine gave her the first excuse. Patsy's phone call gave her the second.

Since there still wasn't a phone in her Ansonia apartment, Ellen Cherry's parents called her, sometimes as often as once a week, at

Isaac & Ishmael's. Out of consideration for customers (in the past, that had been wishful thinking, if not a joke), they usually phoned early, just as she was beginning her shift.

"Mercy me, *you're* sounding bright-eyed and bushy-tailed."

"I am?" Ellen Cherry was disappointed that her supposedly secret glee was so blatantly evident.

"Lord, yes, you are, honey. Now tell me: couldn't be ol' Boomer's back in town, could it?"

"Why, no, mama, he's not. Where'd you get that idea?"

"It wasn't any idea. Just a stab in the dark, that's all. Wondering what'd tipped your giggle box on its side. Leave it to ol' prefeminist Patsy to think there was a blessed man involved." Patsy paused. "Actually, I was kinda hoping Boomer was back over here. For more reasons than one."

"And why is that?" Ellen Cherry asked, mainly to be polite. For the first time in many months, attracting that idiot welder to her side was not a top priority for her.

" 'Cause," said Patsy. " 'Cause your uncle Buddy, as you've always known him, is fixing to go to Jerusalem. Leaving on Monday. Honey, I think he's getting ready to pull off that deal he was talking 'bout at Christmas time. You know, that, uh, Dome of the Rock deal?"

"Yes, mama, I know what you're speaking of. Mr. Hadee says it would touch off a world war."

"I don't know about that, but Bud told your daddy that he wants to strike at the mosque during some big religious festival that's coming up, I believe, next month. He said that the Temple Mount would be really crowded then, so his 'strike' would have more of an impact."

"More people killed or hurt is how that translates. Makes my blood boil."

"I wasn't intending to spoil your good mood. I know you and Bud have fussed over this before. I just thought maybe you should get hold of Boomer someway, and, uh, I guess talk some sense to him or something, 'cause I'll bet dollars to doughnuts that Bud's fixing to try to get Boomer mixed up in it."

"I can't imagine Boomer getting involved. He can be a jerk, but he's not vicious. He's not quite the redneck he pretends to be."

"Well, just the same . . ."

"I'll think about it, mama. I'll give it some serious thought. How're you? How's Daddy? Aside from consorting with Baptist terrorists."

"Oh, we're pretty fine. Verlin's back's bothering him. Claimed he strained it frogging the other night, but I think it's from always setting in front of that blessed television watching ball games. Sets all scrunched down in his chair, like a hound dog passing peach pits. I've tried to get him to work out with me once in a while, but he just snorts. If he saw it was a Jane Fonda tape I was working out to, he'd holler real good. He says women exercising is just like women wearing makeup, they only do it to seduce men. Huh! I had plans of being a professional dancer once." Patsy sighed. "Then that got all shot to pieces." She sighed again.

"Mama, don't. Please don't get misty on me."

"I gave up my dancing 'cause a man loved me so much he didn't want me to dance. My daughter gives up her painting 'cause a man— I ought to shut my big mouth. I don't rightly know why you gave up your painting—"

"I don't either."

"—but I wish you'd get back to it."

"I may do that. I truly may. And you could resume dancing, too. No, I'm serious, mama. You could. You're only a little past forty, in good shape. Sure, they say that dancing's only for young women, but, hey, that's somebody else's rules, not yours. One thing the eye game has taught me, and I guess Boomer also contributed, is that you've got to toss your own salad or else eat with the masses from their narrow trough."

"Then why don't you come down here and help me toss? We could all use us a different set of rules 'round Colonial Pines. It's lovely, though. You remember how lovely Virginia is in the spring."

Mother and daughter exchanged commentaries on the weather, and then Ellen Cherry excused herself. She had to report for duty. Patsy's cheerful nature had resurfaced by the time they hung up, although it worried her that her daughter was once again referring to some funny business regarding a spoon.

Ellen Cherry cracked the kitchen door open and peeked out. Nine or ten men were sitting in the bar watching a Yankees game on the futuristic TV. The dining room was empty. The place probably wouldn't get busy until after eight. Entertainment started at nine. She let the door swing shut and crossed the kitchen to the sinks, where Abu was fiddling with a balky faucet.

"Mr. Hadee, do you think men like Buddy Winkler are actually dangerous?"

Concentrating on the plumbing—he wanted to get it repaired before their incompetent dishwasher arrived—Abu didn't immediately respond. Eventually, though, he looked up and said this: "Anyone who maintains absolute standards of good and evil is dangerous. As dangerous as a maniac with a loaded revolver. In fact, the person who maintains absolute standards of good and evil usually *is* the maniac with the revolver."

His attention refocused on the faucet. The tap swiveled at about the same speed as Turn Around Norman. Abu managed to expose its threads. Then he straightened up to hunt for some machine oil. "Nabila, by the way, saw Reverend Winkler on TV last night. He gave the invocation at the big Republican rally at Madison Square Garden. Evidently, when he was introduced he received an ovation."

Ellen Cherry shook her curls in disgust, then checked to see if any stray hairs had landed in the *falafel*. "Suppose he was exposed as the leader—one of the leaders—of a plot that could destroy famous property and kill innocent victims?"

"So?"

"Well, then everybody would turn against him, right?"

With a paper towel, Abu wiped off excess oil from the faucet neck. His laugh was as dry and scratchy as a roadrunner's toenails. "I would not count on that," he said. "That would depend. If it is committed in the name of God or country, there is no crime so heinous that the public will not forgive it."

By nine o'clock, the I & I was, well, if not jumping, if not rocking, at least hopping like Boomer Petway on one whole foot. Many of Friday night's customers had returned, and some had brought friends along. If the restaurant wasn't occupied to capacity, it held, nevertheless, its largest crowd since Super Bowl Sunday, and there was something of the Super Bowl air of high expectation in the room. As the hour of ten approached, men were on their feet as if awaiting a kickoff. But what they were waiting for was a sixteen-year-old girl whom the bandleader would reluctantly introduce as "Salome."

She appeared without warning and with a minimum of fanfare, dressed in a filmy harem pajama of flaring chiffon over which she wore a considerably more opaque two-piece meta-costume consisting of a brief halter-top and girdle, brocaded in silver and gold and spangled with tinkly disks and flowers. Riding low upon her hips, the girdle afforded an optimum view of belly skin, although her navel was masked by an isolated rosette of brocade, a stylized chestnut burr whose quills protected something round and sweet and altogether fertile, some Mesopotamian seed-nut not yet sprouted. Circling her wrists were alabaster and metal aerodromes housing buzzing squadrons of unseen bees; circling her ankles were beads and bells; while her neck was ringed by a reef of paste jewels from whose nadir was suspended a larger island of gold.

In Ellen Cherry's opinion, the costume was *ongepotchket*—and old-fashioned and corny to boot. However, nobody present was interested in Ellen Cherry's opinion, not even Spike. Here, it should be noted that Salome was barefoot.

From her painted toenails to her head of short, black ringlets, she measured five-three or five-four. Generally speaking, her body was slender and serpentine: her breasts were small and appeared to be still developing, but she swelled at the hips, presenting a pelvis fully capable of accommodating childbirth. Despite rather bushy eyebrows, her face was gorgeous. She had the complexion of a night-blooming lily, dense lips that might have been molded from the meat of muskmelons, a longish nose that in its curl and grace resembled the scroll of a small violin, cheeks and chin whose juxtaposition of delicate bone to carefree baby fat combined the elegance of a racehorse with the robustness of a mule; and mammoth liquid brown eyes, whose luster and latent heat could convince a chemist that chocolate, if not a living organism, was at least a fossil fuel.

But it was her manner as much as her looks that turned men's hearts into squirrel cages. First onstage, Salome appeared like a startled doe caught in the headlights of an onrushing truck. Timid and uncomfortable, she would fidget, flick her hair, roll her eyes, nervously clench her tambourine, pluck at the seat of her girdle, and alternately glare at and shrink from the audience. In no aspect, however, did her shyness or self-consciousness inhibit the free movement of her body once she began to dance. The effect was that of a seduction victim who, because she is virginal, betrothed to another man, or contemptuous of her seducer, mentally recoils from his sexual attentions, only to find her body enthusiastically responding in spite of herself. If there existed in the universe any display with a stronger guarantee of igniting the male libido, it had yet to be cataloged.

In Ellen Cherry's opinion, Salome wasn't much more than a gauche little schoolgirl "picking at her bottom like her drawers are riding up the crack of her ass," but, again, nobody was interested in Ellen Cherry's opinions, least of all not Detective Shaftoe, who, having returned to sit at a front table, got so excited he placed himself under arrest. Salome simply was not a matter of opinion. About an empress, a poetess, a pop star, one might be opinionative, for such women either are frozen in the amber of history or are speeding with one down the illusionary road of one's own time. Salome, on the other hand, had a quality that was timeless. Although innocently young, there was the suggestion of years of experience behind her. She even seemed wise, not in any conscious or formidable way, but rather as if something strangely meaningful clung to her, a secret knowledge or hidden wisdom; a bright creative power and a dark destructive power, neither of which she had to think about, for she didn't think quite so much as she was thought.

Salome shook her necklace: *serpent à sonnettes.* She shook her bracelets: *rattelslang.* She shook her anklets: *culebra de cascabel.* She shook her tambourine: *skallerorm* and *klapperschlange.* And it was clear to every Adam in the restaurant, every Adamu in the bar, that she was the one who'd made friends with the Snake, that she'd let it lick the blood of her first menstruation, that she . . . *oooo eee,* that she . . . *oooo eee,* that she . . . *oooo eee,* that she now knew what the Serpent knew.

The harder she danced, the more vividly she projected the image of the passive, slightly unwilling, recipient of male energy; and yet at the same time (though time had ceased to exist) she represented an agent of calamity, a cunning danger to all men. And through the veil of blue smoke and red light, and white steam off the *falafel* trays, every expressionless face—locked in its zone between ego and release, anxiety and delight—every face was thrust up at her.

So occupied was Ellen Cherry that evening with fulfilling her customers' secondary desires, desires for food and drink (chiefly drink) that she had scant occasion to ponder Patsy's call. Any decision regarding Boomer and whether or not he need be warned of Buddy's presumed intentions would have to be postponed. Her immediate reaction, however, was that her husband—technically speaking, he was still her husband—wouldn't touch Bud's scheme with a ten-foot welding rod, not even if Bud required his services, which he probably did not. The Boomer Petway whom she believed she knew and understood would never buy into churchdom's shame-less flirtation with ultimate cataclysm, let alone hustle to usher in the doom. Or would he? He'd been both tolerant of and generous to Bud in the past, and an awful lot of otherwise sane citizens *had* bought into it, literally, with cash donations that many of them scarcely could afford.

Perhaps the aura of timelessness radiated by Salome was affecting Ellen Cherry in some subliminal way, but it was impossible for her to picture God just stomping on the brakes one day and sending the world flying through the windshield. What was the point? Was life merely a failed experiment destined to be terminated? Since his prophets had forecast a fiery end thousands of years earlier, it would seem that God had known all along that the experiment was going to flop. Why would an omnipotent, omniscient deity go to the trouble to create an infinitely complex universe if he realized from the beginning that it was only going to malfunction and go down in flames?

"Sorry, sir, they don't export Maccabee in bottles. Would you care for a can? Or, we do have Stella in the bottle. That's an Egyptian beer."

She supposed that another way to look at it was that life wasn't an experiment but a test, a test that most but not all would flunk. For those few who passed, there awaited a reward, an afterlife not only experientially superior to life but free of life's planned obsolescence. There was something about such a system that struck her as simplis-tic, if not degrading, but she couldn't put her finger on it, at least not right then.

"Two Maccabees, a Stella, and a brandy Alexandria. No, not Alexander, Alexandria. Don't ask me the difference. If you want," she told the bartender, "I'll ask the guy in the fez on my way to the kitchen."

One thing about which she was reasonably certain, however, was that Buddy Winkler's insensitivity to the beauty in life, his insensitiv-ity to life, per se, was connected somehow to his ironclad conviction that human beings, unlike God, tended to color outside of the lines—and therefore the coloring book ought to be soaked in gaso-line and burned. Time, in his view, was a short, sloppy path from Eve's crayon box to the Messiah's fire box.

At that moment, Salome, her eyes demurely downcast, whacked her well-formed and busy young rump with her tambourine, sending a wave of ecstatic vibration over the tabletops and causing two Cypriot economists to spin on their bar stools. The wave hit Ellen Cherry as she emerged from the kitchen, supporting a laden tray. Outwardly, she paid it little heed, but the shape of eternity outlined by its resonating vectors must have guided a zigzagging mental sequence into place, for she found herself suggesting to herself that *all these folks who're milling about waiting for Jesus to parachute to earth and break up the party are likely to be disappointed.* Personally, she just couldn't imagine a future, regardless how distant, when some waitress somewhere would not be wobbling out of a kitchen on aching arches to deliver yet another dish of, well, if not *baba ghanoug,* some equally unimposing pacifier of the stomach's perennially recurring contractions. She was, nevertheless, compelled to concede that an unending future in which an unending parade of waitresses served up unending plates of hash would strike some people as a pretty good working definition of hell, while still others might ask for no finer paradise.

Information about time cannot be imparted in a straightforward way. Like furniture, it has to be tipped and tilted to get it through the door. If the past is a solid oak buffet whose legs must be unscrewed and whose drawers must be removed before, in an altered state, it can be upended into the entryway of our minds, then the future is a king-size waterbed that hardly stands a chance, especially if it needs to be brought up in an elevator.

Those billions who persist in perceiving time as the pursuit of the future are continually buying waterbeds that will never make it beyond the front porch or the lobby. And if man's mission is to reside in the fullness of the present, then he's got no space for the waterbed, anyhow, not even if he could lower it through a skylight.

Ellen Cherry Charles, no less than Buddy Winkler, participated in history, that modern form of consciousness that glorifies the dismantled buffet, yet blindly craves the waterbed. Unlike the Reverend Buddy Winkler, however, Ellen Cherry had not rejected nature—the living present, the living planet—in order to chase after a transcendent goal. That's why Buddy's behavior confounded her. She was much too busy at the moment slinging *tahini* and mopping up spilled gin to analyze in any depth their temporal differences; indeed, though she had moved a fair amount of furniture in her short life, she may have been intellectually incapable of such analysis, even in serene surroundings. Yet, she was entirely correct to propose that Buddy's disregard for nature, art, and the human experience was tied to his concept of time, especially in regard to an ultimate five o'clock whistle followed by an afterlife.

When the sixth veil falls—and with a barefoot kid called Salome performing the ancient Levantine birth dance in a testosterone-bubbling New York bar, it might no longer be premature to speak of falling veils—when the sixth veil falls, the desensitizing, corrupting illusion of bullet-train history and its apocalyptic destination will surely dissolve.

Roland Abu Hadee once remarked that the reason that Jews habitually accomplished more than Moslems, more than Christians, for that matter; the reason a Jew seldom hesitated to take on artistic, social, or commercial tasks that would frighten off, say, a possibly more qualified Gentile, was because the Jew wasn't betting all of his or her chips on the hereafter; Jews were boldly playing their hands, cashing their checks, *here and now;* they were going for it in their own lifetime because they had never been convinced, as a people, that the banks would be open in heaven.

The patent truth is that nobody, regardless of race, religion, or personal enlightenment, nobody knows whether or not there is an afterlife. Only the dead can say for sure, and they aren't talking. Energy never perishes, so the concept of reincarnation makes a certain amount of sense, but there's absolutely no proof, "memories" of "past lives" (genetic pot shards?) notwithstanding. Despite all absence of evidence, however, there thrives a popular and stern faith in the end of time and in the orchids or onions to be distributed at the finale; and that faith, that wishful—or fearful—thinking, constitutes a veil so thick, so sturdy that it's a wonder we can see to get out of bed in the morning. If nothing else, the sixth veil is an effective sun block. It may also be a shackle and a shroud.

As long as a population can be induced to believe in a super-natural hereafter, it can be oppressed and controlled. People will put up with all sorts of tyranny, poverty, and painful treatment if they're convinced that they'll eventually escape to some resort in the sky where lifeguards are superfluous and the pool never closes. Moreover, the faithful are usually willing to risk their skins in whatever military adventure their government may currently be promoting. When the sixth veil drops, there will be a definite shortage of cannon fodder.

Those in high places are not immune. While the afterlife concept renders the masses manageable, it renders their masters destructive. A world leader who's convinced that life is merely a trial for the more valuable and authentic afterlife is less hesitant to risk starting a nuclear holocaust. A politician or corporate executive who's expect-ing the Rapture to arrive on the next flight from Jerusalem is not going to worry much about polluting oceans or destroying forests. Why should he?

Thus, to emphasize the afterlife is to deny life. To concentrate on heaven is to create hell.

In their desperate longing to transcend the disorderliness, friction, and unpredictability that pesters life; in their desire for a fresh start in a tidy habitat, germ-free and secured by angels, religious multi-tudes are gambling the only life they may ever have on a dark horse in a race that has no finish line. Theirs is a death wish on a very grand scale, an eschatological extension of Kissinger's perverse logic—"In order to live forever, we must die as quickly as possible" —and if time doesn't run out soon, they're going to form a posse and run it out. Fortunately for them, they see signs everywhere that the end is near. Unfortunately, they're virtually the same signs that their ancestors saw millennia before them.

Meanwhile, the thermodynamic and cosmological forces that form the basis for "time" spiral merrily along without going anywhere very much. Just around. And around again. Order expanding into disor-der contracting into order at a rate so incredibly slow that it bores and bewilders us to the extent that we have to invent psychological endings for it. What the sixth veil conceals is not a blank clock but a relieved expression, the expression on our own faces as we meet ourselves coming from the opposite direction, free to enjoy the present at last because we are no longer fettered by the future that is history.

On Sunday evening, there was no music, and Isaac & Ishmael's closed early, right after the Yankees game. Throughout the televised contest, at least once an inning, one customer or another mentioned Salome, usually in a voice that was skittery and feverish, the voice of a prospective bridegroom. Alas, the tambourine lay silent, and neither Abu nor Spike could satisfy anybody's curiosity regarding its mistress's identity. "Well, what nationality is she?" asked a frustrated fan. Abu shook his head. "She says she is a Canaanite. But, of course, that, like her name, is her idea of show biz." Nobody smiled. "She's in the student nurse program at Bellevue," a man said. Everyone looked at him. He was an American, a stocky black man with cotton hair, a relative newcomer to the I & I. "She's a Lebanese national, here on a student visa. During the day she empties bedpans." There were incredulous glances. "How do you know that?" "Maybe I'm a fucking detective," said Shaftoe, and he drained his beer and walked out.

Within an hour, the last cup had been washed, the lights extinguished, and Abu was on his way home. "Mr. Cohen is going over the books," he said to the security guard as he left. "He will be in the office for a while." "What about the waitress?" asked the guard. Abu paused. "Oh? The waitress is still here?" He paused again. "There is no problem," he said at last, and, rubbing his cherry-carrot nose, he climbed into the waiting car.

Thirty minutes later, about the time that Ultima Sommervell was latching her freshly packed suitcase, about the time that the Reverend Buddy Winkler was laying a barbecue-stained Armani jacket in *his* new bag, about the time that Turn Around Norman began to turn in his sleep—a rotation that conceivably could take most of the night to complete—the guard went around back to the courtyard and put his ear to the wall. He wasn't really surprised to hear Mr. Cohen and the waitress riding the dolphin; in his mind, he could almost see them entwined on the office couch, although he couldn't have envisioned that Ellen Cherry was naked except for a spanking new pair of leopard-skin stilettos with emerald clasps, the paper and ribbon that had wrapped them mixed in with the clothing scattered about the office floor. The guard was prepared for the thumps and creaks and meatball ping-pong, the feathery throbs and fermented murmurs that were still lingua franca in AIDS-stifled America, but he was decidedly unprepared for what he heard next, a laudation that prompted him to cross himself and beg forgiveness for the imaginary sin of eavesdropping.

"Jezebel. Jezebel. Painted Queen of Israel. I am praising thee, O Queen of Israel. Whore of the Golden Calf. Strumpet of Baal. Jezebel. Slut of Samaria. Our queen whom the dogs are eating. The watercourse of the Jews is flowing through thee. Jezebel. My Queen. Whose daughter is ruling in Jerusalem. From whose womb is pouring the House of David. Mmm. Jezebel. Priestess of Fornication. Mmm. Queen of Spades. Queen of Tarts. O Jezebel, you are my queen, I exalt thee and praise thy sandals."

On and on in that manner until the guard clasped his crucifix and fled to the street,

On and on in that manner until, blocks away, Conch Shell and Painted Stick were drawn to their rusty window grate as if a magic magnetism was in the air,

On and on in that manner until Ellen Cherry's new shoes were launched into the river of life, amidst a blind boogie-woogie of tadpoles.

On the list of the world's greatest inventions, the mirror is surprisingly high. As invention goes, the genesis of mirrors didn't exactly require a truckload of imagination, the looking glass being merely an extension of pond-surface, made portable and refined. Yet, because it is consulted with such frequency and anticipation by the three billion souls who animate our ball of clay, consulted almost as if it were a powerful deity that can grant favors or take them away; because, whereas most matter absorbs light, the mirror returns light to the world (it arrests light but does not book it, releasing it on its own recognizance); because it also returns, however briefly and superficially, the individual identity that people are prone to surrender to the orthodoxy of the state and its stern gods; because it never fails to provide us with someone to love and someone to hate; the mirror, on the list of great inventions, is rated higher than the thermos bottle, though not quite as high as room service.

"I realize, sir," said Can o' Beans to the mirror, "that the angle of reflection is always equal to the angle of incidence, but *why*? Can you explain it?"

"?ti nialpxe uoy . . ."

"And a further thing, Mr. Mirror," the can went on. "Since you reflect chaos and instability as objectively as you reflect order, since you reflect the novelty and variety that humankind's institutions seem designed to suppress and deny, are you not a dangerous agent of truth? I mean, I know that magicians employ you in their trickery, but isn't uncompromising realism your forte? If humans erect institutions to conceal the unruly aspects of their own minds, aren't you mirrors sort of like holes in the fortress walls? Are you not signposts pointing away from rationality and standardization? Because you chaps show it *all*—good and evil, beauty and ugliness, balance and disarray—with equal emphasis. Or am I making you out to be subversive when actually you're only blasé? No offense intended, sir, in either case."

".esac rehtie ni, ris, dednetni . . ."

Oh, it was pointless trying to hold a civil conversation with a mirror. No matter what anybody said to them, they just turned it around.

This particular mirror, the badly scratched one that leaned against a dank wall in the cellar of St. Patrick's Cathedral, had once been a fixture in a men's toilet upstairs off the apse. In its heyday, it had held in its flat hands many famous faces. Politicians, tycoons, Broadway stars. John F. Kennedy, Truman Capote, Rudolf Valentino, and countless others as glamorous or mighty. Now, alas, it reflected a can of pork 'n' beans. And a sorry can of beans it was, too; a misshapen, savagely scarred plop of metal from which a few scraps of label hung like tassels from a burlesque queen's nips.

If the bean tin was dismayed by its image, it did not let on. In fact, it seemed upbeat and full of itself. The reason for its lofty spirits, despite its pitiful condition, lay in its knowledge that four or five portraits of it existed, splendid oil paintings that captured it in its prime. "What other bean can has been preserved thus for posterity?" Can o' Beans asked rhetorically. "And should my portrait lack the glitter, the chic of traditional society portraiture, so much the better. I am a modern, proletarian icon, and it is fitting that I should be depicted in a brash and modernist style."

In the weeks since he/she had learned of his/her portraits, Can o' Beans had gone to the mirror time and time again, whereas previously he/she had avoided his/her reflection altogether. "It doesn't matter anymore that I'm a wreck," he/she told the looking glass. "I've been immortalized." Then, because he/she was sensitive, he/she would add, "So buck up, dear fellow, and forget your cracks. You, too, may be resurrected in some unexpected way."

Like Spoon, Can o' Beans believed that Ellen Cherry's decision to paint them was indicative of some special insight, some auspicious affinity. "If we can't turn to Miss Charles," he/she said, "then I daresay we can't turn to anyone."

Dirty Sock didn't buy it for an instant. He was impressed neither by news of the paintings nor by Spoon's description of how Ellen Cherry had held her up and studied her with incredible concentration. "The bimbo's just touched in the ol' potato," said Dirty Sock. "All artists are touched in their potatoes."

Ordinarily, Can o' Beans might have launched into a discourse on the notorious thin line between genius and madness, a boundary as much in dispute as any in the Middle East, but that day he/she had had a different point to make. "On the other hand, I fail to comprehend why our venerable leaders persist in believing that human assistance is desirable or necessary. With all respect to Miss Charles and Mr. Norman, it's always seemed iffy to me, and now that Mr. Stick has found us a route to the sea . . ."

"Ever since he whipped that junkie's ass, ol' Stick's been acting like he's touched in *his* potato."

Ordinarily, Can o' Beans might have complained about the stocking's slang, pointing out that a potato was a vegetable and nothing else, a truism to which Dirty Sock might have responded, "Guess it takes one to know one." On that day, however, pedagoguery gave way to concern. "True, Mr. Stick has devoted several weeks to the contemplation of his all too manlike deed," the can agreed, "but he's apparently resolving the matter. At least he's quit lying in the window all day, scanning the horizon for signs of cosmic repercussion, and, of course, seeing precious little except the sides of passing buses. He and Miss Shell are plotting again, and that's what worries me. Why don't we just locomote down to the ships and be done with it? Miss Spoon—doesn't she look pretty now that she's been polished?—Miss Spoon lives in mortal terror that they're going to send her out again, another try at infiltrating the private life of Turn Around Norman. It's for our dear Spoon that I'm concerned."

"Come on, perfesser, you mean to tell me you're not scared about lighting out for the waterfront to sneak aboard some big foreign boat?"

"Me? Fear? What do I have to lose? I was already the luckiest bean can that ever was. And now I will live forever, enshrined as I am on canvas for future generations to meet and to judge."

"Right," growled Dirty Sock. "You and ol' Moaning Lisa."

*   *   *

Spoon's fears were not ill-founded. The stick and the shell were, indeed, considering dispatching her to have another go at Norman's donation box. It wasn't that the Middle Eastern relics were unappreciative of Ellen Cherry's potential friendship, as expressed in her paintings, her eye game, and her erstwhile fascination with the gentleman who turned around for his supper. No, it was that the relics knew something that the others did not.

What they knew was that they were trapped.

That is, two of their company were trapped.

Originally, they had entered Manhattan very late on a rainy, foggy, autumn night. They had lain for days in a culvert near the Jersey-side entrance to the Lincoln Tunnel, waiting for precisely those meteorological conditions. Even at three in the morning, in thick drizzle, however, undetected travel proved more problematic than they had anticipated, and when, on their blind path to the Atlantic, they'd chanced upon the open doors of a holy place, they decided to seek temporary asylum inside.

A van had been parked in front of the cathedral, and a long plastic accordion hose of large circumference ran from the vehicle into the church, as if the serpent of Eden, grown immense and vengeful, had returned to eat up all the world's communion wafers. The truth was, St. Patrick's was having its carpets washed: the hose was funneling a detergent foam. At any rate, the objects had followed the hose through the main door, and, then, having seen cleaners at work in the nave, they had scooted, toddled, and slithered down the narrow staircase that descended from the narthex. In the basement, which had been left open by the janitors, they'd found yet another door, slightly ajar. Painted Stick pried it wide enough for them to slip through and descend a second set of steps.

The doors of the ancient world, to which Painted Stick was accustomed, generally swung freely on their hinges, unless manually bolted or latched. When the door to the sub-basement swung closed behind them, however, there had been an ominous click. Modern doors had catches, it seemed, that engaged automatically. The catch was controlled by a brass knob, round and slippery, and it was quite impossible for the stick, by far the most dexterous of the inanimates, to manipulate it: he had tried on several occasions while his comrades were otherwise occupied. Unless a custodian were again to leave the door ajar, and that hadn't happened in a year and a half, there was no way that the objects might exit through it.

Now, Spoon, Dirty Sock, and, if he didn't mind losing a little more paint, Painted Stick could escape through the window grate. But Conch Shell and Can o' Beans were much too broad to negotiate its grid. Those two were trapped.

Well, the objects had needed some time in which to rest and make plans, and Conch Shell had convinced Painted Stick that the Third Temple of Jerusalem was yet to be manifest, a fact corroborated by Spoon, who had repeated Buddy Winkler's account of the Dome of the Rock. But Temple or no Temple, all of them were itching now to get on with their journey, and the only way they might proceed was if a human being opened the doors or else took a crowbar to the window grate.

Miss Charles had been a likely candidate, but it had been months since she'd stood out front of the cathedral, and Spoon hadn't the faintest idea how to locate her apartment. That meant that they must resort to Turn Around Norman. Or something altogether different.

It was destined to be something altogether different, for the simple reason that one afternoon in midrevolution, Turn Around Norman suddenly scooped up his donation box, flashed his fatal blue eyes, flared his swan-perfect nose, fired a spitty projectile from his bardic mouth, spun on a soiled sneaker, and left the Fifth Avenue stage, never to return.

So abrupt was the performer's departure that it caught the objects completely off guard, although in retrospect they realized that they should have seen it coming. As the weather had warmed that spring, there had been an influx of preachers onto Fifth Avenue, a scattered flock of rackety birds migrating in from some dark, harsh land. At least four of them had settled within earshot of St. Patrick's, and at all hours of the day the objects could hear their magpie cries. "Praise the Lord!" "The Rapture is coming!" "Repent, for the end is near!" "Ye generation of vipers, how can ye escape the damnation of hell?"

As the warnings escalated in volume and frequency, Conch Shell had to reassure Painted Stick that they were standard rhetoric and not bulletins from Jerusalem. To reinforce her assurances, Can o' Beans pointed out that the voices were only reciting biblical verses or parroting shopworn slogans. It hadn't occurred to any of them that the increase in sidewalk evangelism might be bothering Turn Around

Norman, disrupting his timing, cracking his concentration, or tipping the gyroscope that was his heart. After all, that stretch of Fifth Avenue was habitually clamorous. Moreover, in the past, neither competition from other street performers nor the taunts of the cynical had fazed him.

In late May, summer had come to sit on New York's face; hot, moist, sticky, pungent, and oppressive; and with the warmer weather had arrived a warmer preacher, a gaunt man in an expensive-looking suit. His mouth gleamed with golden teeth, his hungry face was tortured with pustules, and his voice was reminiscent of a sad and smoke-filled horn. This man was not given to amateurish sloganeering, but, rather, preached full-blown sermons, elaborate, histrionic, and deceptively slick. Most significantly, he had, with obvious deliberation, stationed himself in front of St. Patrick's, practically shoulder to shoulder with the poignant cherub who oscillated with such supernatural slowness in the street.

For the greater part of a week, Turn Around Norman had gone on with the show, exhibiting not the slightest indication that the intruder had broached his interior shell. Then—presto!—he was gone, leaving the objects stunned. And stranded, in more ways than one.

"We should have seen it coming," said Can o' Beans.

" 'Tis true," Conch Shell agreed. "Pious dogma, if allowed to flourish, will always drive magic away."

Ellen Cherry had written to Boomer, advising him of Buddy Winkler's intentions. Being less certain of Ultima Sommervell's intentions, she avoided any mention of the art dealer. It was not until Boomer wrote back a month later that she learned that Buddy had remained in Jerusalem only ten days, and Ultima half that long. About their visits, Boomer's letter had this to say:

In Jerusalem I get the feeling that I'm leering at the panty outline of history. Something important is taking shape right under the surface, at the crotch of the world, and if the light is right you can detect its general outline, although you don't have a clue what color the thing is or whether it's made out of silk or cotton or rubber or a burlap sack. Anyways, it appeals to the operative in me, and I'm sitting here straining my eyes trying to see the panties better or see all the way through them like they was a veil covering up some fabulous twat, a pussy made out of gold or something, when Bud shows up and he's even more intrigued with the outline than me. He's excited and worked up and talking a mess of double-talk, acting like he's got more secrets than a mongrel's got fleas. He's got a caper on the burner and wants me to help him with it, only he won't say what it is. He indicates that I'll have to use my torch equipment, only not to weld something together but to cut through it, he indicates that me and several other dudes that I'll be bossing will be burning into a place that's got metal gates or bars around it. I hadn't gotten your letter yet, so I couldn't guess what the place might be. I mean he obviously wouldn't be robbing a bank in the name of the Lord Jesus, so I tell him yeah maybe I'll do it, so long as it doesn't interfere with my sculpture. Of course at that point he gives me a sermon about creating graven images.

Well, anyways, candy thighs, after Bud's been here about a week he tells me that the whole deal's postponed and wants to know if I'm planning to stay in Jerusalem until January, which as a matter of fact I am because that's when the monument we're making is scheduled to be unveiled. Ultima, who was here for five days during this same period trying to get me to turn out some New York art, has some information on our monument which I've asked her to share with you if you're interested. Give her a call.

The reason that Bud put off bombing the Dome of the Rock (if you're right and that's what he's got up his sleeve) is due to Israeli politics. Although the right-wing religious parties gained a lot of ground in the last election, it wasn't enough to put them over the top, and Israel ended up with another coalition government in which the hard-liners in the conservative Likud party, which is friendly with the old boys on the far right, share power with the liberals in the Labor party. Now that was nearly four years ago, and everybody is saying that despite the concessions from the PLO and all, that in the election coming up in November the right-wing's going to grab the whole pie, marang (sp?) and all. So Bud reckons he'll have a heap easier time of it with the far right

minding the store, and he's looking to wait until they're inaugu-
rated next January before he commits his naughty act. You get the
picture, honeysuckle drawers?

She did. And there wasn't a rug in it anywhere.

The air pressure inside a champagne bottle is almost identical to
that inside a big truck tire: approximately ninety pounds, for the
record, but there the similarity surely ends. There're bound to be
major differences in the ambiance department.

Most of the period that she had been in New York, beginning
around the time of the sale of the Airstream turkey, Ellen Cherry
experienced a sensation of internal pressure. While the force it
exerted was constant, its character was not. The pressure could be
tingly and giddy, or it could be crushing and dull. In other words,
part of the time she felt like a bottle of champagne, the rest of the
time like a truck tire.

Thanks to her unsettling experiences with the transitory spoon, as
well as her unlikely and rather, ah . . . idiosyncratic affair with her
boss, she'd been a magnum of bubbly most of that spring and early
summer, and the gases that pushed against the walls of her container
possessed enough sparkle to propel her to a phone to call Ultima
Sommervell. Ultima would be closing shop and moving to the Hamptons soon, so if Ellen Cherry wished to quiz her concerning Boomer's
activities, she had to act immediately or wait until fall. She was no
longer desperate, she told herself, merely curious, but she hastened
to arrange a meeting. And she was bold enough to insist that they
meet in the downtown gallery, aware that dogs such as Ultima's
seldom traveled south of Fourteenth Street.

On the day of the appointment, a day in early June when ozone
coiled around every lamppost and sweat ran down to the sea, Ellen
Cherry rode the Eighth Avenue express to Canal Street, then walked
back up to Grand. The first thunderstorm of the season was in the

dressing room, donning its black robes and its necklace of hailstones, strapping on its electrical sword. She glanced at the sky, wondering if she would make it home before showtime. She was wearing a pair of kiwi suede pumps with lime satin bows, a gift from her lover, and although their soles might risk eternity in a burning hell, she preferred that they not be baptized. Oh, Spike would sprinkle them soon enough, but she'd protect them, if she could, from total immersion.

Ultima would be annoyed that Ellen Cherry hadn't brought her a painting or two, but she really hadn't any to bring. She had destroyed the last of the landscapes when Boomer was granted his exhibition, and pictures of a bean can just wouldn't do. For one thing, even though there were significant stylistic differences between them and Andy Warhol's soup cans of decades past, they, nevertheless, would be criticized as derivative. Or so she thought. Imagine her surprise, then, when she walked into the prominent gallery to find its walls covered with blatant imitations of Jackson Pollock, Bridget Riley, Ellsworth Kelly, et al., as well as images appropriated directly, without personal embellishment of any degree, from TV, movies, and advertising. Everything about the show signaled a perverse denial of originality that must have been widespread, since it was a grouping of works by a dozen or more relatively successful younger artists and not the product of one failed imagination. She was staring at an ersatz Joseph Beuys when Ultima called to her from a balcony and invited her up.

Unlike the spacious, dog-inhabited suite at Sommervell's Fifty-seventh Street gallery, the office at the SoHo branch consisted of a desk, a file cabinet, and three chairs, arranged informally on the open balcony. From her seat, Ellen Cherry could look down on the usurped art and puzzle over it as Ultima imparted what she could about Boomer's rather mysterious project.

"It would seem," said Ultima, "that Mr. Petway struck up a friendship with an Israeli sculptor by the name of Amos Zif."

"Amos!" blurted Ellen Cherry. "So it's a male!"

"Sorry?"

"Never mind. Please, go ahead." Out of nowhere, Ellen Cherry experienced a billowing of relief. In fact, her internal pressure, which, due to the proximity of Ultima and the cynically mimetic art, had begun to resume the personality of the acrid, dead air inside a tire, now took a turn toward Dom Perignon.

3 1 9

"This Zif chap was awarded a commission to create a monument, a piece of plaza plop we'd call it in New York, that's to be plopped in a tiny square just west of the Old City, that noisy, smelly place in which, according to Mr. Petway, even Houdini would have suffered claustrophobia. *I* bloody well did. Directly outside of the Jaffa Gate, there's an old Jewish neighborhood that was badly damaged in the 1967 war, and it's in the process of being restored and reoccupied, rather modestly fancy in architecture and rather immodestly ethnocentric in tone. The project directors asked Zif to make a statue that would capture the essence of the land, both ancient and modern, secular and religious. It's being paid for by some wealthy Americans, and that is what they specified. So, he was racking his wits trying to come up with something, and the residents of his kibbutz were feeding him ideas, when our Mr. Petway submitted a design of his own. It succeeded in offending the whole 'kibbutz and caboodle,' as he put it, except for Amos Zif, who adored the idea, as well he might, since Boomer Petway is an American genius and nobody in Israel is making art worth crossing the street for, let alone the ocean. Israel is a Third World country, I might submit, yet too well educated to be innocently charming. There's nothing worse than a backward sophisticate, at least when he comes to art."

"Ultima, you honestly think Boomer is a genius?"

"Don't you?"

Ellen Cherry shook her head. "Hardly, although I might go along with idiot savant."

Ultima laughed a spitty British laugh. "Between you and me, I suspect you're right. Don't you dare tell anyone I said so. In any case, as you must have been informed, he left the kibbutz in the company of Zif, and the pair of them have been collaborating on the monument. It's to be unveiled in January, and they've decided, jolly wisely I'd imagine, to keep its design secret until then. I, however, was allowed a preview of half of it."

"Which half?"

"The bottom, naturally. To be precise, what I saw was the pedestal."

"And?"

"And it was nothing terribly distinguished. There's a large pile of rocks, which I suppose is appropriate, and from the rock pile there rises a vertical, three-dimensional map of Palestine, the ancient Palestine of biblical times, with cities that have disappeared and boundaries that are no longer recognized. The map is fashioned from steel rods, welded together, latticelike. It's tall, perhaps six meters, and I've been led to believe that the statue that is to stand upon it will be of equal height."

"Six meters. What's that in feet?"

Ultima regarded her in the way that a Parisian regards a tourist who pronounces croissant as if the breakfast roll were an irritable female relative. "My dear," she purred, "a meter is three feet plus three inches. Surely you can do the arithmetic."

Kisser of small dogs! thought Ellen Cherry, but she held her temper. "This statue, then. You don't have any clues about it?"

"Not even the U.S. backers have seen a sketch or a model. I do hope it's neither lewd nor ludicrous. There's scant sense of humor in that part of the world. Passion, yes. Humor, no. Anyway, the good news is that our chap is going to take off a bit and make me a couple pieces for my group show in the fall."

Ellen Cherry gestured toward the gallery below them. "Will these artists be included in the group?"

"Many of them, yes. Do I detect a note of disapproval?"

"I guess I just don't get it. Half of them are ripoffs, and the other half are dull and bland."

"No, you don't get it, do you? My dear, you're much too young to be so out of touch with the zeitgeist. Originality is a myth perpetuated by the naive, the romantic, and the unscrupulous. There has been no truly original art since prehistoric times. Every artist has simply reworked the art of his or her predecessors. My artists are unique in that they've owned up to the practice. They've taken it a step further by refusing to participate in the ruse. By simply appropriating the work of artists they admire, copying it and exhibiting it as their own, they are courageously honest—and tragically sad. Their admission of defeat is part and parcel of the melancholia that epitomizes our time."

"Fraught with significance, eh?"

"You sneer at my artists for being passive and unaffecting, but you haven't bothered to ask yourself why they've chosen this look. It is, after all, a purposeful choice. They choose to reject the decadent picture-making of the bourgeoisie. They choose to scorn the aura that surrounds high art, an aura of preciousness and rarity that actually has more to do with art as commodity than art as vehicle for social improvement."

"The kind of art you show uptown."

"Yes, my puppies and I have to eat. Uptown, the art is all aura, and collectors pay dearly to transfer that aura to their homes or offices. Here in SoHo, the art is simply *object*. It depreciates the whole regressive notion of glorification of culture. And why shouldn't it? What is there in our culture to glorify? AIDS? Poverty? Violence? Corruption? Greed? The bomb? Every day there are reports from the Middle East that portend our destruction. It's bad enough that they're destroying themselves over there, but it could escalate to include the rest of us at any moment. It would be socially irresponsible for an artist to produce precious, pretty, elitist commodities in the shadow of Jerusalem."

Ultima lit a pink cigarette and exhaled plumes of perfumed smoke through her fine nostrils. She seemed to be waiting for her little lecture to sink in. Maybe she suspected that it took awhile for information to be absorbed through all that hair. Eventually, she said, "Please don't take my comments as a personal affront, my dear. There will always be a place for the landscapist. But as you leave, have a closer look at the artists that you've belittled. If they have a common message, it is: 'We concede defeat. We haven't a chance against the masterpieces of the past, against the marketplace of the present, against the annihilations of the future, but, nevertheless, here we are.' There's something so poignant and brave and ironic about it that it sometimes makes me weep."

"Yeah," said Ellen Cherry, "I do have to get going. Big storm brewing out there."

After descending the wrought-iron spiral staircase, however, she tarried for a full quarter hour in the gallery, waltzing with the imps that Ultima had let loose in her ivory tower. Hadn't she, Ellen Cherry, also been defeated by art? But to whom had she confessed? Nobody. She had silently withdrawn. Slunk away, as it were. It had never occurred to her to make an artistic statement out of her failure. So, maybe Ultima was right, these artists were more honest, more courageous than she. It took guts to file for bankruptcy of the imagination. Anyhow, whoever said that to be an artist you had to invent? She supposed she had always accepted innovation as a precondition of important work, as if it were a law, but, of course, art didn't have laws. That was precisely what was appealing about it. That was what, in her opinion, made art better than life. Or, if not superior, at least more interesting.

On the other hand, what was interesting about the exact rendering in oils of a subway map? How bleak, how unchallenging, how ordinary, how dumb. Now, if you applied a little eye game to it. . . . She started to blur her focus but quickly refrained. She needed to deal with the work on its own terms. And as far as she could tell, its terms were social, intellectual, and political, not aesthetic. This art existed for the purpose of conceptual argument, rather than for its impact on perception. She was surrounded by ideological propositions in which the ideology was visually static. In other words, the ideas were trapped in the art objects, themselves; from which, due to lack of expression, they could never break free to ride the retinal rails into the mystery tunnels of the psyche.

What these pictures are are tombstones, she thought. *Maybe in their own cynical way they discover value in resignation, emptiness, and meaninglessness; maybe they perform a service in underlining the futility of trying to compete with mass media, but, hey, they're really obituaries announcing the death of the magical power of art. And that announcement could be premature.*

The longer Ellen Cherry thought about it, the more convinced she became that the mission of the artist in an overtechnologized, overmasculinized society was to call the old magic back to life.

Could it be done? Yeah, you pessimistic wimps, it could. Could *she* do it? Probably not, but she could give it a whirl.

She shot through the door. It wasn't raining yet, but the sky was boiling like a pot of *film noir* potatoes. Looking at the sky was like looking through the porthole of a washer in a hipster laundromat. At least three black turtlenecks circled between Ellen Cherry and the sun.

It was barely three o'clock, but SoHo had its lights on. The day was as dark as Jezebel's eyelids. The air was fresh and highly charged. People rushed about in it like apprehensive animals. A lot of the people wore turbans, a lot were wrapped in bedsheets. It occurred to Ellen Cherry that the whole city was starting to look like the bar at Isaac & Ishmael's. She couldn't remember the last time she'd heard English spoken on the streets of New York. On the boom boxes that she passed, each and every one turned to maximum volume as an act of legal aggression, the Spanish singers were rolling their r's for minutes at a time as a result of prestorm static.

She should have gone straight home, unplugged appliances, shut windows, and docked her new shoes in a dry closet, but she couldn't, she just couldn't. She had made up her mind that she was going to paint again; she didn't know what, she wasn't sure when, but inspired by the pessimism of her peers, guided by the strangeness of her experience with the spoon, and letting go of her bitterness in regard to Boomer, she definitely would be painting. And to both celebrate and reaffirm her decision, she thought she owed it to herself, storm or no storm, to pay a long overdue visit to Turn Around Norman.

Norman, Norman. Human pepper mill, grinding away with such breathtaking slowness at the ancient spices that once added the zest of the robust ecstatic to the thin broth of survival. Even if one were unmoved by his actual performance, the kind of concentration and integrity that Norman represented was a model not merely for artists but for. . . . Wait a blue-eyed minute! Where was he?

She had splurged on a taxi in order to beat the rain, and she'd won. The wind had picked up, and thunder was rumbling like a whale with a belly full of Jonahs, but not a drop had fallen, and Fifth Avenue was still relatively crowded. Yet that wasn't Turn Around Norman by the steps of the cathedral, turning in the place where for years he'd turned without fail in all manner of weather; turned daily (except Wednesday afternoons), including Christmas and Super Bowl Sunday. That wasn't Norman, that was somebody else.

Her disappointment changed to disgust. And then to fear. For the Reverend Buddy Winkler recognized her immediately after she recognized him, and he broke off his sermon in mid-admonishment to glare at her in the most hostile fashion. So twisted was his face with hate and anger that his boils squeaked like Styrofoam and his gold teeth nearly wrenched loose from his gums. In a flash, like the frog leg of lightning that kicked across the horizon, Ellen Cherry realized both what he was doing there and why he was glaring at her that way.

Two months prior, when Buddy left for Jerusalem, she had notified the FBI and the Southern Baptist Convention of his presumed intentions. If the federal agents had acted on her tip in any way, she had not been privy to it. Moderate Baptists, however, had been hunting for an excuse to remove Bud from his long-time Sunday slot on the Voice of the Sparrow Network, and they quickly suspended him. By no means was he destroyed financially—his executive position with the Third Temple Platoon compensated him quite adequately —and he continued to make guest appearances on evangelical shows (Pat Robertson admired him for his jingoism, Jimmy Swaggart for his Italian slacks); but Buddy Winkler was a preacher who needed a regular pulpit the way a toilet needed a regular flush. So one day he announced that he was "gonna preach the gospel jest like Jesus done it," and he took to the street. His decision to horn in on "that stupefied halfwit who's probably on some kinda turn-around-real-slow drug" was intended as a small measure of revenge against Ellen Cherry. Now, she stood facing him, not twenty feet away.

"There!" he shrieked. "Brothers and sisters, there she is!" He was pointing at her with a long, bony finger, his voice sounding less like a saxophone than a car alarm. "It's her! The Whore of Babylon of whose filthy fornicatin' wickedness the prophets of God hath warned."

Several pedestrians looked her over, albeit with the feigned air of utter disinterest that is customary among New Yorkers in public places, while a party of Japanese tourists fixed her in the viewfinders of their Nikons. Then, as the first fat raindrops spattered the pavement, he began to inch toward her.

"Jezebel!" he screeched. "Jezebel!"

Ellen Cherry was too shocked to move. "Jezebel!" She watched a raindrop bounce off the toe of her shoe. "Jezebel!" His eyes were murderous, his accusing finger shook like a lie-detector needle at a White House briefing. "Jezebel!"

In the basement of St. Patrick's, Conch Shell and Painted Stick rushed to the grate, followed by their three companions.

"Oh, dear," gasped Spoon. "It's her."

"Who'd you expect?" asked Dirty Sock. "Mother goddamn Teresa?"

Can o' Beans was last to arrive. He/she had been contemplating his/her reflection in the mirror, wondering if Miss Charles had painted him/her from memory or if she'd used another bean can as a model. "This situation is potentially dangerous," he/she observed.

There was a Spoon-rattling crash of thunder, and the rain began to leave the sky like refugees fleeing a revolution, arriving with nothing but the clothes on their backs and whatever skills they might have acquired in their dark villages. "Jezebel!"

The preacher advanced on her very, very slowly, as if he had borrowed a page from Turn Around Norman's book, a book printed on zinc with an ink of cold molasses. But advance he did, jagged wires of lightning twisting like Frankenstein's umbilical cord across his crazed eyes. He was less than ten paces from her when a mighty cloud clap boxed her ears, shaking her from her trance. She whirled and made as if to run, but her shoe heel, not designed for athletic action, gave way, and she fell to her knees. So drenched was she that she had trouble righting herself in the downpour.

"Jezebel!" screamed the preacher above the thunder, and he bounded toward her like an ocelot toward its fallen prey, his mouth wide open, his phallus as hard as a shovel. As he neared her, at full speed, a shaft, a stave, a wooden pole of some sort suddenly shot through the bars of the street-level grate, blocking his right ankle and tripping him flat on his face. His boils skidded along the wet concrete, a tooth punctured his lower lip. He slid directly into Ellen Cherry, but she managed to stand up and yank off her ruined shoes before dashing to safety in the rain.

The objects pulled back from the grate until the preacher, dazed, soaked, and bleeding, stumbled down Fifth Avenue in the direction of his office, stopping every few feet to turn and stare, puzzled, in their general direction. Then, Painted Stick looked at the others guiltily, as if to say, "May the stars above forgive me. I've done it again."

My heart is a Latin American food stall
And your love is a health inspector from Zurich

Pepe, who'd just come on duty in the Ansonia lobby, was playing the recently released Raoul Ritz cassette on his boom box. He had intended to play it for Ellen Cherry, and he'd also intended to ask her at last about the spoon that had wasted Raoul back in April—was it really hers, how had it managed to land on Raoul? he kept forgetting to inquire—but when she walked through the door in her stocking feet, her dress sopping wet, her knees dirty, her stampede of curls looking as if it had finally gone over a cliff, Pepe's mind went blank.

"Miz Charl, holy shit, man! What happen to you, man?"

"Hard day at the office, Pepe." She smiled at him through chatter-ing teeth and padded, dripping rainwater on the tiles, to the elevator.

Upstairs, she drew a hot bath, climbed into it, and had a brief cry. She might have wept longer had she not known that Spike would be by in an hour or two to comfort her. Spike Cohen was good at comforting her. Spike Cohen was good, in general. No starry-eyed old fool, he hadn't lost his head, begged her to marry him, been jealous of every younger man who crossed their path, or showered her with expensive gifts. About once a week, he presented her with a new pair of shoes, but, then, her shoes seemed to have short life-spans these days, and, besides, Spike got them wholesale. Maybe he wasn't Tarzan in bed, but he wasn't Cheetah, either. Any lack of athletic torque or acrobatic flex was compensated for by his tender-ness, sensitivity, and attentiveness. And, of course, by the fact that at just the right moment in just the right tone of voice, he addressed her by a particular appellation of biblical origin, a name that for whatever reason had the power to spin her clitoris like the propeller on a toy motorboat.

Thanks to the increasing popularity of Salome, Isaac & Ishmael's was thriving, attracting many drinkers and some diners, even on those evenings when the girl wasn't dancing. The place didn't get real busy until eight-thirty or nine, so on this, Ellen Cherry's night off, she expected Spike to drop by her apartment about six to spend a couple hours with her. Sure enough, at five-fifty, he tapped at her door with the wedges of a new pair of Maud Frizons. Upon admit-ting him, however, she saw at once that it might be she who had to supply the comfort and consolation.

"Such a pain I got! Sex is out!"

Spike's emerald eyes were duller, sadder than usual, and he walked as if he was helping somebody move a refrigerator. He explained that all week he had suffered intermittent pain and cramping in his lower back, and now it had moved into his— He used the Yiddish word for testicles, but Ellen Cherry got the idea. She was contrite. "Maybe we've been doing it too often," she suggested. "Or too hard." Having never had an older lover before, she was unclear about their durability. She didn't wish to push the envelope.

"No, no," Spike protested. "At tennis I probably already strained something. Oy!"

Spike removed his shoes and reclined on the bed. Ellen Cherry put on her shoes, the Maud Frizons that Spike had just delivered, and lay down beside him. She was wearing her kimono, and panties that were the envy of the less fortunate ones in the dresser. They, the underpants in the drawer, were continually shushing one another as they vacillated between bursts of diet-cola twitter and straining to hear everything that transpired in the bedroom. For his part, Daruma the vibrator sensed that something was amiss and that his giggling *zenbo* were likely to be disappointed. "When radish is cooked, crunch fly up chimney," he said.

The couple shared sips from a flask of rum that Ellen Cherry had taken to keeping on the bedside table. "Anything I can do for you?" she asked.

"No, no," said Spike, gritting his teeth. Then he told her about a reporter from the Village *Voice* who had shown up at the I & I that afternoon asking a lot of questions about Salome. The reporter had seen Salome dance on Saturday night, and now he wanted to write an article about her. "I say, okay, write all you want, but only with her tambourine does she talk."

"That's a fact, Spike. I haven't heard a peep from her in two months. And she's out of there fast as those skinny legs will carry her when her set is over."

"So I tell him, okay, write, write, but be sure you write that a Jew and an Arab together are making it possible."

"Good. I'm sure he will. The *Voice* is nothing if not political. Even its personals are political."

"Oy! Those lonely people what're advertising their own charms, but their shoe size or foot condition never mentioning."

They conversed for a while about how lonely they each had been before they got together, yet how they'd have croaked of loneliness rather than advertise for companionship, and whether that attitude was a reflection of dignity or repression. It was cozy and sweet lying there talking, and Spike's pain, like the thunderstorm, appeared to have subsided. At least, he was grimacing with less force. Ellen Cherry didn't feel quite ready to broach the subject of the Reverend Buddy Winkler's attack, so she talked about Ultima and the show at the gallery.

"Ultima's probably right, her artists are admitting defeat. The extraterrestrial in the woodpile is that they expect to be *rewarded* for those defeats every bit as much as if they were triumphs. You get it? They believe they have an ethical, social right to be exhibited and reviewed and collected regardless of their level of skill or verve, and despite the fact that their work is often a deliberate protest against the whole idea of exhibits, reviews, and collections. Anything less, any favoritism shown those with extraordinary abilities, would be unfair, undemocratic, elitist, reactionary, what have you. Jesus! I wasn't aware that mediocrity was such a virtue. But it looks like both democracy and socialism exist to encourage it."

"Maybe you prefer a kink?"

At first, she thought Spike was inviting her to indulge one or the other of their sexual proclivities, and she was taken aback by his bluntness, but then she caught on. "A king? No, not a king. I don't know what system I'd prefer. But I do know that people who really excel at things—whether it's creating art or running a business— hardly ever make a big fuss about equality, except maybe on the scales of justice. Equal opportunity, yes. Equal results, impossible. The ones who're so upset about everybody not being the same, about competition, about standards of quality, about art objects having 'auras' around them, they're usually people with average abilities and average minds. And below average senses of humor. Whether it's a matter of lifting the deprived up or dragging the gifted down, they want everybody to function on *their* level. Some fun that would be."

"Not to blame, little darlink. It's only the new American dream they share."

"Which?"

"In Europe my family left their toes, but to Ellis Island they brought a dream. The old American dream. Work hard, save your money, be decent, and success you're bound to have. A business of your own. A house. Nice food on the table, carpets, curtains. Maybe two weeks in December in Miami Beach. Only if you're my family you swim with your slippers on. Okay. I grew up with that dream. But these artists you're describing, the self-promoting crybabies what are intentionally being *shlockmeisters* and *gonifs,* they dream the *new* American dream. And the new one is to achieve wealth and recognition without having the burden of intelligence, talent, sacrifice, or the human values what are universal."

"Yeah, I reckon a lot of people are spoiled like that nowadays. In all fields. At all ages, too. But frankly, Spike, I don't really care if artists work a forty-hour week or obey the Ten Commandments. I

don't even give a rat's hair if they pay their dues, just so long as their
paintings go the distance. But if they can't provide me with something gorgeous or astonishing to look at, then don't expect me to
forgive them their trespasses."

"No, no, little darlink. Everybody must be forgiven."

"Including Buddy Winkler?" At this point, she told Spike about
the attack, and sure enough, he was able to comfort her, to make her
feel all right about it, to feel all right even about the retreat of Turn
Around Norman. He held her and slowly commenced to knead the
loaves of her buttocks and the cupcakes of her breasts. Soon, they
forgot the physical and mental things that troubled them, respectively. The dolphin carried them to where the crests were wild and
bumpy and the troughs salty and deep.

Lost in her ecstasy, Ellen Cherry hadn't realized how vigorously
she had begun to buck. Mindlessly, she arched and thrust and
thrashed until his moans—not of pleasure but of pain—escalated
into a scream that froze the sea around her. Gasping, he rolled off
her, off the bed and onto the floor, where in a small pool of vomit,
he lay ashen and unconscious.

"Oh, my God!" she cried. "I've killed him."

The AIDS epidemic, according to the Reverend Buddy Winkler and
his colleagues, was a plague visited upon the earth by Jehovah to
punish the sexually adventurous. AIDS was proof positive, they
preached, that humanity's days were numbered. The fact that the
AIDS toll was a mere drop in the bucket compared to the mortality
figures of the fourteenth century, when the bubonic pandemic wiped
out a third of the world's population, was not the sort of information
to which the oh-goody-this-must-be-the-end mentality paid much
attention. AIDS was tailor-made for the fantasies of the religious
right, because it was genitally transmitted.

To more than one congregation on more than one occasion, Buddy had proclaimed, "Man had congress with sheep and generated syphilis. Man had congress with monkeys and generated AIDS."

"So what does that tell us about chicken pox?" Ellen Cherry had asked one day.

"Yeah," said Boomer Petway, "and how about the first man who ever said he was 'sick as a dog'? Was he confessing to something? Was that the origin of collie-ra?"

Ellen Cherry: "And was Rhett Butler the pervert who spread scarlet fever?"

Boomer: "And if you had congress with jazz musicians, would you come down with thelonious mumps?"

Well, never mind those two. There was, indeed, an epidemic loose in the land, and if it was hardly apocalyptic, if its victims were few compared to pestilences of the past (just as the casualties of the two world wars were slight compared, for example, to those of the Manchu-Chinese War of 1644), it was nonetheless serious and scary; all the more so because it was sexually transmitted. It led children to associate love with death.

However, it was neither AIDS nor ninja nooky that felled Spike Cohen. While a frantic Ellen Cherry was on her way to the lobby to call for an ambulance, Spike regained consciousness and staggered into the bathroom, where he passed a kidney stone as big as the Ritz.

Within a few days, Spike was hurting again. A second stone, a calcium oxalate crystal, to be precise, lodged in his ureter and, like a pirate radio station, went on the air with a sporadic signal and a musical format programmed by Nazi biologists and prelates from the Inquisition. Spike was admitted to a hospital, where, fighting sound with sound, a technician operating a litho-tripter aimed high-intensity sonar at the caterwauling stone. When the bombardment abated and the decibels cleared, the crystalline concretion remained, nesting in the tube between kidney and bladder like a stork in a chimney.

Medical generals ordered an invasion. A spring-loaded wire device resembling an egg whisk was shoved up Spike's penis and through his bladder on a mission to capture the stone. When it was withdrawn, however, its trap was empty, and X rays revealed that the vicious barnacle, a good six millimeters in circumference, hadn't budged. Spike was then readied for full-scale surgery. The operation proceeded smoothly until a doctor with a shaky hand (probably the result of golf elbow) accidentally severed the soda-straw ureter, a boo-boo that went unnoticed by the medical team (probably because it was arguing over the fortunes of the Giants and the Jets).

That evening, Spike developed a headache and a slight fever. The nurses didn't regard the condition as unusual, not even when it persisted. Nearly three days passed before it dawned on them that he hadn't urinated since prior to surgery. A resident physician suspected that a third stone was stuck in the uretero-vesical pipe, but X rays failed to turn up one. Bloodwork was requested. The lab fired back an analysis that made Spike's bloodstream read like the gutters of Calcutta. His nitrate levels were practically off the chart, and small wonder, since urine, unable to reach the bladder, had been emptying into his abdominal cavity at the rate of eight hundred cc's a day. In other words, he had enough hot piss in his stomach to fill the combustion chambers of several powerful motorcycles.

By then, Spike was severely nauseated, his face and extremities were swollen, and he was seized by mild convulsions. Medics swarmed over him as if he were the first tee at a brand-new country club. Simultaneously, he was hooked up to a dialysis machine and given a blood transfusion. On the way to the operating theater, his gurney looked like the lead wagon in a caravan of sterilized gypsies. They cut him open again, drained his stomach, and spliced his ureter. It was touch and go for a few hours, but he survived.

His first words to Ellen Cherry, when she was allowed to visit the following day, were: "Hoo boy! I've been shot in the head, I've been treated for kidney stones. Shot in the head is better."

Robust though he was, the triple whammy of kidney stones, uremia, and encore surgery exacted a steep levy on Spike Cohen's constitution. His eleven-day stay in the hospital was followed by a month's recuperation at his Upper West Side flat. Ellen Cherry nursed him during the day, his son and daughter-in-law at night. His son wasted hours trying to convince him to sue his doctors. "A bad hospital it may be, but the New York state lottery it's not," said Spike. "I'm earning my money the old-fashioned way."

Abu visited the convalescent whenever he could, but he had his hands full at the restaurant. Following the publication of the article in the Village *Voice,* Salome's fame had spread. Patronage of Isaac & Ishmael's had been jacked up another notch. Abu made a rule that nobody could be seated in the dining room unless they ordered dinner, yet even that harrowing prospect failed to dissuade the crowds. By seven on Friday and Saturday nights, there wasn't an empty seat in the place. Bribe and wheedle though he might, Abu could not influence the bandleader to influence Salome to dance on additional evenings. "I will speak to her from the heart," the toothless musician would promise, pocketing the fifty-dollar bill Abu had offered. "But she is a young girl, she has her studies, she needs her sleep."

Neatly dressed in one of the dark blue pinstriped wool suits that he now wore in all seasons, Abu would sit by Spike's bed, cheering him with tales of the I & I's success and of the attention Salome was calling to their exercise in brotherhood. Abu complained often that he couldn't find a competent partner on the tennis court, and that little white lie cheered Spike as well. Abu's visits were short, however. During most of the daylight hours, Ellen Cherry attended to Spike all by herself. She fed him, bathed him, medicated him, mixed him weak rum punches, and read to him from the poetry of Shakespeare and Pablo Neruda.

"When I was a small boy," said Spike, "my favorite poem was 'There was an old woman who lived in a shoe.' "

"I'm not surprised," said Ellen Cherry.

"I also liked the 'this little piggy went to market' routine, but it made my family very nervous. Especially the 'wee wee wee' part."

Although it left her time for nothing else except her job, Ellen Cherry didn't resent the weeks that she spent as Spike's nursemaid. However, the experience permanently altered the nature of their relationship. Her sexual feelings for him simply evaporated. Perhaps it was his helplessness, perhaps it was an overdose of intimacy. She didn't know what extinguished it, but she knew that the fire was out. They avoided any discussion of the matter, yet Spike obviously sensed the plunge in erotic temperature. As much as he might have yearned to, he made no effort to whistle for the dolphin or to throw an electric blanket over its cool, slick back. Ellen Cherry and Spike remained fast friends, but never again did they ride out to mid-ocean, where the salt spray glittered in her neo-hussy rouge as he trolled for that radiant sea-thing that many men have tasted but no man has fully seen.

*   *   *

Spike was as thin and pale as the hoarfrost trim on wolfmother wallpaper when he at last resumed his station behind the reservation desk at Isaac & Ishmael's. It was a peppery Friday evening in early August, and the restaurant was gearing up for a crush of pita snappers and Salome gawkers. Regulars, such as the team of Moroccan irrigation specialists, the UN's Kurdish translator, and Detective Shaftoe, were at their customary bar stools and tables by five o'clock, prepared to wait a full four hours for the first jingle-bang of the tambourine. By six-thirty, a few smitten Romeos already loitered out front, hoping to catch the dancer's eye when she stepped from the black sedan that always delivered her and picked her up, although the only eye that ever regarded them was the pugnacious one of her chaperon, the bandleader's stout sister. Salome neither looked at nor spoke to anyone, but hugged herself, bashful, remote, self-contained, until the band sounded her opening number, at which point she would throw apart her arms and let the glow spread wherever it might, heating the freshly shaved cheeks of diplomats, ripening the green olives in their martinis. "Belly dancers are nothing new in New York," reported the Village *Voice*. "They have bumped and shimmied here since Little Egypt's gyrations upstaged the revolutionary flickers of the prototype television at the 1939 World's Fair. From 1940 on, there have been in the city a minimum of two or three Middle Eastern or Greek clubs featuring practitioners of that ancient art. But Manhattan has never seen a belly dancer such as Isaac & Ishmael's young Salome."

At 6:50, the telephone rang. "Isaac and Ishmael's," Spike answered. "We're full up already." He listened for a moment, then signaled Ellen Cherry. "For you," he called, wagging the receiver. "Sounds like your mama."

"I'll take it in the kitchen. I'm sorry, Spike. I told them never to call here during dinner."

"Not to worry. We're full up."

"Yeah, but I got a ton of *falafel* to sling."

"Not to worry. So, I'll take your tables. It's only for the dancing lady what they're hungry."

"Well now, don't you overdo and have a relapse on me. I want to go buy paints and canvas tomorrow."

Brushing aside a succession of anonymous hands that reached to pat her buttocks or squeeze her thighs, Ellen Cherry made her way to the kitchen, where she lifted the receiver from the wall extension and learned that her daddy was dead.

Embalmed and in his coffin, Verlin Charles still smelled of mildewed washcloth, a defiance of sorts that somehow comforted Ellen Cherry. Verlin was taking it with him, so to speak.

She hovered over the open casket, reminiscing about things they'd done together, things he'd done for her: the dolls and paint sets he provided, the movies she watched from his lap, the drives to Florida during which he so frequently inquired if "daddy's girl" needed a Coke or a hamburger or to pee-pee (when all she really wanted was to perfect her eye game). Tearfully, she shuffled the deck of memory, dealing out the cards of thoughtfulness, fun, and sacrifice that demonstrated his love—yet over and over again the black ace turned up to take the trick: the reminder of that day he had yanked her out of art class, rubbed raw her face, and called her "Jezebel." It seemed to obscure everything else he had contributed to her development and happiness. She wondered if that was natural, if others harbored grudges against essentially loving parents, even after they were gone. If she were to die tomorrow, would she be remembered for a few good paintings, a few acts of kindness, or for her selfishness and spite, particularly in regard to Boomer Petway? She was weeping as much for herself as for her father. When she noticed that the mortician had applied a considerable amount of cosmetics to Verlin's countenance, an ironic smile sliced through the tears.

Patsy came to stand beside her. "It was the football that killed him," Patsy said.

"What're you talking about, mama? Daddy hasn't played football since he was a kid."

"Not playing it, *watching* it. He used up his heart in front of that blessed set."

Later, one of the pallbearers told Ellen Cherry that Verlin had been watching a Washington Redskins exhibition game when he stood and clutched his chest. "Wasn't the excitement," the man confided. "It was the long hours and the snacks."

The Reverend Buddy Winkler avoided any mention of football or television in his eulogy, although he did relate a couple of incidents that had to do with the jigging of frogs. The preacher was eloquent,

even Ellen Cherry had to admit it. His saxophone blew joy into the
dead man's eyes, blew peace into his exploded ticker. With hypnotic
cadences, he reproduced for the bland Baptist mourners the shadow
that a newborn baby casts, then made the shadow grow long and
pointed until it ended like a church spire back in God's own sky.
"The way down is the way up," he said, quoting a Greek philosopher
to a group of people who seldom accepted as truth any word that
hadn't come directly from the Bible or a southern politician.

Ellen Cherry wanted to ask Buddy what he was doing mouthing
the aphorism of a pagan in the house of Jehovah, but she didn't dare
get close to him. At the Charles house following the burial, he spent
most of his time with his arm around Patsy, occasionally pulling her
distraught face to his Armani lapel. Whenever he looked in Ellen
Cherry's direction, his teeth would grind like a slow divorce. Fortunately, he returned to New York the next morning.

The day after that, in the late afternoon, Ellen Cherry went back.
Patsy had insisted. "You got your job, honey. Your daddy wouldn't
want you to miss any more work. You know how he felt about
shirkers and loafers."

Even so, Ellen Cherry was reluctant to leave until Patsy revealed
her own plans to come to Manhattan. "I'm in shock right now. Oh,
mercy, I'm in a pile of shock. But I'll get over it in time, and when I
do, well, there's not diddly-squat for me in Colonial Pines. Maybe I'll
come up there and live around you for a while. Would that be okay?
Your daddy's insurance'll provide a dollar or two and, who knows,
maybe I'll turn a right smart profit on this ol' barn."

On the flight from Byrd Field, Ellen Cherry tried unsuccessfully to
imagine Patsy without Verlin. For that matter, she couldn't picture
the world without him, as insignificant a player upon the world stage
as he may have been. The permanent absence of someone who (from
her perspective) had always been there, shaping her fundamental
experience, her tissue and blood, was overwhelming and unreal. She
felt older, more vulnerable, as if a buffer had suddenly crumbled
between her and the mortal brink.

The day after the funeral, while she and her mother had sat in
front of the floor fan sipping iced tea, Patsy alluded to two miscar-
riages she had suffered when Ellen Cherry was a tot, one of the lost
fetuses, apparently, having been fathered by someone other than
Verlin. It was information that Ellen Cherry neither solicited nor
desired, but when she tried to change the subject, Patsy had an-

nounced, "Now's the time for *you* to have babies, honey. Directly. And you know why? Having babies messes up your life, but when you're young your life's already messed up, so it's easy to fit in a baby or two."

She supposed Patsy was right about the messed-up part. Her life so far certainly hadn't been any clockwork artichoke, although all around her she saw lives far more scattered and confused. Anyway, unless it was another false alarm, the drawstring on her emotional pajamas seemed to be cinching up.

The skyline of Manhattan came into view. Its towers pierced her grief, her introspection, giving her an unexpected thrill. Richmond was so flat in comparison, Colonial Pines such an innocuous splinter on the maypole of the world. She felt rather like a bee returning to a great busy hive, but a hive where the drones pilfered the royal jelly, the workers moonlighted as litterbugs, and the queen reigned only so long as she got good reviews in the *Times*. Jerusalem might be on everybody's mind, but New York was thrill enough for her. "Anything could be happening down there," she marveled, but from her present altitude, of course, she could discern nothing specific. Not one jay feather of smoke, one tabby wail of siren reached her aircraft from the fire that was burning in St. Patrick's Cathedral.

"**E**ither one of you ever have social interaction with a bullet?"

Can o' Beans's inquiry had gone unanswered. Dirty Sock and Spoon had been preoccupied with the crowd that was gathering by the cathedral steps to heed or observe the Reverend Buddy Winkler. A Village *Voice* reporter, the same enterprising newshound who had written about Salome, had published a feature on the preacher, and several TV stations had picked it up (as eventually they would also do with the Salome story). As a result, regular passersby were paying Buddy more attention, and some people were visiting that block of Fifth Avenue deliberately to see the notorious radio evangelist who, in the sandal steps of his Lord Jesus, was now making his pitch in the streets. The resulting increase in pedestrian congestion concerned municipal officials, but due to the prevalence of millennial hysteria and the political power of the Christian right, they had been reluctant to interfere. Secretly, City Hall was hoping that some group such as Freedom From Religion would file a complaint.

"I daresay Miss Spoon would not have crossed paths with a bullet of any caliber, but you, Mr. Sock, did relate that you'd once gone along on an expedition to bag bullfrogs. . . ."

"Jigging," growled Dirty Sock. "They didn't blow 'em out of the goddamned water for Christ's sake." He returned his attention to the sidewalk. "That ol' boy Norman could flat out turn around, but this here fellow knows how to butter his bread."

"Personally, I'd enjoy the opportunity to speak with some bullets, find out what goes on inside those little pointed heads."

The bean can's interest in bullets had been sparked by a news broadcast that had drifted in through the grate. In a widely publicized effort to reduce fatalities among unarmed Palestinian demonstrators, the Israeli military had begun to fire wooden or plastic bullets in its rifles. To the contrary, however, fatal shootings had increased. American and European nurses and doctors doing volunteer service in West Bank hospitals reported that Israeli soldiers, deprived of the power of lead, were now shooting the young Arabs in the head at such close range that even a plastic bullet could cause death or brain damage. "Where there's a will there's a way," said Can o' Beans disparagingly. He/she decided that if he/she succeeded in reaching Jerusalem, he/she would endeavor to interview a bullet or two. Beneath the facade of absolute stoicism that they, like all objects, presented to the animate-dominated world, did bullets have hopes, dreams, and fears? Did the inner life of a wooden bullet differ greatly from that of the one that wore a full metal jacket?

If I ever make it to Jerusalem. That thought (tinged with fatalism, perhaps) scarcely had passed through what, in a bean can, amounted to a brain, when Painted Stick and Conch Shell called him/her, and the sock and spoon, away from their corroded little window on the world to announce that upon that very day they were going to make their move.

*   *   *

"Our timing must be exact," said Conch Shell. "Even so, danger will be upmost. None of you should feel obligated to participate."

So eager were Can o' Beans and Dirty Sock to hit the road (they were mutants now, no longer able to be satisfied with the sedentariness of their kind) that they committed themselves even before they heard the plan. Spoon gave a tinkly little shiver and weakly cast her lot with the rest.

Painted Stick was going to set a fire in the basement. It would have to be set while there was still enough light for smoke to be seen pouring out of the grate, yet close enough to nightfall so that the objects might take advantage of darkness once they were outside the cathedral. Calling upon his knowledge of matters celestial, Painted Stick would calculate the precise moment of truth. Ideally, the smoke should be observed by passersby no more than two minutes before the final colors of twilight faded. An alarm would have to be sounded at once, of course: if the blaze got out of control, the objects might perish, one and all. Spoon alone had a chance to survive an inferno, yet even she might melt into a metallic lump more unaesthetic and more undistinguished than the present configuration of Can o' Beans. Spoon shuddered again. They each heard the tinkle.

"Well now, how in tarnation do you expect to start this here fire?" asked the sock.

"Friction," replied the stick.

"And how . . ." began Can o' Beans. He/she fell silent. Because, as usual, he/she was curious about such things, he/she was about to ask Painted Stick how he would feel if this famous cathedral burned to the ground just to facilitate their escape. But the can decided not to burden Painted Stick, who had whipped one man and tripped a second, with another "moral" issue. Besides, Can o' Beans was well aware that more than one destructive fire of "unknown origin" secretly had been started by inanimate objects. Even humans referred to "spontaneous combustion." They just didn't realize that it could be an act of will.

In a far corner of the cellar, Painted Stick had overturned an old packing crate. The wood shavings that had spilled out were then spooned by the spoon and tamped by the stick into the shell and the stocking, who transported the stuff in their respective cavities to a spot on the floor beneath the grate. "Mr. Sock looks as if he's been taking steroids," said Can o' Beans of his bulging comrade. "Or else he's been fattened for pâté de sock gras." Spoon giggled. Dirty Sock growled.

Atop the heap of curly shavings, which Dirty Sock said reminded him of Miss Charles's hairdo, they had nudged, pushed, and shoved, each according to his or her or his/her own abilities, several dry, dusty hymnals. In the same manner, they added several lengths of wood from a broken pew. Then they stepped back to survey their pyre. "I daresay no scout troop could do better," remarked Can o' Beans.

"You dare said it," said Dirty Sock.

Spoon had giggled again, more from nervousness than amusement.

At twilight, they had assumed their stations. Spoon and Dirty Sock, she all ashiver, he irritated by a piece of wood shaving that had caught in his threads, perched on the ledge before the grate. Conch Shell and Can o' Beans were by the door, positioned so that when it swung open, they would be hidden behind it. Painted Stick was at the edge of the pyre itself, balancing upright on his tapered tip.

They waited.

And waited.

And when the angle and composition of the dying light was to his satisfaction, the stick commenced to twirl. For some reason, each of the others, watching him, thought briefly of Turn Around Norman, although Norman obviously was a slow train to Leadville compared to the rapidly spinning stick. Around and around the ancient talisman twirled, twirling in a frenzy, like a blind man's cane in a whirlpool, like the bit of a diamond cutter's drill.

They watched.

And watched.

And grew anxious.

But at last a shaving began to smolder. Then another. And another. The first spark popped like a baby's bloody head emerging from an oxygen womb. Twins. Quintuplets. Then, an entire population flared, and the shadow of the scorched stick was thrown, tall and mysterious, against a fire-lit wall.

By the time that Ellen Cherry Charles—husbandless, loverless, and now fatherless—returned her seat back to an upright position in preparation for landing at La Guardia, an advance wave of firefighters was cautiously opening St. Patrick's sub-basement door. Precisely at that moment, Spoon, Dirty Sock, and Painted Stick squirmed through the bars and out onto the sidewalk. There they were concealed in a hedgerow of smoke. Policemen already had cordoned off the block. So far, so good.

"If only it will go half this smoothly for the others," said Spoon.

"Yep," said Dirty Sock. "We got it made compared to them two."

Hardly had the objects spoken when a man appeared out of the smoke, a tall, gaunt man who, though attired in a fifteen-hundred-dollar suit, managed to look as cheap as chewing gum. A shock of recognition was followed by the greater shock of capture. Before she could say "Mother Mary" or "white chocolate mousse," Spoon was yanked from the pavement by the man's right hand. Just as suddenly, his left hand snatched up Painted Stick. He squatted for a moment to consider Dirty Sock, but drew back with a show of disgust. Leaving the begrimed garment where it lay, he walked away, clutching and studying the utensil and the wand.

Buddy Winkler had lingered near St. Patrick's that dusk somewhat beyond his usual hour of departure. He had been conversing with a professed supporter, a well-dressed stranger who'd intimated interest in financially supporting any cause that might expedite Armageddon. "Let's you and me talk us some turkey," said Buddy, and, indeed, they had been all agobble when they noticed smoke streaming from a grate at the base of the cathedral. The preacher had been rather surprised by the speed and efficiency with which the stranger used a police call box to summon the fire department.

When the first squad car had arrived, its driver had wanted to question Bud about the fire.

"No, no. This is the Reverend Buddy Winkler," the stranger intervened.

"And who da fuck are you?"

In response, the stranger had removed his wallet and flashed some token of identification that looked suspiciously less like a Visa Gold Card than a badge. The cop nodded and turned his attention to clearing the area. "Reckon I should mosey on out of the way," said Buddy. "Maybe you and me can chew the fat on some more collected occasion." He nodded at the smoking cathedral. "Sure hope the cod-chompers don't lose no prime real estate."

With that, Buddy turned and headed for the barricades. Cursing him, firemen brushed past him on their way up the steps. He disappeared momentarily in belches of smoke. "Bet the archbishop's faggots forgot to turn off the heat under the chowder," he joked. " 'Course, too, they might've been warming up some of that KY Jelly." He'd closed his eyes against the sting of the smoke, and it was at the instant of their cautious reopening that he spotted the things on the sidewalk.

His retrieval of them, two of them, had been purely instinctive, although it quickly occurred to him that the spoon was identical to the one that his wanton niece had painted pictures of, and that the satanic-looking stick was the one that had been used to trip him up a few weeks prior. He'd had a funny feeling about the grate in that cathedral for a while now, a feeling as if something unnatural and unrighteous was being carried on behind it. Something that might have been intended to personally bug him. It wasn't anything he could speak about. He was reluctant to think about it in any but the most superficial way. Oddly enough, he didn't blame the Catholics. Intuition led him to suspect that whatever it was was somehow connected to that lunkhead who used to stand stock-still down the street there, fooling gullible pseudointellectuals such as Ellen Cherry Charles into believing he was turning around. Whatever it was, it was also connected to these things he'd found on the sidewalk. Well, he would paint *their* little red wagon blue! He'd just take their playthings with him! Except for the sock, of course. Let the Devil dress his hoof in that noxious stocking!

Dirty Sock folded himself into a tiny wad and scrunched against the wall. Toward dawn, stymied and alone, he slithered back through the grate into the fire-blackened cellar of St. Patrick's. Some say that he is there still. That he haunts the cathedral like a vile Protestant wraith, causing altar boys to spill the wine, dignified gentlemen to break wind during confession, bishops to lapse into pig Latin, and young mothers to agitate for birth control. It is even rumored that on cold winter nights, he weights himself with a lump or two of coal and plays eerie Hank Williams riffs on the organ. Or that he will slither out of the grate just long enough to wrap himself around the ankle of a matronly shopper, making her squeal and drop the parcels she is fetching home from Saks. "Heh-heh-heh," he's reported to chuckle as he darts back into his den.

Cooler heads say that he's not in the church at all, but, rather, that he's gone to that place where so very many socks go, when, in a manner most unaccountable, they vanish from laundry machines all over America; that he's entered another dimension, as it were; a parallel universe of cotton, wool, and polyester: the Planet of the Lost Socks.

In either case, like numerous pilgrims before him, Dirty Sock was never to reach far Jerusalem. It is possible, however, that Jerusalem will yet come to him.

In regard to Jerusalem, at least, the other locomotive objects fared better than the sock.

Buddy Winkler carried Spoon and Painted Stick to the handsome midtown apartment that the Third Temple Platoon had leased for him (and which he'd turned into a bit of a sty), where, with a mixture of curiosity and revulsion, he scrutinized them for a while longer before shutting them away in his closet. He sealed the door with a prayer. "Lord Jesus, if these here items be possessed of the demonic, please protect your loving and no-account servant from their evil influences."

No sooner had Buddy slammed the closet door than a hysterical Spoon, noting the wide gaps between the louvers, began urging Painted Stick to attack. "Bash him on the noggin," said Spoon, "and let's get out of here!" Surprised by her assertiveness and sensitive about bashing animate noggins, the stick advised her to cool down, to wait to see what fortune would bring.

During the night, Spoon did, indeed, regain a measure of equilibrium, but come morning, when they heard the preacher stir, she began anew her plea for a bash and a dash. "Silence!" ordered the decorated rod. "What can be the matter? Did you not overhear last evening the auspicious designs of our captor?"

The designs to which Painted Stick referred were revealed in a conversation the Reverend Buddy Winkler had had around midnight with a stealthy visitor. "Sorry to ask you to meet me here, rabbi,"

Buddy had said, "but this dad-blasted phone is as good as tapped. An undercover cop of unknown liberal affiliation inveigled me earlier this very day. He was a slick sucker, though I don't believe he more than covered the bottom of his bucket outta my loose pump. Anyways, it's a sign, a sign doubtless provided by the Almighty, that we gotta take us some care. For that reason, I want you to know that I plan to ship this here possibly incriminatin' stuff on over to Jerusalem tomorrow or the next day. Clear it offen the premises. My boy Boomer Petway can just as well store it over there."

"Did you not hear that?" asked the stick. "This man shall be shipping 'stuff' to Jerusalem. And you and I shall ship along with it."

"Oh, dear," Spoon gulped. "But what about the others?"

"There is nothing we can do for them now. Their fate is in the stars. Fortunately, Conch Shell is on the best of terms with starlight."

It took several hours for Conch Shell and Can o' Beans to get out of the cathedral. Soon after the fire hoses were dragged in, they scooted from their hiding place behind the door and began their laborious and frightening ascent of the stairs. Before they reached the basement level, two firemen rushed by without seeing them. In the basement, they hid for thirty minutes in a crate of incense. "Once more I'm thankful I'm not human," said the bean can. "If we had noses, this powder would asphyxiate us. Of course, if we had noses, Mr. Sock might have gassed us long ago."

The firemen made rather quick work of the blaze. All but one of the engines departed. Its crew hung around outside, enjoying coffee and doughnuts and talking football with the cops. They were making certain the fire didn't flare up again. Eventually, the arson squad arrived to launch its investigation. By that time, the shell and the can, like a couple of plaster-cast salmon climbing a dry fish ladder, had clumped safely to the main floor, where they took refuge beneath a pew in the nave.

Gradually, the men cleared out until only one investigator, the archbishop's secretary, and the chief custodian were left. For a time, the objects feared they might be trapped in the nave, destined to be knelt upon at Sunday mass. However, the secretary suggested that the front doors be propped open to air out the place, which smelled pungently of woodsmoke and cremated hymnals. Shortly thereafter,

Can o' Beans and Conch Shell were on the night-town streets, the thousand pulses of the city beating like a thousand phosphorescent wings against their steel and calcium hides.

The balled-up sock was crouched a yard past the Fifty-first Street end of the grate. Turning downtown, as they had been instructed, Can o' Beans and Conch Shell didn't see Dirty Sock. He didn't see them. Keeping to the shadows, they hastily crossed Fiftieth, rounded the corner of Forty-ninth, and ducked into the cement-dusted labyrinth of a construction site. They were sorely disappointed that stick, spoon, and sock weren't awaiting them there.

"Jilted!" said Can o' Beans. "Now what do we do?"

"We shall linger for a bit. There are too many humans about at this hour. But if our companions have not shown themselves by moonset, we shall continue on our own to the river. Thence the sea."

A pensive Conch Shell leaned to rest against a piece of Styrofoam. It proved to be a food carton, left by a gastronomically adventurous construction worker who had purchased his lunch that noon from a nearby Japanese restaurant. The thrust of the shell's spiky whorls tipped the carton over, causing it to expel from its chamber a quivering blob of repulsive white custard. "Go-oo-oo-oo-od-od e-e-e-ev-ev-ev-ning-ning," said the blob, continuing to vibrate like the larynx of an albino soprano.

"And what, pray tell," asked the startled shell, "might *you* be?"

When at last it had ceased to jiggle, the strange life form replied, "You can call me tofu. Or you can call me dofu. But you doesn't have to call me bean curd."

For seventy-two hours, Conch Shell and Can o' Beans scurried from hiding place to hiding place along New York's waterfront, hoping, in vain, for a rendezvous with their fellows. Finally, at approximately eleven o'clock on the third night, an August night, a night as warm and gamey as turtle soup, the shell instructed the bean can to mount her, and with the deformed container nestled in her nacreous cockpit (a little too precariously to be to their liking), she slipped into the greasy harbor and swam away.

The weight of the can forced her to ride low in the water. Every gentle wave lapped against her passenger, and her worry was that the

more powerful waves of the open ocean would wash the can from its
niche. She warned Can o' Beans of the dashings and drownings that
might await them, but when they did exit the harbor the next
morning and the first row of whitecaps set him/her to rattling in her
aperture, he/she yelled "Surf's up!", and whooping like an exuberant
schoolboy/girl, he/she did his/her toeless best to hang ten.

"We travel slowly," said Conch Shell, "and we have such a long,
long distance to go. If we should encounter a storm . . ."

"Let 'er blow!" shouted Can o' Beans. Then, more quietly, he/she
added, "Look, Miss Shell, it's not every tin of prepared carbohydrates
that gets to ride the waves, especially not in such a pretty boat. I
would be prevaricating were I not to admit that both the masculine
and feminine aspects of my nature are aroused by the accommoda-
tions on this cruise. Now don't blush. And don't fret. Think about
the Third Temple of Jerusalem and what role it is that you're
destined to play therein. As for me, my energy has been too long
centered in my intellect. I'm having the time of my life."

Conch Shell said nothing further, but concentrated on the sea and
on keeping her wobbly passenger upright in her crevice. Garlands of
seaweed encircled her like composted leis, crabs serenaded her with
their flatiron fiddles, and schools of shad bumped her along with
their noses. Hardly was she out of sight of the Statue of Liberty than
several cargo ships overtook her. And in the hold of one of them, the
one that gave her the greatest problem with its wake, secreted amidst
odd trappings and paraphernalia in a crate addressed to Randolph
Petway III, huddled a pair of mutated objects of her long and fond
acquaintance.

Husbandless, loverless, and now fatherless, Ellen Cherry became
wife, mistress, and daughter of the I & I. The restaurant's staff had
been virtually doubled, and once more she found herself in a mana-
gerial position. She might have preferred to remain simply a waitress,

but it wasn't possible. By the middle of September, the situation there was almost out of hand, and her expertise and energy were much in demand.

Salome was New York's new queen of the night. Finding her refreshing compared to the aggressive, overdressed publicity sluts who normally competed for the crown, the press doted on her. Yet the more that was written about her, the more mysterious she seemed, and the greater her mystery, the more attention she attracted. In a revolutionary reversal, the hip, the cool, and the famous were among the last to discover her. For months they resisted, but, one by one, two by two, they swallowed their pride, deserted Nell's, 6 Bond Street, M.K., and Payday, to limo and taxi to United Nations Plaza, where, humiliated, they lined up with squares from the suburbs, whining to be let in. Occasionally, a genuine platinum-plated celebrity would appear at the door and petition for admission, but Abu and Spike played no favorites: it was first come, first served at Isaac & Ishmael's, although once Abu did allow Debra Winger to watch the show from the kitchen after she offered to help with the dishes.

In each and every interview they granted, Abu and Spike insisted that there be some mention of the restaurant's raison d'être and of its troubled history. As a result, their experiment in Arab-Jewish camaraderie received notice beyond their wildest dreams. The clippings and videotapes that they collected were dutifully copied and dispatched to Jerusalem.

"Do not get sentimental over us," Abu warned journalists. "We are a tiny and slightly mad oasis in a vast desert. We do what we do, make the statement we make, because of who we are, not because we think we are going to change the Middle East."

Added Spike, "But what we do is necessary already, even if nobody else follows our suit."

In late September, the I & I actually received a fairly major humanitarian award. It was the young belly dancer, however, it was Salome, who was the center of attention. As far as New York was concerned, she was the I & I's meat, and gravy, too; the brotherhood bit was merely an obligatory garnish of parsley.

For a few weeks, the restaurant brought in the orchestra on Tuesdays, Wednesdays, and Thursdays, as well, and hired two experienced belly dancers to shimmy on those nights. In terms of business, the expanded schedule was not unsuccessful, but on Spike and Abu's excitement meter, it failed to even breathe on the needle. The new dancers, veteran performers though they were, were fluoridated tap water compared to Salome's gourd of spiced mare's milk. They were adequate, but as Abu put it, "To the connoisseur, adequacy is insulting." Besides, old customers were complaining that to accommodate the floor show, the super-duper TV was being switched off, usually at the most crucial point in a ball game. Spike and Abu fired the dancers and returned the band to its Friday-Saturday schedule.

The East Indian restaurant next door, completely overshadowed even though it employed a superior chef, offered to sell out to the Arab and the Jew so that they could enlarge their premises. Abu and Spike declined. "What we have already we're sticking to already," said Spike. And what they had was a reticent sixteen-year-old student nurse (Shaftoe was correct) who refused to speak with producers of "The Tonight Show" when they approached her in the cafeteria at Bellevue Hospital, waving a contract so briskly that it cooled off her double order of french fries. (Shaftoe also revealed—nobody knew where he was getting his information—that the girl wore heavy horn-rimmed glasses when she studied or watched cartoons, a fact later confirmed by a writer for *Newsweek,* prompting dozens of men and women with perfect vision to start showing up at UN Plaza in spectacles of consummate dorkiness.)

What they had was a squirmy, self-conscious, adolescent girl who redefined the art of belly dancing without really trying, like a somnambulant who writes original love poems in her sleep. What they had was a virgin (the bandleader swore that she was!) who could make men (and a few women, too) come without touching them, without even looking at them. What they had was a callow child-woman who, wielding a tube of cheap lipstick, marked a ruby X on the sternum of modern, sophisticated, cynical Manhattan, then gunned its heart full of deep emotions and silly ideas.

"The belly dance began as a kind of practical feminist yoga," Abu explained on more than one occasion. "It was developed in the Levant hundreds, maybe thousands, of years ago as a way to tone certain muscles and loosen others, so that women could give birth more easily, with less pain. It also reduced menstrual cramps. Now I am merely guessing, but I imagine that women got together to do these exercises, rather like a contemporary aerobics class, and the menfolk were intrigued in spite of themselves. They found the workouts entertaining or prurient or both. Gradually, belly dancing, like so many other things, drifted out of its original context and became mannered, stylized, self-referential."

"And is Salome restoring some of the original flavor, the old moves?"

"How would I know? For that matter, how would she know?"

"Well, she claims she's a Canaanite."

"A conceit, obviously. Those Canaanites who were not exterminated by the Hebrews were absorbed by them. What Salome said, actually, was, 'I'm one of those Canaanite girls whose mothers picked flowers for the altars of Jerusalem.' A conceit, but I like it. It is musical. A little poem. What I *think* she is trying to say, in her romantic, adolescent way—and I forbid you to quote me on this—is that she is half Arabic, half Jewish. She would have suffered somewhat because of this, and styling herself a Canaanite, a member of a lost race, is her poetic way of dealing with that confusion, that pain. Pure speculation, mind you. Detective Shaftoe, whose information is usually reliable, has said nothing of the sort."

There was a way in which Ellen Cherry grew to resent both the I & I and its star attraction. The more successful the restaurant became, the more of her time and energy it sapped. She was happy for her employers, but once again her return to painting had been postponed (not that any thundering stampede of great ideas was rushing toward the cliffs of her cerebrum, anxious to throw itself headlong into paint jars down below). As for Salome, she, like Boomer, seemed to have succeeded wildly without really working at it (although how could a chagrined Ellen Cherry be sure that Salome hadn't spent most of her young life practicing those moves that she executed with such hesitant if not indifferent grace, and, moreover, wasn't it Ellen Cherry who had asserted that she didn't care whether or not artists paid their dues so long as the end product sprayed Windex on the panes of perception?). Contradiction may be an unavoidable trait in a many-faceted sensibility in an expanding universe, but bitterness is reductive in the most trivializing way, and Ellen Cherry was aware that it was her fate to have to struggle against it. Over and over, she reminded herself how fortunate she was to have landed her life in a situation where strange things could happen to it. "Why, if I hadn't learned the eye game when I was little, I could be in Colonial Pines right now, washing and ironing some clodhopper's shorts."

Husbandless, loverless, and now fatherless, Ellen Cherry couldn't have been unaware that men's shorts definitely were one item missing from any inventory of her world. It was as if some monster Kali-Hoover had sucked all the primary shorts-wearers out of her life. Of course, there was Abu. And Spike, in a recycled guise. And no lack of male energy among the clientele at the I & I. On the other hand, what had become of Turn Around Norman? And that flirty Raoul? They, too, had been vacuumed up off that Middle Eastern rug that seemed to cover the earth in every direction as far as her eyes could see.

She finally got a telephone installed in her apartment so that she could stay in closer contact with Patsy; she exchanged friendly but noncommittal letters with Boomer; she took over the lunch operation at the restaurant, often sticking around late on Fridays and Saturdays to help out with dinner and, in her words, "to watch men go goofy over that spastic little cunt, skinny legs and all"; and—what else? Not much. In her underwear drawer, the gossip dwindled to such a degree that Daruma thought the panties might be actually approaching a Zen state.

"Ripples now vanish from carp pool of mind," said the vibrator approvingly. Out on the Atlantic, however, ripples were riotous, threatening almost incessantly to sweep Can o' Beans from the seashell's hold. And at Isaac & Ishmael's, a new ripple was about to jar things, as well.

The hour was 4:00 P.M., the day Monday, the month September. Late September. So late that you'd have to look closely to distinguish it from October. Dip a slice of bread in batter. That's September: yellow gold, soft, and sticky. Fry the bread. Now you have October:

chewier, drier, streaked with browns. The day in question fell somewhere in the middle of the french toast process. A hint of chilled marmalade in the air.

In the I & I bar, regulars were assembling to watch Monday night football on the mammoth screen. Kickoff was hours away, however, and the lounge chatter ran to other things. To be precise, one other thing.

"She looks so bored all the time."

"Not bored. She looks scared."

"Oh, I don't know . . ."

"Both. She looks bored *and* scared. That's what drives me crazy. She gives the impression that if you took her to bed, she'd look at you like that from start to finish."

"You're right."

"It ees true."

"She wouldn't just lie there. She'd give you a ride like a wild mule. But all through it, she'd look bored and scared. Hoo! It's making me crazy. I can't sleep anymore for thinking about it."

"He ees right. In zee movies, zee women zat are making zee love are looking, how you say, carry away. Zey look carry away and grateful. A mistake. How much more excitement if zey are looking scared and bored. Then men are jump out of zee seats and rush zee screen. Irresistible!"

"It's her age, that's all."

"Yeah, you guys. She looks at you like you bore and scare her because she's young enough to be your daughter."

"If she's my daughter, I'd be in jail."

"That's sick. But me, too."

There was a spill of uncomfortable laughter. A waiter arrived with a tray of *falafel,* the one item on the menu that didn't taste as if it had been scraped off the wick of Aladdin's lamp.

"Anyway, it isn't her face or its expression. It's her body, the way she moves it."

"Oui! Yes. Zose leetle teeties, how she set zem to vibrating! Zey could wheep zee eggs for soufflé."

"I have seen hundreds of belly dancers. Hundreds. My cousin could dance this dance better than any woman in Istanbul. But this Salome girl who dances here . . ."

"She's the best. Her movements are softer and sweeter, but at the same time very, very strong. Her dancing is . . ."

"Zilch."

The man who spoke was Detective Shaftoe. He'd had his face in a beer mug, and it was the first thing he'd said since he ambled in. They stared at him in disbelief.

"Pardon?"

"Zilch?"

"Nothing. The dances she does here are nothing. They're baby dances. In more ways than one."

"What do you mean?" The men respected the opinions of the muscular black man. After all, he used to play football. And he often seemed to know things about Salome that nobody else knew.

"I mean that if you think what she does here is so goddamned hot, you ought to see her do the Dance of the Seven Veils."

Under questioning, Shaftoe admitted that he had never seen this "Dance of the Seven Veils." He'd only heard reports. But his unidentified sources assured him that if Salome ever performed it, which she probably wouldn't, all of the other dances she had done would seem prissy, uncolored, and commonplace in comparison.

The lounge fell silent and remained that way through most of Monday night football.

Word spread like a skin disease in a nudist colony. Hardly a customer, new or old, passed through the door of the I & I without asking Spike, "When's she going to do the Dance of the Seven Veils?" During Salome's performances, between numbers, patrons would call out, "Dance of the Seven Veils!" as if requesting a favorite tune from a rock star. The first couple of times that happened, she looked as startled as if someone had pulled a gun, but later on, when she grew accustomed to "Do the Seven Veils!" the raccoon fingers of a small dark smile would toy with the meat of her upper lip, and ever so gently and briefly, she would shake her head.

A negative head shake was all that Spike and Abu got from Salome, as well. They pleaded their case before the bandleader, who behaved as if his dental deficit was impairing his hearing. "Maybe someday," he would say, a little wistfully, looking off into the distance. "Someday when the apricots are blooming. . . ."

Abu was familiar enough with Arabic idioms to know that that little phrase meant roughly the same as, "It'll be a cold day in hell."

He seized the lapel of the old man's shiny blue suit. "Tell her if she will do the seven veils dance, I will double her pay."

The bandleader tapped his own chest. "Also?" he asked.

"When the apricots bloom!" shot back Abu. "You are being paid extra as it is."

The conductor walked away, leaving Abu to simmer like a pot of *turshi*. Abu conferred with Spike. The two of them were as intrigued with the legendary dance as anybody else. The following week, Abu made another offer. "If Salome will perform the Dance of the Seven Veils just once, we will pay her triple and you double, for that one evening and that evening only."

Showing gums as pink and smooth as Conch Shell's aperture, the bandleader vowed to do his utmost. However, the next evening, the old drooler took Abu aside to inform him that it was no use.

"Not even for triple salary?"

"It is not a matter of money, my generous benefactor. There is involved the matter of tradition. There is likewise involved the secrets of women, little that we men care of such things. There is likewise involved personal disposition. The girl is of high intelligence for a girl. She is the youngest girl to study at the Hospital Bellevue. And she wishes to go to her homeland to be nursing her people. I am sorry, dear sir, but the girl will never do this dance."

"Never?"

"Well. Maybe someday. When the—"

"Apricots bloom." Abu finished his sentence for him and chased him out of the office.

Ellen Cherry answered the reservation desk phone on the October afternoon that the I & I received a bomb threat, the first in many months. Prior to joining in the evacuation of the building, she called her employers at their tennis club. They arrived on the scene in white linen pants and white cotton sweaters. Spike was shod in white tennis sneakers, but Abu had replaced his Nikes with black leather dress shoes. The flashing red lights of the bomb squad van were reflected on their plain toes.

"Somebody is just doing this for old times' sake," Abu said, smiling. "Who would have thought that religious terrorists could be sentimental?"

"No," said Spike. "I'm thinking it's the cops what're making the threat. They got a party scheduled and are short on liquor."

"You all aren't taking this very seriously," said Ellen Cherry.

Spike touched the scars on his forehead. "Of all people, I'm taking it seriously," he said. "But I'm thinking it's just some *shikker* what's mad because our little lady's not doing the Dance of the Seven Veils."

"What is it with this dance?" asked Ellen Cherry. "Everybody's going on about it like it was free sex and ice cream, but nobody knows spit about it."

"It's that shamus what's started it," said Spike, referring to Shaftoe.

"But it is an actual dance," put in Abu. "And apparently it is included in her repertoire."

"Well, what's so special about it? Isn't it out of the Bible or something?"

It was barely three o'clock, but traffic was already gridlocked at the Forty-ninth Street exit from the FDR Drive. The blaring horns and racing engines were so loud that Ellen Cherry flirted with earache straining to hear Abu's explanation. "No, it is mentioned nowhere by name in the Bible, although Josephus the historian records that it is the dance performed by the biblical Salome at the birthday party of her stepfather, Herod."

"The party where John the Baptist's head jumped out of the cake?"

"So to speak. Salome, incidentally, is the same Semitic word as *shalom* or *salem*. In other words, 'peace.' Thus, our beloved city, Jerusalem, is both the House of Peace and the House of the Dancing Girl."

"Of what?"

"The Dancing Girl."

"That's sweet," said Ellen Cherry.

"*I* like it," said Spike.

Abu went on. "The dance itself predates Herod and that particular Salome, his stepdaughter. In fact, it is very ancient and thoroughly pagan. It is connected to the myth of the cyclic death of the sun god. His moon goddess travels to the underworld to rescue him, but to get him back she has to drop one of her seven articles of clothing at each of its seven gates."

"Why?"

"I have no clue. But the reenactment of the story apparently continued well into Roman times. Supported by Hebrews. A dancer would drop a veil at each of the seven gates of the Temple in Jerusalem. At the seventh gate, she was in her birthday suit, though we need not suppose that to be the reason Herod requested the dance at his birthday party. I have read that the veils represented layers of illusion. As each veil peeled away, an illusion was destroyed, until finally some great central mystery of life was revealed."

"What?" asked Ellen Cherry. "I missed that."

Before Abu could repeat the story, word came from across UN Plaza that the police had, indeed, discovered an explosive device planted behind the bamboo matting on a wall near the bandstand. Spike and Abu were astounded. Ellen Cherry thought instantly of Buddy Winkler.

False alarm. The "bomb" proved to be a remote-controlled cassette recorder. Someone, probably a waiter, had hidden it there in order to surreptitiously record the orchestra, Salome on tambourine. "Looking to rake in some extra cash peddling bootleg tapes," Abu conjectured.

"That the old American dream or the new one?" Ellen Cherry asked Spike.

"Better flimflam capitalism than a bomb, already. It's becoming so quiet for the two radishes. Maybe the religious cults are starting to get religion."

"You know," said Ellen Cherry, "I can't figure out the popularity of those cults. Okay, so people can get somebody else to do their thinking for them, what is the big appeal? Are they really that lazy, or is there some secret pleasure in having your mind controlled?"

"I seriously doubt if pleasure is a factor," said Abu. "The level of structure that people seek always is in direct ratio to the amount of chaos they have inside."

"Then ol' Boomer must be as placid as a bucket of doorknobs." Smiling, she mused for a moment about Boomer's antipathy for the straight and narrow. "Too bad you never met him, Mr. Hadee. I have a feeling you two might have gotten along."

Abu and Spike regarded each other oddly. So oddly, Ellen Cherry grew suspicious. She gave them an imploring look. "Shall we tell her?" asked Abu.

"Yeah," answered Spike, "she's deserving to know."

"What is it, you all?"

"Not to worry, little darlink. It's only that in the near future Abu and me may be meeting your Boomer."

"You see, Cherry, last year Spike and I decided to donate a sculpture for a war-torn neighborhood that was being restored outside the Jaffa Gate in Jerusalem. We kept our role anonymous because we were having a little trouble here at the restaurant, and our partnership was somewhat controversial. Through intermediaries, we granted a commission to an Israeli sculptor by the name of Zif, Amos Zif."

"Ah-ha!" exclaimed Ellen Cherry. The light bulb above her head was plainly visible.

"Ah-ha, indeed. Now, we learned soon enough that Zif had, himself, taken on a partner, a non-Israeli, which was fine with us since our basic intention was that the monument be transcultural. We also learned from you that Boomer Petway was collaborating on a sculpture in Jerusalem. Only recently, however, did we put two and two together and—"

"Well, I'll be damned," swore Ellen Cherry. "If the world gets any smaller, everybody is going to have to go on a diet."

"Yeah, but a problem we got. This Boomer of yours is making big chickens . . ."

"Turkey. A big turkey."

"Turkeys and skyscraper pants and income tax forms for double agents, and this is not the monument what we're dreaming of."

"I see."

"We are a trifle concerned," said Abu. "Concerned about image and statement. So we have demanded to examine a model of the sculpture before it goes any further."

"There or here?"

Simultaneously, there was an Arab shrug and a Jewish shrug, fundamentally similar gestures but as different in nuance as a fez and a yarmulke. "A response we don't got yet," said Spike. Then he switched his attention to the bamboo matting that the police had left hanging from the walls in shreds, like the blouse of a horsewhipped adulteress. "How much does plaster cost?" he asked.

*　　*　　*

Arrangements were made to have Isaac & Ishmael's plastered. The restaurant would close during Thanksgiving week so that the workmen could take over. "The staff gets a little paid vacation," Abu announced. The staff received the news with glee—conditions had been hectic that autumn—but some of the customers yowled. Not only would they have to go a week without Salome but also Thanksgiving Day was to football what St. Patrick's Day was to grain alcohol.

"Now I will have to stay home and watch the dime-sized footballs," a Greek delegate complained. "And at halftime I will be expected to pay attention to my wife."

"A cowboy's work is never done," said Ellen Cherry, with a yawn.

"I fear that you have produced a non sequitur," announced an Egyptian doctor, who'd become a real smarty-pants with his English.

"Fuck off," said Ellen Cherry, who was in one of her periodic failed-artist snits.

"Oxymoron!" proclaimed the doctor, and then proceeded to tell her why. "One cannot fuck if one is off, one can only fuck when one is on. On top or on the bottom. Is this not true?"

Ellen Cherry sighed. Thanksgiving was still weeks away.

Meanwhile, the shredded bamboo had been temporarily and sloppily stapled back on the walls. The rooms looked as if they were coated with an especially healthy breakfast cereal, a decor known as "Early Roughage." In this high-fiber atmosphere, Salome continued to dance, although she did not dance the Dance of the Seven Veils no matter how many pleading calls for that dance echoed off the bran.

November. Salome danced, Ellen Cherry managed, and the Israelis voted. Boomer wrote Ellen Cherry all about it. Dirty tricks, faked terrorist attacks, lies, threats, and fear tactics of every polecat stripe. Boomer loved it. Naturally, the right won. Conservatives understand Halloween, liberals only understand Christmas. If you want to control a population, don't give it social services, give it a scary adversary. Communism might have become a passé bugaboo, but ah, now there were the hobgoblins of terrorism and drugs with which to frighten and subdue the unthinking masses. "I learned this from reading spy thrillers," wrote Boomer. "If you want to teach kids how the world really works, take away their civics books and assign them some good espionage novels. By the way, can you send me the new Tom Clancy. Can't buy it over here."

Boomer went on to say that with the right wing finally, firmly in power—it would officially seize the joy stick in January—there was almost certain to be some sort of commotion when his and Zif's monument was unveiled. Then, under the block-print heading FOR YOUR EYES ONLY, he surprised her by describing the monument.

He described it in detail, not only conveying the sculpture's salient formal features but making historical, mythological, and cultural references that he was not likely to have gleaned from any espionage novel. Whatever she thought of the sculpture aesthetically, she had to admire the verbal presentation, and this in spite of the fact that it was executed in a monstrous scrawl. She closed her eyes, and when she did, she saw not the monument that had been so vividly documented but Boomer's own sweet head, hair escaping his scalp like ozone escaping the Arctic. Had her resentment of him given way to longing, a ghostly subconscious longing, a longing that transcended the strictly physical, a longing for his personality, his being, his . . . his *mind*?

Ellen Cherry shook herself out of ludicrous reveries and returned to the letter. It seemed that Boomer was in some trouble with the authorities as a result of a crate of goods that Buddy Winkler had shipped to him. Boomer wasn't familiar with the contents of the crate. Customs officers in Tel Aviv had impounded them, deeming them suspicious. "An investigation is under way, and for the first time in my life I may actually have to stoop to retaining a lawyer. This is the end of something pure and good. Once a fellow breaks down and hires his first attorney, he has gone and booked himself passage aboard the hand basket to Hades."

The epistle closed with a remark of an apparently lascivious nature. Boomer's penmanship deteriorated as the letter progressed, and though she could not wholly comprehend the closure, she would have wagered her last cent that it was lascivious. His signature resembled the mustache of a Latin American dance instructor. To the bottom of the page, however, there was affixed a postscript of almost academically acceptable legibility. Undoubtedly, he had added it after a night's rest. It said:

"On second thought, never mind about the Tom Clancy."

*   *   *

November played out its hand: two dark aces, a pair of shivering treys, and the jack of pumpkins. Salome danced, Ellen Cherry managed, and then the plasterers came and sent both of them home. On the Wednesday before Thanksgiving, Salome (presumably) awoke to study chemistry, change bandages, and sponge froth from the lips of madmen and junkies. Ellen Cherry (positively) awoke to lie abed and brood. After a time, however, she grew bored with despair, got up, performed her toilette, and reheated a pan of I & I *shawarma* for breakfast.

The prospect of breakfasting on leftover *shawarma* was one of the things that was depressing her. It proved to be not all that bad. Any way you sliced it, it beat *baba ghanoug*. She had once served herself a *baba ghanoug* breakfast and had actually swallowed a couple of bites before her taste buds warned her that such behavior was in violation of accords of the Geneva Convention.

She had also been feeling sorry for herself for being alone on a major holiday. Yet, while it was true that her mama had flown to Florida for the long weekend, Patsy would be in New York at Christmas, would, in fact, be moving in with her while she searched for an apartment of her own, a quest that could take about half as long as the search for a cure for the common cold. Ellen Cherry realized that she ought to be taking advantage of this final month of privacy. Besides, she had been invited to share Thanksgiving dinner with Abu, Nabila, and family. So she could stow the self-pity— husbandlessness, loverlessness, and fatherlessness notwithstanding.

Having fallen behind on her rent again, she had also been brooding over finances. But, hey, in addition to vacation pay, Spike had handed her a holiday bonus check in the amount of twelve hundred dollars. That would square matters temporarily. As for the long run, she would find a way to survive. She always had. One thing was certain, though: she would not make paintings for Ultima's gallery simply to try to raise cash. As she'd said more than once in regard to painting, "Having to do it for money is a far cry from having to do it because you have to do it."

Which leads to the fourth member of her blues quartet: art-life gloom. Every other person on the street was the failed consort of one muse or another. One met them everywhere. The would-be guitarist who just couldn't find time to practice, the would-be novelist who developed an allergy to solitude, the would-be actress too weak to withstand domestic and maternalistic urges, the would-be poet who found it easier to get drunk on booze than on language, the would-be filmmaker who for lack of pluck ended up in advertising; the singer, the potter, the dancer who for want of that extra volt of verve, that extra enzyme of dedication, that extra candlepower of courage were doomed to paper the walls of their lives with frustrated fantasies and secret dissatisfactions. Ellen Cherry would breakfast on live cockroaches before she'd turn out like them! She swore it.

Abruptly, she rose and spun one of the canvases that leaned against her walls. Without bothering to change out of her kimono, she grabbed a jar of gesso and commenced to white-out the picture. Had Can o' Beans been told of this, holding on for dear life out in the swells of the far Atlantic, he/she might simply have tumbled out of his/her twat-pink bunker and joined the garbage to which starfishes attached themselves at the bottom of the sea.

An ice fog of gesso descended upon the image. Soon its upper half was obscured. That the words "beans" and "prepared in tomato sauce" were still plainly visible below the cloud would have failed to mollify Can o' Beans. "What if an impatient, impertinent Gilbert Stuart had one fine morning imbued with white stuff the top half of his portrait of Washington?" he/she might have asked. "Could schoolchildren look at a double chin and a round white collar and identify them as being first in war, first in peace, and first in the hearts of their countrymen? What if Leonardo . . ." No, Can o' Beans would not have been appeased, though he/she might have found it curious that half of his/her portrait was left intact.

The explanation was that Ellen Cherry's gessoing was interrupted by a knocking at the door. "Who is it?" she called.

"Delivery."

"Delivery?"

"Florist."

That was strange. Deliveries, flowers included, were routinely left with the doorman. Most irregular. Moreover, the voice (male) had a queer accent, rather like a southerner pretending to speak French.

Buddy Winkler came to mind, though it hardly was Buddy's voice, and she experienced a tingle very close to fear.

Keeping the chain fastened, Ellen Cherry cracked the door. There stood a uniformed deliveryman right out of the twenties. Wearing a teal tunic with two rows of brass buttons, jodhpurs stuffed into high lace-up boots, and an officer's cap with a shimmering black brim, he looked like the Great Gatsby's chauffeur. At the same moment that she classified him as an anachronism, she conceded that any number of gentrified uptown flower shops were capable of forcing a delivery-man to dress in such a foolish manner, and she noted, moreover, that he was cradling one of those long green cardboard boxes in which roses often are packaged. He was also holding a beige paper bag, imprinted with the logo of Barnes & Noble, and that struck her as odd, although if he worked for a general service, she supposed he might deliver books, as well. Still, she didn't like it. There was something wrong with this picture. The dark glasses, for example. The slick little goatee that wouldn't have looked out of place swimming in a Brazilian river. The way he stared at her, nervously licking his lower lip.

With the hand that wasn't gripping the door, she pulled her kimono tight around her throat. If this clown wanted to see tit, he could go to Mardi Gras. She considered opening the door just wide enough to receive the flowers. After all, the jodhpurs had an old-fashioned button fly, not very handy for a rapist. On the other hand, what if the box was from Uncle Buddy, what if it contained some-thing other than roses? No, the guy in the monkey suit was still staring and licking; she had a funny feeling.

"Leave them at the desk in the lobby," she said. After she slammed the door, she put her ear against it. Several minutes passed before he walked down the hall to the elevator. From a window, she saw him leave the Ansonia. He was carrying the bag but not the box. *I guess it's okay,* she thought, but the next thing she knew he had turned and was looking up at her. Ellen Cherry jumped back from the window just as he waved.

She got dressed in a hurry. She wasn't sure why. A pair of panties was yanked from the drawer so fast it made Daruma's head swim. He

perceived it as a blur. "Satori ever fleeting. Clear light enter consciousness like hand of pickpocket. *Om wooga nam.*" His batteries
began to hum. Ellen Cherry pulled on a pair of tights, stepped into a
wool skirt, drew a bulky cotton sweater over her torso. It was not
until she selected shoes, choosing from among those unsullied by
sauce de Spike, that it dawned on her that she had dressed for the
street rather than for the easel.

The gessoing was not resumed. Nor was the picture turned back to
the wall. For the rest of that morning, when she wasn't glancing
anxiously out of the window, she stared at half a bean can. *I guess I'm
not ready,* she thought. *I'm not ready to paint. If I was ready, if I was in
the mood, it'd take more than an incident like this to stop me. Nothing
could stop me. Uncle Bud could be at the door with his britches off and a
frog jig in his fist, I'd go right on painting. Thought I might be ready but
I'm not.*

Shortly past noon, the telephone harmonicaed. It was Abu. He and
Spike were at the I & I, and they wondered if she would mind
coming down. Her counsel was required. It wasn't a restaurant
matter, Abu explained, it was something else. Ellen Cherry didn't
care what it was. "I'll be there before you can hang up," she said, and
exited so hastily that she forgot a jacket and had to return for it.

Passing through the lobby, she picked up the box of flowers.
Presumed flowers. *I'll take it with me,* she thought. *Spike and Mr.
Hadee will know what to do.* The box was light. It didn't tick. It
smelled of refrigeration.

In the Middle East, sand is mixed in with the final coat of plaster.
The sand adds texture, but primarily it adds strength. Sand is to the
plaster what erudition is to the heart. At Isaac & Ishmael's, plasterers
had followed the Levantine practice. It made the place seem more
like Jerusalem. When they had knocked off at noon on Wednesday,
however, one wall still lacked a final coat. The wall behind the
bandstand remained sandless and smooth. "They will be back Monday morning to finish the job," said Abu. "So we shall not be serving
lunch on Monday. You, my dear, get an extra day off."

"Fine. I think I like the smooth wall best, though. It's friendlier, in
a way."

"That is why rough walls are more authentic," said Abu.

"You want Mister Rogers's neighborhood, don't go to Jerusalem," added Spike. "Howdy Doodyville, Jerusalem is not."

"Jerusalem is a city of deep friendships," Abu explained. "But the trowel of history has left even affection a bit rough. In Jerusalem, people will risk their lives for you, but they will not tell you to 'have a nice day.' "

Normally, once started on Jerusalem, Spike and Abu would've had to have their tongues impounded before they'd stop. Today, however, as soon as they had conducted a brief tour of the fresh plaster, they hustled Ellen Cherry into the office, where on a desk there sat a brightly painted metal mock-up of what surely was the Petway-Zif collaborative monument.

Judging from the maquette, the base of the sculpture was just as Ultima and Boomer had described it: a pile of boulders from which rose a freestanding, three-dimensional, vertical map of ancient Palestine (or Canaan). Perched atop the map, its feet planted in a jaunty stance right above the northern city of Dan, was a colossal and altogether outlandish figure. Fashioned from welded steel and cast aluminum, painted in stinging hues, the figure could be said to have the body of a human and the head of a donkey, except that the body had a tail and the head was rather anthropomorphic. Its ears, one erect, one folded, were long and hairy; its eyes bulged crazily; the thick lips of its equine muzzle were parted in an insolent grin that revealed a domino set of protruding teeth, goofus teeth, buck teeth, teeth that would bend the pliers of Nitrous, Greek god of dentistry. This grotesque jackass had a well-proportioned human body, except that where its robe (patterned in Islamic green and Judean blue) hung open, one could see both the milk-swollen breasts of a woman and the relaxed, swinging penis of a natural man. On its left foot, the creature wore a high-heeled slipper, on its right the brogan of a working stiff.

"What do we got here?" asked Spike, "Horace Horsecollar on speedballs? Mister Ed goes to Denmark?"

"You are an artist," said Abu, somewhat tentatively, for he had seen precious little evidence of her art. "What do you make of this cartoon hermaphrodite?"

Ellen Cherry examined the figure closely. Reading about it in Boomer's letter and seeing it in the flesh, so to speak, were two widely different experiences. Not that he hadn't described it accurately, but it was, well, much more vital than she had imagined it, much more dynamic and affecting, even in its reduced scale.

"Hmmm," she said. "Hmmm."

"Hmmm," repeated Spike. "Our little artist lady only has 'hmmm' to say?"

Ellen Cherry ignored him. She scrutinized the maquette awhile longer, shaking the windup toy of her hairdo, although whether in wonderment or exasperation they could not tell. Eventually, she said, "Well, whatever it is, it isn't cartoonish. It's really quite powerful, in both a kinetic and a totemic sense."

"See?" said Spike. "What am I telling you? It takes an artist to *hok a tchynik*."

"Then you do not know what it is, either," said Abu.

"Oh, but I do," Ellen Cherry corrected him. "Oh, but I truly do."

The country of Palestine, which had been called Canaan, was named for Pales.

Pales was a deity. The ass-god. Or the ass-goddess. Usually he was male, but sometimes she was female, and sometimes its gender was a tad ambivalent.

The name Pales was Arabic, having come out of Libya, but the Hebrews loved the long-eared bisexual no less than the Arabs. Tacitus, the Roman historian, wrote that the Semites fell into venerating the ass because had it not been for wild asses, they never would have survived in the desert. It was probably more complicated than that.

The ass was a savior who provided milk, meat, shoe leather, and transportation (what the Bible calls the "golden calf" was actually the golden ass, since there were never many cows in the Levant).

The ass was also obstinate, silly, and sexually crude.

Embodying all of those characteristics, Pales was trickster, fertility spirit, and sacred clown, presiding over humankind's unruly passions, giving mortals what they needed, but not before having some fun with them.

Ellen Cherry explained all this to Abu and Spike, just as Boomer had explained it to her. "In the left hand there, the female hand with the long fingernails, that's a pitcher of milk and a jar of honey. Those wavy white rods in the masculine hand are supposed to represent the hot desert wind. I guess they used to call that wind 'The Breath of the Ass.' That wind always brought trouble."

"How could something called 'The Breath of the Ass' help but bring trouble?" said Abu. "Still, it's musical. A little poem."

"That wind I know already. In the Sinai, I felt it. Oy! Such a wind! It irritates the mind as well as the body."

Having informed its financiers what or who the statue represented, Ellen Cherry went on to explain why it had been chosen. "Boomer says it ought to remind Arabs and Jews of their common roots, that once upon a time they worshipped the same deity and that a lot of stuff they still have in their religions can be traced back to their common cult. He says it should remind them that this land they've fought over so bitterly was named after a braying ninny. And that that ought to tell them something. Among other things, it should tell them not to take themselves so seriously. Ol' Boomer and Zif hope that both Arabs and Jews can look at this creature, all goofy and vulgar, and maybe find some humor in their own folly. And that at the same time that they're laughing at themselves and how they allowed a simple case of sibling rivalry to escalate into such a long-lasting, world-threatening mess, they can also reaffirm their original sexuality, which, Boomer says, means reaffirming their ties to nature. He says that one of the main problems in Palestine or Israel is that everybody, Arab and Jew, lives in the abstract, lives in political and religious ideology rather than living in physical bodies connected to the earth."

She paused. "Well, there you have it. Personally, I don't know donkey poop from oat bran when it comes to ass-gods, or any of that other *National Geographic* jive. But I do know what works on an aesthetic level, and as nutty as this piece is, as a work of art it ain't bad. It ain't half bad."

Around and around the maquette, Spike and Abu walked.

"It has a certain élan," admitted Abu. "A crazy throb of life."

"It's speaking to our fundamental unity," said Spike. "That I like."

"Yes," Abu agreed. "But there will be misinterpretations. And there will be trouble."

"Hoo boy! You said it. The Breath of the Ass."

*   *   *

Around and around the model, Spike and Abu walked. Ellen Cherry went to the toilet. Coming and going, she paused to admire the smooth white wall behind the bandstand. When she returned to the office, the men were still circling the androgynous ass, trying to determine if they liked it or not.

"By the way," Ellen Cherry inquired, "how did you get the maquette?"

"Rather mysterious," replied Abu. "A messenger unexpectedly delivered it."

"Oh. You'd intimated that Boomer or Zif or both might bring it over."

"Yes. But a messenger delivered it."

"Oh."

There was a rum bottle on the desk, and Ellen Cherry helped herself to a shot. When it reached her stomach, she experienced an instant flash of heartburn, as if the rum was chemically antagonistic to some component of the *shawarma*. She burped. The burp, though dainty and subdued, jarred something in her thinking process. "What did the messenger look like?" she asked.

"Sorry?"

"The messenger who delivered the model. What did he . . . ?"

"Now that you mention it, he was rather quaint. He was in full livery."

"Did he have a beard?"

"No."

"Are you sure? No goatee?"

"No. He was clean-shaven, was he not, Spike?"

"Like a matzo ball."

"Well, was he wearing dark glasses?"

"Yes. Yes, he was. How do you know this?"

"Anything else?"

"No."

"No tan paper bag?"

"Why, yes, he did have a bag under his arm."

"Yeah, and when he set down the model, a book fell out of it. It was the new best-seller by that guy Tom Clancy."

"Well, I'll be. . . . I *thought* I saw him limping when he left the Ansonia."

"What is this, Cherry?"

Ellen Cherry whirled to the sofa and snatched up the florist box that she had forgotten there. She tore off the lid. Inside were a dozen

red roses, their stems longer than the virile ears of a jackass. And
there was a tiny envelope. And in the envelope, a card. In a cement-
mixer scrawl, it read:

Love & Lust From
the Master of Disguise

"That son of a bitch," she said, laughing. "That complete idiot son
of a bitch. He's having entirely too much fun."

First, she telephoned the Ultima Sommervell Gallery. Ultima was
said to be in a meeting.

Next she called the Ansonia. "I'm sorry, man," said an unfamiliar
voice, "Pepe's in a meeting, man."

Was this what they meant by trickle-down economics? She poured
herself another jigger of rum. Quietly burping a vapor of molten
lava and dragon snot, a venom of fire ant, an essence that certain
Middle Eastern governments might surely have converted to weaponry, she got hold of her emotions. Her intuition told her that
Boomer was already on his way back to Jerusalem. An inner voice
whined that he might have been around long enough to ball ol'
Ultima, but she scolded herself that she had a lot of nerve fretting
over infidelity on the very sofa where she and Spike. . . . Ellen
Cherry let go of the whole business. She laughed again and took a
drink of rum.

Then she made another phone call. "David Davis Artist Supplies,"
a geezerish voice answered. It was ol' Dave, himself. Obviously, Dave
Davis, proprietor of her favorite materials outlet (and unrelated to
the late Mel Davis, whose dog boutique invariably gave her the
willies), ol' Dave was not in a meeting.

Ellen Cherry checked the office clock. It was two-thirty on the day
before Thanksgiving. "Are you still open?" she asked.

"You bet we're open, and we're facing it all."

"I'll be right in."

One last shot of rum and, leaving Spike and Abu in orbit around
Pales, she hailed a cab to Lafayette and Bleecker to invest her rent
money in the retail sector of private enterprise.

*   *   *

Many New York artists preferred to patronize Pearl Paints at Canal and Broadway, but it was David Davis for Ellen Cherry Charles. She liked the fact that it was old, funky, and underlit. She liked the fact that ol' Dave maintained personal relationships with artists and that the clerks, who were usually too busy to wait on her, dressed in black sweatsuits, as if they were stagehands in some kabuki theater of art supplies. It was the kind of store in which she had daydreamed of shopping when she was still a girl in Colonial Pines, a slightly otherworldly place that outfitted the brave and the anointed for magical quests.

There was a room at David Davis devoted to brushes. Hundreds of them in all sizes lay in the subterranean dimness, their glossy bristles pointing at the shopper as if the shopper were auditioning before an audience of hedgehogs. Walking into the brush room, Ellen Cherry always felt like a moth who had fluttered into a fur coat. Today, burping, each burp a demitasse of napalm, she selected more than a dozen fine sable brushes, mostly in the broader widths.

A clerk, gliding into the room as if to roll scenery aside so that costumed samurai might battle with palette knives, actually asked if she needed assistance. It was uncharacteristically uncrowded. No last-minute shopping frenzy at David Davis, no artist cooks seeking materials with which to improve the appearance of a turkey.

She moved on to the acrylic department. Now came the fun part. Without regard to price, she began to pull jumbo jars of paint from the shelves. And, burping all the while, her esophagus smoldering like a soggy fuse, she chanted the names of the colors as she dropped them into her basket.

"Indian red," she sang. "Mars red, venetian red, cadmium red, vermilion, and rose madder." There was alizarin crimson, magenta, and that thorn in the backside of the sinful, sister terra rosa.

There was cobalt blue, cerulean blue, prussian blue, ultramarine blue, and, with just a soupçon of garlic, french ultramarine blue.

"Hansa yellow." She liked the sound of that one so well she sang it twice. "Hansa yellow" (patron saint of jaundiced piano players). Then, "zinc yellow, lemon yellow, yellow ocher, mars yellow, naples yellow, and brilliant orange.

"Thio violet, prism violet, mars violet, cobalt violet, dioxazine purple."

Next, those nightmares of newlywed homemakers, raw sienna and burnt sienna. ("He likes his medium rare, boo-hoo.") Raw umber and burnt umber ("There, there, dear, we'll send out for pizza."), van-dyke brown, brown madder, thalo copper, silver, gold oxide, and payne's gray.

"Viridian, o viridian! Green earth, cadmium green, hooker's green" (protectress of novice prostitutes) "and sap green" (patron saint of voters who believe all Irish-American politicians are honest).

"O sing mars black, lamp black, ivory black, and titanium white" (blessed are the Caucasians who went down with the ship). "Sing iridescent white and light portrait pink."

What did she forget? Lily white, basic black, snow white, black beauty, white christmas, black friday, white supremacy, black power, the color purple, people-eater purple, the color of money, long green, lawn green, lorne green, *Lohengrin,* the color of your parachute, the color of my true love's hair, puce, mars puce, mars chartreuse, mars bars, little-boy blue, blue bayou, blues in the night, paint-the-town red, do-it-up brown, james brown, dorian gray, red skelton, red october, tom clancy red, better-dead-than red, better-ill-than teal, greenberg, gold-berg, long-john silver, mellow yellow, electrical banana, yellow peril, yellow fever, mayonnaise yellow, mustard, relish, and onions.

Ellen Cherry's head was spinning. She felt dizzy and faint. She should have known better than to mix rum and art supplies. With effort, she hauled her purchases to the checkout counter, where she parted with considerable cash. After the transaction, Dave called her a cab. She waited for it on the street so that she might inhale some crisp, cool air.

By the time that the taxi deposited her back at Isaac & Ishmael's, her vertigo had subsided, and her heartburn was but a dying ember. Spike and Abu had gone, as well. "I'll be doing some decorating," she informed the skeptical security guard, and she let herself in with her key. She wasted little time, but unpacked her supplies, arranged the paint jars in a row at the rear of the bandstand, fetched a stepladder from the pantry, turned up the thermostat, stripped down to her underpants, and went to work on the wall.

Whistling, humming, bobbing, weaving, scratching, contorting, swill-ing diet Pepsis, playing the eye game just like she used to do, she painted until well past midnight. Then she collapsed on the office couch where she and Spike Cohen had . . .

She awoke at dawn, toasted some pita bread, washed it down with milk, and surveyed what she had done. For the most part, it pleased her. There were contours that needed thinning, volumes that needed weight, lines to be shortened or lengthened, passages of color to be tinted or shaded: she was a bit rusty, after all. Yet, on the whole, it pleased her. And, of course, there was a lot of blank picture plane left to cover. The wall was eleven feet tall and fourteen feet long.

After calling Nabila to say that she would have to forgo Thanksgiving dinner due to a headache, she hopped back on the ladder and painted all day. Most of Thursday night she painted, and Friday and Friday night, Saturday and Saturday night, Sunday and Sunday night. She took daily sponge baths in Abu's beloved sink, but never changed her underwear, and long before Monday, it looked like . . . well, if Joseph had been a cross-dresser, the Bible might have made reference to his panties of many colors. ("The girls in the drawer are not going to believe this," said the polychrome briefs. "Om wooga nam.") The I & I she cleaned out of diet Pepsi and Coke, leftover *falafel, tahini,* and, yes, even *baba ghanoug.* By Sunday, she was having an hourly coffee with rum, just to keep the motor running.

When at 8:45 on Monday morning Spike showed up to admit the plasterers, Ellen Cherry was so deep in sleep that an industrial crane couldn't have lifted her out of it. Spike hovered over her, cursing the kidney stone that had knocked him loose from her embrace. His fingers itched to touch her nipples, although one of the nipples was gold oxide and the other mostly french ultramarine blue. Her feet, too, were spattered with paint. Nevertheless, Spike bent and kissed lightly his favorite toe. Then, he covered her nakedness with his *ongepotchket* coat and went to the kitchen to phone Abu.

"Our little artist lady has struck!" he announced. "The big one she's dropped."

"Send the plasterers home," said Abu, when he had learned the details.

When Ellen Cherry finally awoke, the bar was packed with men watching Monday night football. Each of them had noticed the new mural, but only one of them, Detective Jackie Shaftoe, followed it as avidly as he did the game.

Ellen Cherry dressed and slipped out the back door, through the frosty courtyard. She was still exhausted, but there was a zip in her step. She could have kicked the moon.

*   *   *

Now, Spike and Abu had two confounding works of art on their inexperienced hands, and throughout the week they studied them with equal zeal. The husband's piece, the sculpture, was the critical work, of course, since a decision about its deployment had to be made. On Thursday evening they made it.

Abu explained to Ellen Cherry their rationale. "Concerning this Pales character, I cannot suppose how much research your Boomer conducted—"

"Probably not very much. I'd guess he just stumbled across the story somewhere and took a shine to it."

"But we skipped tennis today so that we might verify his claims at the library."

"And did he have it straight?"

"Hoo boy! He told only the tip of the iceberg."

"Indeed, dear Cherry. It seems that the cult of the donkey deity extended throughout much of the ancient world. I was surprised to learn that Palatine Hill in Rome also was named for the clownish Pales."

"To our credit maybe—maybe not—we Hebrews tend to regard him as male. 'Iao,' we call him."

Ellen Cherry sang, "And on that farm he had an ass, Iao, Iao, O."

"You're laughing, already, but you may not be so wrong."

"As you accurately reported, Tacitus wrote that the Semites fell into venerating the ass because had it not been for wild asses they never would have survived in the desert. It was probably more complicated than that. How complicated? Well, it isn't enough that the children of Lilith, Adam's 'bad' wife, were born with donkey haunches or that Samson slew the Philistines with the jawbone of an ass or that Jesus chose to enter Jerusalem on the back of one of those scrawny steeds, but very early images of the Hebrew Messiah depicted him as an ass-headed man crucified on a tree."

"That's *wild*."

"Even earlier, in Egypt, there was an ass-headed deity my ancestors called Set, who was crucified annually and wounded in his side. On more than one Sunday morning in spring he rose from the dead."

"You're kidding."

"You're kidding, she says. That, little darlink, is what I'm saying to the next goy what is accusing my people of Christ-killing. You're kidding."

"As a goddess, Pales was the protectress of herd animals, thus insuring the survival of the tribe. As a bisexual, Pales was served by both priests and priestesses, usually dressed in big wooden donkey masks. The temples where Pales was worshipped gave us the word 'palace.' "

"Fascinating, you all."

"During the Festival of Palilia, which was appropriated into the Christian calendar as the Feast of Saint George, some rowdy games were played in those temples."

"I'll bet."

"Today's innocent children what're attending birthday parties where Pin the Tail on the Donkey is played—hoo!—they don't know what they do."

"Iao Iao O," said Ellen Cherry.

Since Pales had been an important religious figure, one whose pale specter still haunted the Western and Middle Eastern worlds, and since he—or she—was almost entirely forgotten, to a large extent deliberately obliterated by revisionist theologians, Spike and Abu thought that it might be a swell idea to revive the figure.

"It is dangerous to forget the past. Of course, it will be controversial, but it is such a lively sculpture, if the narrow-minded fundamentalists can rise above their insecurities, even they might enjoy the antics of our prancing donkey."

"A kick in and from the ass," said Ellen Cherry. "Well, I applaud your decision. There's a jarring poetics of spatiality in this piece. By that I mean the implicit assumption of unified form in space is exploded by the presence of three independent components—the rocks, the map, and the figure—that are only subliminally connected, but which playfully echo the constant clash of images and their meanings in the human mind."

Spike and Abu looked her over.

"Hoo, such *hoking a tchynik*," said the one.

"What's a girl like you doing in food service?" asked the other.

"But you know, you all still haven't told me what you think of my mural."

In truth, they weren't really clear about what they thought of it. Certainly, it would never occur to them to drape or replaster the wall, for that might hurt Ellen Cherry's feelings; and they had to admit, moreover, that the painting added color and energy to the room. Whether or not they understood it, appreciated it wholeheartedly, or supported it against the attacks of others, well, that was a horse of a different collar.

And it did invite a few attacks. Among the staff and clientele there were several who delighted in the mural, many who found it easiest to ignore it, and several who were affronted, even angered by what they took to be an insult to their ideas of art and their perceptions of reality. At various times, Abu and Spike fell into each of those camps, though seldom for longer than an hour.

When a British employee of the UN remarked, "My seven-year-old daughter could have painted that," Ellen Cherry responded icily in the only way one could to that most hackneyed and yahoo-brained of reactions to art:

"Maybe she could. But she didn't. And I did."

During cocktail hour on Friday, as the bar was filling with regulars, there was considerable banter concerning the painting, much of it lighthearted, none of it informed. After a particularly snide evaluation by the fat Egyptian doctor, Detective Shaftoe rose to his feet, lifted his can of beer to the mural, and said softly but very emphatically:

"Museum quality."

Then he sat back down.

The sullen, burly American black with the white hair and oft-broken nose was known to be a man who spoke only when he had something to say. The others respected his opinions. If Shaftoe pronounced the painting worthy of being hung in a museum, there wasn't a fellow in the room inclined to disagree. But the majority in the bar was also in harmony with the bartender when, after a deferential pause, he said:

"Guess that's why I don't go to no museums."

"*Any* museums," Dr. Farouk corrected him. Can o' Beans would have loved the guy.

The viewer's eye entered the painting through the beak of an owl. It was a nighttime painting. Although the scene, if one could call it a scene, was interior, the stars were nevertheless plainly visible, and the furniture was flecked with foam from the moon.

Through a diamond-shaped window, animals could be seen snoring on a hillside.

There were prominent architectural overtones, but the picture, if one could call it a picture, might also be read as a landscape. Wasn't that an oak tree shading the cookstove, and wasn't the oak choked with mistletoe?

Gooey and thick, the paint had been applied with luxurious abandon, and yet the mood it evoked was not of modern luxury but of preindustrial grandeur; the black, muddy, smoky grandeur of life at the edge of great forests. Pastoral pageantry. The woodcutters' ball.

To the extent that the imagery suggested a rediscovery of a forgotten past, it likewise suggested that that "lost" past was the perfect expression of contemporary urban sensibilities. From where had the city-dwellers come, after all? What was the metropolitan equivalent of jollifications around the bonfire or of the fanged things that ambushed maidens on their way to the well?

Though the painting was heavy and dense, pulled by gravity like the skin of a crone, nothing stood still in it. The mushrooms, the fetishes, the wool and the wine, the mascara jars, the poppies, the crickets, the poison arrows, the bravura helixes of juicy smoke all spun like the stars: onward, outward, inward, backward, sideways, upside down, and forever. The iron sword that was embedded in the trunk of the oak was as vibrant as the little silver spoon that bounced on the buffalo hide, the golden cradle that was balanced in the crotch of the tree rocked so hard that the sky rocked with it, a zodiac transformed into a music hall.

Despite its complexity, its nocturnal richness, there was something slaphappy if not slapdash about it, something careless and childlike. Itch as it might with stellar information, buckle though it might under a weight of ashes, adobe, and bone, it also was as topsy-turvy as a nursery rhyme; it was kachina pinball, an episode from chipmunk television.

It was not unlike—and one is forced to say this—the room of the wolfmother wallpaper. Salome, when she arrived for her Friday night performance, took one long, captivated look at it and consented to dance the Dance of the Seven Veils.

She didn't perform the Dance of the Seven Veils that night, as Abu was led to believe she would. "Will she be doing it tomorrow night, then?" he asked the bandleader at the conclusion of the show. Salome had already departed. She seldom spoke, in any case, partly due to shyness, partly to the fact that she had a pronounced lisp, partly to some cultural code to which she was said to adhere. "Will she be doing it tomorrow?"

"Such is not the case."

"Next week, then?"

"Such is not the case."

"Well, *when?*"

"Further into the future."

"Oh, I get it. *Mish mish.* When the bloody apricots bloom."

"No, no, my benefactor, no. The month of the dance shall be January. The date of the dance shall be the twenty-third. The day of the dance shall be Sunday. The hour of the dance shall be three o'clock P.M. in the afternoon."

"Hmmm. I see. Well, that is precise enough. I will not trouble you to explain how she arrived at that particular time, although I should point out that that is a good seven weeks away."

"She is of need to prepare herself," the bandleader said. There was no enamel in his mouth to stand in the way of his saying it.

Management hadn't planned to reveal it right away, but word leaked out faster than radiation from a government reactor, and by showtime on Saturday, the whole restaurant, from kitchen to admission line, was squeaky with Seven Veil helium. Nearly everybody had the date wrong, however, and those few who pinpointed the day set the hour anywhere from dawn to midnight. So, Abu borrowed the microphone from the bandleader and, standing tall and dignified, his nose a fluorescent traffic cone in the spotlight, he cleared his throat and began, "Ladies and gentlemen, Isaac and Ishmael's, your home for the multicultural cuisine of Jerusalem, is proud to announce . . ."

He closed to a glove factory of applause. Even the hip refugees from Payday and Nell's, people who prided themselves on never expressing enthusiasm for anything (unless alone in front of a mirror), slapped one damp palm against the other, although they were careful not to emit a hoot or whistle. The place was so noisy that only those near the front of the bar heard Detective Shaftoe when he exclaimed, "There's a catch!"

Among those who did hear him were Spike and Abu, the Greek delegate, the Egyptian doctor, the Cypriot economists, and a table of Israeli regulars from the Peace Now organization. Each of them looked at Shaftoe expectantly, a little anxiously.

"There's a goddamn catch to it!" he repeated. There was a note of betrayal in Shaftoe's voice, a note of helplessness and skepticism, as if even he couldn't believe what his police-trained memory was telling him was true.

The Super Bowl.

The Super Bowl.

The Super Bowl, the Super Bowl, the Super Bowl, the Super Bowl.

By innocent coincidence or diabolical design, Salome had scheduled the Dance of the Seven Veils to commence simultaneously with the kickoff of the Super Bowl game.

Conflicts flared almost instantaneously. On the one side, there were those for whom the legendary Dance of the Seven Veils had taken on the proportions of fabulous personal fantasy—romantic, erotic, opulent, mysterious; resonant with long-lost exotica, secrets of the Bible and secrets of the East: they would have crawled ten kilometers on a carpet of dog poop and razor blades to witness it, were it the genuine article; and with this devastating nymph who called herself Salome, there was no question of authenticity. On the other side were those for whom the Super Bowl was the most anticipated event of each and every year, the culmination of five months of thrills, endless statistics, ego boosts, and severe disappointments; a major holiday, no, *the* major holiday, a day when routine and care were suspended; when the nation, the world, came together as one; a festival that cut across national, racial, and religious boundaries; a ritual during which no time existed except the artificial time on the game clock, a symbolic battle in which only token blood was shed and for the duration of which the grip of death on the human psyche was relaxed and put aside: Isaac & Ishmael's still had the biggest, sharpest television screen in midtown Manhattan, and this group had every intention of watching the game on it.

It was not, however, a matter of two warring camps, the one demanding Salome, the other, the Super Bowl. At least, not at first it wasn't. In the beginning, the majority of the I & I's regular patrons straddled the fence. They wanted the game *and* the dance. Sgt. Jackie Shaftoe, for example, couldn't even conceive of having to choose between them.

To their credit as humanitarians, Spike and Abu acted to nip the divisiveness in the bud. That very night, seven weeks before the twenty-third of January, they sought to avert conflict through compromise.

Salome's ride was late that night, so she waited in the office for her chaperon to come through the courtyard and fetch her. That is where they approached her. She was breathing hard from the exertion of the performance, and her body was so bathed in sweat that her clothing stuck to her, causing her thighs to present themselves like mackerel fillets on a platter, and her nipples to protrude like rubber erasers through wet Kleenex. A pearly mustache of perspiration accentuated the ripeness of her mouth, making it appear as if it had been sucking on a peach, and her hair was plastered against her neck as if she had just emerged from a bath—or a wedding bed. To Spike's and Abu's great relief, she'd covered her *marquise au chocolat* eyes with thick spectacles, through which she was busily reading an Uncle Scrooge comic book. Had it not been for the glasses and the funnies, they might not have been controlled enough to approach her at all.

As it turned out, it was futile anyway. In her dewy lisp, she told them politely, "My schedule is fixed, sirs. It's in the stars. I dance then or never."

What could they do but assure her that the date was fine, was perfect, was hunky-dory, was resplendent with lucky omens, and wore a carnation in its buttonhole? They waved meekly as she slipped into a heavy wool coat and, glasses steaming over, vanished into the courtyard on the arm of her protectress.

Over the next couple of days, Salome's decision was relayed to the regular clientele, who now numbered between thirty and forty men and a half dozen women, where it was generally accepted, though not without grumbling and grousing.

"She could do that dance any old time she pleases. Right? So why does she have to do it while the game is on? What's the deal?"

"As zee inspector says, it ees a catch. A treek of some kind. She ees sabotaging zee football."

"No, no, come on. There's no hidden agenda. She just doesn't care, that's all. She's a chick."

"I resent that. Millions of chicks watch the Super Bowl. Someday we may be playing in it."

"Ha-ha."

"Fat chance."

"When the apricots bloom."

During Salome's performances the following weekend, several patrons yelled relevant comments at her, some of them pleading, some openly resentful. She paid them scant attention. In fact, she was dancing better than ever, with more vim, more daring, more open-heartedness.

"She must be working up to the Seven Veils," said a fan.

"Naw," the bartender disagreed. "The bandleader says that she just gets off dancing in front of that painting."

Salome and Sergeant Shaftoe weren't quite the only living souls to respond enthusiastically to Ellen Cherry's mural. An artist, a collector, and a trio of gallery poufs took their eyes off the shim-sham-shimmey long enough to hurdle along the starlit obstacle course of Ellen Cherry's creation, sliding on a sheet of pure color here, banging against the shadowy edge of a rectangle there, in pursuit of her elusive organic forms. They were impressed enough to later discuss the mural down in SoHo, presumably within earshot of Ultima Sommervell, because one noon the dealer showed up at the I & I for lunch.

"Darling, how simply interesting. I daresay this is your finest work. It is. It's a breakthrough, don't you think?"

"It's pretty much the same as I've always painted."

"Oh, but scale can make a difference. Size *is* important, no matter what our apologist sisters say." Ultima laughed a spray-the-roses, there-will-always-be-an-England sort of laugh. "It's more than the large format, though. It's your syntax. The way in which you've orchestrated a structural quarrel between the metaphoric and the metonymic. What is this I'm eating?"

"It's called *baba ghanoug*."

"Jolly well named." With her fork, she pushed the puddle of beige stuff aside. "In terms of content, you seem to cross, recross, and sometimes erase the boundaries between interior and exterior, between past and present, between the abstract and the concrete. Without resorting to the cheap theatrics of surrealism, you've painted a portrait of nighttime consciousness, which is to say, of the feminine side, of the right brain, of intuition."

"Well . . . this picture *is* more out of my intuition than out of my experience," Ellen Cherry conceded. "Say, maybe you'd like to sample some—" But try as she might, she couldn't think of anything more horrific than the *baba ghanoug*.

It wasn't that Ellen Cherry was unappreciative of Ultima's *hoking a tchynik*. The dealer had eyes, no doubt about it. But Ellen Cherry hadn't analyzed the painting, and she was less than eager to entertain anybody else's analysis. On a conscious level, she wasn't sure what the painting meant or even where it had come from, she knew only that it was a work of complicated and unexpected beauty and that she was somehow responsible for it. Beauty! Wasn't that what mattered? Beauty was hardly a popular ideal at that jumpy moment in history. The masses had been desensitized to it, the intelligentsia regarded it with suspicion. To most of her peers, "beauty" smacked of the rarefied, the indulgent, the superfluous, the effete. How could persons of good conscience pursue the beautiful when there was so much suffering and injustice in the world? Ellen Cherry's answer was that if one didn't cultivate beauty, soon he or she wouldn't be able to recognize ugliness. The prevalence of social ugliness made commitment to physical beauty all the more essential. And the very presence in life of double-wide mobile homes, Magic Marker graffiti, and orange shag carpeting had the effect of making ills such as poverty, crime, repression, pollution, and child abuse seem tolerable. In a sense, beauty was the ultimate protest, and, in that it generally lasted longer than an orgasm, the ultimate refuge. The Venus de Milo screamed "No!" at evil, whereas the Spandex stretch pant, the macramé plant holder were compliant with it. Ugly bedrooms bred ugly habits. Of course, it wasn't required of beauty that it perform a social function. That was what was valuable about it. Even more than virtue, it was its own reward. To be sure, there were those who maintained that beauty was in the eye of the beholder, and there were beholders who thought her mural was the print of the paw of the pukemaster, but those guys could just kiss her feisty fanny, which *everybody* agreed was beautiful.

Neighbor against neighbor, countryman against countryman, brother against brother, boss against employee, husband against wife. If conditions at Isaac & Ishmael's sound like civil war, then those are the boots it must wear, because as the year flipped from old to new on its solar hinge, those were how conditions were.

Instead of Fort Sumter, it was a none-too-posh cocktail lounge; instead of a garrison, it was a motley crowd of Americans and foreigners watching TV; instead of a cannon, the shot that touched it off was fired from a timekeeper's buzzer. It happened on a weekend afternoon, the day that a National Football League team from New York City—whether the Jets or the Giants isn't really important— won the playoff title in its conference (the first time that had happened since 1986) and the right to play for all the marbles in the Super Bowl game.

"New York's in!" screamed one of the locals. "Now, by God, we *got* to watch the game."

"Absolutely. Salome must drop her veils some other day."

"Well, she's not going to change her time and that's final. So maybe you should watch the game some other place."

"Some other place?" The fellow was incredulous.

"Perhaps she should stage her sleazy striptease some other place."

"She dances here, not some other place."

"Well, I watch football here, not some other place."

"So it is a 'sleazy striptease' now, is it?"

"You guys got pussy on the brain."

"And you gentlemen have zee football on zee brains."

"It's not football, damn it! It's the Super Bowl!"

"It's not zee pussy, it's zee Dance of zee Seven Veils."

"Come on. Smarten up. The Super Bowl is the pure spirit of America. It sums up this country, it's what we're all about. You miss the Super Bowl, you miss the whole point of being here, jack."

"Ha! You think we are in this country to watch wealthy gorillas play schoolyard games?"

"No, I guess you must be here to watch teenage pussy shake a tambourine."

"Dickhead!"

"Your English is improving, frog mouth."

"I was under the impression," said Dr. Farouk, "that this was a democracy."

"Fuckin'-*a*, it's a democracy."

"Then we must vote."

At that point, Spike and Abu stepped in. "Okay," said Spike. "Okay. We'll have an election, already."

"But not today," put in Abu. "There must be time to weigh the issues, time for each side to make its case. Think about it, discuss it, and in two weeks you shall vote. Mr. Cohen and I shall remain neutral. We shall tally your votes and declare a winner."

All agreed that that was fair. All but one, that is. "It isn't going to work. You can vote between money for schools or no money for schools, you can vote between Jesse Jackson or some jive-ass Republican, but can't nobody with a drop of juice in 'em vote between the Dance of the Seven Veils or the Super Bowl." As usual, Detective Shaftoe was correct.

As was customary in modern election campaigns, fair play was shunned from the start. Spike and Abu were forced to waste an inordinate amount of time working to insure an honest poll. Their efforts were about as effective as Mother Hubbard's pet care. Proponents of both sides were bringing in relatives, friends, and casual acquaintances, and trying to palm them off as eligible voters, which is to say, regular patrons of the I & I. It was difficult to sort them out, for to Spike most Arabs looked alike, and Abu had the same problem with Jews. Race or national origin had little to do with which side people took, however. There were North Africans who compaigned diligently for football, Americans who passionately endorsed the dance. And vice versa. Straight women and male homosexuals were solidly behind Salome. Lesbians supported the Super Bowl.

In the flush of excitement that followed New York's victory in the playoffs, the majority leaned decidedly toward the ball game. Then came Friday night, upon which Salome, though as pouty and uncomfortable as ever, danced as if she were bareback on a bucking python, danced like a police whistle in a raid on a bordello, danced like a self-winding watch on the wrist of Saint Vitus. The pendulum swung.

"But I just don't see how I can deliberately miss the Super Bowl," said one perplexed gentleman. "It seems . . . unnatural."

"Consider this, my friend. When was the last time you saw a Super Bowl that wasn't as dull as bouillon?"

"Well . . ."

"Be honest. Ninety percent of the games have been boring."

"Lots of important things are boring. Church is boring. That's no excuse for not going. The UN is boring."

"Salome is not church, and she's not the UN—"

"You can say that again."

"Right you are."

"—and the Dance of the Seven Veils will never be mundane."

"Couldn't be."

"Hardly."

"Not a chance."

"Yeah, but still . . ."

As election day drew near, Spike and Abu carefully calculated the outcome. After much observation, private polling, and scientific conjecture, they concluded that twenty-five percent of eligible voters favored the game, thirty percent favored the dance, and the remaining forty-five percent not only were undecided, they were so ambivalent, so torn, that they probably wouldn't vote at all.

"Any way we dismember this chicken," said Abu, "it is going to be an unhappy bird."

"Oy!" exclaimed Spike. "Palestine it's resembling."

Ellen Cherry had watched the fluxions, the dirty tricks, the acrimony and confusion with detached amusement. Personally, she wanted the dance, but only out of curiosity, and she was curious only because she'd learned that her mural had influenced Salome's decision to perform it. Of course, she had never been especially attracted to athletics. One of the few things she had always admired about Boomer Petway was how he'd lain down the shot put and taken up the tango.

One day she had asked some men at the bar, "What would happen if God snatched your balls away? You know the balls I'm referring to. Suppose a spaceship flew into our atmosphere and beamed up every ball on the planet. Every last football, baseball, tennis ball, basketball, volleyball, golfball, shot put, softball, squash ball, soccer ball, pool ball, bowling ball, even croquet and polo balls, all of them. What would happen? Would the male population go slowly berserk? Would blood flow in the streets? Would you boys just curl up and die? Or would it expedite the evolution of a higher species of mammal?"

A few of them had looked at her sheepishly, the others as if she were dangerously dumb.

"Spaceships do not exist," said the Egyptian doctor dryly.

"They better not beam up no *goof*balls or you in big trouble," warned Shaftoe. Those who were familiar with the expression had a hearty laugh.

For weeks the controversy had raged around her, yet if Ellen Cherry found it impossible to ignore, she found it entirely possible to belittle. There were more primary concerns snapping off of the synapses beneath her pecan and chicory curls, not the least of which was Patsy's impending arrival, bag and baggage; lock, stock, and barrel; hook, line, and sinker; bell, book, and candle; Merrill Lynch, Pierce, Fenner, Smith and Non Sequitur.

In preparation for her mama's Christmas Eve entry into the nonstop espresso machine of Manhattan, she had whited out with gesso all the nude portraits of Boomer Petway. That operation had served the dual purpose of concealing her artistic adoration of Boomer's heavy equipment (although she had every reason to suspect that Patsy's captivation with the manly apparatus exceeded her own) and of providing her with fresh blank surfaces upon which to paint. She was cramping and bloating with the urge to paint, a kind of PMS, and one of her fears was that with Patsy in the apartment she would lack both the privacy and the space.

She'd then proceeded to white-over the pictures of the dirty socks and the bean cans, including the half-can that remained from her last foray into gesso. (Thousands of miles away, a deformed, barracuda-bitten, and thoroughly naked Can o' Beans—the last remnants of his/her identifying label having dissolved in the tepid waters of the eastern Mediterranean—issued a sudden groan, as if telepathically receiving the news. "Hold on awhile longer, you must, you must," commanded Conch Shell, who even then could detect the sonic vibrations that advertised the surf smacking a pier in Tel Aviv.) Next, Ellen Cherry had turned to the spoons. One by one, she covered them up, trembling all the while, until there was but a single spoon portrait remaining. That one she had half a mind to preserve as a reminder of the bewildering impact upon her life of the spoon's enigmatic appearances and disappearances (she still suspected that Secret Agent Petway was somehow responsible) and, just as significantly, of the oceanic rapture and arcane knowledge with which the spoon had rewarded her when she had subjected it to the eye game. Upon reflection, however, she'd decided that there were things in this world upon which it was best not to dwell lest they attach themselves to one's keel like barnacles, and slowly cause one to leak, to list, and eventually to sink. She had regained much of the equilibrium she'd lost since moving to New York and didn't wish to risk being thrown off balance again by the weight of a weird dessert spoon. But wait a moment! There were ways in which that spoon, the very weirdness of that spoon, had assisted her in righting herself. Hadn't the spoon pierced, as if it were a fork, the rigidity of her ego, and wasn't a tight ego the source of many an individual's misery; and, furthermore, hadn't she intuitively painted a spoon into her mural at the I & I? In the end, she chose to save the one spoon picture, but to keep it safely turned to the wall.

There was one painting left with which to deal: the portrait of Boomer with the seven various tongues. That one she delivered to the Sommervell Gallery. Ultima found it inferior to the I & I mural, into which she continued to read social and political meaning even while complaining that the mural accentuated feminism's soft dark underbelly. Nevertheless, Ultima was certain that the portrait was commercially viable, due mainly to its subject. Boomer's reputation loomed even larger on the New York art scene since he had deserted the scene for Israel. "Were he Jewish," said Ultima, "his flight to Jerusalem would have produced only nods and clucks. But here we have a white southern hillbilly Gentile. . . . Well, my dear, our Mr. Petway does keep them guessing." The portrait sold within forty-eight hours for five thousand dollars, allowing Ellen Cherry to escape eviction. It would have been awkward had Patsy arrived to find her camping in the streets on Christmas Eve.

Prior to Patsy's arrival, a letter had arrived from Boomer. Ellen Cherry had written to him, as well. Their letters had crossed, perhaps over the Atlantic (whose chops Conch Shell and Can o' Beans had managed to negotiate just ahead of wintry storms), perhaps over Jerusalem itself, over Gaza, over *intifada,* over stones, sheep heads, honey cakes, rubber bullets, and the endless caravans of ancient superstitions.

Boomer had reported that the Pales sculpture was finished and soon to be installed. Its unveiling was scheduled for the final week in January. After that, he would have some decisions to make. In the meantime, Buddy Winkler would be coming over, though probably not until after the inauguration, toward the middle of the month. In the last paragraph, Boomer wrote rather movingly about the sweet torture of having glimpsed her again, although only after first crowing over the success of his masquerade. "Looking at you in your kimono, it felt like some backyard chef was sprinkling meat tenderizer on my heart," he scrawled. "A month-old baby could of gummed my heart up like pablum. An old boy with a bleeding ulcer could of digested it easy as cream."

As for Ellen Cherry's note, it was succinct enough to fit on a Hallmark card. "Dear Husband and Master of Disguise," it read. "Thanks for the lovely roses. I knew it was you all the time."

Patsy's plane had been an hour late, touching down at noon on the day before Christmas. Her emotions were as frizzled as her hair. "Another hayseed blows into Big Town," she announced as she came through the gate. "Lord, honey, why didn't I stay down yonder where I belong? I'm way too old and got way too much insurance money to be let loose in a meat grinder like this. I feel like handing over my purse to the first ol' boy I meet on the corner, save him the trouble of fleecing me."

"Aw, mama, you underestimate your shrewdness and overestimate your net worth. You're going to be broke in no time, all right, but it'll be landlords and Bloomingdale's that get your stash."

That night they fried chicken and trimmed a delapidated little spruce that looked more lost and scared in New York than Patsy did. They drank a fair amount of eggnog with rum in it and ended up crying, mostly over Verlin, although a dozen tears were reserved for Boomer Petway and a half dozen for men in general.

The next morning, Patsy was a bit more intact. "If Bud can get by in this huge ol' place," she said to her bacon, "then so can I."

"You'll do fine, mama. But please let's not talk about Uncle Bud."

"He'll be expecting to see me."

"Okay, if you want to, but not under my roof."

They switched the topic of conversation to Isaac & Ishmael's and Ellen Cherry went on at some length about Salome, her wide following and narrow calves, and the furious flap that was festering: the Dance of the Seven Veils vs. the Super Bowl. Patsy was fascinated and asked lots of questions. "I could of been a dancer myself," she said plaintively, her fork circling the high-relief of her waffle like a disabled warplane circling a mountainous region, searching for a place to land.

Her first week in New York, Patsy Charles refused to leave the Ansonia unless in the company of her daughter. While Ellen Cherry was at work, Patsy would clean the apartment and dance to Neville Brothers tapes, naked except for white go-go boots. Once, standing at the window, she'd said to Ellen Cherry, "It sounds so harsh out there. It's a wonder it hasn't rubbed calluses on you."

"It can do that," said Ellen Cherry. "It can also polish you, make you shine. I remember what Boomer wrote to me once about the Middle East. 'The rougher the world gets around me, the sweeter I seem to myself.' I guess it's all in how you receive it."

"That Boomer."

"Yep," she sighed. "That Boomer."

Eventually, Ellen Cherry began to take her mama to the I & I with her. Patsy helped out in the kitchen and bussed tables in the bar. It gave her something to do and allowed her both to study her daughter's mural and to witness firsthand the terrible row over the dance and the game. She understood the magnetic pull of football since it had, in her opinion, been the death of her husband, but it wasn't until she actually saw Salome perform that she could appreciate the spell the girl cast upon an audience.

"Lordy mercy," said Patsy. "She's a half-cooked little fritter, but a fellow'd have to be coated with Teflon not to let her stick to his pan."

A few days later, there was a brawl in the bar. It started when a Super-Bowl-hating woman raked her husband's cheeks with long crimson fingernails, and quickly spread to other tables before Detective Shaftoe broke it up by firing his snub-nosed .38 in the air. The slug ricocheted off a pipe in the ceiling and struck the mural. A sound came out of the bullet hole like the faroff howling of a wolf.

* * *

"That settles it," said Abu, when he and Spike showed up from the tennis club. Shaftoe and the security guards were still arguing over the detective's right to bring a gun into the restaurant. "That settles it. We are canceling the election."

"Hoo boy!" said Spike. "We sound like a banana republic."

"But you have a plan," Abu reminded him.

"Correct. We're kaputting the election and moving on to Plan B."

Plan B was Spike Cohen's idea. So disturbed was he by the discord that the conflict between the game and the dance had generated that he had volunteered to purchase several large, expensive, industrial heaters and a canvas canopy so that the giant TV set might be moved temporarily into the courtyard behind the I & I. It wouldn't be nearly as comfortable as indoors, but there would be food and beverage service at card tables, and those customers who still couldn't settle on one event or the other might move back and forth, if it suited them, between the Dance of the Seven Veils and the Super Bowl.

As the fateful Sunday was now only eight days away, almost everybody seemed grateful for the compromise. "Looks fine," muttered Shaftoe. *"On paper."*

On Monday, January 17, Patsy had lunch with Buddy Winkler. She begged Ellen Cherry to go with her, alas, in vain, so she ventured forth alone and, after nine or ten timid attempts, succeeded in flagging down a taxi. To Patsy's surprise, the address where the cab deposited her was that of a Middle Eastern restaurant. "Why're we eating this kind of food?" she asked, once she had flustered the good reverend by giving him a hug.

" 'Cause I'm going off to Jerusalem in the morning, and I need to accustom my taste buds. I got lots to do over yonder, and I can't afford to be distracted by queer and unappealin' sustenance. Your next question, I reckon, is why I didn't choose to acclimatize my palate in that greasy Gomorrah where Verlin Charles's only girl is breakin' her dead daddy's heart."

"Why no, Bud," said Patsy, "I was fixing to ask who dressed you. I mean, that there's a right pretty suit you got on, but that necktie looks like something the cat drug in, and isn't your shirt a tad heavy on the starch? I was fixing to ask if you couldn't use a woman's touch. In regards to your wardrobe, I mean. But now that you've gone and tol' me you're lighting out for Is-ra-el, I reckon my question has got to be, 'Why?' What is it that you're aiming to do in that troubled place? I *know* why you wouldn't take your lunch at Isaac and Ishmael's, although Verlin Charles did eat there on one occasion. And that brings up another question, *two* other questions. Can hearts really break once they're dead and gone? And do you suppose that when Jesus Christ comes back to rule in Jerusalem, the menu over yonder will then feature biscuits and ham gravy?"

The Reverend Buddy Winkler just stared at her, shaking his head, as if he were a kindly but exasperated teacher of arithmetic regarding a pupil more interested in flipping spitballs than in mastering the life-enhancing practicalities of long division. The waiter appeared, and they each ordered *shish tawook* with cucumbers.

"I reckon you find it better at Isaac and Ishmael's," Buddy said when it was served.

"To be honest, no," said Patsy. "Theirs tastes a bit like kerosene."

"How could anything taste right in that atmosphere? Where that hussy dances?"

"You know about Salome?"

"The whole blessed town knows 'bout that little harlot. Can you imagine? Namin' herself after the second most evil woman in the Scriptures! A deliberate insult to the memory of John the Baptist. If I wasn't sure the world was endin' soon, this evil 'round about us would plumb spoil my appetite."

"It's right around the corner, is it, Bud?"

"Oh, Patsy, you can't believe how slick everything's fallin' into place." With a wooden kabob skewer, he tapped the tabletop (no bamboo place mats in *that* Middle Eastern restaurant). *Tap tap tap.* "All the prophecies." *Tap tap tap.* "Fallin' into place." *Tap tap tap.* "One by one." *Tap tap tap.* "Pretty as a speckled pup." He laid the skewer down. " 'Course the Kremlin is foulin' things up, wouldn't you know? New regime in there with 'glassnose' or whatever, talkin' peace and disarmament, tryin' to cool things off. Naturally, the Russians don't want the fiery end to come, they're atheists, they're gonna burn. Russia is deliberately slowin' down the process. They're the ones monkeyin' with God's timetable. And that's why I got to do . . . what I got to do. Get things back on track. Over in Jerusalem, they eat these here cucumbers for breakfast. For *breakfast*! Have you ever . . . ?"

"You're gonna fool with that Dome of the Rock."

"Hush. I can't say nothing further. That daughter of yourn has become a thorn in my side. She can't be trusted. Let us lament the iniquities into which the paintbox of Jezebel has led her. Let us—"

"Let us change the damn subject before I get my dandruff up. I'm not putting up with you bad-mouthing Ellen Cherry."

"Oh, Patsy."

They finished the meal in silence. As they waited for the bill, Buddy said, "I want you to know I'm real thankful that Verlin remembered my mission in his will."

"Your mission's got a highly substantial cash flow, don't it, Bud?"

"Armageddons do not come cheap."

"Tell me this: what if your violent scheme succeeds and you blow the Arab thing to pieces and make the trouble over yonder even worse than it is already—and then the Messiah still doesn't come?"

After a short pause, during which he employed a kabob skewer to pry a microchip of green pepper from between his gold teeth, Buddy said, "Then I reckon I'll have to step in and be the Messiah."

With such horrified disbelief did Patsy look at him that he drew his palm instinctively, self-consciously across the wafflescape of his face and said, "Don't worry, the prophecies don't fib, and if they do, then life don't mean applesauce and never did." He snatched up a saucer of *baba ghanoug* and held it so close to her eyes that she had no choice but to gaze at the dead civilizations submerged in its goop.

That evening, about the time that Patsy was telling Ellen Cherry that Uncle Bud's ambitions might well be bigger than she had ever imagined ("I thought he just wanted to see himself on the TV"), about the time that the reverend was laying out a bulletproof vest in the bottom of his traveling bag, there came a sharp rapping at his door. Two men stood there, one of whom Bud recognized as the fellow who'd engaged him in questionable conversation the evening of the fire at St. Patrick's Cathedral. Smiling politely, they displayed plastic cards identifying themselves as employees of the Central Intelligence Agency. They asked to see first his driver's license, then his passport and airline ticket to Jerusalem. The driver's license they returned, the passport they confiscated, the ticket they tore into confetti.

"We'd appreciate it, Reverend Winkler, if you'd please come with us," said the familiar one.

"Looky here, I got me a whole pisspot of the finest Hebrew lawyers in this city, and when they get through with you boys, you gonna wish you been home watchin' 'I Spy' reruns with the little woman." He reached for the telephone, but a fist closed around his wrist, immobilizing it.

"You don't want to discuss this with your attorneys, believe me you don't. In a few hours, you'll understand why. Now get your overcoat. We got a plane to catch."

It wasn't until he saw the Washington Monument, illuminated by floodlights, that Buddy realized in what direction they had been flying. (Their Lear jet, which bore the corporate logo of a newspaper chain that the evangelist believed to be headquartered out West somewhere, had taken off from a military airfield in New Jersey.) In a few minutes, they crossed the Potomac River and completed their descent.

A stretch limo, so glossy black that Buddy mistook it for a shadow, was waiting on the tarmac. "Least you're kidnappin' me in style," muttered Buddy, who'd been unusually subdued during the flight. The car already contained one passenger, a guy in sweats, or, more precisely, a gentleman in powder blue Gucci running togs. He was sipping from a can of Miller Lite. When Bud grew accustomed to the dim light, he recognized the boyish good looks of the vice president of the United States.

"Care for a brewski, Reverend Winkler?"

"Well . . . I don't normally touch alcohol, but, okay, thank you, sir."

One of the agents, who had joined them in the gently rolling acreage of the backseat, pulled another can of Miller Lite from an inset refrigerator and popped its tab. Buddy took a long, anxious swallow.

"Tastes great," he said.

"Less filling," said the vice president.

Buddy did not think to argue.

For an hour they drove around in the frosty Virginia night, past sub-division after sleeping subdivision, each as restrained in temperament as the British-sounding name it bore (Pickwick Farms, The Greensward, Dippingdale Creek); past drive-in picture shows with lifeless screens, past massive shopping malls designed to resemble colonial towns, now dark and deserted, their cash registers cooling down like runners after a marathon. They drove the speed limit, no faster, no slower, stop-ping only once, in the parking lot of a colonial-style McDonald's, where the vice president got out and urinated into the shrubbery.

As they drove, the vice president talked. His voice was cheerful in a flat sort of way, but with an adenoidal edge that under the proper stimulus might whine with a kind of Eagle Scout hysteria. He thanked the preacher for his tireless ministries on behalf of God Almighty and Freedom Land. He was not only sympathetic, he said, to Buddy's plot to bomb the Dome of the Rock (with which he seemed to be familiar down to the last detail) but also grateful, he said, and admiring. It was a job that needed doing, according to the vice president. But, unfortunately, not just yet.

"You see," said the Veep, "and I'm speaking to you in strictest confidence, we have a president of this republic who's a hypocrite."

"Now, Mr. Vice President . . ." cautioned one of the operatives.

"A fine and good leader in many respects," the young statesman continued, "but in certain matters of utmost concern to, ah, true Christians everywhere, he's, sadly, not with us. He pays lip service to those, uh, matters of faith, but the truth is, Reverend Winkler, our President just does not believe even the teeniest bit in the prophecy. Well, that's not quite a fact, he does believe a teeny bit in the prophecy in a, uh, abstract, distant, on-paper sort of way; he just doesn't believe in the fulfillment of Ezekiel in our time. Why, I don't think he *wants* the fulfillment of Ezekiel! I don't think he wants the Rapture. You should see the way he rolls his eyes at me whenever I bring it up. I feel sometimes he's mocking me. Mocking *us*."

"You don't say?" clucked Buddy, his head buzzing with scriptures and historical facts that he could quote to the President to prove that Ezekiel's visions were rising like catfish all around them, that fire and brimstone were set to rain, and that those disarmament treaties that delayed that earth-burning rain succeeded only in spotting points to the anti-Christ.

As the limo glided past the neo-Tudor edifices of Tally Ho Estates, the vice president explained that were Buddy and the Third Temple Platoon to attack the Dome of the Rock in the near future, there was every indication that the President would join with Russia, would side with the evil Gog, itself, to try to forestall the nuclear purge of which Zechariah had spoken so graphically, and which the destruction of the heathen mosque *ought* to precipitate, if things were allowed to run their rightful course.

The Veep warned Bud that to level the Dome of the Rock while the current president was in office was to risk gumming up the works. He asked Bud—he ordered Bud—to be patient just awhile longer, to wait until there was someone more enlightened in the White House. And he indicated that that might not necessarily be as many years away as Bud might think.

The lights of the airfield, haloed like Nordic madonnas in the frosty air, could be seen again when Buddy was warned, further, against the prideful folly of unilateral action. "I admire your courage, but, look, Pat and Jerry have got a, uh, stake in this, too, and frankly they're a notch higher up the chain of command than you. We have to all pull together. Understood?"

"Guaranteed, sir. Verily, verily I say unto you—"

But before he could so much as blow the spit out of his saxophone, the vice president interrupted. "Say, reverend," he asked, "who do you like in the Super Bowl?"

"Indianapolis," blurted Buddy hopefully, then instantly regretted it. Something in the Veep's tone when he said, "That's real cute, fellow," led Bud to believe that the Colts hadn't made it that year.

When the limo came to rest on the tarmac again, Buddy's host pumped his hand. "God bless you," he said, and the door flew open as if on cue. Forty yards away, the Lear jet was already warming its engines.

"Any questions?" an agent asked, as Bud was buckled into his seat.

"Nope. Well, er, yeah, there's one puny item that's been a-troublin' me. You boys obviously been nosin' 'round inside my apartment.

Now, I ain't complainin'. Y'all had to do it, y'all was jest doin' y'all's job. Y'all been in my place on more'n one occasion, most likely, and I was jest wonderin': at any time did you happen to remove from the premises—for your own good reasons, naturally—a spoon, a little bitty silver spoon, and a colored stick? The stick wouldda had funny little horns on it."

From the way the agents looked at him, and then at one another, Buddy couldn't help but fear that whatever credibility he had had with the powers on high had probably now been squandered.

What was that sound? That rustling noise? It could be heard in the icy North, where there was not one leaf left upon one tree, it could be heard in the South, where the crinoline skirts lay deep in moth-balls, as still and quiet as wool. It could be heard from sea to shining sea, o'er purple mountains' majesty and upon the fruited plain. What was it? Why, it was the rustle of thousands of bags of potato chips being pulled from supermarket racks; it was the rustle of plastic bags being filled with beer and soda pop and quarts of hard liquor; it was the rustle of newspaper pages fanning as readers turned eagerly to the sports section; it was the rustle of currency changing hands as tickets were scalped for forty times their face value and two hundred and seventy million dollars were wagered upon one or the other of two professional football teams. It was the rustle of Super Bowl week, drowning out the sobs of the homeless, the jabber of the mad, the death rattle of AIDS victims, and the sad, disgraceful news from Israel a.k.a. Palestine; drowning out, too, the motorboat idlings of happy infants, the whoops of lottery winners, the buttery grunts of lovers, the prayers of the traditionally devout, and the chants of those who repeated (and repeated) exotic syllables in meditation centers, rustic retreats, and at least one underwear drawer; drowning out commercial negotiations, classroom lectures, rap, rock, and reg-gae, not to mention normal dinner table conversation. The rustle caused symphonies to cancel concerts, brides to postpone weddings, and persons unlucky enough to have been born on January 23 to despair of anybody remembering them that year. The rustle grew in volume as the week passed, not only in America but in numerous foreign lands, although the pitch was obviously more mighty in New Orleans, where the Super Bowl would actually be played, than in, say, Ouagadougou, where fans who normally spoke Fulani or Bobo would yell "Touchydown!" in the TV bars of tiny tropical hotels.

Yes, hundreds of concerts, weddings, birthday observances, and political speeches really would be rescheduled so as not to be eclipsed by the Super Bowl, which would be watched by one hundred and forty million Americans. Yet, at Isaac & Ishmael's, the Jerusalem-style restaurant diagonally across the street from the United Nations head-quarters building in New York City, Salome, the belly dancer, hadn't budged, despite the rustle all about her. She would dance at three o'clock, and those who wished to watch her had better be there. Others could watch football in a windy courtyard or camped on some sofa, dipping carrot sticks into bowls of weary substances only marginally more appealing than *baba ghanoug*.

One victim of the I & I dilemma thought he had it figured out. "We've been overlooking something, chaps," he said. "I mean, how long is this Dance of the Seven Veils going to last? Twenty minutes? Not much more than that, I'll assure you. We can have our cake and eat it, some of us. Me, I'm watching her dance, then I'm popping outside for three fine quarters of football plus the halftime show. I'm paying Dr. Farouk to hold me a seat."

Shaftoe chuckled sardonically. "You think you're the first sucker to think of that? Farouk's probably gone and sold that seat he's holding to a dozen fools like you. He's from that part of the world, man. He knows that that dance can go on for hours. And once you start watching, baby, you don't walk out till it's over. Not for nothing."

"Surely for the Super Bowl . . ."

Shaftoe laughed again. "She-ee-it. What you know about football? Why, I—" The detective fell silent and returned to his beer.

On Friday night, Salome's performance was not up to par. Moody and distracted, she shimmied at half-speed and twice dropped her tambourine. She glanced repeatedly at the mural on the wall behind her, but it neither relaxed nor inspired her. On Saturday night, the night when New Orleans, New York, and at least one other American city were practically one giant Super Bowl party, she failed to show up at all.

"She has the small fever," the bandleader explained.

"The girl always looks like she has a slight fever," said Abu to Spike. "That is what is so arousing about her."

Singer Bonnie Raitt, one of the celebrities in attendance, got up and entertained the audience by improvising blues to a Middle Eastern beat. She was a hit with both the suburbanites and the hip, as well as the tourists, but the regulars went home early, grumbling about Salome.

"What if she doesn't show up tomorrow? What if she chickens out? Suppose she's got the flu?"

They turned to Shaftoe, but he had nothing to say.

On Sunday morning, the sun came up like an engineering project, hoisted with considerable strain up a scaffolding of thin, icy cloud. The sun seemed huge and flat and rough and pale, like the face of a newly constructed dam. Behind it an Amazon of snow roiled and spat, churning to get free.

Patsy was Ellen Cherry's alarm clock. Always awake by seven, Patsy would arise to run through her Jane Fonda workout. Then she would shower, apply cosmetics (never without the thought that Verlin might be spinning in his grave), prepare breakfast, and wake her daughter. On this morning, when Ellen Cherry finished in the bathroom and sat down to cinnamon toast, she found Patsy flipping through the yellow pages, hunting for a Baptist church within walking distance. She had to admit that it was as much habit as anything else.

"Forget it, mama. You want to go to services next Sunday, fine, we'll find you a place. But, hey, today's the big day at the I and I. I mean, *the* big day. People are gonna be going crazy down there. I'm going in early, just as soon as I eat. You ought to go in with me, because we can use the help, and it might even be interesting, you never can tell."

However crazy Ellen Cherry imagined the scene at Isaac & Ishmael's might be, it was crazier, still. When she arrived, Patsy in tow, at five past ten, there already was a line out front, stretching down the block and around the corner onto East Forty-ninth. Those who had queued up for the telecast could be distinguished from those intent upon the notorious dance, the former being loud, half-tipsy, and attired in deliberately sloppy duds, while the latter were more refined in deportment and dress, although they, too, maintained a festive air. A third and less populous group seemed anxious, hesitant, nervously subdued. They were the ones who had yet to make up their minds.

Escorted by security guards, Ellen Cherry and Patsy hurried down the alley and into the courtyard. It had been transformed into an outdoor café, covered by an awning striped in the colors of the New York team. The hefty heaters were humming and glowing, each instantly zapping the odd blowing snowflake that drifted into it like a moth into a flame. The mural-sized television set was already on, as if to gather momentum. Mother and daughter paused for a second to look at it. Some sort of pregame spectacle was being telecast, a preview, the announcer said, of the halftime extravaganza, which that year was to salute America's growing Hispanic community. Ellen Cherry believed that she recognized the featured performer. "Well, I'll be double damned!" she marveled. "That looks like ol' Raoul. Raoul the doorman."

Spike increased the volume, whereupon the hunk in the tight silver jumpsuit with the red Puerto Rican sash, the homeboy who was surrounded by scores of dancers and rock 'n' roll musicians and who, except for the absence of a porkpie hat, so resembled Raoul Ritz could be heard to sing:

> *My heart is a Third World country*
> *And your love is a tourist from Switzerland.*
> *Never trust a country that won't allow live poultry*
> *To ride on its buses.*
> *Oh, never trust a country*
> *That won't permit live poultry to ride on the bus.*

Inside the kitchen, Roland Abu Hadee was actually in his shirt-sleeves. The jacket to his conservative pinstriped suit dangling from a hook, Abu was grinding chick-peas with one hand, chopping cucumbers with the other. Nabila, his wife, also was helping prep for the chef. Patsy patted them each on the back, grabbed a knife, and joined in. "Anything a southern gal knows, it's how to cut up a fryer," she said.

Ellen Cherry went into the dining room to lend Teddy a hand with the setups. "I didn't know Raoul Ritz had a hit song," she said.

"Where've you been?"

That was a good question. She looked to the mural for a clue. She had to enter it through the beak of an owl.

Other staff members began filtering in. They all worked furiously. While the game and the dance weren't scheduled to commence until three, the restaurant would open its doors at noon. Spike Cohen made certain that they opened on time.

The crowd, many of its members distinguished officials of the United Nations, galloped in like a stampede of wild mustangs. They pushed, shoved, and fought over the prime tables like teenagers at a heavy metal cafeteria. Many ended up in the courtyard by default. It was less contentious out there than in the dining room and bar, probably because every seat within a quarter mile of the giant TV was a good one. Nobody had spotted Detective Shaftoe on line outside, but suddenly there he was, perched on the bar stool closest to the bandstand, ordering *falafel* and a Maccabee. One of the Greeks suggested that he had hidden all night in the men's room. "You dudes been reading too many Trojan horse stories," said Shaftoe. In any case, he'd made his choice.

At 12:12, Spike instructed the security guards to block the door. There were at least a hundred people still clamoring to get in, but the occupancy number dictated by the fire marshal already had been exceeded. Those who had gained admission to the dining room and bar were whooping and chattering. Beneath the rambunctious gaiety, however, the atmosphere was decidedly tense. Some patrons seemed secretly afraid to be there, although the root of their fear was not easily determined. Perhaps they were worried about violence. Perhaps it was something less solid.

Spike went out on the sidewalk to meet the press. "The Super Bowl's showing out back," he explained. "Inside, the little dancing lady is doing something special. In a nutshell." He shrugged. The reporters weren't satisfied. They had gotten wind of the Dance of the Seven Veils and badgered for details. Spike told them what he knew, which was precious little, then switched the subject to the I & I experiment. "In the past, my Arab partner and me have said it's a gesture only that we're making here, that we have no illusions about changing the large picture. To tell you the truth, I'm not so sure. This continent of North America, what did it used to be? A torrid swamp, am I right? For millions of years it was a jungle. Then in one minute, one minute, it was all covered up with ice from top to tush. You know your history? Very, very fast, things can be changing. A continent. A human life. So, the Jews and the Arabs are at each other's throats for years into the thousands. So what? So what it's so long? It could change in one minute. One minute, I'm telling you. It's for the remote possibility of that minute that we stay in business."

"But, Mr. Cohen, when Salome drops the seventh veil, will she be nude?"

"Mr. Cohen, you got a silver platter in there?"

"Hoo boy!"

After reiterating that the media was banned, at Salome's request, Spike went back inside.

"Nothing here," a reporter grumbled. The others agreed.

Meanwhile, Ellen Cherry was locked into fast-forward, moving like a slapstick character in a silent film. Orders for food and drink were buffeting her like the surf at Drowned Waitress Beach. In her career in food service, she had never worked at quite that pace.

"Jesus!" she exclaimed. "If this keeps up, I'll be medical waste by the end of the day. They'll just shovel me into that incinerator out back of Bellevue."

For better or for worse, it would not keep up. In fact, Ellen Cherry was to discover that while fans in the courtyard would continue to munch and swill throughout the Super Bowl, appetites indoors would taper off dramatically. Once the first veil had fallen, hardly anyone called for anything, except mercy.

At 2:54, there was a roar out on United Nations Plaza, causing the revelers in the I & I to suddenly stiffen and crane their necks. There was a certain amount of concomitant spillage. It sounded like a ruckus out there. The dining room, conversely, was silent and edgy. At 2:55, the front door was flung open by a security guard, and the word "koksaghyz" was coughed into the restaurant, followed by the word "megakaryoblast."

That's how they looked, Salome and her chaperon: like strange words on a road sign or a page that a reader could only wonder at but hardly define or pronounce. Many in the I & I thumbed hastily through the pocket dictionaries of their life's experience, searching for meanings to which they might relate. But would "koksaghyz" seem any less exotic once one learned it was a dandelion of Central Asia? And to be informed that a "megakaryoblast" was simply an immature megakaryocyte was not much help at all. Better, perhaps, to take the words at face value, to let the senses deal with them, or the tip of the spine. The rational mind just got in the way. Besides, a better word for the chaperon, throwing her elbows and swinging her dog coffin of a purse, may have been "ducatoon." At least "ducatoon" was evocative of her waddle and her squawky aggravation.

But never mind the megakaryoblastic ducatoonish behemoth. Once she had escorted her charge to the bandstand, she vanished behind the orchestra and was forgotten. All eyes were on the koksaghyz; tender, solitary, trembling in the smoke. And speaking of eyes, eyes were nearly all that one could see of her. Salome was so thoroughly swaddled in scarves of gauzy purple silk that only her hands, her bare feet, and her eyes were exposed. Every ring, bell, and bracelet had been removed from her extremities, and her eyes, which resembled shot glasses of warm Hershey syrup, were given over to ansoopia, which is to say, were rolled almost violently upward (think of the heavenward eyeballings of first-time sinners or the traumatic posturing of El Greco saints). She just stood there fidgeting, the ansoopial

koksaghyz, fixed upon the ceiling from which the bamboo had
flown, stood there wrapped like a conch-shell burrito in the purple-
red dyes of Canaan/Phoenicia, stood there for several minutes, picking at her seat, regarding the fresh plaster, until at exactly 3:00 P.M.,
at precisely the moment that the New York kicker's toe met the
ovoid flank of the virgin football, the orchestra struck up her tune.

For the first time, Salome looked at the audience. The French
undersecretary winked at her, and Shaftoe sucked in his breath. Of
the faces that stared back at her, two of every three were male, and
although they had chosen her over the Super Bowl, still, most were
flushed with the ruddy concerns of their gender: concerns of possession, profit, and conquest. Salome turned slowly to the mural, where
a more lunar sensibility was represented: a loose poetic text of
seasons and renewal. Imperceptible to the audience, she emitted a
soft, low howl. She rattled her tambourine.

Then, she danced.

This is the room of the wolfmother wallpaper. The room where your
oldest living ancestor, the monarch amoeba, holds court in the
irrigation ditch at the foot of the bed.

> *Yeeh yeeh yeeh yeeh yeeh*
> *Yeeh yeeh yeeh yeeh yeeh yeeh yeeh*
> *Zinga doppa dop lop zinga*
> *Eh, eh-eh, eh eh zeeee*

As her bare feet slapped the floor in time to polyrhythms more
ancient than Petra, Salome whirled and dipped and whirled again,
slapping and whirling simultaneously, and, moreover, pushing and
contracting her pelvis, as if straining to expel a child. Her eyes were
wide and hot, and the purple scarves swirled all about her. She
danced thusly for close to twenty minutes before the first veil fell.

For some reason, Ellen Cherry, Spike, Abu, and practically everyone else in the room had assumed that the first veil dropped would
be an upper one; specifically, the one that obscured her nose and
mouth. They assumed erroneously. When it finally fell, fluttering to
the floor like the skin of a moonsnake, it bared not her face but her
loins. The audience was stunned. Worried about their cabaret license, Spike and Abu panicked. Shaftoe's battered brow furrowed

with concern: he was, after all, an officer of the law. Ellen Cherry blushed. She had sunbathed nude with waitress girlfriends in Seattle, but she'd never really focused, been virtually forced to focus, on another woman's pudendum. It was both fascinating and discomfiting. She was glad that Patsy was out back in the courtyard.

Everybody was shocked, even the unshockable. Yet nobody acted to stop the performance. Nobody. And Salome went on whirling and dipping and swooping and arching, and each time that she arched, they found themselves looking into the prettiest and pinkest little slit that anyone could ever imagine, its folds delicate and mysterious, its tiny stinger aimed at them like the gun barrel of a felonious orchid, the curly pelt around it as sleek and moist as the welcome mat at the Bermuda Triangle Hilton.

The veil had not lain long on the floor when Ellen Cherry began to . . . well, to receive ideas. Spontaneously, without preamble, things occurred to her; thoughts entered her mind, one might say, except that they were both more vivid and full-formed than the thoughts that she was accustomed to entertaining, and they were permeated with information that she hadn't realized that she possessed. It was as if they were somebody else's thoughts, zapped by ray into her brain, where instantly they took hold and became her own.

Earth, it occurred to her, was a sexual globe. Unique, in a solar system of dead rocks, snowballs, and gasbags, Earth was a theater, a rotating stage upon which a thin green scum of organic life acted out countless, continual scenes whose content, whether explicit or oblique, was almost wholly sexual. In the biospherical epic, the players were either Seed Packages or Egg Cartons (a few versatile actors such as the amoeba could perform both roles, but it was a dying art), and the scenery, props, and costumes were designed to enhance or facilitate the coming together of hero seed and heroine egg. The colors, the smells, and the sounds of organic things had evolved as sexual attractants, created to keep the trillion romantic plots moving toward a trillion more-or-less happy endings. Recent observations of the behavior patterns of bonding molecules showed that even on the molecular level, intricate and tricky courtships were constantly tran-spiring: there was molecular rejection, for example, and presumably molecular heartbreak. Within a broad age span, sexually inactive organisms—plant, animal, molecular, or human—could be said to be aberrations, freakish or pathological misfits out of tune with the harmony of life.

Despite an often ostentatious masculine display that would indicate otherwise, the sexual drama (or melodrama or farce) was largely, historically, directed by the female. That was particularly true among human beings, in which species the male had gone to ludicrous and often violent lengths to compensate for what struck the more insecure of men as an inferior sexual role. One of the lengths to which they went was the establishment of patriarchal religion and the recasting of a father figure as the producer of the show, although from the very beginning, the cosmogonic principal had been feminine. Those men, envious and anxious, not only fired the Great Goddess (who smiled upon all manner of sexual expression, including that which moderns were to label "promiscuous" and "pornographic"), but they also spent thousands of years and billions of dollars trying to conceal the fact of her existence.

And this further thought occurred to Ellen Cherry after the falling aside of Salome's first veil: that whenever society demonstrated signs of rediscovering the goddess, of returning to more feminine value systems, the patriarchally conditioned psyche generated diseases, literal diseases such as syphilis in the hotly romantic nineteenth century and, in the wake of the Sexual Revolution of the 1960s, AIDS. Those diseases were caused not by sexual license but by the *fear* of sexual license, by the conservative DNA's inability to adjust to hedonism; and they were compounded by guilt over the suppression of the Great Mother and the denial of the sensuality with which she so frequently underscored her coexistence with the void. Eventually, AIDS was destined to run its deadly course, however, and eventually every manner of carnal play would go back into full production, for like it or not, gentlemen, that was the way of her world.

Yes, that's it! thought Ellen Cherry Charles.

> *Yeeh yeeh yeeh yeeh yeeh*
> *Yeeh yeeh yeeh yeeh yeeh yeeh yeeh*
> *Zop de bango zee whee winga*
> *Eh, eh-eh, eh eh haiii*

This is the room of the wolfmother wallpaper. This is the room where the boys slept inside their blowguns to avoid being bitten by the bats, for whom the girls sewed tiny velvet suits.

Vulva exposed and sweetly agape, Salome danced on, whirling and arching, until, after another twenty minutes or so, a second veil was pulled loose and tossed gracefully to the floor. This veil had covered her waist and belly, a belly that seemed at once round and flat, a haptic demimound already familiar to her fans, although until that moment they had never drawn dew from the saucy well of its bare navel. Almost immediately, Ellen Cherry received another intellectual transmission.

"Human beings do not have dominion over the plants and animals." That was the message that seemed to flash on her mental screen.

Human beings did not have dominion over the plants and animals. Every daisy in the field, every anchovy in the bay had an identity just as strong as her own, and a station in life as valuable as hers. To disrupt the daily lives of trees and beasts, to take the lives of trees and beasts (except when necessary for basic shelter and sustenance), to drive whole species of tree and beast to extinction was arrogant, profane, and ultimately a boomerang honed for suicide.

Plants and animals—perhaps even minerals and inanimate objects— were in partnership with humans. Moreover, they, not us, were the senior partners, as a result of their experience and their perfection. Plants, especially the psychoactive vines and fungi, had a great deal to teach humanity; in fact, if humanity hoped to evolve rapidly enough to keep philosophically apace with its technological advances, the expeditious and postverbal insights provided by psychotropic vegetation might well be its only salvation. In any case, the welfare and wishes of the inhuman must be taken into consideration by any civilization with legitimate chances for survival, although the issue was not merely pragmatic but moral and aesthetic. Humanity was a function of nature. It could not, therefore, live separately from nature except in a self-deceiving masquerade. It could not live in opposition to nature except in a schizophrenic crime. And it could not blind itself to the wonders of nature without mutating into something too monstrous to love.

Yes, that's it! thought Ellen Cherry.

Yeeh yeeh yeeh yeeh yeeh
Yeeh yeeh yeeh yeeh yeeh yeeh yeeh
Wop za whoppo zeena za-za
Eh, eh-eh, eh eh eeeng

This is the room of the wolfmother wallpaper. The room swept by a broom made from language. A room where the dust mice are as luminous as grapes.

The third purple cloth to float free from the whirling form of the dancing girl—Salome was whirling more now and arching less—had been wound about her neck and shoulders. Sure enough, as it settled upon the floor, like the filmy soul of a dirty sock landing in a polyester paradise where such earthly woes as toe jam and clothes dryers were only bad memories; sure enough, as it settled in a gossamer heap near the scuffed black shoes of the mesmerized Shaftoe, Ellen Cherry felt another brainful coming on.

She understood suddenly, and for no particular reason of which she was aware, that it was futile to work for political solutions to humanity's problems because humanity's problems were not political. Political problems did exist, all right, but they were entirely secondary. The primary problems were philosophical, and until the philosophical problems were solved, the political problems would have to be solved over and over and over again. The phrase "vicious circle" was coined to describe the ephemeral effectiveness of almost all political activity.

For the ethical, political activism was seductive because it seemed to offer the possibility that one could improve society, make things better, without going through the personal ordeal of rearranging one's perceptions and transforming one's self. For the unconscionable, political reactivism was seductive because it seemed to protect one's holdings and legitimize one's greed. But both sides were gazing through a kerchief of illusion.

The monkey wrench in the progressive machinery of primate evolution was the propensity of the primate band to take its political leaders—its dominant males—too seriously. Of benefit to the band only when it was actively threatened by predators, the dominant male (or political boss) was almost wholly self-serving and was naturally dedicated not to liberation but to control. Behind his chest-banging and fang display, he was largely a joke and could be kept in his place (his place being that of a necessary evil) by disrespect and laughter. If, for example, when Hitler stood up to rant in the beer halls of Munich, the good drinkers had taken him more lightly, had they, instead of buying his act, snickered and hooted and pelted him with sausage skins, the Holocaust might have been avoided.

Of course, as long as there were willing followers, there would be exploitive leaders. And there would be willing followers until humanity reached that philosophical plateau where it recognized that its great mission in life had nothing to do with any struggle between classes, races, nations, or ideologies, but was, rather, a personal quest to enlarge the soul, liberate the spirit, and light up the brain. On that quest, politics was simply a roadblock of stentorian baboons.

Exactly! Yes, that's right! thought Ellen Cherry.

Eeena eeena eeena eeena
Eh eh-eh eeena whop

This is the room of the wolfmother wallpaper. The room where volcanoes filled the ashtrays with their fine cinders, and the keyhole itself was a fumarole.

By her own admission, art was the lone subject in which Ellen Cherry was at all educated (unless one counted waitressing, and, of course, one could not count waitressing). It could be said that she was a specialist. Or, less charitably, charged that she was as much of an idiot savant as Boomer Petway. Outside of the realm of the artistic, she'd been a bit of a ditz. Yet, she felt now as if she had reached an understanding in several significant areas, had reached it suddenly, effortlessly; had reached it—and this was the queerest part—during the hour and twenty minutes that she had spent watching Salome dance. If there was a connection between the revelations and the dancing, she could not conceive of it. She had to admit that the girl, despite her snotty disposition and skinny legs, was amazing, whirling like that for well over an hour, but Salome's impact certainly was not on the *mind*. In fact, the girl was making her rather horny, she who had never been tempted by other women before. And that made it all the more extraordinary that she was simultaneously entertaining big abstract thoughts. Only they weren't self-generated thoughts so much as they were— Well, it was as if a coating of something was being peeled off of her corneas and she was seeing things for which the eye game had barely prepared her.

It occurred to Ellen Cherry then that not one customer had ordered so much as a glass of water in a very long while. She wondered if they, too, were receiving wisdom from the Dance of the Seven Veils; if anybody else was hosting those verbose epiphanies.

From face to face she glanced. They were definitely absorbed. That surly old black detective appeared absolutely paralyzed, his can of Maccabee welded to his lips. And Dr. Farouk, who'd slipped in from the courtyard between quarters to take a quick peek at Salome, had frozen in his steps, his fez-topped bulk blocking the passageway. Above the sound of the orchestra it was difficult to hear clearly, but indications were that the Super Bowl crowd out back was hectic and merry compared to the almost reverential mood of those indoors. Still, it was impossible for Ellen Cherry to ascertain if anyone was sharing her insights. To do so, maybe one would have had to have been recently exposed to close encounters with a spoon.

Eeena eeena eeena eeena
Eh eh-eh eeena zop

A fourth veil came undone, circled several times the gyrating torso of the dancer (it had somehow been wrapping both of her arms) like a gaseous cloud of star stuff orbiting a galaxy, before finally breaking the gravitational attraction and wafting toward a new home on the edge of the bandstand. Ellen Cherry understood then that religion was an improper response to the Divine.

Religion was an attempt to pin down the Divine. The Divine was eternally in flux, forever moving, shifting shape. That was its nature. It was absolute, true enough: absolutely mobile. Absolutely transcendent. Absolutely flexible. Absolutely impersonal. It had its god and goddess aspects, but it was ultimately no more male or female than it was star or screwdriver. It was the sum of all those things, but that sum could never be chalked on a slate. The Divine was beyond description, beyond knowing, beyond comprehension. To say that the Divine was Creation divided by Destruction was as close as one could come to definition. But the puny of soul, the dull of wit, weren't content with that. They wanted to hang a face on the Divine. They went so far as to attribute petty human emotions (anger, jealousy, etc.) to it, not stopping to realize that if God were a being, even a supreme being, our prayers would have bored him to death long ago.

The Divine was expansive, but religion was reductive. Religion attempted to reduce the Divine to a knowable quantity with which mortals might efficiently deal, to pigeonhole it once and for all so that we never had to reevaluate it. With hammers of cant and spikes of dogma, we crucified and crucified again, trying to nail to our stationary altars the migratory light of the world.

Thus, since religion bore false witness to the Divine, religion was blasphemy. And once it entered into its unholy alliance with politics, it became the most dangerous and repressive force that the world has ever known.

Yes! I see it now, thought Ellen Cherry. *The religious training I was given as a girl was a form of child abuse.*

And she thought she heard somebody next to her say, "Yeah! That's right! I see it now."

Eeena eeena, eeena-eeena ai
Eh, eh-eh, wop wop haj

In the room of the wolfmother wallpaper, a woodpecker flies in through the transom and leaves three farts: one on a hot skillet, one in a bottle, and one between the strings of an autoharp. Room service.

The founding of a religion is an elaborated version of pitching coins into a wishing well or spitting off a bridge, Ellen Cherry was thinking. *I guess people have an innate superstitious urge to want to fill a void.* As she was thinking this, Salome began shedding veil number five, releasing it as she whirled. It had concealed her ankles, calves, knees, and lower thighs, that section of the dancer's body that Ellen Cherry had snidely characterized as overly thin. With the falling of that scarf, there vanished the last vestiges of any illusion one might have retained about money.

Whenever a state or an individual cited "insufficient funds" as an excuse for neglecting this important thing or that, it was indicative of the extent to which reality had been distorted by the abstract lens of wealth. During periods of so-called economic depression, for example, societies suffered for want of all manner of essential goods, yet investigation almost invariably disclosed that there were plenty of goods available. Plenty of coal in the ground, corn in the fields, wool on the sheep. What was missing was not materials but an abstract unit of measurement called "money." It was akin to a starving woman with a sweet tooth lamenting that she couldn't bake a cake because she didn't have any ounces. She had butter, flour, eggs, milk, and sugar, she just didn't have any ounces, any pinches, any pints. The loony legacy of money was that the arithmetic by which things were measured had become more valuable than the things themselves.

There then followed some fairly standard wisdom along the lines of how it was easier for a camel to pass through the eye of a needle than for a rich man to enter the kingdom of Heaven (when one considered how often that currency served as the paper representation of a big rigid ego, and how that heaven, on the other hand, was the loose state of egolessness, one saw what Jesus was driving at), to which Ellen Cherry was positive she overheard Spike Cohen exclaim, "Hoo! How true it is!" Then, the tambourine banged like a fist on a jewel box, and Salome entered the extended series of exquisite whirls that would climax with the dropping of the cloth from her breasts.

"Mmm. Nice tits," remarked the bartender, a sentiment that echoed around the room. They were a young girl's tits, only slightly larger than Ellen Cherry's, but they were as perfectly formed as the wheels of a bicycle and seemed to subscribe to no theory of gravity. Glistening with perspiration, they resembled oversize tulip bulbs bathed by a fine spring rain. They heaved from Salome's exertion like jellyfish in a choppy tide, a condition that some found prurient and others distasteful. In any case, none took their eyes off her, even though a brassy fellow yelled from the courtyard door, "Hey! New York just kicked a field goal to go ahead!"

Eeena eeena, eeena-eeena haj

Beneath the floorboards of this room, schoolgirls operate a diamond mine. Every card on the table is the queen of diamonds. And the wallpaper howls at the moon.

Revelations were starting to overlap. Ellen Cherry was just thinking about how no amount of money could buy security, and if it could, it would be a bad bargain at any price, since security was a form of paralysis, just as satisfaction was a form of death; she was thinking something in that category when the sixth veil flew away from Salome's likable, lickable breasts, and abruptly her mind was occupied with notions of time, history, and the afterlife. She saw that the past was a recent invention, that people sacrificed the present to a future that never really came, that those who tied all of their dreams to an afterlife had no life for there to be an "after" of; saw that time was a meadow not a highway; that the psyche was an all-night restaurant, not a museum or a church; and that on every conceivable level, belief in a hereafter was hazardous to health. Moreover, the world would not be destroyed, at least not until the sun pooped out in about two billion years—and by then there would be other options.

"But what about Judgment Day?" Ellen Cherry found herself whispering.

Every day is Judgment Day. Always has been. Always will be.

"Anything else?"

Yes. Just this. The dead are laughing at us.

"Wow," said Ellen Cherry Charles.

For hours, the Reverend Buddy Winkler had been pacing the floor of his office. Cracking his knuckles. Grinding his gold teeth. Scratching his face until the pustules broke and bled. He was just so blessed dad-blamed all-fired *frustrated*! He could hardly stand it! Lordy lordy lordy lordy law. All those many long lonely months, years even, that he'd been preparing himself, priming himself, honing himself for one monumental and glorious act: the bringing down of the Dome of the Rock so that the Third Temple might rise in its place. This very day, Sunday, January 23, was when the holy explosives were supposed to go off. Today! And here he was, hamstrung, impotent; stuck among the niggers and the dope fiends and the sodomites in New York City, not only deprived of the opportunity to personally fulfill his God-appointed mission but unable to be on hand in Jerusalem in case the rabbis and yeshivas went ahead and bombed the damned mosques without him (which probably would not happen, the CIA would see to that).

Lordy lordy law, he was fit to be tied. He was about to explode his own self. He needed an outlet for the righteous energy, the redemptive fury, with which Jehovah had flooded him.

It was going on five in the afternoon when Buddy hit upon the idea of venting a little spleen on Isaac & Ishmael's. If ever an establishment needed a sharp whack with God's flyswatter, the I & I was it. Those peacenik humanists! That dancing girl! That blabbermouth Jezebel of Verlin Charles's! Yep. Bud allowed as to how he might amble down there and wag a finger or two at their shame. He telephoned several of his Zionist friends, but they were all watching the Super Bowl. So were his contacts in the Little Matches of Jesus. Okey-dokey. Let the fools sully the Sabbath with their trivial games. Buddy would go it alone.

> *Yeeh yeeh yeeh yeeh yeeh*
> *Yeeh yeeh yeeh yeeh yeeh yeeh yeeh*
> *Zinga dopla dop lop zinga*
> *Eh, eh-eh, eeena-eeena ai*

This is the room, all right, but the candles have burned down, the lamps are dry, and the blue neon has blown a fuse. The wallpaper might as well be stone. In the blackness there can be heard a low, perpetual rattling and a *click click click click*. It is Jezebel's bones. Or else the rolling of the dice.

The teenager was completely naked then, except for the short purple veil that masked her face. Abu and Spike were beyond worrying over the illegality of the situation. Detective Shaftoe certainly wasn't about to arrest her. He was himself in irons. Nobody moved, and above the whine, drone, and drumming of the orchestra, no sound was audible except for Salome's labored breathing. She had been dancing for more than two hours and obviously was near exhaustion. The dance appeared to be winding down. The whirls were elongated, slow and dreamy now, although they'd lost little if any of their impact. She turned as if knee-deep in fruit pulp, and the hypnotized audience followed her as helplessly as if she were the cufflinks of Mandrake the Magician.

Earlier, much earlier, in the afternoon, Ellen Cherry had considered applying the eye game to the dancer, but decided it would have been akin to painting a second smile on the Mona Lisa. Now, she was incapable of that kind of self-control, even if she had deemed it desirable. Her mind was calm, yet humming with activity, and Salome seemed to hold on to it with small sweaty fingers, the way that she held on to her tambourine.

When the seventh veil flew away from Salome's face, it was as if the girl had opened her mouth and burped out a bird-sized butterfly. Ellen Cherry's first thought was, *How beautiful she is!* Her second thought was, *Everybody's got to figure it out for themselves.*

Yes, that was it. The government wouldn't take care of it for you, no matter how much you'd paid into Social Security, or how many votes your political action committee may have bought. You couldn't learn it in college, colleges chose largely to ignore it. Churches, conversely, were falling all over themselves to save you the trouble of thinking about it; they would hand you an answer as neat and tidy and definitive as your horoscope in the daily paper—and, unfortunately, just about as useless because it was just about as generic and every bit as speculative. Great books, paintings, and music were helpful, in an inspirational way; nature, even more so. Valuable clues were constantly dropping from the lips of philosophers, spiritual masters, gurus, shamans, gypsy circus girls, and wild-talking tramps in the street. But they were clues, only. No self-proclaimed holy man could cut the mustard for you, and the ones who were truly holy would tell you so. Nor could you turn it over to some chatty, disembodied entity channeled from the other side. (The dead are laughing at us, remember.) You couldn't even learn it at your mammy's knee.

The illusion of the seventh veil was the illusion that you could get somebody else to do it for you. To think for you. To hang on your cross. The priest, the rabbi, the imam, the swami, the philosophical novelist were traffic cops, at best. They might direct you through a busy intersection, but they wouldn't follow you home and park your car.

Was there a more difficult lesson for a human being to learn, a paradox harder to accept? Even though the great emotions, the great truths, were universal; even though the mind of humanity was ultimately one mind, still, each and every single individual had to establish his or her own special, personal, particular, unique, direct, one-on-one, hands-on relationship with reality, with the universe, with the Divine. It might be complicated, it might be a pain in the ass, it might be, most of all, lonely—but it was the bottom line.

It was as different for everybody as it was the same, so everybody had to take control of their own life, define their own death, and construct their own salvation. And when you finished, you didn't call the Messiah. He'd call you.

Um, well, okay, thought Ellen Cherry, *I guess I understand. But wait a minute. This isn't all? Surely there's more? There must be something else.*

The dance was ending. Salome executed one last passionate pirouette, slapped both feet resoundingly against the floor, then staggered to a stop. She stood facing, but not looking at, the audience; her eyes downcast, her mouth gasping, her entire respiratory system convulsing, her legs wobbling as if about to give way. Oddly, nobody, not even her chaperon, made a move to support her or to cover her nakedness. The room was silent, transfixed.

Ellen Cherry's condition was not measurably superior to the dancer's. She was tremulous, flushed, in a kind of trance. She was in the room and not in the room. Her mind whirled endlessly upon a dance floor of ideas. Instinctively, she sensed that once the last of the veils had dropped, some greater, more all-inclusive secret should have been exposed; she should have been squinting at the contours of the Mystery. Thus, she squinted at poor Salome, who continued to stand there, shaking, panting, dressed in angel chaps of sweat. And she thought, *Come on, now. What's the punch line? There's got to be something else.* Until, finally, a voice inside her said:

"We're making it up."

Who? What?

"Us. All of us. It. All of it. The world, the universe, life, reality. Especially reality."

We're making it up?

"We make it up. We made it up. We shall make it up. We have been making it up. I make it up. You make it up. He, she, it makes it up."

Okay, I'm an artist, I can accept that. In theory. But how do I apply it to my daily life?

"You'll have to figure . . ."

It out for myself. But hold on. Please don't go away. Can't you at least leave me with some advice?

"You need more?" (The inner voice was incredulous.)

Yes. Please. A little more. A speck more in the line of practical advice.

"Very well. The trick is this: keep your eye on the ball. Even when you can't see the ball."

You're kidding, thought Ellen Cherry Charles.

Ellen Cherry made for the door. She had to get out of there and get out fast. All that had transpired seemed perfectly natural to her, as natural as daydreaming or brainstorming or the eye game; she was overwhelmed, to be sure, but hardly frightened or bewildered; she was, in fact, in a state rather next to wahoo. But she needed to change spaces, to get some air.

Others, perhaps as many as twenty, followed her out. And when she turned the corner and headed up East Forty-ninth they did likewise. It wasn't as though they were interested in her, but, rather, that she was in the lead of a group that was being swept along by its own stupefied momentum.

The group was far enough down the block that it failed to hear the commotion back at Isaac & Ishmael's.

At exactly the moment that they were turning the corner, Buddy Winkler had pushed his way into the restaurant. When he had spotted Salome, still standing there naked (her chaperon was in the act of draping a coat about her), he'd rushed the bandstand, nearly falling over Roland Abu Hadee, who, for some reason, was on his hands and knees, picking up the discarded veils. Some witnesses later testified that the Reverend Buddy Winkler had shouted, "Beast! Great Fornicator! Whore of Babylon!" Others would claim that he was merely sputtering and growling. In any case, he charged the girl and grabbed her by the throat.

Detective Shaftoe shot him dead.

The two security guards ran in, guns blazing, just as they had seen it done in the movies. Salome was shot accidentally, Shaftoe more or less on purpose.

*　　*　　*

4 1 4

Both were critically wounded but, in time, recovered.

Jackie Shaftoe, once he could walk again, retired from the police force and devoted his days to painting, with moderate success. His major influence, he was ever quick to point out, was Ellen Cherry Charles. He never attended another football game nor watched one on TV.

Once she could breathe without the aid of a respirator, the Jewish/Arab girl who called herself "Salome" was whisked by her guardians out of the country, presumably to Lebanon—once known as Phoenicia, an extension of the land of Canaan.

Scattered snowflakes as large as postage stamps were spinning in the dusk, but the temperature was rather mild, a benefit to Ellen Cherry, who had neglected to don her coat. She did shiver slightly as she passed the Mel Davis Dog Boutique, but it was not due to the weather. *If we're making everything up,* she wondered, *why are we making up doggy salons?* Sushi bars, she could understand, which was nice, because she and the motley band of ecstatics who tagged along with her must have passed a dozen of them, closed for the Sabbath, the green furnaces of their *wasabi* banked against the night.

As the group neared Lexington Avenue, it became aware that a great many automobiles were blowing their horns. That was unusual for a Sunday evening and had not the "pilgrims" been so blissed-out, some of them might have taken it personally. On Park Avenue, sedate Park, the automotive blare increased, and on Madison, people were yelling from the windows of hotels and cars. Approaching Fifth, Ellen Cherry paused to listen. The others paused behind her. In the distance, a great din could be detected, a singing and cheering and banging sort of din, as if, in a parking lot many blocks away, the

Woodstock rock festival was being reenacted. At last, the "pilgrims" had a destination. They crossed Fifth, then Sixth, and turned southward toward the roar, their waitress, Ellen Cherry, leading their advance.

Times Square was in turmoil. There were thousands, perhaps tens of thousands, there. A huge noisy surge of humanity clogged every artery, like animated cholesterol, halting vehicular traffic for blocks in all directions. Drivers leaned on their horns, but less in anger or frustration than in joy. As for the multitudes on foot, they whooped like warriors on an ancient rampage, danced, jumped up and down, slapped one another's palms repeatedly and ritualistically, and raised their index fingers in the air. Grinning boys of many races chugged beer from quart bottles, and intoxicated girls flashed their bare breasts at the mobs, just as they might in New Orleans at Mardi Gras. Mardi Gras, in fact, was what it resembled, except for the occasional dancing snowflake and the absence of masks. It was a celebration, a mighty, riotous jubilee—and the dazed group from Isaac & Ishmael's jumped to the conclusion that what was being celebrated was the end of illusion, the undraping of the Mystery, the genesis of a grand new age.

Even Ellen Cherry, momentarily, thought that the spontaneous outpouring had been unleashed by the Dance of the Seven Veils. Gradually, however, it dawned on her that what was being celebrated, what had whipped the population into exultant frenzy, was New York's victory in the Super Bowl game.

Symbolically, perhaps, Ellen Cherry swam against the current, fighting her way out of Times Square even as hundreds fought their way in. At one point, her forward progress arrested by a knot of Jersey guys through which she could not slice, she used the delay to scan the front pages of newspapers at a kiosk. A prominently featured article bore a Jerusalem dateline. In its lead paragraph, it reported that a squad of Israeli soldiers had employed a bulldozer to bury alive a half dozen West Bank Arab youths (one as young as eleven) whom they suspected of stoning military vehicles. In the second paragraph, it described how a pair of Palestinians had stabbed to death four innocent Israeli civilians and an American tourist at a sidewalk café in Jerusalem. As the Arabs shoved their long knives into stomachs, hearts, lungs, they had shouted, "God is great! God is great!"

Sickened, she turned, found a seam in the mob, and snaked through. She pushed, and was pushed, back to Fifth Avenue. There, she walked to the north, the crowds growing thinner, the din fainter with each step. By the time that she reached St. Patrick's Cathedral, she was virtually alone on the sidewalk, although Times Square roared behind her like a distant waterfall of parrots and soup pots, and every other passing motorist had his palm on his horn.

At St. Patrick's she slackened her pace. Instantly, she saw, or thought she saw, a flash of purple fabric behind a shin-level grate. It so resembled one of Salome's falling veils that she was convinced that she was hallucinating. *I'll probably be seeing them everywhere,* she thought. *I'm really in a state.*

Ellen Cherry walked a few yards further, stopping at the place where Turn Around Norman had performed. Deliberately, she planted her feet as precisely as possible on the spot where his feet always stood. She closed her eyes and even tried turning a fraction of an inch to her left, but her slow motion was far too fast.

"Turn Around Norman," she said aloud. "Where does magic and beauty go when it's driven from the world?"

At the grate, there was another flicker of purple, but she wasn't inclined to investigate. She just stood there, a snow stamp pasted to her forehead as if she were about to be mailed to the Yukon, wondering about Turn Around Norman until there was nothing left to wonder. Then, recalling the newspapers that she had seen, she wondered, *Why are we making up a mess like the Middle East?*

The dance was over. The veils were all dropped. The cascade of epiphanies had ceased. The inner voice was mute, and that was fine, it had given her more than enough guidance, more than enough understanding, more than enough to figure out for herself. Neverthe-less, she believed that she would try to summon it one more time. Standing in Turn Around Norman's footprints, she squeezed her eyelids and began to hum an approximation of the music that had filled the I & I all afternoon.

> *Yeeh yeeh yeeh yeeh yeeh*
> *Eeena eeena, eh-eh, haj*

What about this Middle East business? Why is it making everybody crazy? Why is it so awful? Is it really totally hopeless? I need to know.

For a long while she heard nothing except Super Bowl fallout. It didn't surprise her. She brushed a snowflake from her nose (Antarctica, twenty-two cents). What could she expect? Ah, but then an answer began to build in her brain, slowly, organically, like bees excreting comb.

Consider the anatomy of the Middle East, said the inner voice. Hasn't it been called the Fertile Crescent, the primordial uterus from which the human race emerged? Well, look at it today, consider it now. Of all the places on the planet, it is the most feverish, hot, pain-racked, tense, dilated, bloody, traumatized, stretched to the point of ripping. Remind you of something? The "trouble" in the Middle East is nothing but natal contractions. The world is in labor, and the Middle East, quite obviously, is the vagina out of which, if it doesn't abort, the new order of humanity must be born. The labor is difficult and long, and it may get worse before the vagitus is heard, but don't despair over the Middle East: something great, something wondrous, something completely unimaginable is there aborning.

Are you putting me on? asked Ellen Cherry Charles. But then a carload of loudmouths drove by, chanting the score of the Super Bowl game, and she heard nothing further, nor could she generate another pertinent thought.

The next evening, she flew to Jerusalem. Her mama paid for part of her expenses, Spike Cohen paid the rest. Her benefactors drove her to JFK and saw her off.

On the way home from the airport, in the backseat of a limo, Patsy and Spike fell in love. They later married, settling in Brooklyn Heights, where Patsy took belly dancing lessons and where her white go-go boots finally got the attention they deserved.

The mere thought of it would one day cause Ellen Cherry to lose her lifelong fondness for shoes.

Rusty metal caught the morning sun like a ruby brooch catching the eye of a burglar. Had Can o' Beans been human, he/she might have stretched and yawned. It was a new day in Jerusalem, a city that, in one state of disrepair or another, had seen so very many new days; and in a rock pile a couple hundred yards west of the Jaffa Gate, the bean tin, or what remained of it, greeted this morning, as it did every morning, with the rusted-out, inanimate equivalent of a grin.

The Atlantic, from whose waters Conch Shell could not fully shield it, had taken a terrible toll on the can. Oxidation had enveloped it like an orange mitten enveloping a fist, and then disintegration had set in. "I'm just a tired old bum beside a railroad track," Can o' Beans told a beloved companion. "A busted, rusted derelict fit for nothing but the two-bit harmonica junkyard blues." Of course, that lament was fanciful, if not wholly tongue in cheek.

The hope that Israel's arid climate might extend the tin's life expectancy for another six months could not alter the fact that it was a goner; encrusted, crushed, cracked, and worn as thin as the whiskers on a billy goat. Still, it was happy with its final resting place. Can o' Beans, you see, loved, absolutely *adored,* the statue of Pales.

Painted Stick and Conch Shell, who had had little trouble locating each other once they were back on their old stomping grounds, had invited him/her to accompany them to the Dome of the Rock, where now they were in some manner or other unofficially ensconced, awaiting the advent of the Third Temple, in whatever form it might take. Grateful for their offer, Can o' Beans had nevertheless declined. "I'd just be in the way," he/she said. "I have nothing to contribute. And the Messiah, should he—or she—or it—decide to put in an appearance, doesn't need rubbish like me underfoot. Besides, I like it right here in this little plaza. Just look at that statue! How mischievous it is, how lurid and full of life. And it's androgynous! It's AC/DC! In regard to gender, that donkey covers the waterfront. This is *my* Temple of Jerusalem."

The sun climbed higher over the most revered, most bloodied town on earth. The sun felt at home in Jerusalem. The sun had connections there. And though it was a long way from a Safeway shelf, Can o' Beans felt at home there, too. He/she sat among the rocks, as still as an inanimate object ought to be, enjoying the warmth, admiring Pales, and observing the people who came to photograph or point at Pales, many of them with an air of outrage.

About that time, Can o' Beans noticed Boomer Petway. He/she noticed Boomer not because he/she remembered him from their Airstream turkey ride—Boomer was in disguise now and hardly could be recognized as the fellow who'd deserted him/her in that cave after so thoroughly and entertainingly partaking of his wife— but, rather, noticed him because of his gait. "Isn't it odd," he/she said to his/her nursemaid and companion, "that every morning about this time a different person comes and walks around and around the monument with the same identical limp. Oh, what a marvelously weird place this is!"

Jerusalem didn't seem so weird to Ellen Cherry. Where she sat in the overgrown garden of the little stone house that Boomer had shared with Amos Zif, the vectors of death cults, past or present, did not reach her. The February sunshine was just strong enough to buzz in her plasma, and the light was almost impossibly clear. From the weedy patio, there spread a field of rosemary and thistle. Honeysuckle wound bureaucratically around the trunks of Persian lilac and wind-bent pine. Birds chirped messages older than prophecy, older than tourism, and even the furry black centipedes that scurried along the crumbling garden wall appeared benign. She sipped her tea, drew on the pages of her mental sketch pad, and absorbed through every pore that she could open, the ancient golden light.

Ellen Cherry was awaiting the return of her husband. Each morning, after they'd had their sex and breakfast, Boomer dug into his spy bag, selected a disguise, and went down to the plaza by the Old City's Jaffa Gate to ascertain that nobody had bombed, censored, or vandalized his creation during the night.

From the moment of its unveiling, a fortnight prior, the piece had generated an uproar. Much of the adverse reaction was elicited by Pales' two-for-the-price-of-one frontal nudity, but many also took offense on racial grounds, the figure being both Arabic and Jewish. However, few in government or elsewhere had yet caught on that the prancing donkey-person represented for Arab and Jew a common ancestral deity, because few had been taught that it was for the prince of jackasses, the buck-toothed empress of jennies, that their solemnized and contested land had, appropriately or not, been named. When that information emerged, either Jerusalemites would lighten up or the *falafel* would really hit the fan. In anticipation of the latter, Zif had embarked on an extended tour of France. Boomer wasn't worried. What could they do to him? He'd been ordered to leave the country in thirty days anyhow, as a result of the shipment of Armageddon paraphernalia that he had received from the late Buddy Winkler.

In spite of everything, Boomer had hopes for the survival of his sculpture, so he ventured out morning after morning to survey its condition. When he came home, he delighted in making love to Ellen Cherry while still wearing the disguise *du jour*. She admitted that that could occasionally be exciting, such as the time that he'd been in drag as a nun, but today he was dressed as a municipal rat catcher, and she knew that she was going to have to draw the line.

Beyond that, the future was uncertain. Doubtlessly, she would leave Jerusalem along with Boomer, although her curiosity about the new dimension of being that was aborning there had hardly been satisfied. They talked about building a house near Seattle somewhere; a roomy, rustic lodge on one of those evergreen hills, if they could find one that the timber companies hadn't skinned alive. There, with her eye on the ball, she would paint. She'd paint and paint and paint. She would dedicate herself to . . . well, she'd have to call it "beauty," for want of a better word. She wouldn't be sentimental about it, or self-righteous, or even spiritual and pure. And she wouldn't get defensive when ridiculed or misunderstood. Beauty she would not carry like a banner, nor would she take refuge from the world in it like a hermit in a shack. Beauty would just be her everyday thing.

Meanwhile, there was so much to think about. All that had been revealed to her—and to who knew how many others?—when Salome danced the Dance of the Seven Veils. Those revelations might require her to grow in unexpected directions. The others might similarly grow. What effect, if any, that mutant growth might have on the culture at large, in the earth's "Final Days," remained to be seen. Meanwhile, the garden there in Jerusalem, the sunny patio there at the cervix of the world, was a fine place to ponder it all.

Ellen Cherry was relaxed, calm, at peace. The roller coaster ride was over. Those years of feeling on top of things one week, squashed by them the next, had fallen away like the pages of a calendar. Those bizarre events that had haunted her in New York were swiftly fading memories. From now on—she could sense it—her existence would be stable, maybe even staunch; the life of a relatively normal artist in which relatively normal events transpired. She sighed like a feather pillow being fluffed by an old Norwegian maid. She took a long, slow sip of tea.

Moments later, Boomer bolted into the garden. It didn't much look like Boomer but it was he. He was carrying something, presenting it to her like a gift. God, she hoped it wasn't the tail of a dead rat.

"Looky here, bagel britches!" he practically shouted. "Looky what I found for you lying in the rubble on the edge of Pales Plaza. It's a spoon! A little ol' spoon! Exactly like the one we lost in that cave that day! I mean *exactly*!"

MP 5V